THE BODY TEMPLE

The Body Temple

MAX RANKENBURG

ISBN 979-8-9925921-2-2

eISBN 979-8-9925921-3-9

First Printing, 2025

What?

Know you not that your body
is the temple of the Holy Ghost

which is in you
which you have of God

and that you
are not your own?

You were bought for a price:
glorify God in your body
and in your spirit
which are God's.

1 Corinthians 6.19

All that you put into a place, everything you give to the work you do
– it's impossible to account for. It's impossible to say:

"Here you are. This is it. *This* is what it amounts to."

Because there is always something else. There is always something
more. You think you have it, but something gets away. Something you
didn't know was there. It will wake you in the night.

Terrance Goddard, *A Carpenter's Handbook*

Contents

desert, out of the city. It was the Wild West still, with cowboys and Indians and men on horses, guns in their belt. I fell asleep. When I woke we were already in the mountains. Again, it felt like we'd entered a different world, come across a continent to another country. The air was cooler there. And the sky, unlike in the desert, where the glare hurt your eyes, the sky in the mountains had this deep, deep blue, a mesmerizing color that, with the peaks up and around the horizon, drew the eye, gesturing, as if to say, "Come higher, come up."

I do not remember being frightened before seeing the house. But there was something to the atmosphere, to that environment, the solitude of the narrow little road wending its way upward. Maybe I did look back, down the road we'd come, and think about the city, about our little house on Orchard Avenue, so far away.

Ascending the driveway we passed a large cart, full of stones, drawn by a mule. A group of men were working there, building a wall or reinforcing the side of the road, I don't know what. They stopped what they were doing as we passed. I imagine for some of them the sight of our car was a first. It wasn't ours, of course, it was the Whitehall's – we didn't own a car until a few years later, when my father moved to MGM and got into sound – but that didn't matter. I felt like a prince in the back seat, high off the ground, looking down at these silent filthy men, that bug-eyed mule, Nancy's hand in mine.

Then we saw it, the Drammond House. I remember glancing forward, over my mother's shoulder, and seeing, first, these trees, the woods, but then – then there was something out there, something running through the trees, keeping up with us in the car. We were not going very fast. The driveway was steep and narrow, after all. But what was it, in the trees, coming along with us, racing us to the top of the hill through the woods? Then it came to me: "It's a car. Like ours." But how? What was this car doing in the woods, driving, it seemed to me, directly through the trees? How was it possible?

They were windows. It was the house, right there, behind this thin wall of trees. And it was our car that I saw, its reflection skipping along, window to window, one sheet of dark glass to the next, until we came to the top of the hill and turned away, and the house pulled away from the driveway, and we stopped in this wide, shaded front yard.

It came out of nowhere, see. We were in the desert, and then ascending the mountain, and then on this driveway, entering the little woods, passing the men working on the side of the road, and ascending still, and then it was there, beside us before we even saw it. Like it was part of the woods, cut from the rock of the mountain. Which it was, at least in parts.

It has been said that the house is very large. The Drammond House is an extremely big place. But this description is inaccurate. Unless you've been there, and seen it with your own eyes ... But what does that mean? You can't. All you have is me, and this account. So I'll try. Like this. Imagine a skyscraper. One hundred floors. Now tip this building on its side. Call that, "The South Wing." Now take another skyscraper and tip this on its side and press the base of this building up against the base of the other. Call that, "The North Wing." Imagine where they meet, these two structures, another tower, not as high perhaps as a skyscraper, but high enough to strain the neck. Like a cathedral chopping a hole in the sky. The place also had an east and west wing, and gardens, courtyards, towers, parapets, terraces. And that's just a rough sketch of the exterior. The inside of the place was something else altogether.

There was also a basement to the house, naturally. Although this word, basement, does not truly describe what's beneath the place. It is perhaps impossible to say what's beneath the Drammond House. I have studied the issue. Made a map, as you've seen. And thought about this question all my life. And now, rather than feel like I'm coming closer to the truth, rather than wish I could live a little longer, another decade, and finally figure things out. ... Rather, I'm terrified of the question. What's down there? It has destroyed part of me, taken so much of me, thinking about what's down there. Now, it is not that I don't want to think about it anymore – no. There's no helping that. The train's left the station, as they say. No. I wish I had never started, I wish, like in that myth, I had never opened the box and released such horrible things, wish I had never stepped foot in the place, wish I had never even known it was there.

◇

I was a ten year old boy. Things are larger and more complicated and mysterious when you're young.

The lady of the house had prepared a table outdoors, in the front yard beneath these magnificent oak trees. Her name, I later learned, was Corinne Kearn. She was not, properly speaking, the lady of the house, but only the housekeeper. There was no lady, it turned out. And the lord of the manor, so to speak – because there was no such thing in California at that time as lords and manors, but to my mind that didn't matter – he was off, abroad somewhere, a chemical engineer, I recall someone saying, who was more often in the Middle East or South America than he was at home.

So Miss Kearn, with a small staff, attended the place. She would receive guests, fix rooms, have meals prepared. All of that. I guess it was a popular weekend retreat for studio men like my father. And I must say, Miss Kearn and the house she kept did possess a certain refined quality of the old world, something my parents had grown up with and lost. So it appealed to them in that way, reminding them of the wonders of their childhoods, of the majesty of the world before the war.

I remember Miss Kearn at the base of the semi-circular twin staircases, before the house, her expression, her imperturbable poise, her ageless face. A beauty, she was, even to my ten year old eyes. Tall, a long face, large dark eyes, her black hair pinned back over her ears, up off her long neck. Another woman, hardly up to Miss Kearn's shoulder, stood by her. A squat blockish thing, her unfocussed eyes, a drooping eyelid, a kind of idiot's sneer in the lips. The kitchen maid, it turned out. She answered to Elaine.

It was, I think, Mr Whitehall who introduced Miss Kearn to his family and to my parents. Gently she took each of their hands in hers. As for the children, she looked us in the eye and nodded her head, expressionless. Nancy took a step behind the leg of her father.

Then we sat at the table and food was brought out from inside. We ate. Shadows shifted high in the trees overhead.

After the meal, the adults had liquers and coffee. The men smoked cigars. I whispered in Nancy's ear. We would go exploring.

"Don't go into the woods," my father said as we excused ourselves. "You don't know what's out there."

I recall him pulling me up close, his large hand brushing hair aside from my brow, like this ... And how he twisted his face up into something menacing. "You don't know what's out there. What man-eating creatures hide in the shadows."

He was an actor in his youth. He lived for moments like that, when he could playfully threaten and taunt me with a fantastic image. To keep me awake at night, truth be told. Though it was not that my father frightened me, not that exactly. I knew he was just telling a story, making things up. I knew the difference between what was real and what wasn't. Rather, it was the image he evoked, and how he could manifest such a thing in words, so quickly and so easily, that caught my attention, that fomented in an instant other images of my own invention.

"What hides in the shadows." As a boy, saying words like that to myself, lying in bed in the dark, would conjure all sorts of things, objects, creatures and the worlds they lived in. Such words as those, and I can hear his voice still, stayed with me for years to come. Later, when I was older, the words would find correspondences in the world, such as in an account I read of the burning of Dresden, in nineteen forty-five:

> They come at night
> and take away the dead

But how was he to know that? How was he to know the effect his words would have on his son? He couldn't. He was a simple man, finally, who, after accepting his failure as a stage actor, became what was essentially a carpenter. He was a builder, a man good with his hands but not one to carefully read through and think about symbols.

Interpretation was not his trick. So he could say things, his innocence, I suppose, giving him license to, like "You don't know what's out there. What man-eating creatures hide in the shadows," knowing that the words should do something to the boy but not knowing precisely what, not knowing in fact what the words even meant. They were like the wooden braces you put behind a backdrop or beneath a stage. Replaceable, interchangeable pieces. They weren't his words, but only something he'd heard, something he could use on his boy like another father might use the belt. To keep us in line. He was a simple man, a poor man, finally, all his life.

We went around the side of the house, along a path. I remember how, turning around a sharp corner, the sound of the adults at the table vanished altogether, in an instant. They weren't that far away. But it was something of the trees, and of the building itself, something that dampened sound, the presence of others. And in no time at all it was as if Nancy and I were all alone in a strange, magical world.

There was grass along the side of the house, a margin between the building and the woods of about twenty feet. The grass was a light green, cropped low, dry, I recall, the earth hard. I wanted to walk, to try and go around the house, to see the backyard. She wanted to get inside. "What for?" I asked. "I don't know," she said. "Just to see. Maybe there's a game room." "We shouldn't," I said. We walked on. The windows of the house were high and dark, clean, long pieces of glass, reflecting the woods across from us. I remember thinking how empty the place appeared, and how strange, such a large house in the mountains, with nobody inside. Was it frightening? As I think back on it, it should have been. But I really can't say if I was frightened then. I guess I was a little blind. And in any case, I was with Nancy, and I found comfort in that, and I had to act brave, for her.

Though, as I remember it, she did not seem the least frightened. She went up to the house, climbing various stairways, to look through the windows. She'd press her nose to the glass, cover the sides of her eyes.

"You shouldn't do that."

"I want to see."

"What's in there?"

"Nothing. Stuff. A piano."

And down she'd go, and onward we went.

After a while we sat down on the grass to rest. Lying back I saw the sky far above, the sharp horizontal line of the house's summit on one shore with the turbulence of the trees on the other.

"Close your eyes," she said. I did as I was told. She touched my nose with a blade of grass. "Do you think I'm pretty?"

"No."

"Prettier than that lady?"

"You're just a girl."

"Would you like to kiss me?"

Did she actually ask such questions? Probably not. But who can say? I did lie on the grass, and she did touch my nose with a blade of grass. And she did, after a moment, regardless of what I said, lean down and kiss me on the lips.

I got up to go into the woods. I'd had enough of answering her questions, putting up with her taunts, of playing, it's easy to see now, the husband-wife game.

The trees were not dense, and there was little undergrowth. I immediately found, within view of the house and of where Nancy still sat on the grass, talking to herself, warning me, no doubt, that what I was doing was forbidden, a dead tree with a hole in its trunk. The hole was large enough for a boy my size to climb into. I wasn't about to do that, of course, but it did cross my mind. I leaned in. The darkness wrapped around my head, shoulders and hands. Did I close my eyes? Not at first. There was a sound, something down in the tree. A rustling, maybe, of something moving, coming up, an animal. But then, to my ear, there was something else. And then, I recall, I did close my eyes, listening carefully.

"Nancy!" I said, looking back, "shut up! I found something."

Deep down, distant, quiet, something rumbled, turned like a motor. It was not the earth, not something of the earth. It was an engine I heard underground, far away. I leaned in farther, my waist pressed against the tree, the rim of the hole. No. I'm certain. I'm telling you. I heard it: there was something mechanical down there, under the tree, in the earth. It was like – a locomotive, a steam engine as it leaves the station, a massive block of metal slowly gathering momentum. Cheeoooo – cheeoooo – CHEEOOOO.

"Nancy! Come here. Look at this."

The girl reluctantly came. "You're going to get in so much trouble."

"Look. Listen. There's something in there."

Fearlessly, she grabbed the sides of the hole in two hands and pressed her face down into the darkness.

"What is it?" she said over her shoulder, "I don't see anything!"

"Listen. There's a sound."

"Stupid," she started to say.

Was it the hiss of the creature or the girl's scream that I heard first, I don't recall. But in an instant Nancy cried out, threw herself backwards, falling, sobbing, and this huge fucking raccoon the size of a Labrador pulled itself from the hole, hissing like a cat, his teeth bared, one of his humanoid claws reaching out for me.

She hurt herself, falling, scratched her knee and the side of her hand. She was crying as I reached down for her, took her hand, pulled her quickly along, away from the animal that, after its initial emergence, and our retreat, seemed pleased with what it had accomplished, and disappeared, descending into its dark dwelling.

"I'm telling! I'm telling!"

Back on the grass, apart from a little blood on her knee, the scratch on her wrist, dirt on the back of her dress, Nancy seemed more or less back to normal.

"I can't believe you did that to me!"

"I didn't know it was there. I swear."

"You knew! You knew it was there!"

"I didn't. Nancy."

But she was off, running back the way we'd come, her bony elbows and thin arms flapping at her sides like a bird's broken wings.

"But did you hear it?" I asked her. "Nancy!"

I took my time getting back, preparing my defense. My father, I thought, I could appease, convince. My mother would be a different matter. And she'd take Mrs. Whitehall's side, I had no doubt. There'd be no arguing with her, them. And my father, in the end, would have to take her side. Would they whip me in the company of others? Probably not. But inside the house, where there was ample room for corporal punishment, I would very likely get what I deserved.

As I came around the corner of the house I heard the commotion. Everyone sounded worked up.

"It was just a raccoon," I said, practicing.

But there was no need for a speech, my defense, or argument of any kind. Because the commotion I'd heard was not for Nancy, her bloody knee and scratched wrist, her tale of my mean assault against her in the woods. No. It was nothing of the sort.

The girl stood aside, hands in her pockets, chin down, watching the adults, who were all talking at once, surrounding what looked to me like one of the workers we'd seen on the driveway, coming up. I went over to the crowd. I noticed a man with a bloody rag pressed to the side of his head. But the crowd surrounded a different man, one of the workers, another bloody rag wrapped around his hand. The color had drained from his face. He staggered as he approached the house.

I went to Nancy. "What happened?"

"The man's hurt. His hand."

"What happened to him?" I asked, pointing at the fellow with the rag on his ear.

My father came over, his eyebrows up. "Oh, there you are," stepping between Nancy and I. "You missed it. A real bout between man and beast, I'd say."

"Pop," I said, which was what fathers were called in Los Angeles at the time, "what happened to him?"

"Get this," he said. "The mule took a bite out of that one's ear." He pointed at the lonesome looking fellow with the bloody rag on the side of his head. "And when he whipped the creature it leapt forward, pulling the cart and pulling a rope that the other fellow was at that moment fastening." The man, and attending crowd, were climbing the winding steps toward the entrance to the Drammond House.

"But what happened?" I asked.

My father looked at me, down at me. I remember the expression on his face. As if he'd just then discovered my presence. "Why," he said. "It cut his finger off. The knot. It closed." He demonstrated, fists in the air as he pulled an invisible rope and knot tight. "Like this. Snip."

"Cut his finger off!"

"Snip."

I looked at Nancy. She looked like she wanted to say something, fear in her eyes. But she didn't speak.

Then my father looked at the girl, at her knee, the dirt on the back of her dress. "And what happened to you, dear?" He looked at me, smiling in the corner of his mouth. "What were you two up to? You didn't go into the woods, did you, like I told you not to."

"Sir."

"I fell," said Nancy, her eyes on the group of people going inside. "We were playing tag and I tripped. And fell. It's nothing, Mr. Manning. Just a scratch."

"My, my," said my father. "When it rains it pours. Let's get you inside and clean up."

·◻·

Why do I tell you these things? I've half a mind to stop here. It is not easy to talk about these things, remembering something that happened so long ago. You say, "It helps to talk about it." Really? Does it? Tell me. Because the pain never goes away. Whatever else changes, the pain is always there. I believe that now. Once I was like you, thinking about catharsis, thinking about the passage of time and how, as is said, we heal in time. That's a lie. There is immortality in life, as you might imagine as I tell this story, but it is not what you think. Not of the spirit, not of beauty. Nothing like that at all. Look at me, doing this, telling a story you've heard again and again, and for what? For you. I do this for you.

And what you can do for me, is promise me that you'll never, never go out there.

But I'll be dead someday, long before you, so that's on you.

We went inside. I noticed blood on the floor, dark drops of it marking points in a line across the entrance hall, through an archway, down a dark hallway, into, what I recognized even at a distance, a kitchen. That's where the Whitehalls and my mother, the injured man and some of his coworkers, and Miss Kearn had repaired to. I could hear water running.

A great staircase rose before us, forking right and left halfway between the ground floor and the first. A balcony wrapped around the first floor, and then, further up, another balcony lined the circumference of the second floor. Higher still was a third balcony, and fourth, fifth – need I go on? There was a small dark room on our right, what I took to be a closet. I did not look inside. And to our left, a larger room opened up, a lounge or study, large red and blue couches beneath these tall windows, a long wooden table, a globe.

I followed my father into the kitchen. Nancy was directly behind me. The injured man was crying softly, moaning, breathing quickly. Mrs. Whitehall, I think it was, was fastening something – a bandage, I mean, not the finger itself – onto the man's broken hand.

Nancy whispered at my shoulder. "Where's the finger?"

I looked at her, bewildered.

The adults agreed that the man needed to be immediately taken down the mountain to the village, where there was a doctor. I guess – I didn't ask – they would take the man's finger along, too, and try to refasten it. They can do that, I've heard, if it's done quickly enough after an accident. Stitch things back together.

"Come on," Nancy said in my ear. She took my hand.

We stepped through a narrow doorway into an adjacent room, a scullery, I seem to remember. The counters and sinks were clean, quiet, unused for ages, it seemed like, white dishes stacked neatly on shelves. Through another door we found ourselves in a small, modest dining room. A large wooden table was pushed against one wall, places set for two. There was a cabinet against the other wall. Its doors were closed. Nancy opened one and looked inside.

"What is it?"

"Glassware."

Then, as before, when we were outside, the sound of the adults behind us diminished to nothing, and Nancy and I had the place to ourselves. She moved forward with less caution, excited, impatient.

"Wait for me."

But she wouldn't. She almost ran into the next room.

"Nancy. Please. Don't run. We shouldn't be in here."

In the following room, it was like a creamery, I guess you'd call it, the place smelled like cheese, and Nancy was at the end of it, on a little stool, opening an ice box.

"Nancy, don't."

"Ewww," she said, dropping the lid closed, hopping off the stool, running ahead.

Then I was frightened. I remember thinking, passing the ice box, wanting to look inside but also not wanting to, wanting to be with Nancy, to explore the house with her, with her alone, but also wanting to be back with my father and the others – I remember thinking, "What's come over her? She's like a different person all of a sudden. She's not listening, or doesn't hear you, doesn't even want to be near you." And then the thought: "We're going to get lost."

I followed her into another room. I saw her go into the room. But once I was in the room, I couldn't find her.

"Nancy?"

I continued on a little faster then, not wanting to be left behind, and also wanting to stop her, to seize her and take her back. It was not right, what we were doing, running through someone else's house like that, and running through a house like that one. "Nancy! Stop!"

"Henry! Come on!"

She called me from the next room. But when I got there the room was empty. "Where are you?"

"Henry!"

She was farther away, her voice getting smaller.

"Where are you?"

I thought I'd made a wrong turn, gone into the wrong room. So I went back to the previous room, what looked like a formal dining room. There was another door, I saw, closed, in a shadow. I went through there, into a hallway.

"Henry! Where are you?"

She was far, far away then. She'd gone too far on her own and I wouldn't be able to catch up with her, find her.

"Stop playing!" I said to the empty hallway.

Distantly, softly: "Hen-ry!?"

I thought: "If you go on, looking for her like this, you'll get lost. And you won't be able to find your way back. And then both of you will be lost. Turn back and get someone."

I went back the way I'd come. "It's not funny, Nancy," I called out. "I'm going back."

"Hen-ry!?"

"I'll get someone," I said, though not too loudly, not wanting to frighten her, exactly, implying that something was wrong. Not wanting to frighten myself with the same implication.

I followed the steps I'd taken almost exactly on my way back, naming things to myself as I went. "The stool, the ice box, the table, the cabinet."

The adults had quietly gathered in the entrance hall. The injured man's hand was wrapped thickly in a white bandage. Another man, one of the workers, had his hand on the injured man's shoulder, guiding him along.

I went to my father, who was at the moment engaged with Ms. Kearn, the housekeeper. She was telling him with evident pleasure a story about the house. "And she couldn't stop," the woman said, smiling, drawing close to my father, looking him directly in the eye. "She told them, it was the house that meant everything to her, and that should they stop before it was complete... Well. For someone who had invested so much of herself, years of her life, into the place, it would mean – she said it – it would kill her."

"You don't say."

The woman looked down at me, the curve in her lip unfaltering, her story hardly interrupted. I could have been a dog at her knee.

"But then, as things go, they did run out of money and resources, and they had to, they had to stop. After which the house... The house speaks for itself."

My father shook his head, whistled. "Over two thousand rooms," he said. "I can't imagine..." Then he noticed me, at his elbow. "Did you hear that, Heinrich. Two thousand rooms in the place. *At least!* For a hundred years they were building. ... My son, Heinrich," he said to the house-keeper, tousling my hair.

I told him that Nancy was lost.

"What did you say?"

I told him again, whispering. "I don't know where Nancy is."

"Were you playing games?"

"No."

"Then where is she?"

"I don't know."

I was close to tears then. I was more sad than I was scared, and I was scared. But I felt – how can I say it? – something like betrayal at Nancy's disappearance, her running off like that. After all, she had asked me to come along. But then she abandoned me, hid from me. It was cruel. At least that's what I recall feeling.

My father did not appear concerned. He thought about what I'd said, looked once more at the housekeeper, said something else about the house, and then, pushing me gently before him, said, "We should go. Let's find Nancy."

Ms Kearn, I remember, who'd listened to what I said without comment, raised her hand and caught the other woman's attention. The deformed one. Elaine. I do not re-call anything being said between the women, but Elaine then shuffled off.

We made our way toward the door, my father still in conversation with the housekeeper.

"What about Nancy?" I said, looking back. The place was growing dark. The others were already outside. "Pop! What about Nancy!? We can't – "

The man stopped moving forward, held his breath, looked down at me sternly, and said: "Heinrich. Do not interrupt me when I'm talking."

I bit my tongue. I looked at the woman, who, in the entryway seemed suddenly very tall. And she looked down at me, this tilt to her head, something of pity, misunderstanding or curiosity. Like she'd never seen a child before.

Then Mrs. Whitehall stepped away from the others, quickly came across the porch to where we stood, her hand out, her eyes on me. "Darling," she said, zeroing in, beginning to lower her face to mine, a finger drawing a strand of her blond hair over her ear, "where's Nancy?"

I was about to say that I didn't know. I was about to say that she was lost in the house. But I couldn't speak. My tongue was stuck to the roof of my mouth. "I – "

"There she is," said my father, turning back.

Elaine had Nancy by the hand as she guided her from the kitchen, into the hallway, into and across the entrance hall. The girl looked unharmed, indifferent, inscrutable. She didn't look at me as she passed and took her mother's hand.

My father and I were the last of the company to leave the house. I went down the stairs before him. I can still hear him talking with that woman, the housekeeper, on the porch above me. He was really taken by the house, the story of its strange construction, by the housekeeper. I remember, I had stopped on the stairs, wanting my father to come down with me, to be with him, and hearing his voice above me, and hearing the woman's voice too, not making anything out clearly, and not hearing anything from the others, who were back at the car, and then hearing a bird cry out in the trees, darkened by twilight, above, and in the overpowering silence that ensued, the absence of the bird, the distance of my father from me, and in my uncertainty of which way to go, up or down, I noticed near my foot a crack in the marble stair, a fine, simple, jagged line. The light was dim but I could almost see inside. And never in my life had I ever felt so alone, and never since have I felt as alone as I did then, looking at that stupid crack.

In the backseat of the car, whispering, I asked Nancy what had happened. She wouldn't say. She looked at her hands, her lap, touching the scab on her knee. She looked at me, blinking quickly, her glassy eyes marked, even I, a ten year old boy, could see, by something she'd seen.

"What happened?"

Her lips moved, like this, about to release. But she remained silent. For the length of the trip back, she was silent. Hours later she fell asleep and rested her head on my shoulder. I remember that. I felt like I loved her. I did love her. I was ten years old.

Then I fell asleep. My father woke me when we were home and carried me from the car inside.

She never told me what happened, what she saw in the Drammond House. Never. And I know she saw something because slowly, by increments, I realized that she was a different person. A harder person. No longer a little girl, the Nancy Whitehall I'd known. No longer wanting to play husband-wife games. Indeed, when school resumed a few weeks later, I hardly saw her anymore, hardly spoke to her.

⌂·

I was at Jack Moreland's place, in New York. This was ninety-one, ninety-two. I overheard this man and woman talking about Hollywood of the thirties. And then he, the fellow, I forget his name, recognized me and knew that I'd grown up around there at the time, and he started asking me, you know, this and that, did I know this person and that person. It struck me as rude bordering on offensive, what he did, pulling me over and putting me on the spot like that, and I was not in a good mood to begin with, so I did my best at answering his questions without committing to participating in whatever it was he and the lady had been discussing. And I was just about out of it when the lady said, snapping her fingers, "Whitehall. That was his name. Lawrence Whitehall." To which he said, "That's right! And did you know he had a daughter, Nancy, who married– "

"Of course," the lady said as she pinched the bridge of her nose and nodded. "That's who it was."

"They lived over on Grove Street for fifty years," the man said, "she, writing all those books right under our noses," he said.

"She seldom came out, I heard."

"But he loved her, desperately. I know that. I saw that on many occasions. He was a –"

I stopped listening. I checked an impulse to toss my drink in the man's face. For what reason? I can't say. To shut him up. Words are too much sometimes, truly.

She died a few years ago. She moved to the city for college in the late thirties and never left. And I guess she found this man, and lived over on Grove Street with him for all of her adult life. A writer of some acclaim, it turns out.

To think she was right over there, all this time. I might have passed her on the street. When I was there, in the city, which wasn't often, but still. Though if I did I probably wouldn't have recognized her, and she wouldn't have recognized me. And she wouldn't remember my name. And we'd pass each other, just two old people going their ways.

She became a recluse in the last decade of her life. I've confirmed this with a few others in the years since that show, what I overheard. So chances are I never passed her. But I'm certain I've walked by her place. And to think she was there, up there, behind one of those windows. Writing. Remembering. Or trying, as I do, to forget.

□

Did I do what? Read what she wrote?
Why would I do that?

Part One

Marianne

~ 1 ~

The woman said he might go back to Manning's, looking for her, and that's what he did. That's where they found him.

The sergeant got up before dawn and walked over to Griffith Park. He walked up to the observatory and looked out over the city. The sky was bronze blue, clean and deep. The world just coming around, rising up.

He walked home. He kept a canary in a cage. He fed the bird, whistled quietly for it. The bird whistled back, singing. He took a shower. When he got out of the shower the young woman who sometimes came by had gotten up and made a pot of tea. She helped the sergeant dress. The man had no left arm. He wore black slacks, a clean white button down shirt. They pinned the left sleeve to his belt just above the left-hand pocket of the slacks. She helped him into a black coat. He buttoned it at his sternum. She straightened his collar. Bending the left sleeve of the coat at the elbow, she drew the sleeve horizontally across the sergeant's stomach and pinned the cuff near the right-hand pocket.

The woman brought the tea to his office. He drank two small cups slowly, in silence. His desk was covered end to end in papers, books, magazines. The wall beside the desk was likewise covered in papers, newspaper clippings, photographs. In one of these his daughter smiles brilliantly at the photographer, running towards him. It was her fifth birthday. They'd gone to the zoo, invited some friends. They made colorful hats for everyone out of tissue paper.

He stood over the desk. He looked at a notepad, some things he'd written down the night before. He lit a Marlboro.

At a quarter to eight he left the house. An old Mercedes Benz, black, dusty and worse for wear, was at the curb. A black man was driving. He reached across the passenger seat and opened the door. The sergeant, a compact Japanese man, lowered his head for the brightness of the day, and quickly walked to the car and got in.

~ 2 ~

"Last February, my wife, Lucy, she went to Hong Kong. For a conference. It was – the first, a Thursday. I took her to the airport."

When they picked him up he came without a word, like he was expecting them. He took a coat and stepped outside, turned to check if the door was locked.

At the station they sat him down, gave him a cup of coffee. He was polite, attentive.

"We have some questions maybe you can help us with."

A tall black man sat across from him. A Japanese man stood in the corner, by the window. There'd been a woman in the room briefly, asked him to sign some papers. He did. She left.

"I know," he said.

It was about a man named Joseph Manning. He was visiting from Germany, come out for his father's funeral. He was supposed to be on a plane back right about then. They'd seen the ticket. But the man hadn't turned up.

There'd been a fight, apparently. The woman – Charlotte Graham was her name, they'd pulled her over late Saturday night, driving erratically, her face smashed up, almost two hundred thousand dollars in the backseat of the car – had given them an earful the day before. Named these two men: Joseph Manning, first, the one who'd beat her, and Raymond Byrd, second.

So they got Byrd.

He didn't ask for a phone call. No lawyer. No resistance. He looked like a man who wanted to talk.

Gerald McNeal was the detective seated across from Byrd. In his experience, you get a man in and ask him a simple question, and he goes back seven, eight months, starts telling you about this long weekend, visit from an old friend, with the wife in China, you interrupt him. Get him on task. Focus. This time around he didn't do that.

"She's in genetics," Byrd was saying. "The human genome thing? Heard of it? Don't ask me. She's the doctor in the house. Tells me that in the future we'll be able to order our kids like sandwiches at the deli. Like cornbeef on rye. A kid."

~ 3 ~

She kissed me at security. I watched her go. We've done this before, many times.

She'd be back on Wednesday. I said I'd pick her up.

From the airport I went down to a place called the Samaniego Gallery, off Sawtelle. This painter, fellow named Heinrich Manning, was there. He wanted to show me something.

I have a painting of his on the wall in my office. This abstract thing. Rectangles and lines. Black and white. There's some blue in there if you look closely. These boxes going off to nowhere. I don't know. It grows on you.

For a few years in the nineties I made more money than I knew what to do with. So I bought art. These paintings, one of which is from this guy, Manning. Frankly I wasn't crazy about the piece when I first saw it but now, like I said – we've come to terms.

That was then. So Manning – this is last summer, a year ago – he calls me one day, out of the blue.

"Raymond Byrd? This is Heinrich Manning. You have a painting of mine. I have its partner. You'll want it. You must see it. You really must come by and see it."

So down I go to have a look.

I like it. It's similar to what I already have but seems to – I don't know... It's hard to talk about art... Seems to move in various, odd directions. Creating, Manning said,

"This space. Here. Feel that? How it's pulling," the old man said, turning his fists in the air as if tightening an imaginary knot.

Heinrich Manning's a big man, an old man with these huge hands, thick arms. A man who knows how to tie knots, I thought, listening to him, watching him.

Pulling?

But he was asking too much. And he knew it, and he knew I knew it. So I was going to step out, wait awhile, wait for him to call back. The old man liked me, I could feel it.

"Working on anything new?" I said.

He looked down at me, closed and opened these tired blue eyes. He knew I wasn't going to buy his painting and he was ready to let me go, cut me off. He'd wait for me to come back.

"I stopped painting," he said. "Years ago. I build now."

"Build what?"

"Heh. None of your goddamn business is what. It's a house."

I thought about that. From paintings to houses. "A house? Is that art or architecture?"

The man looked at the painting before us. He raised his chin, sawed his teeth together, said, "You always ask so many questions?" He faced me but didn't look at me, his eyes on someone over my shoulder. "Do I even fuckin know you?" He moved his lips, uncovering yellow crooked teeth. Then he looked me in the eye, quietly said: "It's a very *complicated* house. Impossible to – "

Then the old man broke into motion, his head turning, his huge chest and shoulders following. "Where's Charlotte?" he said. "I need to... Charlotte, come here!"

His assistant was across the room, engaged with a young couple. Her mouth closed at Manning's summons. She excused herself and came quickly forward. She looked my way, nodded – I'd spoken to her on the phone – faced the old man.

Manning growled at the woman, put a hand on her shoulder, spun her around, both of them walking away from me.

I watched the two, the giant old man looking down at and holding in place the slender woman who worked for him. This small, subservient thing in a skirt, hose and heels.

Then I left.

I returned to the gallery the day I took Lucy to the airport.

Manning had called again. "Raymond Byrd? This is Heinrich Manning. You have a painting of mine. I have its partner. You'll want it."

The same exact speech I'd heard before, word for word.

I reminded him that I'd already seen the painting, and that we'd met. "How's the house coming?"

"Come to the gallery, Raymond. I want you to look at this painting. You're making a mistake, not taking it."

I wasn't going to argue with the man. And I wasn't going to buy his painting – circumstances hadn't changed in the six months since we'd last spoke. But I decided to go to the gallery anyway. If, for nothing else, to talk with the artist's assistant, and connect the woman I'd seen with the voice I'd only heard on the phone.

This time I found myself alone with the painting. Manning made an appearance, but he was busy with someone else, here and there and then gone. I could hear him grumbling, cursing elsewhere in the gallery.

"We haven't properly met." She'd come up suddenly. She stood at my shoulder.

A calm woman, she spoke quietly, clearly. She wasn't American, I immediately heard.

"Charlotte Graham," she said, extending a hand. I took it. She smiled. She had a large chin and big mouth. A slender build, like a runner's.

"I remember," I said.

"Heinrich tells me you're being difficult."

"Because I won't give him my money?"

"He says that you *want* the painting. You just don't realize yet that you want it. True?"

Large brown eyes, gentle eyes. She looked at me as if reading something on my face. Not intrusive but discomfiting, the woman, for her directness and beauty. I had to look away, at the painting.

"I think I told him," I said, checking on her in the corner of my eye – she hadn't moved – "I can't afford something like this now."

"I see."

I faced her and this time she looked away. "That's good to know," she said. "Most people..."

"All I'm saying is – had we spoken a year ago, I wouldn't be so difficult."

She faced me. I was learning quickly, acclimating to that gaze, those eyes.

She seemed trustworthy and kind. Naïve, I would have thought if she were younger. But she wasn't that young. Thirty-five, say. So what was it? Sincerity, or tactics? Some women are like that with everyone. Which means it's not trustworthiness or kindness you see there.

"I'll tell him that," she said.

I might have said more, to keep her company for a little longer. But Manning, barking her name somewhere in the gallery, interrupted.

Her eyebrows rose, her smile fell. "The master."

"Is he always this way?"

"No," she said, stepping away, "only here, when he has an audience."

She approached an entrance to the adjacent room. But before she'd stepped around the corner, Manning quickly appeared, towering over her, reaching for her, growling as he tucked her inside his massive arm, putting his body between us. He glanced my way, mumbling words that only the assistant could hear. Then the two of them disappeared into the other room.

~ 4 ~

There was traffic on the way back. Bumper to bumper. The 10 eastbound. It was probably close to noon by then. Maybe an accident? Roadwork? It was beginning to rain, a mist blowing over the highway.

We'd stopped. Everything locked up. One's thoughts wander. I was thinking of Charlotte Graham, of being elsewhere, of Lucy... I don't know what I was thinking. It was something Lucy had said that morning, as she rushed around gathering things. Small details. Women and travel. And time, let me add. Are we really so similar, after all? I had the ticket in my pocket. I knew the gate of departure and the boarding time. That's what she was racing around for. The ticket. I held it out. She stopped in her tracks, mouth dropped open. Then she rushed forward, pinched my chin, pecked me on the cheek. "You think of everything, don't you."

No, I should've said. I don't think of everything. Far from it.

But it's these little things, you know. She meant no harm. It's just something she says. Maybe she's half-right.

I do think more about such things, like tickets and times of departure, than she does. But not everything.

The traffic broke apart, everyone accelerating like mad. To beat the next guy.

And the car in front of me stopped on a dime. I hit the brakes. I guess we weren't going that fast. But my tires were old, balding. I skid and hit him. I could see the other guy, his eyes filling the mirror over his head in the instant before impact. And then the crunch and jolt. You'd feel more on a city bus. And the eyes again. If a look could speak: "You motherfucker!"

"Human genome," I said to myself. "Perfect kids. Perfect drivers."

His was a Corolla. Somewhat new, I guess. From the 90s. They all look the same.

I drive a Volvo. A '78. It's a solid car. I got it in college, in Berkeley. The world ends tomorrow and all you'll find will be cockroaches and Volvos. And they'll run.

We pulled over. The guy jumped out, skipped back to his bumper, squats down, shaking his head, talking to himself. This diminutive man. Indian, bald as Ghandi, he waddles up to my window, starts up before I've even said a word. A thick blue vein, like a lightning bolt, cut down the middle of his forehead. I got out, looked at the damage, ran a fingertip over a groove in his bumper. Apologized, accepted blame, gave him my insurance card. I asked for his but he didn't have one. I don't know what the law is in this regard. If I give him mine does he have to give me his?

In the end it didn't matter. In the end he drove away and I never heard from him.

He was writing down my information, talking quickly to himself in his language. I was holding my wallet, thinking nothing in particular, thinking how much I could use a new wallet, watching the leather disintegrate before my eyes. That cold flat drizzle blowing in my face, the line of traffic bumping along. People going places.

I noticed then, behind my Master Card, a business card I'd tucked there some months before.

Marianne Heaney
Vice President
Office of Development
Los Angeles Philharmonic

There was a thick crease, like a paper scar, down the middle of the card. I'd folded it over at some point. Unfolded it at another. Slipped it there, behind the credit card. And nearly forgotten about it.

She'd rung me. Marianne. This is from years ago. She'd moved to town from New York, started something at the philharmonic. In development, whatever that is. We got a coffee. Talked about our lives. Fifteen years, we agreed, since we'd seen each other. She looked great. She'd married an engineer. Not a builder. A sound guy. Recording, with Sony or something, and something to do with one of the studios. They had a kid, a boy. She took a picture from her purse. There he was. Big head of brown hair under a red cap, dopey smile, squinting, a baseball bat on his shoulder.

On the back of the card she'd written a phone number.

The Indian was all worked up, bouncing on the balls of his feet. "Yi'know what that's gonna cost me, man! Hey man! You even from around here!?"

Then he got in his Corolla and drove away.

I sat in the Volvo and watched traffic tick by, letting the soft rain do its thing on the windshield. I dug around in the glovebox for some cigarettes I kept there. I couldn't find them. Lucy must've taken them, tossed them. She's always getting on me about that.

"It hurts *everything* in your body," she'd say.

"A cigarette a day never hurt anyone."

"But it's not a cigarette a day, is it? Is it?"

I turned on the radio, flipped across the dial, stopped on something I knew. That's a viol da gamba. The composer is... He's French. It's the renaissance. Marais? I knew these things a long time ago. The modern cello is the descendent of the viol da gamba. It's a beautiful instrument, the viol, to see and listen to in a live performance, if you have the chance. Softer than you'd think, looking at it. Big thing, small sound. Like an old lumber jack whose voice has worn out. He wants to talk but doesn't have it anymore. You have to lean real close to hear the story.

Marianne played the cello.

~ 5 ~

"Ray. What a surprise." I could hear she was in her car. "Listen!" She was almost shouting. "I have this meeting way the hell out in Tehachapi. You free? Feel like going for a drive?"

Maybe the sun was shining on the other side of the mountains.

I went home, shaved, showered, trimmed my nails, fed the cats. I made a pot of coffee and sat down to think things over.

A deck extends from the back of the house. Boards keep coming up. They're warped. I hit them down every few weeks, put in new nails, but it doesn't matter. Up they come. The whole thing needs replacing.

Down a few steps there's a lawn. In the winter it finds a shade of green. Silver, bluish, the color of ash. My lawn. I run a mower over it sometimes not because it needs cutting, it never needs cutting, but just to act like I care for it. It's something to do. Lucy gets a kick out of it.

Rain blew up against the window. Such a soft mist, falling without a sound, blowing like sand for three days.

The most rain we'd had at once in years, I remember hearing. Should've done something to my lawn.

The house was quiet. The cat drank her milk, her tongue, machine-like, stabbing at the surface –

tack tack tack tack tack tack tack –

It's not that Lucy makes a commotion. No. She's a quiet, gentle woman, after all. No. It's something about being alone in a house in LA on a rainy Thursday afternoon. Not hearing the neighbors, not hearing traffic, not hearing anything but the operation of my cat's tongue on a bowl of milk. *Tack tack, tack tack.*

We have two cats. One, the younger, eats like that, with or without company. The other is cranky and only comes out when nobody's watching. I can hear her at night, when I'm in bed, lurking about the place, clicking her teeth in disgust. But that's cats for you.

~ 6 ~

Traffic had thinned out by the time I got north of the city. Rain continued to fall and blow, the sky already tipping toward night even though it was only midafternoon, three at the latest.

I met Marianne in Mojave, at this bar, I forget the name. Big windows along the street, nobody out for the weather. We had a couple beers, talked about her new job with the symphony. She had to take these road trips out of the city every week, going to find the money lenders.

"It's a job," she said, speaking of what she did, development, which has nothing at all in common with what I did in software. I made interfaces. Marianne collected money for the future. "I'm good at it, and it pays well. I'll move on when I'm tired of it. I do miss the city."

New York, she meant, which made sense. Los Angeles, at times, can hardly be called a city at all. It doesn't have a real boundary, like Manhattan. It just goes on and on and on, eventually petering out in the desert. But even then, and you don't have to look too closely, you can still spot it, LA, dragging its heels in the dust, looking for water, for something to suck.

"You got somewhere to be?"

She caught me daydreaming, elsewhere.

"No. Why?"

"There's a place in the mountains, this mansion." She drank her beer, ran the tip of her tongue quickly over her upper lip.

"A mansion."

"The Drammond House, they call it. Heard of it? Let's go out, take a look."

At the end of the bar sat an old man and woman. He was thin as a blade of grass, bowed over like he was asleep on the back of a horse. He wore a cowboy hat. I could hear him wheezing as he laughed at something the woman said. Then he got up and shuffled over to this jukebox and put on Patsy Cline, "Walkin' After Midnight." Then he shuffled back to the bar and held his hand out to the woman, palm up, like something from Romeo and Juliet, and she took it, and they started dancing this easy three-step, the old man's eyes on the woman's face, and then down, somewhere between her breasts and chin, going back, years back.

I go a-walkin', after midnight, in the moonlight –

I didn't want to go out to this house. Something had come over me, a change of spirit. Maybe it was the drive, or the rain, or the desolation of this bar which hadn't changed in fifty years, or remembering the quiet in my house that morning. To enjoy a peaceful weekend alone with the cats. I'd read something. Stay in bed all day. Order takeout.

I looked at Marianne, into her large dark eyes, at her lips, at the clean curve her hair made hooked over her ear, at the paleness of her neck where it fell behind the hem of her black shirt, looked at this woman who did not want to not go home for the evening, to her kid, to her sound-engineer husband, who wanted instead to take me to a mansion in the mountains and start something. So I changed my mind. I guess that's what happened. Because I said: "That's a great idea."

It was cold outside. A stiff wet wind blew out of the west. Raising her voice, she offered to drive. She was in a silver Jaguar. She was climbing in, hardly waiting for any response from me. I looked at my battered Volvo, fingered the keys in my pocket. What was there to think about? The cats? They'd survive a day or two alone. They'd done it before.

Marianne glared at me through the windshield, her mouth going but nothing but wind and rain in my ear.

I got in. The heater was blowing. Something by Edward Elgar was in the player. "What is this? I know it."

"The Enigma Variations," she said. "This one's Henry Somerset. A childhood friend. He died in the war."

She pulled onto Route 14 and gunned it, tore across that desert like there was no tomorrow.

~ 7 ~

Before you get to the place, midway up the mountain, above Lake Isabelle, you pass through the village of Maiden. It's little more than a gas station, a mini-mart, and a diner called Rosalee's. We stopped at the diner for coffee.

The lights were out. The place looked closed.

"Help you?"

We didn't see her at first. The waitress was sitting in a booth, in a shadow at the end of the counter. She'd raised her chin, looking at us. Rain fell gently against the window behind her.

"You open?"

She stood up, walked our way, a paperback in hand. "Guess so," she said.

"There coffee?"

"I'll have to make it."

"Do that," said Marianne.

The girl looked at Marianne and blinked. Then she rolled her eyes, set her book facedown on the counter, and stepped away into the dark kitchen. A moment later she called out from the dark: "You're not ordering anything to eat, are you?"

"Not if there's a grocery here."

"There is. But he's – what time is it? He's closed."

"Then we might."

"You can't. Cook's gone home."

"Not even a sandwich?"

"Nada."

"A slice of bread with cheese?"

The girl made a racket fixing coffee. She was reading something by Edith Wharton. Know her? *Age of Innocence*. No? It wasn't that.

Marianne looked at me and said softly: "What a bitch."

A few minutes later the waitress came back with two steaming mugs of coffee. She set these down before us, reached beneath the counter, tossed a couple packs of sugar by the mugs. "Take milk?"

The girl disappeared once more into the kitchen. When she came back she had a cup of coffee in hand. We drank in silence. The wind howled outside.

"Where you headin'?"

"A place called the Drammond House," said Marianne.

The waitress held her mug up to her mouth, blowing curlicues of steam off its surface. She raised her eyebrows, looking at Marianne. She had blue eyes. "Why would you go out there?"

"Is it far?"

"No. Just up the road. I bet it's closed. For the season. Should've called ahead."

"So there's an inn there?"

"Used to be. I can't say now. Anyways, snow's expected tonight. You could be out of luck. If it's closed."

"We'll manage."

"Say," said the waitress, "where you from? And don't say the city, that's obvious. But I know you're not from there."

Marianne glanced at me, faced the waitress, her eyes tightening. "How's that?" she said.

"Just something about you."

"What about me?"

"Something."

"Something?"

The waitress didn't speak. She drank her coffee, looked at me. "You're pushy."

"Pushy," said Marianne. I could hear her enjoying this, itching to start something.

"You don't make an effort at politeness."

Marianne reached out and put a hand on my shoulder, leaned toward me, leaned forward, on the counter, her mouth falling open, smiling. Warming up. "Politeness" she said to me. "Am I not polite?"

"I wouldn't put it that way," I said. The waitress chuckled.

"What is this place?" Marianne howled, turning to take in the diner, this dim cold room, the late rainy Friday afternoon. "What have we stepped into here?"

"Rosalee's," said the waitress. She smiled ear to ear. Lovely girl, red hair, blue eyes. Reading Edith Wharton, too, of all things. I wanted to stick around and talk to the girl.

Marianne got up quickly, said, "I'm from Newark. Heard of it? Land of push 'n shove. And now I gotta piss. Which ways the?"

The waitress raised a hand, pointed.

When we were alone, the girl said, "I didn't mean to offend her."

"You did sorta call her impolite."

"Well I didn't mean to."

I'd finished my coffee. I showed her the bottom of the mug. "Don't worry about it," I said. "She's always that way."

The waitress disappeared into the kitchen, came back with the pot, poured me another cup.

"So it's not far, this mansion, the Drammond – "

"The Drammond House. You shouldn't go up there. That's all I'm saying."

"Oh? Why's that?"

"It's closed, for one. Because it's winter and there's no business. Second... "

I waited. I studied the bright enamel on her large front teeth. There was something in the face, something she was hiding.

I said: "It's not haunted, is it?"

That brought her back. She glanced at the book she'd been reading, still face down on the counter. "Haunted? No way. Nothing like that. It's just – just a big old house. Not much there. And it's falling to pieces. They'd tear it down but I guess it's a historical landmark so – you know – there's all kinds of bureaucracy that needs to happen before they can do anything. And it's so far away from everything. I guess nobody cares that much." A car passed outside, behind me, the hiss of its tires drawing the waitress's gaze up over my shoulder. She raised her chin and started to wave, but then it was gone. "So it stays there, year after year. Rotting, growing, going back to the earth."

"Growing?"

"You know what I mean. Decomposing, joining the ecosystem, organically. It makes sounds."

Organically?

"What kind of sounds?"

Marianne came around the end of the counter. She said, filling the place with her voice, her presence, "You got ants all over the bathroom."

"They do that when it rains."

"Well you should spray. It's filthy."

"They gotta eat too."

"What?"

She stood behind me, her hand on me. I could feel the heat of her body in her hand, feel her strength. I could smell her.

"You're taking us to a haunted house," I said.

"It's not haunted," said the waitress. "There's no such thing. It's just big. Like I told him, it's best not to go up there. But if you do – stay close, don't get lost."

Marianne pulled at me. "Let's go before it's dark. Before it snows."

"Listen," I said to the waitress. "Could we buy some – "

But she was already shaking her head. "I can't. Nico'd hide me if he found out I was in the pantry."

"I'd pay you, of course, for the coffee and – "

"Just the coffee. It's two dollars."

I put two bills on the counter. The girl kept her eyes down. I turned away and followed Marianne out the door.

"Stay together," the waitress said.

"What's that?"

"Stay together. You go in – you'll see. Easy to get lost, so – don't wander off."

Pulling up the road, Marianne said, "What a character. Didn't know they had white trash out here." She laughed, mouth wide open, looking my way for a response. "*Nico'd hide me*," she said, snorting. "What does that even mean?"

I'd glanced back at Rosalee's, the inside of which was suddenly dark. But there she was, the waitress, a dim slender figure by the door, watching us drive off. Closing, I suppose, for the night. We, her last customers.

Except for the car I'd heard passing when in the diner, seeing the girl's slow reaction, we saw no sign of another living soul in Maiden that evening.

"Rotting, growing." The girl's words hung in my head like curious birds coming down in the dusk. But then, as happens, I thought about other things, like taking off Marianne's stockings.

~ 8 ~

We continued up the mountain by the only road. I asked Marianne if she knew where she was going. She said she did. But to any stranger observing us it would appear that we were heading nowhere but deeper into the wilderness.

There was no sunset, no obvious evening. One moment it was a late Friday afternoon, and then it wasn't. The light just went out. Night was upon us.

The road was narrowing, with the bare face of a cliff rising on the right, and scrub and thin pine trees on the left. Not much farther ahead, I imagine the road turned to gravel and then, further on, to nothing more than an animal track.

I wanted to turn back. But then she stopped the car, leaned my direction, her cheek up to mine. "There it is." She pointed through the windshield, at an opening in the cliff, up a path, a slim line of blue light from the head-beams illuminating what looked like a stone column.

We got out. The air was cold, fresh and thin. I could feel the altitude in my hands, my head, a slight dizziness as I climbed from the car.

What Marianne had seen was in fact a column, one of a pair, between which crossed a large iron gate. The metal was so old that, when I grabbed it, flakes of rust crumbled in my hands. It was locked.

I was about to say: "Let's go back. Let's go down to the lake. There must be a hotel there we can stay at."

But she said: "I'll leave the car here. We'll walk up."

"But the gate's locked."

"So we'll go around."

The woman had this idea – of going to this place, the Drammond House – and I knew, recognized in an instant, that there was nothing I could possibly do to stop her. That's the way she was.

She got back in the car, pulled it up the road a little ways, turned around, brought it back, parked on the opposite shoulder.

There was a small archway on the other side of the column. Under this was a second gate, smaller, newer. It was unlocked. It pushed open without a sound.

We went up the driveway. The rain had stopped but the wind continued to blow, cutting at us as if we were naked, animals far out of their element.

We walked for what felt like a long time. I don't know how long. Thinking about it now, and going back to do that walk several times since, I think it was probably no more than thirty minutes that we hiked. Probably closer to twenty. But we weren't walking quickly, and we moved carefully for the growing darkness and the cold.

"I'm sorry I got you into this," she said.
"What do you mean? Into what?"
I took her hand. She held on firmly.

~ 9 ~

The Drammond House saw us before we saw it. It materialized out of the woods, the mountain.

When we stopped in the front yard, I saw that the building went down the hill we'd just climbed, in the trees. We'd been walking by it and hadn't even seen it there.

Big? Enormous. What can I say? They don't make buildings like the Drammond House any more... *Gargantuan*.

It was dark then. And the house was dark. So perhaps in my memory of that evening I was seeing things that weren't there. But it's a big place, no question. On and on and on, down the hill, into the woods, wrapped, I later discovered, around the mountain. Church Dome Peak they call it. I don't have to explain that.

Marble steps twisted down from the building, like arms coming to embrace you. We went up. From the front door hung an iron knocker, a creature, part man, part horned animal, with a heavy ring in its mouth.

"What's that?" she asked.

I look closely. "A bull."

I raised and lowered the ring several times. No answer.

"No it's not. It's a man, except for... It's from mythology."

"Got me there."

She looked in a dark window, tapped at the glass.

"She was right," I said. I stepped back, tried to take whole place in. "Closed for the season."

"But we came all this way."

So we made our way around the house. There was a path. We walked for, I don't know, five, ten minutes, the Drammond House running on and on at our right. Stairs would go up now and then, to cool dark doorways, various porches and terraces. These windows black as onyx looking down on us.

No – I was ready to go. The place was abandoned. And it's not the kind of house you want to just spend an evening around, exploring. Like a ruin. It's not a ruin. No. It was dark, and cold, and there was this – *building*, huge and dark and silent rising over us. I wanted to go home.

But she insisted. "Maybe we'll find someone."

"Like who?"

"A caretaker."

"A caretaker?"

Behind the building we found a garden, a lawn, a field running down a hill to a line of trees. It was quiet back there, peaceful in a way that the front of the house was not. And the air was different. Sweeter, warmer. There were rose beds, I saw, to one side, stems capped with dying blossoms.

And there was a light. Not in the house itself, but down at the end of the lawn, in the trees. There was another building there. There was also, we both heard at once, music, a piano, someone playing a piano. We approached, descending the gentle slope.

In the woods, in a small clearing, stood a neatly kept cabin. Smoke rose from a stone chimney. There was light in the window. The piano and pianist were inside.

Marianne climbed a step onto the porch. The piano instantly stopped. Neither of us moved. Inside, a man called out: "You are late!" We could hear him coming to the door, the floor creaking beneath him.

The man who opened the door was old, bald except for some long white hair over his ears, a long narrow face, hooked nose, strong body. He was shirtless.

He stared at Marianne for a moment, and then looked down at me.

"Who are you? What do you want?"

"Is the inn closed?" said Marianne.

"The what? The inn? Course it's closed. What you doing here?"

"I was told there was a place to stay."

"Lady," said the old man, "you aren't listening to me. The house is closed. Go back to where you came from."

Marianne turned, looked at me, pouted.

"You play very well," she said, facing the old man.

He snorted, paused. "Bitch of a piece. I'll die before understanding half of it."

"What is it?" I asked.

He pointed his nose at me and blinked. He said: "Beethoven." He was chewing something, moving his teeth, watching the two of us carefully. He didn't wait for an answer. "The place is closed. I suggest you head back before the snow starts."

"Couldn't you – "

"I said no."

I heard the fire inside his cabin crackle. I heard, just behind me, something quietly snap. A man, a young man, had approached. "Sam," he said. "I'll show them in. We can fix something."

He was a slight man, thin, swarthy, something elegant about how he dressed, his posture, the way spoke.

"Martin," said the old man, raising his voice, "I told them the place is closed. It's closed. We have no... It's not right making exceptions for strangers."

"There's going to be snow soon," said the man. He looked at me, held out his hand. "I'm Martin Sanchez. I'm the houseman." I took his hand. Small, fine bones, a gentle touch. "Welcome to the Drammond House. If you'll follow me."

Marianne stepped from the cabin porch, came to me, and we walked away.

"You better be gone in the morning," said the old man, to our backs. "It's not fit having people this time of year. When we're not equipped."

We started up the hill, over the lawn, with Mr Sanchez.

The old man, Sam, called out weakly behind us: "You'll come back, won't you?" And Sanchez turned, glanced between us, raised his hand, nodded, waved once.

"His name is Sam Gretton," Sanchez quietly said. "He's the groundskeeper. He is not fond of company, as a rule. He's good with plants and animals. If it were up to him, the house would be locked, the key thrown away."

As we approached the house I heard Mr Gretton resume playing his piano.

~ 10 ~

The door we passed through entered a large kitchen. Sanchez went before us and turned on a light. It was a long capacious room, with countless counter tops, shelves along the wall, sinks, cupboards and cabinets, pots and pans and strainers and other kitchen implements hung from the ceiling. Our guide continued quickly across the room to a counter where he pressed his finger down on a golden bell. It rung once, sharply. The sound wavered on the air for half a minute. The man stood, eyes toward the ceiling. We waited. He pressed the bell a second time.

A white swinging door opened and a woman entered. She was short and stocky. A long gray nightgown draped over her shoulders. Her short brown hair was pulled into a stiff pony-tail high on the back of her head. Her nape was shorn punk-style or as if she'd just come back from surgery. The woman stood there for a moment, her mouth open in a strange half-awake grin, her yellow teeth pressed squarely together. She was nodding, but in agreement or on the edge of sleep I couldn't tell.

"She answers to Elaine," Sanchez said. "She is the cook and the only maid of the house."

The houseman looked at the cook and only maid, and the woman, stooped and unsteady on her feet, looked at the houseman, waiting, it appeared, for orders.

Marianne approached the woman in two long steps. "Good evening," she said. Elaine pulled back.

Sanchez raised a hand. "She's mostly dumb. Sometimes you'll hear her repeating words to herself, things she hears. It is best, Ms Heany," the houseman said, gently placing a hand on Marianne's wrist, "to let her be."

Then another woman appeared. I can't recall from where. The kitchen, lit by these long florescent ceiling lamps, was a cool, quiet, spacious room, our presence, the four of us, hardly a disruption. We were just passing through. It was clearly a place that once upon a time had been very active, a kitchen for a staff of a hundred people, a kitchen to feed the guests in a full hotel. It almost felt like we were trespassing, in a room that had long since been closed off.

But then she was there, this other woman. The housekeeper. Corinne Kearn was her name. She introduced herself, smiling warmly as she came toward us. "I'm the housekeeper. I understand you'll want a place to stay for the night."

She was tall, with long black hair twisted into a bun. Long face, a big chin, dimpled in the center, full lips, these dark wide-set eyes with smooth, low, drowsy lids, a beautiful woman, I recognized in the same moment that, touched I suppose by her smile or the sound of her voice or her poise or the way she seemed to glide over the floor – her dress went down to her heels – I had the oddest sense of her kindness, her sympathy for us, complete strangers.

I took her hand and introduced myself, introduced Marianne. The housekeeper looked at each of us in turn, deep into our eyes, a beguiling smile on her lips, a look that suggested she knew us, or had known us, and was trying to place a face to a name. I thought: "You'll want to come back here. You'll want to talk with this woman, to get to know her. Find out her story, where she's from."

That's the way she is, Corinne Kearn. She has – how can I put it? – a presence. She's the kind of woman who steps into a room and elicits quiet, sudden attention, the wonder of her audience.

~ 11 ~

The one called Elaine led us to an elevator. It was an old machine. Small, cramped inside, terribly quiet for the cushioned the walls. A dusty deep red velvet. A thin worn carpet of the same bloody color. Tarnished brass trim. A brass lever, like you see on streetcars, which our guide firmly gripped and pulled into her gut. There was a jerk, bounce, and up, slowly, we went. Over the door a dial, a hemisphere marked over its edge by Roman numerals, began to measure our progress.

"Amazing that this thing still works," I remarked. Elaine looked at me from the corner of her eye and said nothing. "What floor is it we're staying on?"

If memory serves, thirty – XXX – was the last digit on the dial, farthest to the right. But I might be wrong. Because the machine didn't work properly. The needle stopped two thirds of the way across. At two o'clock, say. And though we continued our ascent, the dial, broken, only clicked and bumped, the needle twitching, leaning forward and snapping back. *Click. Click. Click.* Marianne took my hand. Her palm was damp.

Then with another bounce and jerk, we stopped. The door opened and I stepped out into a dimly lit hallway. Marianne followed closely and Elaine came last, rushing forward to get ahead of me, choking, snorting, humming quietly in her throat. She hurried down the hall. We followed.

The room was long and narrow, a bed taking up the space of one end, a chair, table, cabinet on the other. There were two windows. Night had fallen. I can't say if they looked on the front of the place, the back or one of the sides of the building. I've since learned that the Drammond House has courtyards, exterior spaces enclosed by the building. So we could have looked over one of those. But as I say, it was night, and cold, and the window was frosting up, and outside it was dark, very dark.

Standing at the door, her yellow eyes on the floor, Elaine waited. Marianne said that the place would do. Elaine nodded and gestured and we followed her down a long dim hallway. She opened a door, flipped a switch in the wall. The bathroom, a bright, clean, tiled room. Then she took me by my hand and led me further down the hall to another door. It was a closet. Folded neatly on shelves inside were blankets of various sizes and textures.

Elaine looked up at me, gave me her ghastly grin. I thanked her. We parted outside of the room.

"What a creature," Marianne said.

"She's not so bad. She does her job."

"But those teeth. Did you see the scar on her neck?"

"The girl's harmless. Anything to eat in there?"

The woman had opened a panel in the wall revealing a small bar. What was there was covered in dust. She took down a bottle of Tanqueray, wiped it off, overturned two glasses, blew these out, filled them, held one out to me. "We drink our dinner tonight. Chin chin."

We had a couple martinis, took a hot shower, climbed into bed, and finally got around to what we'd come up the mountain for.

Afterward a ravishing hunger overcame me, as sometimes happens. I pulled on my pants and shirt and stepped into the hall.

"Where you going?" she said from the dark at the end of the room.

"To find something to eat. I'm dying."

"Come to bed. It's late. There's nothing there."

The hallway was lit near the baseboard, tiny lamps cut into the wall in uneven intervals. I went down toward the bathroom, to the closet with the blankets, past that, down to the end, where the hall made a smooth turn to the left. There was a staircase there, winding steeply up and down. The elevator was in the opposite wall.

I went up to the next floor, I don't know why. Upstairs, another hall, where it was dark, impossible to see a thing. Wind outside howled distantly. Down I went.

I climbed into the elevator. I touched the cool old skin of the lever. But I did nothing else. Marianne was right:

There'd be nothing there, in the kitchen. If I could find the kitchen.

"Don't wander off," the girl at the diner had said. Her face flashed before my eyes. Her red hair, blue eyes, her lips.

I went back to the bedroom, climbed into bed, nestled up to Marianne's big back.

I woke in the middle of the night. Maybe I'd heard something. The place was freezing.

I went out into the hall, down to the linen closet, took out a blanket, went back to the room.

"Where'd you go?"

She was on her side, the blanket pulled up to her chin, her eyes wide in the dark.

"It's cold. Here's another blanket."

"Don't leave without telling me. Without waking me."

I arranged the second blanket on the bed and climbed in. But then I couldn't sleep. After awhile I got up again, went to a window. I raised it. Immediately a hard cold wind blew in, howling.

"For Christ's sake. Close the window!"

Pushing the window down, however, it caught, stuck in its track. Snow blew inside, dusting the floor, my feet.

"Raymond, please!"

"It's stuck."

But then it came undone, slammed downward, the glass rattling crisply in the pane. A heavy silence came over us. The world in the window was dark, empty, reduced to nothing but the far-off muted growl of the wind around the building outside.

Lying awake, I strained my ears for the sound of the wind, for the occasional rattle of the window – simple reassurances that the world, the natural world, was still there, outside, just beyond this thin pane of glass. Because otherwise, inside – ... It was unnaturally quiet in the room, in the hall, in the house, everything wrapped so tightly and carefully in the structure, the countless walls, ceilings and floors, entries, exits, levels.

At one point, it was so dark in the room I could hardly make out the window. But then, rattling, it was there, over there, where I'd left it.

"There's always the window," I said to myself.

"What?"

"Nothing. Go to sleep."

But then she couldn't sleep. We lay there together, staring at the dark, listening to each other breathe. After awhile – I was nearly out – she pushed me over on my back, climbed onto me with a grunt, and we had a second round. She was playfully loud that time. So was I, probably. Who would hear us?

It took me a while to finish. But when I did we both collapsed, fell instantly asleep, into a deep dark slumber.

~ 12 ~

It was before dawn when I woke. She lay beside me, on her front, her face away from me, arms out, heavy, low in the mattress, motionless.

I heard something across the room. But it was still too dark to make anything out clearly. When I heard it again – what was it? Something mechanical, like a vacuum cleaner running in some distant corner of the house, or like someone snoring in a room on a floor above us, or below us – I climbed from bed, approached the opposite wall. Down at the floor was a vent, a black grill. It was shut. I opened it.

"So there's a heater in this place. Of course there's a heater."

But no heat was coming up. Nothing came out. Dark, stale air, all the way down.

"In its day," I started thinking, staring into that dark hole, "a whole crew of maintenance men must have worked down there, keeping things like the heat running in this place. A whole underworld of maintenance people. Underground keepers, they'd call them." Sam Gretton was the general of the outdoors, and there'd be somebody else in charge of the underground, of an army of jockey-sized, pale and blind men in overalls, mole people scurrying about the catacombs beneath the house, keeping the heat and electricity and water running.

Then I heard it. What had woken me. My thoughts froze in place. In the empty shaft, deep in the house – not a draft, not a furnace. Maybe I was hearing things. I put my ear to the vent. Sure enough: somewhere in the house, down below, something moved and caused a low, rumbling rhythm, turning, like an engine. It was very dim, whatever it was – dim enough to be practically nothing at all, nothing more than my imagination.

A motor, an old locomotive, some kind of respirator.

"What're you doing down there?"

Marianne was seated at the end of the bed, her large frame spread wide and hunched over, looking worse for wear. Tits down her to navel, dark bags under her eyes. She's a brilliant woman in many ways. But not in the morning. She gets up like a bear waking for spring. Slowly, ravenously.

"Ass in the air," she said, snorting, clearing her throat, scratching her crotch. "You look like you wanna get buggered. You wanna get buggered?"

"There's something down there."

"Sure there is. A broken furnace."

"No. Listen. I hear it."

The woman yawned, licked her teeth, stretched, stood up and shuffled over. We both regarded the vent in the wall for a minute. "What is it I'm listening for?" She yawned again, scratched herself some more, gave me this look like "I leave you alone for two minutes and this is what you get into?" She knelt down, turned her ear to the vent. She put a hand against its black metal face.

"I guess it's not broken," she said. "Feel that?" She looked up at me.

Warm air was gently blowing, filling the room.

She went to the door, unlocked it. "I gotta use the loo. Come with me."

We showered, dressed, prepared to make our descent. Maybe we'd find something to eat.

But there was no need for that, to go looking for the kitchen and the one they called Elaine, the cook, the maid. Because when I opened the door, there she was, a tray in her hands, nodding to herself.

"Elaine," I said. "What a pleasant surprise."

"I'll die if I stop," the woman quietly said.

"Sorry?" I hadn't expected her to say anything. And what she'd said, if I'd heard her right, didn't make a whole lot of sense. *I'll die –*

"I'll die if I stop."

The words came out so quickly, muttered, but articulate, almost sing-song.

"What'd she say?" asked Marianne, who was at the window across the room.

But Elaine said no more, her lips moving and her eyes on a distant point, dumb once again.

"I think she said," I said, stepping aside so the maid could come in and set the tray – with coffee and croissants and butter and fruit – on a table, "she lives for mornings like these. To serve gracious guests like us."

And at that Elaine chuckled, gargled something in her throat. She looked me in the eye as she left the room and laughed inside her broken mouth.

The coffee was hot and good, and the croissants were delicious, fresh, homemade.

~ 13 ~

The snow had stopped falling. The sky was low, cold, a monotonous hard gray. A solitary crow, out of sight, cried out three times, to no response. It was Friday, February second.

"How do we get out of this place?"

We'd finished our breakfast, stepped into the hall. Marianne was looking at the closed doors of the elevator. Nothing was happening.

We descended a couple flights. The hall we entered was larger, wider than the one we'd left. We stopped at a balcony, looking up and down an atrium, a large circular window high overhead in the ceiling. The groundfloor was far below. The place was quiet, vast, empty.

We found a different stairway and descended again. After awhile Marianne grew uneasy.

"I wish there were someone here to help us," she said.

The stairs we descended turned around and around in a tight coil. I was in front of her. I paused for a moment, on the stairs, looked up at her and said:

"Dear, there's nothing to worry about. Remember, they're closed. Off season. The staff is away. We'll have to make do on our own. And we'll find our way out. If we just continue down, right?"

She stood over me, behind me, glared down her nose at me. "Don't *dear* me, Ray. And I'm not worried... I just think they could be more professional about this. To let two strangers wander around the place. She brought us breakfast, after all."

We continued on our way. We saw that morning, descending and exploring various floors, many rooms, all kinds of rooms. I recall what looked like an auditorium, and a study, a women's parlor, some kind of workshop, and next to that a tall, long and narrow closet full of empty and dusty wooden shelves and tables, and a room like a hothouse, made entirely of glass, and a long wide arcade, the arched ceiling filled by hexagonal windows, the floor tiled in the same black and white pattern.

Marianne was not as interested in these sights as I was. Descending another stairway, she pushed me in her hurry, saying, "This is crazy, Ray. We are lost!" And then, stepping in front of me and almost running: "Will you get out of my way!"

"Marianne. Wait – "

But there was no holding her back. She was panicking. I could hear it in her voice, see it in her eyes, in her flushed cheeks. I could smell it on her as she stepped before me and hurried away.

I ran to keep up with her. "Marianne. There's no need to – "

"We've got to get out of this place! I need to get back. I have to go to work, Raymond. I know that doesn't matter to you, but it matters to me! Now we gotta find a way out. This is absurd!"

"Marianne!"

She was running. I was running, on her heels, trying to restrain her, but also beginning to feel something about her uncertainty. We were in fact lost, if not knowing where you are in a strange house counts as being lost. But I didn't see, precisely, a need to panic about this. It was a house, after all, with a ground floor, and windows, and multiple entries to the outside. What could be so hard about getting out?

She'd got ahead, down some stairs. I couldn't see her. I could hear her running, but she was so far ahead of me on the stairway that I could no longer see her.

"Marianne. Wait for me! Why are you running!?"

Yes. It's a simple question. Nobody runs inside a house. Unless something's on fire or there's an intruder. It's just not something we do inside. Run. But the Drammond House is not like any house you've seen. It's a big place. Very, very big. And there's room to run. Still, why was she running? Was she trying to get away from me? Trying to get somewhere before me?

Was she trying to get away from something else?

I couldn't keep up. I could still hear her, up ahead, but nothing else. "Marianne!" I recall a sense – dizzying, in its way, as we turned and turned and turned again, descending those various flights, taking three or fours steps along a short hallway or into a recess, finding another flight of stairs and descending again – "Marianne, please!" – that there *was* something, something behind us, pushing us along. Though it was, I'm certain, a figment of my imagination, the combined effect of responding to her excitement, and running, and losing our way in the house, and hearing the fear in her voice – naturally, I came to feel as if there were something malevolent behind me, on my heels. There was nothing there, but that didn't matter. It felt like something was there. And, no, I did not turn to look. I was afraid I'd lose Marianne.

I did, finally, lose her.

"Okay, dear, you win! Enough's enough."

I could hear her somewhere up ahead, getting farther and farther away from me. But, strangely, I didn't really care. If she wanted to play games, fine. What was she going to do? *Leave without me?* Abandon me in the place?

I'd stopped in a map room. A beautiful room, if you go for maps, as I do, but also as good a place as any to pause and catch your breath and think things over. "Who knows but here's where I'll find a description of the place, a little sketch of the house. For emergencies."

"I'm in the map room!" I called after her, my voice curiously flat and small. Although by that point I don't think she could hear me. If she could, she wasn't listening. Or she ignored me.

There were maps of all shapes and sizes and ages suspended from the walls, stacked on tables. There wasn't, however, following my cursory inspection of the room, a map of the house, any indication to me of where I was in the Drammond House or how to find an exit.

On a large green table a map of the moon was laid out. I spent a minute looking it over. "Mare Fecunditatis." Strange name, if you think about, for a plain on the moon. What scientist came up with that?

When I decided to move on I found my way down to the entrance hall and kitchen without a problem. And there she was, off to the side, in a library, seated. And there, too, somewhat to my relief, was our host, the housekeeper, Corinne Kearn.

The two women were on a couch beneath a tall tree shrouded window, talking.

"There you are," I said, and Marianne turned, glanced my way, and then turned back to Ms Kearn, to whom she was speaking. I approached the two women. I was interrupting something, I saw, as Marianne continued to talk with the housekeeper even as I crossed the long chamber. I couldn't hear what they were talking about.

Then Ms Kearn said, standing: "Mr Byrd. I hope you had a pleasant visit. It wasn't too cold, then?"

"Not at all. We kept each other warm. And I took a blanket from the linen closet. Thanks. We were just heading out."

"So soon," said the housekeeper. She smiled, looked down at Marianne, who remained seated. Her long face, that high brow, those wide set soft eyes, the woman could stop time with a look like that.

Nobody said anything for half a minute, the two women silent in that peculiar way women have after they've confided secrets to each other, not looking at anything in particular but always returning their gaze, in flashes, to the intruder, the one whose entry inadvertently forces the sealing of the pact, makes the secret a secret by virtue of his presence alone.

I said: "I'll settle up, then."

"Very good." The housekeeper left the room and we followed.

In a small room not far from the kitchen, where the women remained, chatting, looking on the garden in the back, I met Martin Sanchez, the houseman. I signed my name in the register and I paid the bill, which wasn't much at all. The man did not say a word.

"Thanks for helping out last night," I said.

"Don't mention it."

Sanchez looked tired and preoccupied. The healthy swarthiness I'd seen in his face the night before was gone. The face was ashen and swollen, the color of dirty snow.

"So you live here. All year round. You and Elaine, Corinne and the gardener, what's his name – "

The man paused before saying anything. His tired eyes flit about, looking for something in my face to focus on.

He said: "Gretton. Sam Gretton is the groundskeeper. And no, I do not live here – with them."

"You live in town then, down in the village? I can't imagine you commute – "

"Mr Byrd," he said. "I don't see how that's any of your business. Where I live."

What goes on in our private lives is of little interest to anyone. And that is why one's privacy is of everyone's interest. "You're right," I said. "It's not ... But thanks, again, for your help. It would have been a long drive back in the storm, at night."

I was thinking of Gretton, in his cabin, at his piano. "You're late!" he'd said, obviously expecting the house-man. If it had been up to him, we wouldn't have stayed the night. We would have returned to the car, driven down to the desert, and gone back to the city, and gotten a room at a decent four-star place, consumed a stimulating fusion meal at a four-star restaurant, gone through the motions, and then, the next day, gone our separate ways. And she'd still be here.

Sanchez stepped away, held a door open for me, extended his arm. I followed. He led me through the entrance hall and out the front door, to the porch. The women were there, close together and talking like reunited old friends.

~ 14 ~

Wet soft snow dropped in handfuls from the trees as the sun dragged itself up from behind the mountains in the east. The driveway was wet, steaming. Gretton must have been up early.

Marianne was irritable on the way down. Silent, in her head, marching ahead of me.

"What is it?" I said. "Now you regret coming up here. You were the one, remember –"

She spoke, hissing, over her shoulder. "You can be so fucking rude."

"Rude?"

"What is your problem?" she snapped. She stopped, held her hips, squinted at me.

"My problem?"

"You were so rude to Corinne. She's so generous, and only wanted to help, and you –"

What was this? Had I suddenly, in secret and without my realizing it, married this woman? You go with a married woman who's not your wife to a place in the mountains to have sex because you're not married to her. To remind yourself of what it was like before you gave up

81

your life for the other person, and to be with a person who wants the same and who knows how to give it and who knows how, the next day, to walk away with a clear conscience. And not be a bitch about it.

I said: "I don't know what you are talking about. I was not rude to the woman."

"You were. I saw the way you looked at her. But it shouldn't surprise me. You. Ray. You really are like that, aren't you?"

"Like what, Marianne?"

"The way you looked at her! You haven't changed a bit."

"Changed a bit? I change all the time! What's wrong with you? It wasn't my idea to –"

"You're going to come back here, aren't you? To get after her."

"After Corinne Kearn?"

"I can't believe you."

She turned from me, continued marching down the hill. I tried getting a straight answer from her but she had nothing more to say. Except, once we were in the car: "Shut your fucking mouth, Ray, and don't say a word until we're back in the city. I can't – "

She'd turned the car on. Her palms were hard against the wheel, her long fingers stretched out. She looked at those fingers as if counting, double-checking, ten digits. "This conversation is over."

The deep murmur of the Jaguar's engine on a cold morning. The plaintive piping of a mourning dove some-where in the trees outside. I thought about Lucy, my wife, wondered what she was up to this lovely Saturday morn-ing. When was her presentation? I'd promised to call af-terward. But I had no idea what time it was in Hong Kong. That was something, I thought to myself, I should know. "You think of everything," I could hear my wife saying.

Marianne turned the car off, looked into her lap. I thought she was about cry.

"Marianne?"

She touched her chest, pressed a thumb against the base of her throat. Quietly she said: "I forgot something."

"What?"

"I had a ... a necklace. Didn't you see it?"

She looked me in the eye for the first time in hours. This strange light in her eyes, on her open lips. She pressed her tongue against the back of her teeth, about to speak.

"I didn't see a necklace," I said.

"I had a necklace. This morning. I took it off when ... It's there. In the bathroom. I remember seeing it. I set it on the counter next to the sink." She got out of the car. She was talking quickly, frantically. "I know it's there. I'll be right back."

She started jogging up the driveway to the Drammond House.

I got out, called after her: "Marianne. Wait. I'll come with you. Wait."

"I'll be right back," she said. She turned, walked backwards up the hill, twisted her lip in this sad, insincere, hateful smirk. "It's nothing, really. Ten minutes. Twenty, max."

The dove cooed above me, invisible in the limbs. I looked at the tangle of branches and oak leaves, at what I thought was the bird, listened and attempted to whistle back his lonesome melody. He remained silent as he listened to me. Then he moved, and I saw his head appear through the leaves, his piercing black eye taking me in, head atilt, perplexed by the sounds of the man beneath him. Then I stopped and waited and he went again as I listened. We did this a few times, back and forth.

When I started up the driveway after Marianne, the bird flew off and the woods were quiet.

~ 15 ~

Why didn't I go back in the house to get her necklace? I would have, if she'd asked me to. But, reflecting on the moment now, something had come over Marianne. I don't think she wanted me to do anything for her then. The feeling I had was that she wanted nothing more than to get moving, to return to that bar in Mojave and drop me off at my car and leave. Why? Who can say? The workings of a woman's psyche are one of the great unfathomables, and there's no point banging your head against the wall trying to undo it. Just let it be, I say.

When I came to the house the front door was closed and locked. I raised and let drop the iron hoop in the creature's mouth. It wasn't a bull, after all. More like a goat, but not that either. It *was* mythological, as Marianne had said, but I couldn't recall the particular name. Nor was the ring in the mouth simply a hoop of metal. It was a snake.

The knocker cut the air of the front yard with its sharp report, but nothing happened. I waited.

I left the porch and went around toward the back of the house, down what I thought was the path we'd followed the night before. It was a long walk. I kept the house on my right, and in sight, for what it was worth. Soon the path narrowed, the trees and shrubs rising up, growing thicker with every step. And soon what had been, the night before, a rather wide grass covered passage narrowed to little more than a track, a crack through the woods for animals. I was about to turn back when the path ended and I, with a single step forward, found myself in the enormous backyard of the Drammond House.

It was like a city park. I hadn't noticed its size and the diversity of flora the night before, coming back with Marianne. It was largely overgrown, with trees, old and young, alive and dead, coming up throughout the yard between, and sometimes in the midst of, a network of gravel paths. The green lawn, a gentle slope running down to a stand of redwood trees, was well kept, cut low, as was the vegetable garden at the top of the slope, in the shadow of the house. There was also, to one side of the garden, a bed of roses and other flowers, some of which, the damndest thing, were in full blossom.

I made my way out onto the lawn, for a better view of things. At my back, in the woods, a solitary crow barked a couple times, quickly rising and crossing the sky, alerting others of my presence.

Coming to the middle of the lawn, and just about to go up to the house, I noticed a figure farther down the hill, laid out flat. It was the groundskeeper, I saw, approaching him, Gretton, prone, his face turned away from me, his right arm deep in a hole. The man hardly moved as I approached and I couldn't help but think he was dead.

"Mr Gretton?"

There was a neat pile of black earth below him, and beside that a muddy spade and an old wooden toolbox.

"Say, Gretton!"

The geezer raised his head as if remembering something, hearing me from far-off, but he didn't turn my way. Then he went back to whatever it was he was doing in the hole.

"I'm looking for Marianne," I said. I could hear the old man muttering, cursing under his breath.

His face still in the hole, mouth in the grass, he said, "You wanna do something useful, hand me that pipe wrench."

I pulled the wrench from his tools and dangled it over his shoulder. The hole he'd dug was deep. Near the bottom a thick brown pipe shot through the earth at an odd angle.

He took the wrench, struggled with the pipe, cursed it, and waited, holding his breath. Then he grunted, pulled the wrench up, tossed it into the pile of dirt, and slowly climbed to his feet, clutching his knees, straightening in choppy intervals. His arm was brown and wet with mud to the shoulder. He took a soiled rag from his back pocket and wiped his hands. When they were sufficiently clean he twisted the rag in both hands, wringing water from it.

He looked at me, one eye lower than the other, a curl in his lip. Then, hands on his hips, he looked at the hole. I stepped closer and looked at the hole with him.

Water slowly filled the bottom of the hole.

"God damn it," he said. "It's lower down. It has to be lower down."

"It's a broken pipe?"

The look he gave me was answer enough.

"The fuck you want?" the old man growled. "Can't you see I'm working?"

"I was – "

"I heard what you said, Mr Byrd. That a concern of mine? What your ladyfriend does –"

"You didn't see her – "

"The place is closed, Mr Byrd. We don't take visitors this time of year. Far as I'm concerned, you aren't even here."

He took a pack of Camels from his breast pocket, shook one up between his lips, put the pack back, raised a lighter, lit up. He watched me through a cloud of blue smoke. He sighed and in a gentler tone said:

"It's a soft spot. An old pipe, ground down to nothing, somewhere down there. Deeper."

On the redwoods at the bottom of the yard a horizon of faint blue shadow lowered like a curtain. The sun, through a razor thin break in the clouds behind us, was coming up over the house. In a few minutes the shade on the trees would fall to the lawn and creep upward, toward where we were standing, and then slip beneath us on its way to the house. But then, almost in the instant I noticed it, the shadow on the trees disappeared and the world grew darker and colder.

Gretton smiled, sawed his jaw back and forth. He said: "This line, I thought I turned it off years ago." He drew on his cigarette, touched the bridge of his nose, closed his eyes. "So much plumbing down there, under us. Unless you hit one you can't say which is on and which off. ... But those trees yonder," he said, raising his muddy hand, a hooked finger, "the redwoods. They got these roots that get into everything. Everything, Mr Byrd."

Tall green triangles in the dim morning light, perfectly aligned, motionless, like trees a child might draw. My Back Yard, by Raymond Byrd.

"It's something else," Gretton said. "You get a leak. The smallest thing. It could be anywhere. Even up here, thirty meters away. Anywhere out here. And those trees, I'm telling you, they'll find it. It's amazing. You'd think they had a plan."

"A plan?"

"You know. Purpose. A manner of approach," he said. He smoked. "But they're just trees. I should've cut 'em down years ago. Now the missus likes 'em."

That would be the housekeeper, Kearn, I thought. Since Gretton appeared to live alone in his cabin back there, in the trees.

"I'm not sure," he said, gesturing at what he'd exposed, our attention once more on the hole at our feet, on that black line of pipe, on the pool of muddy water beneath it, "if that's the one. There's another pipe, something older, beneath it. Could be that. Could be there's yet another, a third beneath that. ... What I should break down and get is one of those devices, like a metal detector but for water. Something that senses the leak and tells me exactly how far off it is. Because this way... Damn it all... Look at me – I could be here all day, digging up the entire yard looking for this cracked pipe. All these goddamn pipes running everywhich fuckin' way, you'd think – "

The old man stopped and turned his hooked nose and pointed chin my way. He smiled, held his cigarette out, said: "But listen to me. You don't need to hear any of my complaints. And don't let me get started. What you're here for is that – "

Up in the house something clapped loudly, snapped in the air like a gunshot. I turned to look, as did the old man. It was a dark, monstrous edifice, the house, its wings stretching lazily out over the earth.

"That'd be Elaine. Has these unsteady hands. Poor thing. Drops things. Really gets the missus worked up. You'd never tell, of course, appearances being what they are," he said. "They're good at it." The old man sighed.

"Good at?"

"But I was saying – " The groundskeeper finished his cigarette, pinched out the butt out between his muddy thumb and finger and dropped it into his pant pocket. "That woman of yours – "

"Marianne?"

"She was just up here. Not ten minutes ago. Looking for you."

"Marianne came here? She was looking for me? "

"She was here, sure enough. Standing right where you are. Mister Gretton, Mister Gretton," the groundskeeper said, his voice rising into a mean and nasally imitation of Marianne, "have you seen the man I was with – "

"So she got her necklace?"

"Her necklace? I have no idea what she got or why she was out here. But I sent her back. Said I hadn't seen you and that you were probably out front, down at the car."

That was fast, I thought. Recalling just how difficult it had been for us to get out of the house. That she had somehow managed to return to the room so quickly, take her necklace, find her way out of the place, come out into the yard to speak with the groundskeeper, and then walk back – without my having seen her.

She must have gone through the house. Not around, as I had.

"She must be inside, then," I said.

"Nah. She went around. I saw her. I tell you – not ten minutes ago. There she went."

The groundskeeper pointed, nodded.

"But Mr Gretton. I just came around the house and I didn't see her. She must have gone through. I'll go see."

"It's best to go around," Gretton said.

"But that's the way I just came," I said. I started up the hill, toward the house. "I'll just see if maybe Elaine saw her."

"She's down at the car, I bet you."

"I'll just have a quick look."

"Mr Byrd," the old man said, "I bet she's waiting for you right now. Down at the car. Wondering where on earth you've gotten off to. It's much easier – "

I looked back at the old man. He'd picked up the pipe wrench. It looked heavy in his small hand, pulling at his filthy arm, asking by its weight alone to get back to work. "You really should go around."

I could feel Gretton watching me as I approached the house.

Near the top of the lawn, near the garden, the temperature fell quickly. And the closer I got to the house, to what I thought was the kitchen, the entrance we'd used the night before, the heavier the air felt around me, and the deeper the silence, like entering a tomb. Corn, tomatoes, squash in the garden, all of it dying, perfectly motionless, like a still life painting.

I climbed a short stairway, came to a door. It was locked. Through a window I couldn't make anything out. I rapped on the glass. "Elaine? Ms Kearn?"

Nothing. I returned to the garden, continued along the house and passed through a high archway, entered a courtyard, a filthy marble fountain in its midst. I looked up at the walls of the Drammond House, at these countless dark windows. Up and up and up, the sky a small dim patch of gray far overhead.

"Ms Kearn?" I called out. "Mr Sanchez? Marianne?"

My voice echoed upward along the building.

I saw what might have been Corinne Kearn at a window four or five stories up. But then, staring at the window, at shadows, at a dark glare off the glass, I realized there was nothing there.

But then, again, I noticed a figure in a different window.

"Ms Kearn? Hello? It's me. Raymond Byrd. I'm looking for Marianne."

The glass was empty. I was talking to shards of light, to reflections, curtains shifting on drafts inside the house.

I started back, going around the place, as the groundskeeper had told me to do. It then occurred to me that there must have been two paths around the house. Marianne and I must have walked right past each other and not even known it.

As I came to the end of the building I looked down the slope of the lawn at the old man, on his belly once again, his arm sunk to the shoulder in the earth. A fragile figure, in the end, I didn't imagine Gretton had the strength to do much more than maintain the lawn, garden and roses, to fix leaking pipes.

The groundskeeper barely moved in his position on the grass. After a moment it seemed as if he were sinking into the earth, his body ever so slowly deflating, collapsing, the dark green of the grass rising up over him. I imagined – envisioning, as it were, his burial – that he'd been there, at the Drammond House, for a long, long time. Sam Gretton could have a been a boy in the house once, a servant of some sort – he wasn't the type to be served – and he just stayed on and on for years, the remainder of the century. Someday soon he'd end up at the bottom of a hole like the one he'd dug.

"Say, Gretton!" I called down to the man.

"Eh?" The groundskeeper looked up from his work, turned his head my way, but otherwise stayed on the ground.

"It's a beautiful lawn you keep. And the roses, too. And the garden. How do you do it? It's January."

When the old man didn't answer, I thought he hadn't heard me. But then he spoke, coughing, clearing his throat, taking a deep breath, shouting: "It's geothermal, Mr Byrd. The ground stays warm all year round."

I nodded and waved and turned away, started back around the house.

"It's not magic," I heard him say behind me. "It's volcanic!"

The front of the house remained closed and locked.

I made my way back down the driveway. Before reaching the road – the large main gate before me, the pedestrian gate to its side wide open, I suppose I or she had left it that way when we last passed through – I noticed something different. Something, apart from the gate, wasn't right.

It was her car. The car had been on the shoulder, facing down the hill, on the other side of the road, well in view of the gate. I'd sat in it just an hour before. I'd seen Marianne get out of the car, walk across the street, go back through the gate, and start up the driveway. I'd gotten out of the car, crossed the narrow road, called to her, watched her for a moment as she continued up the hill. She'd turned, said something to me, smiled.

The car had been right there.

But then I saw it. Either I didn't remember things right, or it had moved a little further down the road.

And she was in it. And it was on, the motor idling. That explains things.

As I stepped through the gate, however, I watched, amazed, as the car pulled away.

"Marianne!"

The red flicker of the tail light as she took the first bend, disappearing from view.

"Wait! I'm right here!"

I chased after her, running down the mountain. But there was no point. The car was gone. Marianne, waiting for me, must have decided that I had somehow left without her.

~ 16 ~

"Help me understand this."

The black man across from Raymond Byrd raised a hand, closed his eyes.

"What's that?"

"You left the place without her."

"What do you mean *I left the place without her*? – She left without me."

"Sure about that?"

"What's there not to be sure about, I saw her drive away."

"You saw Marianne Heaney inside the car that drove away."

" ... It had to be Marianne."

"But you didn't see the driver. You didn't see who was driving the car."

"No. I didn't. But it looked like Marianne. It was her profile."

"You saw her profile? You were close enough to the car to see the driver's profile and call out to her and she didn't see you, she didn't stop?"

"From behind ... I think it was Marianne."

The black man had been taking notes. Then he sat back in his chair, looked at the notepad on the table, set the pen down beside it. "What happened, Mr Byrd?"

~ 17 ~

I walked down the mountain to the village of Maiden. That diner, Rosalee's, was open. Busy, for a place like Maiden, for that time of year.

I went in. Took a booth. A huge teenage boy served me, a brown scab under his ear dripping puss down the side of his thick neck.

"Where's the girl?" I asked. The boy poured me a cup of coffee.

"Which one?"

"The redhead."

"Oh, Jill? She's off today." The boy spoke slowly, like he was nearsighted and trying to read the chalkboard from the back of the room. "She does weekdays, mister. When it's slow. She likes it when it's slow. Jill's not really a people-person. She does some Fridays, I guess. You know. If we're slammed."

"You a people-person?"

"Yessir."

"You get tips here?"

"We pool'em, mister. I bring home – I dunno – twenty five on a good day."

"And what's today?"

"Don't know yet. Still kinda early. Maybe lunch'll pick up."

"What happened to your ear?"

The boy's round head turned bright red. He said: "Oh, that. That's nothin'." He touched the scab, wiped his finger back and forth on his greasy apron. "Bit of impetigo. Doctor gave me a cream. Said it should clear up in a few days."

"You an athlete?"

"Yessir." The boy smiled.

"What? Football?"

"Football and wrastlin' mostly. Weights in the spring."

"I see."

"Say," said the boy, "you gonna order somethin'?"

"No." I sipped the coffee. It was scalding hot. The boy started to turn away. I stopped him. "Listen. A silver Jag didn't pull in this morning, did it?"

The boy blinked several times. I could see the gears turning in his piggish eyes. He squinted, thinking hard. "Jag as in the car *Jag*, Jaguar, right?"

"Right."

He thought about it some more.

"Nah. Didn't see any."

I drank my coffee. The boy waited for me to say something else but I had nothing else to say.

Outside the diner I waved down a truck that looked like it was leaving town. I got a ride to Mojave, where I'd left my car the day before. It was a filthy, dejected looking machine, what the Mojaveans would have taken for an abandoned vehicle in another day or two and towed away.

I got home in the late afternoon. One of the cats met me at the door. Can't say it was happy to see me. She was hungry. I fed her, looked around for the other.

The place was cold and dark. It felt like I'd come home from a month long vacation, that emptiness coming up in my stomach that says: "Go back. Don't unpack, don't look at the mail, don't open the fridge. Take your bag and go get a taxi and get out of town and don't come back."

I took a long hot shower, put on some sweats, checked the messages – there were none, nothing important – ordered a pizza, opened a beer, and turned on the TV.

Later that night I took Marianne's business card from my wallet and called her cell. No answer. Then I called Lucy's hotel in Hong Kong. There too, no answer.

I fell asleep watching David Cronenberg's *Rabid*. It's a zombie picture. But the best part has nothing to do with zombies. It's the thing in the woman's armpit. When she has sex, she takes the guy's face and presses it into her armpit, feeding the creature. I tell you, you see that and you'll either wince or laugh or do both, but the next day, without a doubt, you're thinking of armpits.

~ 18 ~

Wednesday evening I met Lucy at the airport. I was there early. She looked good, if a little tired. She came through the doors at customs moving like she meant business. She spotted me in an instant, came right up, wrapped an arm around my neck, pulled herself against me in a tight hug, a kiss on the cheek, one quick on the lips, and she was off, eyes forward. That's Lucy at the airport for you.

She was quiet on the way home. I asked her about the conference. She said it was fine, said nothing in particular. Generalities she hoped I'd understand and, if not, at least find sufficient. I guess I did.

She asked me about my weekend. I made something up. Generalities I hoped she'd understand. She asked why I hadn't called after her presentation. I said I forgot to and that when I realized that I'd forgotten it was too late.

"I did call. Saturday evening," I said. "You were out."

"That's not like you. To forget."

"I didn't forget. I remembered – but it was too late."

The questions ended there. It was no trouble, her asking about my weekend and why I'd forgotten to call –

I'd expected as much. In fact, I was a little surprised she dropped the matter so quickly.

It was raining. Traffic on the 105 dragged along and then finally came to a standstill. The tinkle of rain on the roof and windshield, the slow archs of the wipers making their repeated passage, I started thinking of the Drammond House, of its old elevator, of the peace of falling snow, of the furnace that turned on when Marianne bent down to touch it.

I started to say something but stopped. Lucy had fallen asleep.

We got home close to nine-thirty. She stepped in the shower. I fixed dinner. Grilled prawns and bell peppers, fried potatoes, a mixed green salad, a pinot out of Temecula. One of her favorites.

I was setting the table when the telephone rang. I picked up. Silence on the other end. Not perfect silence, but the faint hush of someone with a phone pressed to his ear, to someone listening and waiting and thinking.

"You gonna say something?"

Click.

My wife picked at her food but drank with a healthy appetite. She was unusually quiet. I watched her replay something that had happened at the conference in her head. But I didn't say anything.

We ate in silence. When it looked like she was finished, I said: "I'll clean up. You look tired. Why not go to bed, I'll join you in a bit."

She stood, looked down at the dinner she'd hardly touched. She was about to say something. I could see it in her. "Thanks, dear."

She turned away, started into the other room. "What happened?" I said.

"With what?"

"At the conference. Something happened. They promote you? Or are we both on vacation now?"

Her shoulders fell. The woman took a deep breath. "The presentation went well. Much better than expected. But – yes." She sighed, eyes down. "Things happened. I'll tell you about it tomorrow. I'm beat."

But the next day we got up together at half past six, as we did most weekday mornings, and, as usual, I walked down to the corner Starbucks for a latte and to read the paper, and she did her yoga routine on the living room floor. And at quarter to eight I took her down to the station where, ten minutes later, she'd get the train for Irvine, where she worked.

I tried Marianne several times throughout the day. She didn't answer. I didn't think too much of it. She didn't want to talk. So be it. I did want an explanation as to why she left me on the mountain, at the house. That was audacious. But that too, in a week or so it wouldn't matter. Generally I don't dwell on things like that. And in a certain way, it didn't surprise me, Marianne's move. It's something she'd do. She's not the kind of woman, Marianne, to – how'd the waitress put it? – make an effort at politeness.

No. You rub her the wrong way and she'll leave you on the mountain. You can walk home.

That evening we went down to this bar I frequent to hear some music. I knew the pianist. We didn't stay late.

I didn't ask her to say any more about the conference. But I could tell something was eating at her.

The phone rang again later that night. The same caller, I assume, since he, or she, didn't say anything.

"Marianne?" I asked.

But nothing. The caller hung up.

A week passed in this manner. By appearance, we were carrying on with everyday life. We even went out to the movies on Valentine's, saw something by Woody Allen, I think it was. She likes Woody Allen.

Then, Friday of that week, the sixteenth, we sorted things out. I still hadn't reached Marianne. And, anger or not, it wasn't like her to cut herself off so suddenly without an explanation. She's a loud woman. She gets in your face about things. So something wasn't right. I'd phoned the office of the philharmonic and found out that she hadn't been in all week.

I started thinking: "If she's missing, then I was one of the last people to see her. Who else saw her? Who saw us together?"

I was considering my options, reconstructing our two days together scene by scene, when Lucy called to say she'd be late at work. She called again around eight to say that she was getting something to eat down there, with friends, and that she'd be on the last train up, at the station around eleven-thirty.

Yes. I felt like I was being pulled in two different directions at once. If I was going to find out anything about Marianne, I would need to tell Lucy what happened. Especially if Marianne was missing. I would not be able to keep that a secret.

In general, I'll say here, I do not keep secrets from my wife or from others. I'm not very good at it, keeping secrets. It's not that I have a bad memory or enjoy *chatting* with people. I don't enjoy chitchat, usually. So what is it? I don't see any reason in concealing information for specific purposes from those I interact with.

Did I cheat on my wife before Marianne? Yes, I did. Did I tell my wife? No. I did not. Does that count as keeping a secret? Not if the fact that I had sex with those other women without telling my wife is not concealed information. If Lucy had asked me, I would have told her.

And so, anticipating a situation in which it would be better for both of us if I told Lucy about Marianne, I decided to tell her.

At the same time, I wanted to wait. Because I suspected that Lucy was not being entirely candid with me. I can't say what I suspected her of doing, but I knew, or sensed, rather, that what my wife was up to that evening was not work related.

As it turned out, my patience paid off.

~ 19 ~

Shortly past eleven that night I got ready to go down to the station to meet Lucy. I was putting dishes away in the kitchen. The music was up rather loud and I didn't hear her come in. I nearly jumped from my skin, dropping a glass in the sink where it shattered, when she stepped into the kitchen and said,

"I took an earlier train, and a taxi."

"Can't you make some noise when you come in unexpected. Holy Christ!"

Her cheeks were flushed. She seemed distracted, not tired, her eyes all over the place, nervous. "Why's the music so loud? You always do this when you're alone?"

I was picking shards of glass out of the sink.

She dropped her bag on the counter, took three long steps into the living room, twisted the dial down on the stereo. It was Shostakovich, the piano preludes and fugues. The silence that then filled the house was cold, jarring.

I leaned on the counter, looked at my wife. "Have a good time?"

"Yeah." Breathlessly, wringing her hands. "Ray. Listen."

But before she could start the telephone rang. I could see it light up before it made a sound, as if my attention was so focused part of my mind was a second ahead, in the future, engaging the world before the arrival of my sluggish body.

We watched the phone ring for an instant. A giant cockroach could have come through the door and attracted less attention. I thought: "Here we go. The revelation." I picked up.

"May I speak to Lucy, please." He was English.

"Who is this?"

"Is this Raymond? My name is Paul Wise. I'm in love with your wife. May I speak to her, please?"

"Come again?"

Lucy said, her eyes closed, reaching toward me: "Ray. Can I have the phone?"

"You're what!? Who is this?"

"Raymond."

"Who are you!?"

"Raymond."

There was something about the way the man said my name – how can I put it? –

"My name is Paul Wise. I work with Lucy. I'm sorry but – "

I was seeing red. I was lifting this man by his throat, throttling him in my imagination.

But then, as quickly as it had arrived, the wrath dissipated. Everything was suddenly very clear. I recall feeling queasy, a little sick at the understanding that had come to me like a lightning bolt.

I replaced the phone in its cradle. I faced Lucy and said: "That was Paul Wise. He asked for you. I think there's something you need to explain."

There was something. Her story was both incredible and absolutely mundane. I wanted to laugh and cry, both for many reasons. It was not unlike, this scene in the kitchen that Friday night, leaving the Drammond House, descending the driveway with Marianne. Shocked and confused, suddenly, violently thrown into a different world. A parallel universe where almost everything is exactly as it is here, in our universe. But for these small differences, these other, meaningless, quotidian acts that we've committed, that have as a result built up an entirely different string of consequences, a network of relationships and understandings. And I was in the wrong place, the wrong universe. I was being confused with that other Ray Byrd. Not this one. The other guy, the one who went up to the Drammond House with Marianne Heaney – but didn't come back.

She told me that she was in love with this man, Paul Wise, and that she wanted a divorce so that she could marry him.

I'll say that once more. My wife, Lucy, told me that she had fallen in love with this man who she had met some months before and that she now wanted to end our marriage so that she could begin a marriage with him.

I didn't know what to say. Suddenly, you're thinking, this parallel universe theory – not so crazy, huh?

I looked around for something to drink. I took a bottle of Cutty Sark from the pantry, poured myself a full glass, drank it down, poured another. I poured her one too but she didn't touch hers. Had I heard her correctly? Divorce? So that she could –

There was almost something idiotic about the scenario. Divorce the man you're married to so that you can marry this guy you've fallen in love with. I don't know. The logic here is utterly bizarre. What's a marriage if you go around wanting to fall in love? What's a divorce, for that matter –

She raised her voice. "I'm in – "

"I heard you the first time."

Of course I'd heard what she said. We don't have communication problems, Lucy and I. In that way. In saying what we want, what we expect of the other. Lucy was like that – probably more so than me – she'd say things like that.

"I'm in love with another man."

She'd told me before. There's the rub. Let me explain. Let me say. She'd told me before. It was around the New Year, she'd said: "There's a new man in our office. He's from Oxford."

"Oh, is he. What's he do, what's his name? That Oxford, England, or Mississippi?"

"Paul Wise. England. He does ... "

I don't know what she said. Stem-cell something. Cancer something. It's not important. I could tell, listening to her, that what the man did was not important.

"I'd like to have him over," she said. "You'll like him."

"I'm sure I will." I didn't say that.

But I could hear it, what she wanted me to say, her hand on my arm: "You'll like him."

As if it's a wonder for me to like another man, to like one of my wife's colleagues. As if I had some kind of record of losing it, attacking like a dog, whenever she brought a male colleague home.

I thought about it later that night. This new man, from Oxford, who Lucy wants to have over.

And then I thought nothing of it. The next day it was as if nothing had been said. We were up early, as always, and she caught her train at ten of eight.

But that was then. What happens in the span of three weeks, twenty days? What happens in the lives of a man and woman, a married couple, an American man and American woman in a suburb of Los Angeles, a couple without children, a couple whose combined incomes puts them, let's say, in the upper tier of the middle class, of the so-called well-off part of the middle class? What happens to such people in any span of twenty days?

"Once again?" I said.

"I'm sorry, Ray. But there's nothing we can do. I want to be with him."

"What's that mean? Nothing we can do? You want to be with –"

"Don't be difficult."

"Don't be difficult? I won't be difficult. But you need to explain yourself. You can't just tell me I want a divorce because I'm in love this English doctor and expect me to stand here and say, Okay. Great. Have at it. ... I want an explanation."

"It's not like that," she said.

"Not like what? What's it like, Lucy?"

Then ensued a surprisingly civil discussion of the matter. We sat down. She talked. I drank and listened. It was very simple, I came to understand. We were to separate, first, and then, should this new love of hers turn into something more lasting – which it would, she assured me – we would divorce.

Divorce, amicably, she said. Should her new boyfriend turn into something more lasting. Her words.

And if he doesn't? I didn't say that. But the thought, naturally, did rattle around my head. If it doesn't? Then she comes back to me? And I take her back? And I take back this woman who abandoned me for that other man, to try him out, this woman who tried out the other guy and didn't like what she found? Take back this woman who's had – ...

I don't want to sound vulgar. It would be easy to sensationalize the scene and make the two of us look like vile human beings. But we aren't that. I'm not that way, nor is Lucy. Furthermore, the salacious details might distract you from what came next.

Where it came from, I can't say. I was more than a few glassfuls into the bottle and teetering. But it came, all the same, out of the blue, dreamlike in its suddenness, and strangeness, and frightening naturalness.

"Okay," I said. "But give me this. I'll let you do what you want with Mr Wise. But in exchange, I need something from you first. I want a date. I want a weekend with you."

She didn't move, didn't blink. For a moment I wondered if she'd even heard me, my proposal, wondered if I'd even said the words. But then she spoke, breaking the spell, leaning forward over the table, her lips twisting as she quietly said:

"You think you'll win me back, Ray, is that it?"

"I'll let you have whatever you want, Lucy. I promise. But give me a weekend first. Let's get out of town."

Was it premeditated, this plan of mine? Of course not. How? I didn't know Lucy was going to come home that night and thrust Paul Wise in my face. I was about to confess to her. So how could I – plan such a move? The idea, the place, as if in a flash of lightning that illuminates the world in a blue drowned reflection of day, came instantly to mind. There it was. Stranger things happen.

Okay. Maybe there was some priming of the machinery. I did have the house in mind, after all, did have Marianne's disappearance pacing back and forth in some corner of my brain. "Get her up to the house," the voice in my head said. "She'll lead you to Marianne. You'll stay with her, won't let her out of sight. And if what happened to Marianne happens to her, you'll figure everything out. And if you're lucky – "

Lucy agreed to the proposal. We'd go the following weekend. Which was fine with me, since it gave me time to do some more digging on the Marianne issue, and Lucy time to come to her senses. I didn't tell her where we were going. "I'll surprise you, sweetheart."

I am not a lucky man. This buddy of mine, from way back, high school, this guy would win everything. Dumb luck, the dumbest, the most amazing kind. It didn't matter what it was. If numbers and chance were involved, Jack would win. His number was always coming up. I mean ... it was frightening, this guy's luck. You might as well just hand your money over to him, if a bet was involved. Just hand it over. He would win. He always won.

I'm not like that. It's not that I have bad luck. I have neither good nor bad luck. It's like attached ear lobes. Some people get 'em, others don't. You might say, being generous, I have your average luck. Sometimes I win, sometimes I lose. But more often, it seems, I lose.

We went to the house. They met us at the door, Kearn and her creature, Elaine. As if expecting us.

We got a room, a room very similar to the one I'd been in before. We went through all the steps. Hardly a variation on what I already knew.

And then, the next day, I lost her.

There. I said it. I lost her, my wife, Lucy. We went into the Drammond House together, and I came out alone. As before. As always, I've come to realize.

... What happened to him? Jack? ... Yes. That's the thing. Testicular cancer. He died a couple years ago. He was – I don't know – fifty. Early fifties. I went to the funeral, saw some guys there I hadn't seen in thirty years. We barely recognized each other. Nobody said a thing. We

all wanted to, of course, but the joke was ... No. I couldn't.
And none of them could either, I guess.

~ 21 ~

I lied. There was a variation, the second time around.

I got lost, to begin with. I don't know how it happened. From Mojave to Maiden, in the mountains, it's almost a straight line. Rather, there is only one way from one village to the other. But I missed the turn.

Marianne was gone. And after calling her office a second time, and speaking to the same person, and sensing that she remembered me, my voice, I decided that calling a third time wouldn't help matters. The woman was gone. I felt somewhat responsible for her disappearance, of course, but I couldn't describe – to you, now, or to myself, then – exactly how I was responsible. We'd parted. I saw her walk up to the house. The gardener saw her, or said he saw her. And I saw her, as I said, drive away without me.

Someone drove her car away. I thought it was Marianne.

It was raining, as before. As we passed through Mojave, passed the little cantina Marianne and I had stopped at, where, I reflected, the story, so to speak, had started – what was the Patsy Cline song that the old guy put on the jukebox? I can hear her voice but not the words... – and entered the desert, everything began to look the same, in-different. I had that woman on my mind. I was driving back to the Drammond House to find the woman I'd lost. My wife, Lucy, seated beside me, grimacing in tolerance of my surprise weekend getaway, she might as well have not even been there. That would've been better, in fact – had I gone back alone. None of this would have happened.

Night was falling quickly and she was losing her pa-tience.

"You're lost. Admit it. Pull over. I'm asking for direc-tions. What's the place called again!?"

And then we found ourselves in Maiden, outside of the diner I recognized from before. Rosalee's. A light was on inside.

"Stop the car. I want to make sure we're going in the right direction. This is just ridiculous, Raymond! You're driving me out here into the middle of fucking nowhere, and for what!?"

I parked the car. She leapt out, ran through the rain to the entrance of the place, disappeared inside. I almost let her be. I almost decided then that she was right, that it was a stupid idea to take her so far out, for a weekend, for my – whatever you want to call it.

I got out of the car, walked up to the place in a cold rain. It was warm inside, busier than before. Another girl, a Mexican, not the redhead, the Wharton reader, was rac-ing about, steaming plates in hand. Lucy was at the counter, leaning in, looking one way, then the other, wanting someone's attention. I walked past her, back to the toilet, closed myself in, took a piss, looked at the ants on the floor and thought about Marianne, about what I had done.

When I came out Lucy was talking with the redhead. She must have been in the kitchen. The waitress noticed me before Lucy did. When I came to the two of them, Lucy said quickly to the girl, "Thanks for your help," and turned away from me, stepping behind me, toward the door. I started to say something to her but she was clearly in a hurry, wanting to move on. I watched her go back out into the rain toward the car.

"Get you something?"

The waitress looked me in the eye, cocked her hips, raised her chin. Something in the expression, in her lips. She remembered me.

"I'm not sure," I said.

"Well if you figure it out – "

The girl blinked her big blue eyes.

Suddenly I wanted to be elsewhere. Maui, on a sunny beach, a hat on my face, dozing to the sounds of the Pacific.

Through the window of the diner I could see Lucy in the car, low in the seat, her head a dark white and blue smudge in the glass.

"So you're going back there," the girl said.

"Back?"

"Because you lost the other one."

"... What're you talking about?"

"You lost that woman. That's what happens there. You go in with someone... You come out alone."

"I don't know what you're talking about."

"Don't go up there."

Then she was looking at me directly, standing straight, leaning into the counter. She'd lowered her voice. That wasn't the waitress talking, giving me advice. It was something else. A young woman whose name I didn't know. She was warning me, one human to another.

"You're mistaking me for someone else."

The girl was holding on to her side of the counter. She had long thin fingers, her nails painted red.

"I know what you're doing," she said. "It won't work. You're going to lose her. You're going to lose her, and the next one, and the next after that. Don't go up there, Ray."

"You remember my name."

"Go back to the city."

"What do you know about that place?"

"Go back to the city."

A big man in a dirty white shirt and greasy apron came out of the kitchen, quickly stepped up behind the waitress, put a hairy hand on her ass, said into her ear almost in a whisper,

"Jill. The good Lord gave you two legs and two arms for one purpose and that's to deliver what I cook and to recover soiled dishes. You clock out at the end of your shift. Then you can do what you want so long as you love God. That clear?"

Jill rolled her eyes and stepped away.

Nico, the cook, I remembered, then said to me, his fat lips sputtering: "Something you need?"

When I got back in the car Lucy immediately said: "She said it's up the road. Not far."

"I know where it is."

~ 22 ~

I parked at the bottom of the driveway, as Marianne had before. It was dark then, pitch black outside. The rain had stopped.

Lucy looked at me. I waited for her to say something, to curse me again. But she didn't say word, a cold hardness in her face, her lips. She got out of the car and closed the door.

We went up the hill in silence. I took her hand. Her skin was cold to the touch. I expected her to pull away. She didn't. Not at first.

She stopped. She was looking into the woods to our left. I thought I could make out the house further ahead.

"Let's not stop," I said. "It's right up here. I can see it."

She dropped my hand and stepped into the dark wet woods.

"Lucy!"

I followed her up a narrow path through the trees.

"Lucy! Now we'll get lost. Please – "

"I saw something," she said. "A light."

"There's nothing out here."

She was moving away from me quickly, practically running up the mountain, the cold dripping woods.

For a moment, I lost her. I couldn't see her. "Lucy!"

The path entered a meadow. Lucy was there, just ahead, at a tree, among these black, round, gnarly things, an old orchard. Trees large and small overladen with rotting fruit. Sharp green grass grew high through the sagging limbs. The trees looked not wild but weary and neglected. One had fallen over, the earth torn up around its long limp roots.

I came up behind her. She was holding the tip of a branch, her face up close to the tree. She sniffed, glanced back at me, said: "It's an apple. They're apple trees."

"Imagine that."

"You can't find apples like this anymore."

My pants were drenched. I could feel water running along the bottom of my foot.

"You think they still produce?"

She looked at me. She was about to speak when a man in the orchard turned on a flashlight, covering us in a long cone of white light.

"It's private property, you know," the man said.

Lucy held a hand to her brow. She grimaced. Anger flashed in her eyes.

It was Gretton in the orchard. I recognized the voice. I said: "We were hoping to stay at the Drammond House. If there's something available."

"It's closed," said the groundsman.

"I'd heard," I started to say, but Lucy interrupted –

"We could at least come in to dry off and have something warm to drink."

The groundsman didn't speak. The light held. Water dripped from the limbs around us.

"Is it far?" my wife said, stepping forward, into the orchard, toward the man.

Then Gretton lowered the light and turned and slowly made his way into the woods. We followed. After a few minutes the woods parted and the house rose up suddenly, a massive wall of black stone and glass.

A lamp burned on the porch above us, and standing alone in the pool of golden light it cast was the houseman, Martin Sanchez. He smoked, watched the damp dreary night, his dark eyes lowering as we came to the stairs. And then it was hardly a glance, his eyes tipped down as if we were nothing more than two ants on the marble step. "Look at you," he said.

I heard Gretton make his way off into the night. Sanchez watched him momentarily but otherwise hardly moved as we ascended and stopped beneath him, soaked to the bone like two old dogs. Then, flicking the cigarette off the porch, he said: "I'll find some dry things for you."

We followed the man through the front door. The foyer was cool and dim. The houseman had stopped. Noting our presence in the corner of his eye, he slowly reached up to the wall, over a wooden cabinet, and pressed his finger against a brass button. A moment later a small bell quietly rang out, and the sound hung, reverberated over us as we entered the front hall, faced the stairs rising to the first balcony. On the ground floor only a few lights flickered and burned. Rooms and halls, their entries completely dark, surrounded us. But above, on some of the countless floors, lights burned, flickering here and there. We both stopped, eyes up in awe at the vast atrium, at the distant circular ceiling where rain, in complete silence, fell sparkling against the glass. Sanchez continued forward, away from us.

"What is this place?" Lucy said.

"It's the Drammond House."

"It's ... "

"Stay with me," I said. "Don't get lost."

"Mr Byrd," Sanchez said from the other room.

"Stay with me, Lucy. It's a big place."

"How does he know you, Ray?"

Good question, dear.

"I made a reservation."

"But – "

We moved forward, toward the hall, if I remembered right, that would take us to the kitchen. When I saw Lucy hesitate, her head still spinning as she tried to take the whole place in, I told her: "Come on. Tomorrow we can explore."

It was not the kitchen we entered but a small office, a room, no more than a recess in the wall, with two small entries, each in opposing walls. Sanchez was seated at a desk there, writing, a hooded lamp burning hot over his hand. I noticed on the desk, beneath the man's arm, a white and black layout of the building, a map. But I knew instantly that it wasn't the entire house.

The houseman turned around and pushed forward a register. The line I signed was the second on the page. The first had a name I didn't recognize, a name I could hardly read. Dr. something, it said.

I thought of turning back a few pages to see if I could find my previous entry. But with Lucy at my shoulder, I didn't.

"So there's a map of the building," I asked the houseman.

He blinked, eyes on the register, on my signature. "Of some of the building," he said. Then he looked up at me. "We're closed, you know."

"So I understand. But with the night as it is –"

The little man shut his eyes, seemed to be listening to something far away. Then he opened his eyes, turned them coolly on my wife, and said: "With the staff as it is, Mrs Byrd, we must close the house in the winter months." He opened a drawer at his side, reached in, moved his fingers as if petting spiders. Then he withdrew the hand and held out a key. "But we do keep a couple rooms prepared. For such occasions."

Sanchez gave me a hard look. His head began to tilt to one side, the gesture of a question. But he didn't say any more.

We went back to the entrance hall. The housekeeper was there, with Elaine, the maid. The latter was breathing hard and trembling, her lips gleaming with saliva.

"Mr Byrd," said Corinne Kearn, "you made it."

"I'm Lucy Byrd," said my wife. She stepped around me, reached out for the housekeeper, and took the tall woman's extended hand. "We got lost."

"That happens," said the housekeeper. "At night, up here... Sometimes it's hard to find your way. The mountains, and the woods – "

"Exactly," said my wife, raising her eyebrows, looking back at me, taking, it seemed to me, to my absolute bewilderment, a kind of fancy for the housekeeper, in a mere handful of words. Resentment – I'll call it that – turned over in my guts.

You'll like him, she'd said.

Sure I will.

"And I told him," Lucy went on, "as soon as the sun goes down, it's going to be impossible to find anything up there. No no no, he says, I know where it is. Give me this, he says, my sense of direction is a thousand times better than yours."

The women smiled. Elaine bounced on the balls of her twisted feet.

Lucy said: "So we had to stop and ask directions. No no no, he says. I know where I'm going. I know where it is. But only then, down at," she said, raising a finger in the air, pointing toward the entrance, "that – the diner."

"Hmm. Rosalee's, it's called," said Kearn.

"Right. There. The waitress helped us. Nice girl."

"Jillian."

"The redhead?"

"Her name is Jillian Veldt. We know her."

"Well if it wasn't for her – gosh," said my wife –

and I'm thinking: *Are you fucking kidding me!?*

" – we'd be in Yellowstone by now."

"Yellowstone is a thousand miles away," said the house-keeper. "I think you mean Yosemite. So give your husband that, Mrs Byrd," she said, her chin coming my way, her eyes on mine, "maybe he does have a better sense of direction than you, than you realize."

Sanchez, who stood at my back, cleared his throat, and was about to say something when Kearn said: "So you haven't eaten?"

"No," said Lucy, looking at me as if expecting me to explain why we hadn't eaten. She added: "But it's too late now."

"We didn't," I said, "but at this hour, and on a night like this. Really, a warm bed, a cognac. Ms Kearn. We'll be fine."

"Elaine," said the housekeeper, looking down at the maid, "you'll bring supper to our guests. There's confit de canard," she said, facing us. "You eat duck, don't you?"

Sanchez offered to take us up to our room, but Kearn insisted. The houseman retreated a step and lowered his chin. We followed the housekeeper through a door and down a hallway, to the elevator. I happened to look back to where we'd come from – already knowing, as I did, some of the tricks of the house, and since the elevator, if it was the same one I'd used before, wasn't where I thought it should be – and saw that the houseman remained where we'd left him. He looked at me from the end of the hall, a small man, a tiny figure, like some dim, peripheral face in a crowded group photo, poised but with a manner I thought of at the time – as if he had something urgent to say, as if, I thought, he'd wanted to pull me aside to tell me something apart from the others – of loneliness. The houseman might have had a friend in the groundskeeper, Gretton, but inside the house he struck me as a lonely man, as not fitting with the rest, with his role, title, re-sponsibilities, whatever those were at a time like that, in the off season.

Then, with a ding, the old elevator arrived and opened, and we climbed in, Lucy, myself, the inimitable Corinne Kearn at my back.

"You going to finish that?"

The duck was greasy and salty. Utensils, silver and clean, came with the dish but my wife chose to eat with her hands, like an animal. And when she was finished with her portion she reached onto my plate and took what I'd left. Her lips glistened, covered in brown duck fat, black chips of herbs stuck in her front teeth.

It was not the room I'd been in before. The hallway looked the same, as did the bathroom down the hall, but the room was different. Wider, taller. There was a fireplace at one end of the room, a pile of dusty wood on the hearth, a large bed on a raised platform at the other. Between two windows a long oak table was pressed against the wall. Above this hung a tapestry. Its decades old image had faded, what had once been reds, blues and greens now dusty and brown, a uniform amber. The light at the end of a summer day. You had to look closely, for its age but also for the dimness of the room. It portrayed a man with a flute. A shepherd. He played beneath the limbs of a large tree. Dancers, women, circled the tree, their knees up, hands up, their clothing falling from their buoyant bodies. Their feet had once been red. Not in slippers, but with blood, I imagine. When women danced with shepherds barefoot in the hills.

Despite the blaze I'd started in the fireplace, the room was cold. Stone, smooth, dark, like a cave cut from a glacier.

I listened to my wife eat. I poured myself what remained of a Château Margaux that had come with the duck and stared at the tapestry on the wall. "Who's that, you think?" I nodded at the figure beneath the tree.

My ravenous wife glanced at the image, shrugged, stuck a bone in her mouth and pulled it out clean. "A shepherd," she said.

The rain had stopped. I opened a window, stuck my head out, leaned on the sill. Clouds, low and heavy and black, covered the sky. The house beneath me and above, farther than I could see from my small perch, was dark and silent. Like a stage set in the wee hours of the morning, the theater empty, everything locked up, everyone home, asleep.

When she finished eating, Lucy curled up on the sofa before the fire. I went to her, pushed her legs over and sat heavily beside her. We watched the fire burn, listened to the fire hiss and crackle. A small pile of wood remained. In another two hours it would be gone and the fire would die and the room, ice cold and dark, would be little more than our tomb for the night.

What time was it? When would the sun rise?

"You cold?" I asked her. "I'll find a blanket."

"What will we do when there's no more wood?" she said, reading my thoughts.

I put my hand on her leg, caressed her hip. The fire sparkled in her eyes. "We'll keep each other warm," I said.

"You'll have to get more wood." She looked at me, a cool distance in the gaze, pulling back. "Great place you found here, Ray." She stared at the fire. She looked old and tired. She said: "Who told you about it?"

The room didn't have a bar, as the previous one had. A stiff drink or two would hit the spot.

"I saw an ad."

We sat in silence after that. The fire dimming, the cold of the house coming up out of the floor. Occasionally something far off in the house would stir – a door clicking closed, water momentarily running, whining in the old pipes – and I, or she, would look around, expecting more, wanting to hear more, the voice of another person, something warm and alive to remind us of why we were there, to muster our strength to get from the dying fire to the bed. But nothing would follow these occasional interruptions. The silence of the house returned.

She yawned loudly, her teeth popping from her mouth, and got up, went over to her things. "Where's the washroom? Think I'll clean up and try to sleep. I hope we can leave right away in the morning. There're things I want to do."

I took her down the hall to the bathroom. She closed the door in my face.

"Come back to the room when you're done," I said.

She was pissing. "Where would I go, Ray?"

"Don't wander off. It's a big place."

In the room I put the remainder of the wood on the fire. I got into bed. The gold light of the blaze made the figures in the tapestry – the shepherd, the dancing women – spin back and forth in shadows, coming to life. There was something momentarily pleasant about the scene. The warm firelight filling the room, a little color returning to the drab fabric.

I must have fallen asleep. When I woke the room was dark and cold. Lucy was in the bed beside me, sitting up, her hand on my chest. Her eyes were wide open, spoons of darkness.

"You'll have to get more wood," she said.

"It's not that cold. Under the cover."

"Ray. Ray. Wake up. It's freezing in here. Get the wood. Start the fire."

In fact, it was cold, quite cold, in the room. And without heat of some kind, in a few more hours neither of us would be able to sleep. So off I went, with a glance back at the warm bed where my wife lay, the down blanket pulled up to her eyes, into the Drammond House alone.

The houseman, Sanchez, had mentioned something about wood for the fire, in a room off the kitchen. But where was the kitchen?

I waited at the elevator. It appeared to be out of order. Or shut off for the night. Our hosts must have assumed we wouldn't need it, would have no reason to go out into the house in the middle of the night.

There were stairs just a step away, descending around a curve into darkness. I thought of Marianne and our morning together, racing down, down, down into the house through those dozens of rooms.

I pressed the hard black button of the elevator, hoping against hope that it would work, looking at those stairs, Marianne's face filling my thoughts. I'd never see her again.

The elevator arrived, the doors opening in silence. I stepped inside, pulled the lever.

A minute or so later the machine stopped, the doors opened and I stepped out. I immediately knew that I'd gone too far. And what I should have done was get back into the elevator and gone up, and gone either to the first floor, where I'd try to find the kitchen, or back to the room, and to Lucy, and I'd tell her that couldn't find any wood and that we'd just need to sleep clothed. We could ask for our money back the next day.

I stepped into a dimly lit hallway. The first thing I noticed, indicating to me that I was somewhere beneath the Drammond House, was that air was warm and humid. The second thing was the sound. There was an engine, a soft hum, the turning, churning, boiling of a furnace or ...

The walls and floor, ice smooth cement, were painted a dark aquamarine green. It could have been a hospital but for the relative silence and absence of anybody else.

I went down the hall. The first door I came to was metal, like in a ship, warm to the touch. Locked, no surprise. The next door, the same.

I walked for a minutes in this way, trying doors, quietly making my way into this level of the house. The sound of the engine, whatever it was, didn't change in volume or pitch. It simply continued, doing its work, as engines do.

Then I came to an open door. The room I entered, made of the same poured cement of the hallway, was dimmer than the hall, nearly dark. But there was little to see. Hardly a room at all, the niche led almost immediately to an archway and descending staircase. The stairs were stone, large black volcanic blocks, and, in the low light, they appeared to be wet, glimmering with moisture.

I could hear water, then, dripping, gently splashing. And I could smell it, too, the salt and sulfur of a spring. And then – poised at the top of these steps like a sleepwalker, half awake, half dreaming, about to make his move – I heard someone, what could only be the sigh of a human, a woman. It was not my imagination, it was not a machine, it was not the water, and it was not an animal. There was someone down there.

"Guests are not permitted in this part of the house."

I turned quickly. It was the houseman, Sanchez, right in my face, and I probably would have slipped and fallen had the man not immediately reached out and took me by the arm.

"I was looking for wood."

"You should have rung. Guests are not permitted here."

He pulled me quickly, firmly, small as he was, from the room, pushed me into the hallway, back in the direction I'd come from.

"Rung you? I didn't – "

"She didn't show you?"

"She?"

"Elaine didn't show you?"

"There's a phone?"

"I'll speak to her. I'll bring the wood. Now go back to your room."

It could not have been the same elevator I took a few minutes earlier. The elevator Sanchez pushed me into looked like the one I'd used but we'd come to it much too quickly, almost as soon as we'd left the alcove, where he'd found me.

The doors closed between us and, following a gentle jerk and bounce of the contraption, up I went.

~ 24 ~

W as it my floor? Was that my room? If I opened the
door and stepped inside would I find my wife asleep
in bed? I don't know how these things work.

The bathroom I passed looked like the one on our floor.
I reached into the darkness and turned on a light. Sure
enough: ours. That was my toothbrush balanced on the
marble sill above the sink, beneath an old silver venous
mirror.

I looked at myself and thought about what I'd done,
what I was doing, thought about my wife and the impossibility of saving my marriage, thought about Martin
Sanchez, who had probably just saved me from, if not serious injury, further complications and deceit.

A few more hours. Then we can all part ways.

There was someone in the hall. Humming, or crying.

"Martin?"

The hallway outside the bathroom was empty. My
room was only a few steps away. But the sound I'd heard
had been distinct. There had to be someone there.

I walked toward the elevator, to the staircase. Nothing.
Nobody.

But then, again, the sound. Someone was crying, sobbing quietly.

"Lucy?"

The door was smaller than the one to our room, and flush with the wall. You wouldn't know it was there if you weren't looking for it. It opened outward, revealing a narrow hallway that seemed to run parallel to the one returning to the bathroom and to my room. I stepped inside. A wooden staircase immediately rose steeply upward. The sound I'd heard, a woman crying, was louder here. She was upstairs.

It was a tiny bedroom at the top of the stairs, with a small blockish bed, a table, a black circular window looking onto the night. On the bed, beside a clutch of limp-headed dolls, sat Elaine, her big shoulders bouncing and convulsing as the girl quietly wept. Her pink cheeks were wet with tears.

"Elaine," I said, entering the room. The ceiling was low. "What happened? What is it?"

The maid sobbed, her face a ruin, the mask of sadness. She began to lift her hands from her lap.

I went to her, sat beside her on the stiff bed, put an arm around her shoulder.

"Elaine? Tell me – "

Quickly, though without aggression, the girl turned to me, ducked her head, wrapped her strong arms around my body, her ear to my chest.

"I'll die," she said, whispering.

"You'll what?"

"I'll die if I stop," she said, her thick lips to my sternum.

"If you stop?"

I tried to raise her head, push her away, to speak to her face to face.

"I'll die if I stop. I'll die if I stop."

"Elaine!"

She moved quickly, with surprising strength and the effortless grace of a cat, and in a moment she'd climbed over me, straddling my hips, her mouth against my throat, under my ear.

"I'll die if I stop." Her breath was hot and rank in my face. Her teeth snapped before my eyes.

"Elaine!"

She began to lift up her shirt, to press herself against me, all of her weight coming up over me.

She hissed, pulling at my hair: "I'll die if I stop!"

"Elaine!"

"Ray!"

"Get her off me!"

It was Lucy at the top of the stairs, panting, her eyes flashing.

At the appearance of my wife Elaine transformed, melting as it were into the sobbing idiot I'd discovered a minute earlier. She fell into my wife's open arms, blathering, sobbing.

"What happened?" Lucy said to me. "My dear," she said, stroking Elaine's big head.

"I found her this way. I heard her crying. I came – "

"What did you do?"

"Lucy! I heard her crying. So I came up the stairs. That's what I – "

I got up from the bed and the two women sat down, Elaine cradled in my wife's arms. Elaine sucked loudly on her thumb and looked at me, menace and cruel understanding in her pale eyes.

But then she stopped, the performance coming to a sudden end, and pulled away from Lucy. She sat up quickly and folded her hands in her lap, her fat face empty, devoid of any semblance of warmth, life, sadness.

The houseman, Sanchez, stood in the entrance to the girl's room. He looked at Elaine, at Lucy, at me. Then he looked at the maid again, his eyes holding the girl for a spell. Then he turned, descended, said: "I brought up some wood, Mr. Byrd. I've started the fire in your room. It should burn until morning. Please, follow me. I am sorry for the disturbance."

~ 25 ~

Faint, steel gray light in the window. Not day, not night. There were voices far off in the house. Someone yelling, shouting. Screaming. Something crashed to the floor.

But it was distant, this ruckus, so far off as to be nothing more than an invention of my weary brain, fragment of a dream.

It came in brief intervals. Bursts of muted sound.

Lucy slept beside me, curled on her side under the blankets. I could feel the warmth of her breath on my arm.

Then it came again, this noise. Someone shouting, a woman it sounded like – a young woman, it seemed to me then – and a moment later, something violently breaking, an object thrown. Crash! Then silence, deep and frightening. Painful, in a way. I wanted to hear more. I couldn't sleep.

I was going to get out of bed, put wood on the fire. But I'd wait another minute. See what happened.

I had closed my eyes. I stroked Lucy's long thigh. She had lovely legs, Lucy did.

Maybe I was falling asleep, finally, when it happened again. A woman shouting, people fighting somewhere in the house. I'm fairly certain it was a woman, but memory does things to stories like this one. It could have been man, I suppose. But it was too high a voice to be a man's, even if he was that angry and excited. No. It was a woman. And it sounded, this second time, as if she were barking. Like a dog.

Brap! No! I said! ... Brap! Ark! Ark!

But softly, and so small and distant as to be hardly audible, or only audible in the silence of dawn in a house like that, with the woods and mountains, and the building, all around.

Lucy didn't hear a thing.

I asked her a few hours later, when I woke a second time. She was already awake, looking at me.

"Did you hear the noise? That shouting?"

"No."

She got out of bed. She was naked, which surprised me, the room being so cold earlier.

She went to the fireplace, squatted like a farmer, put wood on the black remains and, lowering her head, blew on the embers. A moment later a flame caught. She remained before the fire, squatting, her head down, her big knees up around her body.

"I thought you were cold," I said.

She turned her head, gave me an ear. She said: "I am. What d'you think I'm doing?"

"But you're naked. When did you – ?"

Then she turned around and looked at me. "I was hot. ... Now I'm cold again." She stood, turned, looked at the fire.

Wet milky light filled the window. I couldn't tell if it was the sky or part of the house, wrapped in cloud, that I was looking at.

She said: "I know what you did."

"What'd I do?"

"I know what you're doing now."

"What's that?"

"You brought someone here. When I was in Hong Kong."

There's nothing like an argument with your wife first thing in the morning to make you feel old. "Let me go back to sleep and dream!" you say to yourself. But there's no going back. You might try but she won't let you.

So why stay? Why not leave her and go back to the solitude and peace and quiet of singledom?

There is no going back. There is no such thing, any longer, as singledom. We need each other, even when this need destroys us, and even when we know the need is destroying us.

"No I didn't," I said.

"You did. And... And now... "

"And now? What now?"

"Now you think you can... "

"Think I can what?"

The fire was burning properly then. Lucy turned and came toward the bed. She went to her side, looked at me, fury in the hardness of her mouth and eyes, bent down, picked up her clothes, started dressing.

She said: "That girl told me."

"That girl? She's mute."

"Not her, Ray. The other one. The waitress."

"What waitress?"

"You know the one."

I thought about it. I thought about what she thought I was doing. She was the one who... After all, she's the one who wanted a divorce so that she could go off with Paul Wise and make... I didn't want a divorce. I didn't want anything – except for things to remain the way they were.

No. That's not entirely true. In fact, what I wanted in that moment was to get out of the Drammond House, with my wife, in one piece.

"So you don't deny it," she said.

"I've never seen that waitress before in my life. She thinks I'm someone else."

Lucy went on, quietly: "And what if that girl, Elaine, said something?"

"She doesn't talk."

"Sure she talks. You heard her. Last night. She's not mute. She just has a problem."

"The girl's nuts."

"She's not nuts. She just has a problem talking."

"You saw her, Lucy. All that baby-acting. Sucking her thumb! And then when Martin showed up, how quickly she composed herself. It was all for show! She's nuts. They should lock her up." I got out of bed and pulled on some clothes. "Let's get out of here. No breakfast, no nothing. Let's just leave. I'm sorry I brought you here."

But she wasn't finished. She'd thought carefully about what she wanted to say. How long had she been up, watching me, thinking? "Elaine repeats things she's heard. Didn't the houseman say that? She's not crazy. Just troubled. What were you doing in her room, Ray?"

"I told you. I heard her crying. I went to see what happened. I didn't know it was her bedroom up there. I didn't know it was her, Elaine. All I heard was – "

"Who's Marianne, Ray?"

Something in the fire popped and hissed.

"Marianne Heaney is an old friend. We went to school together. Why do you ask?"

"She's the one you – "

"Who told you about Marianne? How would she know?"

"Paul. He told me."

"Paul! How would – "

"Who is she? Where is she now? Why didn't you – "

For moment I had an opening. She'd let her guard down. I could hear it, see it in her posture. Even if she knew that it was true that I'd brought Marianne to the house, even if I told her straight out that that's what I'd done, she didn't, for an instant, seem to care. But I missed my chance.

"It's true," I said, "we made a date, to go to this concert. She – "

"I don't know what you think you're doing, Ray, but it won't work. I don't care what it is you're trying to do – coming up here, bringing me up to this awful place... I don't care. We're finished, Raymond. You're a despicable man. I don't know why I've stayed with you as long as I have. I've had enough. When we get home I'm taking my things and leaving. I won't talk with you any more. Get a lawyer."

She'd brought along one bag. She'd hardly opened it. Now it was closed and she was taking it and leaving the room.

"Lucy, wait," I said. "Wait for me. Don't go down by yourself."

She left the room, disappeared in the hall. As quickly as I could, I packed my own things and raced after her. She was waiting at the elevator. "Please," I said, "I'm really sorry about what's happened. Sorry we came up here. It was a terrible idea. You love Paul, fine, I accept that. ... You can go. I won't stop you." She was tapping her foot impatiently. She glanced at the staircase. If she decided to take the stairs down I wouldn't be able to stop her. And I'd lose her, I was sure of it. I was about to reach out and take her hand.

The elevator opened. We stepped inside. The elevator closed and began a long slow descent.

~ 26 ~

The kitchen wasn't far off. The housekeeper was there, loudly reprimanding Elaine. We passed through various rooms, down several hallways, following the sound of Kearn's voice. Then, pushing through two tall white doors, we were there.

Kearn stood stiffly before the maid, whose face was flush and wet with tears. Sanchez stood at a distance, by a window, half-turned toward us. Before I or Lucy said a word, Kearn stepped forward quickly, lowered her chin, stopped before us, looked me in the eye, my wife in the eye, and said: "Mister and Missus Byrd. I want to apologize for what happened last night. Elaine knows that she shouldn't bother our guests, knows that her proper place is... in no place, invisible. But she is willful and... It's hard, as I hope you can understand. She's not like the rest of us."

I thought she'd say more about Elaine, describe what had happened to the young woman. But she didn't. Her gaze wandered in thought. Then, collecting herself, taking a long deep breath, she looked up, turned aside, said: "There are muffins, fresh butter, and apples. Please sit. Elaine will be with you in a moment. Coffee?"

I was about to thank the woman for her courtesy and to excuse us from breakfast, as there was something urgent we needed to return to in the city. But Lucy followed the housekeeper sweetly, and took a seat at small round table near a window.

I followed her, and, without sitting, leaned down and said: "I think we should be going."

"There're muffins, Ray. And fresh butter."

She avoided my eyes, looking elsewhere.

"I thought you had – "

"Don't be rude, Ray," she said, facing me. "Sit down. At least have a cup of coffee."

There was no point arguing with her over whether to stay for breakfast or not, though part of me wanted to smack her senseless and carry her on my shoulder out the backdoor – out of frustration but also fear, a sense that the closer I got to leaving the house with Lucy the closer I came to facing what it was I couldn't face, a destiny, a demon, the magic of the house itself. But I sat down. I drank a cup of coffee. I didn't touch the muffins, butter, or fruit.

Elaine stood behind me, at my shoulder. I could hear gas bubbling in her stomach. I could see when Lucy, in flitting glances, would look up at the girl.

The housekeeper stood behind Lucy, at the far end of the kitchen, in plain view. Tall, still as a statue, she watched me drink my coffee and wait for my wife to finish.

I heard people talking outside. Gretton, the groundskeeper, and probably Sanchez. Though if the old man talked to himself while he worked that wouldn't have surprised me.

My wife finished her breakfast. She licked her lips, wiped her mouth, and quickly stood.

"Okay," she said.

On our way out we did not speak. The housekeeper followed us to the door.

I stepped outside first. The world was damp and gray. For an instant I thought, "I did it. I've got her."

But I found myself alone on the front porch. Lucy was still inside, in the foyer. She stood in a shadow, watching me.

"I'm going to take a cab, Ray."

"You can't. There aren't cabs here. Come on."

"No," she said. "Listen. It's no trouble. You go on. I think I'd like to stay a bit longer. And take a cab back."

A bird started singing in the woods. Gretton, raking somewhere nearby, started whistling to himself. The world was coming to life.

It's no trouble, Ray.

"Then I can stay a little longer too," I said. "I can wait here. And then we'll – "

I took a step toward her, entering the house. Lucy backed up a step and raised her hand.

"No," she said. "You don't have to. Please, Ray. Don't. I know you have things you need to do. I know you wanted to get back to the city early. So. Please. Just – "

"Okay. Why don't I take you down to the village. Down to Mojave. There you can get a cab. Up here, you'll be waiting all day. I can take you. Down the mountain. And then you can come back on your own, whenever you want. But – "

"In fact," said my wife, as if the idea, so perfect and clear and inarguable, had just dawned on her, "Corinne mentioned that later they'll make a trip down to the village for some things. So I can get a ride from them. And then in town surely I'll find a taxi. Or maybe there's a bus back to the city." Her eyes sparkled.

Then the housekeeper, Ms Kearn, appeared. She'd been behind Lucy, there all along. And though I had seen her I hadn't fully recognized the woman, her quiet presence. She took a step forward as if entering from another room. She was truly a tall woman, a big woman.

I said, "Lucy," and again I stepped toward her, into the entrance of the Drammond House, and again my wife took a step back. I remember feeling, then, as if I were on an edge, as if watching a child step near the edge of a precipice and not realize the danger she was in, thinking: "Don't react. Don't startle her. Walk toward her, reach out, and take her. Quickly."

"Lucy." She looked distracted, a fleeting moment of confusion on her face as the housekeeper began to come between us. "I know you are angry with me," I said, "But... Please... Let me."

"Mr Byrd," said the housekeeper, "it wouldn't be any trouble at all, Lucy's coming with us. Really, no trouble at all."

"Thanks, Ms Kearn, but it won't be necessary, because – Lucy's – "

I was following the women – being led, I should say – back into the house. The foyer expanded around me. The entrance hall, like a cathedral, was only a few steps farther. Lucy, who had somehow positioned herself behind the housekeeper, was out of reach and nearly out of sight. By some trick of light, the incredible dimensions of the place, my wife with every slow step backwards seemed to be getting smaller and smaller, sinking into the depths of the house.

"Enough's enough, Lucy! Let's go. Come with me – "

Corinne Kearn wears a fragrance. It's gentle and quiet. You need to be in close to smell it, sense it. Wisteria. But something else, as well, something deeper. Hotter. Burned.

And she was close, then, directly in front of me, between me and Lucy, and as I raised a hand for my wife I found myself nearly touching the housekeeper, Ms Kearn, my hand rising along the side of her arm, to her shoulder. Her long face, dark eyes, that big dimpled chin, her inscrutable poise.

"Lucy? Please – "

My wife, lunging at me, doubling over: "FUCK OFF, RAY!"

That had never happened before. And it took me a moment, a few seconds to gather my thoughts, study this livid creature that was screaming in my face. It wasn't my wife, wasn't Lucy saying those words. No way. Lucy was a scientist. Lucy was an honest woman who didn't hide her feelings but who also wouldn't let anger overcome her, control her like that. The woman screaming at me was not my wife. That was something else –

"I – "

The housekeeper made a sound in her throat and lowered her chin. She raised a hand, her palm toward me, not touching me, but stopping anything I might try. "We'll take her down, Mr Byrd," the woman said.

Over the housekeeper's shoulder I watched Lucy's back as she walked further into the house, across the entrance hall. Not hurrying, not in anger. Simply walking away. And then the one they called Elaine was there, approaching her, a big smile on her twisted face, the creature reaching up with both hands, as if to be lifted, for my wife.

"Lucy – "

"Mr Byrd?"

"But – "

"The groundskeeper, Mr Gretton, will be going down the hill in an hour or so. He'd be happy to take Lucy down to Maiden, where she can call for a taxi from Mojave. It is no problem, Mr Byrd, no problem at all. In fact, to save time, we can call the taxi from here. How's that sound?"

She had a long neck, a long face, a high brow. Blue eyes but with spots of gray, dark speckle in the iris. Byrd eyebrows, thick black hair pulled loosely back into a bun. I wanted to throttle her. At the same time, I was curious, not in a violent way, but in that other way – wanting to touch and see, like a child. She hardly moved when she spoke. And the words were flat, indifferent, almost whispered.

"Okay," I said. "Okay. Gretton can take her down."

I left. The woman watched me leave. I could feel it, her eyes on me, her pride like a force of nature pushing at my back, taking the ground I was giving up.

~ 27 ~

I didn't leave right away. I sat in the car and waited at the bottom of the hill. Rain gently fell, blowing in the air like sand. Everything was cold, quiet, holding its breath with expectation.

Of course they didn't come down. Gretton, my wife. They'd never come down, never go into town, never call a cab. I knew that but at the same time didn't know it. The idea hadn't become a reality. But then it did, then it was, as I sat there in the car listening to the tickle of rain on the roof, watching another day disappear.

I drove down the mountain, pulled in at the diner, Rosalee's. It was busy, the windows steamed and dripping. I went inside and found a seat at the counter. After a minute the redhead came over, stood at attention before me, snapped her gum.

I spoke first. I said: "You from around here?"

"What kind of question is that?"

"It's a simple question."

"Nobody's from around here, mister. We all come here and then never leave."

"So where you from?"

156

She snapped her gum, smiled in the corner of her mouth. She said: "You must like that place. To keep going up there."

"What place's that?"

She looked at the notepad in her hand, tore off the top page, spun, stuck it on a wheel in the kitchen window, spun back, said: "You know. The Drammond House."

"Not particularly."

"You a reporter or something?"

"No."

"Because you keep coming back. Only people who do that are writers of some kind. Students, too, sometimes. Anthropologists. Architecture... But you're too old to be a student."

"... What do you know about the place?"

She glanced over my shoulder, looked aside, down the counter. She couldn't stand around chatting. Nico'd be out soon.

She leaned forward, the button in her jeans scratching, clicking on the counter's edge. "It's not goin' too well, is it?"

I looked at the girl. Jillian was her name, I remembered Kearn saying the night before: "Jillian Veldt. We know her."

I didn't say anything.

"You and that lady... Your wife, I assume. She's not out in the car, is she?"

Another waitress, the Mexican girl I'd seen before, brought a plate of pancakes to the man seated next to me and let it fall with a clatter. An old wiry fellow, he rotated the plate ninety degrees, took up his knife and fork and chopped the stack down the center in one deft stroke. Then he poured a string of syrup over the split surface. Before proceeding he paused, looked at me in the corner of his eye.

"Lucy left earlier," I said. "Took a cab. But how'd you know she was – "

The waitress smiled, showed me her teeth.

"Sure she did, mister. Took a cab. You think I'm dumb? We see things, waitresses do, learn how to read people. Their wants and desires, dreams, plans for the future, fears. You get to recognize all these things serving food..." She played with a strand of her red hair, curling it up on her finger. She had a brown freckle on the side of her neck. She went on. "Like that other woman you brought here. I knew immediately what was happening there."

"That so. How?"

"Simple. You were smiling. And so was she."

I ordered pancakes. The waitress disappeared, reappearing for only a moment minutes later to deliver my breakfast.

"Great hotcakes here," said the man next me, eyeing mine.

They were pretty good.

When I paid, Jillian said: "If you're thinking of going back there, I wouldn't." She looked me in the eye. Big lovely blue eyes in her narrow face. She wasn't smiling then. There was no joke to the warning. "Sometimes they come back," she said. "But usually–" She gave me my change. She shook her head.

~ 28 ~

I waited outside the gate until dark. Nothing came out. Nothing went in. Then I started thinking: "Marianne didn't leave this place without me. They took her. She's up there. And now Lucy's there too. She wasn't going to leave. I don't know why she decided to stay but she did. Take a taxi! You think I'm stupid, Corinne Kearn?"

Witch.

"Lucy might despise me – and she cheated on me – and most other men would do the right thing and let her go – do what she wants. But I can't. They can't have her. I won't let this happen."

I got out of the car and walked up to the house.

I thought of cutting through the meadow Lucy'd found, go through the orchard like we did before – to avoid coming up to the front door – but with the darkness, the woods, the rain, I had no clue as to where the path was.

But the problem of the front door turned out to be no problem at all. The place was dark and quiet. Lights out.

I tried the door. It was locked. I made my way along the side of the house, following a narrow green lawn.

I'd walked for maybe ten, fifteen minutes, when I came to a tall and narrow stone archway, a flight of wet black stairs. Up I went to the first floor, a weedy terrace. Passing through another arch I entered a courtyard, a small garden, bare and black lemon trees.

The house surrounded me. There were windows on all the floors, going up farther than I could make out. It was quiet, still. Rain dripped from the eaves.

The windows were dark and cold. The house appeared abandoned, lifeless. I went toward a door and noticed, as I approached, my reflection in the window approaching, growing larger.

When I looked inside a man stood there, looking back. It was Sanchez, the houseman. He opened the door, regarded me stolidly for a couple seconds, and quietly said: "What are you doing here?"

"I was looking for my wife. She didn't come down."

"You shouldn't be here."

"Mr Sanchez – Martin, is it? – I'm sorry to disturb you at ... But ... I know I shouldn't – "

"You are trespassing."

He looked at me and waited, as if I would defend myself against the charge.

"This is private property," he said. "I could call the police."

A gust of wind blew behind me, dusting both of us in cold rain. The houseman closed his eyes.

"Please," I said. "Have you seen Lucy? I just – "

Then the man stared at me without moving. He said: "Come with me, Mr Byrd." He turned and without a sound made his way into the darkness of the house. "I'll show you out. Follow me."

The houseman led me into a hallway and through an office, and then a library, what could have been a classroom, and into a room made entirely of pink marble. Then, midway down another hall, he stopped. He tilted his head to the side, listening. It was some kind of alarm, an electronic buzzer chirping fitfully far off in the house.

Sanchez turned, faced me, pointed at a bench near the wall. "Sit," he said. "Wait here. Don't move."

I did as I was told. The small man continued a short ways down the hallway, and then turned, pushing open a door. He glanced back at me and then stepped into the other room. "I need to take care of something," he said. "I'll get a lantern."

With a click, the door he passed through closed and I was alone in the hallway.

After a moment the buzzing sound we had heard stopped and I heard Sanchez quietly responding to someone's questions. I couldn't make out the words, the sound of the man little more than a mumbled whisper.

As I listened I began to make out other sounds. Rain falling hard outside; a fire popping and crackling in a fireplace nearby. And then laughter. Distant, very quiet, but distinct. The sound of a woman laughing. Then the hushed, calm, relaxed murmur of two women talking. I couldn't tell what was said. One was older than the other. It was the older one who had laughed.

Upstairs, directly above me, a door closed. Someone moved away, down the length of the hall.

Then the house was quiet. The rain, the fire. Little else. There was hardly a breeze, the old tired air of the place still and heavy. Then the voices I'd heard suddenly became much sharper and closer. Down the hall, at some distance beyond the room the houseman had entered, a woman step from a room. She was immediately followed by another woman who, from my position, looked a lot like my wife.

They walked down the hallway two, three steps. The leader was reaching for a door across the way.

I stood up. "Lucy. Wait." Quickly I made my way down the hall.

Either the women hadn't heard me or my wife chose to ignore me. In any case, they were gone. The door I thought they'd used was locked. I stood in the dim hallway, listening carefully, my ear to the door. The voices were once again distant, muted.

I tried another door, farther down. It too was locked. How many more could there be? I tried another. It opened onto a descending stairway. I glanced back, wondering where the houseman was and why it was taking him so long to return. If he came back ...

"I'll just be a minute," I told myself. "I'll only go a little ways. And then come back. I'll be right back. He'll probably still be on the phone. Keeping me waiting here."

I could call the police.

Sure you will, house man. Let's get the police out here. Into the house, down in the basement. See what we turn up –

Then it was the women again, the older one, once again, laughing.

They couldn't have known I was there. They seemed polite, at ease, in the middle of something. They weren't laughing at me. It was something else, a joke that Lucy had made.

She was enjoying herself.

Why not let her be?

"Because she's my wife. And they'll do something to her. She needs me."

She didn't sound like –

"She does!"

The question was, finally, if they had gone this way, down these stairs. I couldn't be certain. It seemed, when I looked back at the bench I'd been told stay at, that I'd come too far down the hallway.

But the other doors were locked.

"So she had a key."

So you agree: they didn't come this way.

There was something else, then, another sound coming up the stairs. A rumbling, an engine somewhere deep beneath the house had started.

Do as you're told.

"I just need to – "

You are trespassing!

"It'll just be – "

I stepped through the door, began down the winding stairs. I heard the door close behind me and then the rhythmic turning of the engine below me, though still quite soft and distant, was all I could make out.

~ 29 ~

I descended for some time before coming to a door. It was locked. I continued down. The next door I came to was open. The hallway I looked into was dimly lit and cold. For whatever reason I decided that it wasn't the floor I wanted and so continued down. The next hallway was much like the first. As was the one after that.

The level I finally stopped at was warm and humid. I could hear, in addition to the rumbling of the engine – which was no louder than before, though distinctly an engine of some kind – water running, splashing. I thought I could hear voices. But the mind plays tricks with us in solitude, in places like the Drammond House where one can walk for hours, an entire day perhaps, without coming upon another soul.

Or days. Come to think of it – of how far down that stairway went – of how many other stairways there must be, of how many levels below the surface of the earth the house descends. Not to mention what rises above, the parts that can be seen with the naked eye.

The hallway led past dark empty rooms, past other halls, chambers, stairways, closets and recesses. Rooms, rooms, rooms. I should have turned back.

"Turn. Go straight. Get to the stairs. Go up. Up up up," I told myself.

I should have left string. Like – what was her name? – Arachne, going into the maze after...

I turned down a short hallway. There was a metal door at the end. It was locked. There was a vent cut in the door, beneath my knees. I crouched, listened, looked.

Behind the door was a large room. Byrd tiles, a pool, a spring. I could hear the water moving, pouring, splashing periodically. There were also voices. Swimmers, bathers. Women, all.

In fact I could make out very little through the vent. Several thread-thin lines of dim light, of steam. But near its lower right corner, the vent was damaged slightly. On hands and knees I bent down, focused on this opening. The floor, I recall, was warm, almost hot to the touch.

Using my housekey I tried to pry the metal back, to make something of this aperture.

The water moved in slow black waves. The door was so close to the pool had I been able to reach through the vent I could touch the water.

Near the back of the room a platform rose above the water. Someone was on it, seated. The steam and darkness of the room made it difficult to discern anything clearly – but it seemed to me that there was a woman on the platform, something tall, upright before her, between her arms and parted legs. And then, gently, faintly, I could hear it, the sound of the instrument, like a cello, and her voice, a wordless melody.

In the same instant someone came to the door and stopped before it. I found myself looking at a thin white ankle. Practically in my ear, its owner said: "You make it sacred."

She was on the other side of the door, mind you, and the door was locked, but the woman could have been on top of me, her words that clear, that close to my ear. "You make it sacred."

For a long second I didn't move. I studied this ankle, the top of her bare foot. And then I began to smell her – musk, sweat, the salty vapor of sex.

Without a sound I rose from my position on the floor and took a step back. The woman on the other side of the door was whispering. Someone else was there.

The handle in the door moved, shifted incrementally. The door remained locked. The whispering continued.

And then, stopping my heart, clear and cool as ice, the housekeeper said: "Ray? Is that you?"

She was there, Corrinne Kearn, just on the other side of this door. And she knew it was me, knew I was there. And in a moment, I had no doubt, she would open this door and take me.

I could hardly breathe, my heart in my throat. It took all my effort to move, retreating backwards step by careful step.

"Ray?" she said again. And again, the handle in the door shifted downward, wanting to open.

When I stepped into the hallway, glancing to my right, into its empty depth, coming back to life, realizing what I'd done, what I was doing, and what, at least in my imagination, would happen to me should that door between me and Kearn suddenly open.

I turned and ran.

She said, as if just behind me: "But why, Ray? Why?"

And then the other, repeating her strange remark: "He makes it sacred. Sacred!"

I could see the end of the hallway up ahead, the entry to the stairs I'd come down.

Behind me, a door was opening, metal sliding over and cutting into the tiled floor. A warm draft quickly came over me, on my neck, pushing at my back.

The stairway was within reach.

She was behind me, above me, her voice in my ear: "What are you looking for, Raymond? Why are you down here? Is it Lucy you're after?"

I took the stairs two at a time, not daring to stop and look back. How she could be so close to me I couldn't fathom. And a part of me realized that the voice was in my head, a figment of my imagination. But another part of me realized the trick in this thought, the unreal hope – and this part wanted to stop and see it and face it.

And die, most likely.

I couldn't breathe, my lungs in tatters, my heart about to explode, the stairs going on and on and on. Up, up, up! How many doors and halls I passed ascending, I couldn't say. It seemed that there were a lot more of these than there had been before. But then – back then – there wasn't a ghost at my shoulder, in my ear.

"What did I tell you!"

Something came down. Light as a feather, but sharp, like a sliver of glass. It caressed at first, but then pricked, penetrated, burrowed into the side of my neck. Without looking, I reached up and took her hand in mine –

Sanchez met me at the top of the stairs, where I collapsed. Without a sound, he closed the door behind me.

I looked up at the man, gasping for breath. He lit a cigarette and regarded me impassively. He closed his eyes, opened them, said softly: "What did I say?"

I struggled to speak. The houseman closed his eyes tightly. Then he looked at me, took a long deep breath, smoked. He said: "Don't move. That's what I said. I told you to sit on that bench and not to move. And what did you do?"

"My wife."

"You moved! You went downstairs."

The houseman crouched, his hands on his knees, lowering his angry face. In a level tone, he said: "People get hurt, Mr Byrd. Wandering, in this house, alone."

"My wife is down there."

"Are you hurt, Mr Byrd?"

I picked myself up, faced the man.

"Sanchez. My wife – she's down there."

The houseman stood back, tucked in his chin. He smoked, watched me carefully. "No she isn't," he said.

"But – "

"No buts, Mr Byrd. Your wife is not here. She's gone. Now, if you would, please follow me."

The houseman walked down the hall toward the bench he'd left me at. There was a lantern on the bench. He lifted this and opened a door across from the bench. He held the door open, waiting for me. I followed. The door closed behind us and the houseman led the way.

We walked for several minutes in silence. Then we entered a wide chamber, tall dark windows on three walls. We came to a door. I could see dark figures, towering trees, waving in the wind outside.

"What do you mean, she's gone?" I said.

"She's not here."

"So she left?"

The houseman opened the door. There was a small round porch. At the bottom of a short staircase stood an old man. Gretton.

The houseman gave me the lantern. Quietly he said: "Your wife is not here, Mr Byrd." I took the lantern and stepped outside. "Don't come back."

I looked from the houseman to the old man at the bottom of the stairs. The old man's face was swollen and pale, half asleep.

Behind me the houseman said: "There's a path. It will take you to the bottom of the hill. To your car. Stay on the path. Sam will accompany you."

It was cold outside. A mist blew, whipping, curling in the air around us. The old man looked at me and groaned. He nodded to his right, wanting me to go first. I looked a last time up at the house, at the enormous glass room, the small entry the houseman stood in. Sanchez took a step backward and closed the door. He stood behind the window, the darkness of the house condensing around the small man like smoke.

"Go on, Byrd," said the groundsman. "It's cold out here."

~ 30 ~

I woke one night, it was maybe a week later, hearing something in the house. I hadn't been sleeping well.

It turned out to be nothing. The cat, the older one, lurking in the darkness, growling to himself bitterly.

I hadn't heard anything from Lucy. Or Marianne. I was beginning to think I'd never see either of them again.

Maybe I should have been more concerned. Seeing as I'd been with them, at that house, when they disappeared. I should have called someone, gone back there.

What was her name? That waitress? *Jillian.*

Don't go back, she'd said.

"Don't come back," the houseman had said.

The waitress knew something. Even if I didn't go back to the house, a chat with Jillian wouldn't hurt.

But I waited. I don't know why. Didn't feel urgent. I kept telling myself: "They left you. Not vice versa. They wanted to stay."

I could still see my wife's face, when she turned and screamed at me.

It wasn't her. They did something to her.

Someone from her office called. "Is Lucy feeling alright?" the woman said. "She didn't pick up anything while overseas, I hope."

Only an Englishman.

"No," I said. "Lucy is fine. ... It's only – well – we're going through a divorce, see – so she's, well – she's moved out."

The woman didn't speak. I could hear a TV playing in the background, a child crying. Quietly, she said, "I'm sorry."

"I have her number around her somewhere."

"Oh, Mr Byrd, you don't – "

"No, it'll – "

"Please, really, it's okay. But we'll see her later in the week, you think?"

"I couldn't say. Miss – "

"Betty. My name is Betty."

"Okay, Betty. I'm Ray, Lucy's husband. Though as I – "

I thought of mentioning Paul Wise, Lucy's new man. There was a good chance Betty'd know him or have heard of him. Didn't they work together?

But then – then...

"She'll be back soon. It's just the moving, see. Dividing things, sorting. It's not so – ... You don't have to hear this. So if I see her, I'll be sure to tell her you called."

"Great," said the woman. "Again, I'm sorry to hear – "

Anyways, I was having trouble sleeping. Seeing things in my head, hearing things that weren't there. I can't say I had bad dreams – I don't remember if I dreamt. But I certainly felt... disoriented, that first week, returning, alone.

I took a notepad and pen from her desk, went to the kitchen table, sat down, stared at the blank sheet and thought of names, thought of all the people who had seen me at the house or going to the house with Marianne and Lucy.

There were the people at the house, of course. The staff. Kearn and Elaine and Sanchez. Gretton, the gardener.

Those women I'd seen, in the hallway, though I don't think they saw me.

The woman behind the door, at the bath.

"You make it sacred."

I wrote the words down near the edge of the page, a separate idea, another mystery. *The sacred*. That bath or whatever it was beneath the house –

Who was she?

And then there were the people at the diner. Jillian, and the other waitress, Nico the cook, the pimple-faced boy, the old man I'd sat by, he'd overheard, he must have overheard our conversation.

And with Marianne, there was that other place, down in Mojave. The cowboy sitting at the end of the bar, the woman he danced with.

Not many people, as I thought about it, looking at my list, though there could be more. Many more. At the house. In the diner. It was busy.

The trucker.

It's hard though, retracing these things, walking backwards in our memory to see for a second time what happened. Not only do you begin to doubt yourself, second guess yourself – *Did she touch you as you ran away? Was she flying?* – but you find yourself wanting to stop, unable to go on.

It was like *this*, we say to ourselves, remembering. But not like that. *Definitely* not like that. It couldn't be. It wasn't.

And what kind of memory is that?

~ 31 ~

Paul Wise, Lucy's man, he knew about Marianne.

I woke up, the words already out of my mouth, like water in the face: "What about Paul Wise?"

I'd hardly asked myself this question when the answer came to the door.

"You must be Paul."

"Where's Lucy?"

He was a fat man. Not a huge man but going soft. He had a wide, pink, sunburnt face. Thinning red hair. These yellow teeth splayed everywhich way. English. An Englishman, did I mention? From Nottingham or some place. Robin Hood country. Looking into that ruin of a mouth I could almost see the bandit and his merry men looking back at me.

"Where is she?"

He had these small narrow set eyes. He spoke without blinking, staring.

"You mean Lucy? Haven't seen her for days. Since she got back. When she told me about you. The scientist."

"So you know who I am. It's Wise, Paul Wise. I want to see Lucy."

What could I tell him? I stood there dumbfounded, facing the man as I faced the occasional salesman or Jehovah's Witness, waiting for the pitch. What do you say? Your wife goes missing and her lover comes to the door looking for her. I shouldn't have been surprised. I wasn't, really.

"Listen," I said, "She's not here. After that night you called, we talked about it, she packed some things and left. I assumed she was with you."

I stepped away from the door, back inside to the kitchen, took a cigarette from a pack I'd bought the day before, lit up. Back at the door, the man hadn't moved. He could've been cut from stone.

I said: "You didn't see her at work."

Then his eyes started moving, shifting, looking at me, down, over my shoulder into the house. He was losing something. The courage he'd spent days mustering up to come see me. He blinked quickly, violently. A glance aside, thinking, he said: "She hasn't been in. I haven't seen her. She hasn't returned any of my calls. Since..."

I smoked. Sausages sizzled in a pan in the kitchen. It had rained all day. Now the sky was black and silent. The world was soaked into passivity. The city seemed miles away.

The man wasn't chewing gum but he made a move with his mouth. His yellow teeth snapped together. He looked me in the eye and very clearly said: "What did you do, Raymond?"

"What did I do?"

"You tell me where she is or – "

"Or?" I smiled at the man and an instant later regretted it. The idea of getting into something with Paul Wise over Lucy just seemed kind of silly to me. It wasn't something I'd actually considered. But then, in that instant, hearing some sort of threat in the man's words... Well, it all seemed kind of silly. Lucy, the Englishman, the house.

I wasn't sleeping much at night but it wasn't because of Paul Wise. What could he do?

"Paul. I'm sorry. I shouldn't have... I'm – "

He was working his mouth again, building the phrase before he let it go.

I said: "Why don't you come in, have a drink."

"If you've – "

"Paul. Don't get worked up. It's quite simple, actually. So. You coming or going, because I got meat on the fire that needs attention. Drink?"

The man grimaced childishly, raised his chin.

He came inside, gently closed the door and came into the kitchen without a sound. I pulled a chair out for him at the table and he sat down heavily, the wind wheezing from his lungs. The cat – the young one – ran over and circled the legs of his chair. He was distracted, reaching down to pet the animal.

I was cutting parsley.

We see these things – this memory, the scene – and wonder about other possibilities. If I had killed the man, for example, then, there, in my kitchen – would I be here, talking with you?

"Wine? Whisky? Calistoga?"

He had a whisky with ice.

I'm not a murderer. Even in other possibilities. I could never do it.

He finished the drink quickly, stood up, went to the bottle and poured himself another. He was moving differently then, relaxing. Two guys drinking, cooking meat, talking women.

"I'm sorry about what's happened," he said, eyes down. They were words he'd practiced, come over wanting to say. They meant nothing.

I said, chopping parsley: "Look. I'll take you to her. She's at this – it's a retreat, I guess you'd call it. For women. You understand. Some kind of cleansing she felt she needed. Not of you, I mean. Surely. But still. Having come all that way to tell me what she told me, and then to deal with me! Women. Problem is, Mr Wise, that you'd like to understand her. Like to know why she did what she did, disappearing like this. But the fact is there's no understanding them. Give it up. Anyways, she's yours. You win. I won't fight her, won't fight you. It would've happened, I suppose. You get to know a person, you can feel these things coming. She didn't have to tell me. I would've guessed... So. You eat meat? You free Friday? I'll take you there, to the place."

He finished his second drink slowly, watching me, thinking. Then he got up and left without a word.

~ 32 ~

"Did your wife go somewhere with Paul Wise?"
"My wife is at the Drammond House."
"But is it possible that – "
"I told you. I brought her to the house. She didn't come out."

"So you say. But maybe she left without you. Like Mrs Heaney. Maybe she told Paul where she was going and what you were trying to do. Hoping to accomplish, bringing her out there. Meaning, she'd already made up her mind. She'd play along. And when she had her chance, she meets Paul. They left together without telling you."

"Without taking anything? Saying anything? She hasn't... Why would she do something like that?"

"... You said it yourself. There's no plumbing the woman's psyche. So who knows what she did, Mr Byrd. I'm only offering a possibility, a suggestion."

"Possibilities... You're still wrong. What you're suggesting – it doesn't make sense."

"... No, Mr Byrd. What I'm suggesting makes perfect sense. It's what you've said – with this haunted house story of yours – that doesn't make much sense. And now

I'm going to make another suggestion, take it as you like. ... I'm not accusing you here of anything, but try and look at it from my point of view. You have this woman, your wife. You have yourself, the husband, who has not been, let's say, the greatest husband in the world to his wife. You mess around. You lose touch with the woman you're married to so that one day she comes out and says, blowing you away, she's in love with another man. Okay. So now there's another man. So you've got *your* secrets – call them what you like – and she's got hers. Paul Wise. You'll like him, she said. But you don't like him. You can't stand this guy. Everything about this man makes you sick. And he's the one who's stolen your wife's heart. Okay. I'm just saying, look at it like this. Because... Lookit, it's not the first time a marriage has broken up over... It's *okay* to feel angry at this guy, angry at her, to want... I'm just saying, look at it from where I'm sitting. Your wife is missing. Not to mention this other woman, Marianne. Your words, Mr Byrd. You sit here telling me that after she told you about her affair, you arranged to take her out to the country for a nice get away. To try and patch things up. Okay. Makes sense. But then she doesn't come back. And then the other man... Don't tell me."

"I know what it looks like."

The black man seated across the table from Raymond Byrd opened his eyes very wide, stared at Byrd for half a minute. Byrd looked at the detective, at the surface of the table, at the other man in the room, the Japanese man standing in the corner by the window.

The detective said: "I'm not accusing you of anything. We're just having a conversation, you and me. I wanted to learn something about a man named Joseph Manning, and I was told you might know something of his where-abouts. So I asked you. And you start telling me this far out story about a big house up in the mountains, and this woman, and your wife, and this man. And don't let me forget this painter fellow who, I take it, is Joseph's father. So you're working up to it. That's fine. Take your time. Like I said. It's not the first time a marriage has broken up. These things can be complicated. I know. But now let me be frank with you. You're digging yourself a deep hole, Raymond. You realize that. You realize everything you tell me about all these people who are not Joseph Manning I'm going to come back to, later ask you about. After you give me Joseph Manning."

"I'm... I'll tell you what I know."

"I know you will. In fact, despite myself, I believe al-most everything you've told me so far. You're either a very good liar or – "

The black man smiled, leaned back in his chair. It was a warm handsome smile.

"Or kind of foolish," he said. "You do realize what you're doing, telling me about these missing people."

"I do."

"I think you do. Which makes me wonder, Ray, why you'd do something like that."

~ 33 ~

The houseman opened the door. Behind him the Drammond House was dark and quiet. A cool breeze blew out from the inside.

Hardly moving at all, Sanchez regarded me and then Paul Wise, and then me again. He was still, lethargic, dressed for work but as if he'd just stepped from bed.

"Martin," I said, "this is Paul Wise. He would like to see Lucy."

The houseman blinked, took a deep breath. Then he looked at Wise and said: "This way, please."

He led us through the entrance hall and down a corridor. Wise fell behind, looking up in awe, turning as he walked, trying to take the whole place in.

At a bench outside of the houseman's office, Sanchez told us firmly and quietly to sit and wait for him to return.

We sat. We waited.

After a couple minutes I rose and started down the corridor. Wise followed. I stopped at what I thought was the entrance to the basement I'd used the previous time.

I didn't have a plan, exactly. And perhaps somewhere in my mind I thought we might actually find Lucy, actually return with her.

My hand on the door to the basement, I said: "Paul, listen."

"Didn't that man ask for us to wait?"

I looked at Paul Wise, the scientist. Momentarily I wondered how the man had first met my wife. He didn't seem like the kind of man who would come on to a married woman. Lucy must have made the first move, which she was capable of.

I said: "Sanchez asked us to sit and wait. But that doesn't mean he wants us to sit and wait."

"What?"

"He's the houseman, Paul. Most of what he says is just formal. For show, for his guests. Nothing more."

"But he *did* tell us to wait for him."

Would I leave the man there, in the house? I had no intention of doing this.

Had the scenario crossed my mind? Yes, truthfully, it had.

"Listen to me, Paul, very carefully. We're going to take these stairs down into the basement. But it's more than a basement. It's more like... Another building. Like catacombs. It's very big and rather confusing. I need you to pay attention and stay close to me. Lucy is down there."

I seemed to have the man's attention.

"If something happens ... If we get separated ..."

"What could happen? Why would we be separated?"

"*If something happens,* you come immediately back here, come back the way we came. And *get out* of the house. The exit is through there."

I pointed down the corridor to the entrance hall, foyer and, a hundred meters distant, a narrow and rectangular block of darkness, the door we'd come through.

"Is that clear?"

"I think so."

I pushed the door open and we began our descent.

The engine, heart of the house, far off, strong and hypnotic, ran as before. Soon the air warmed and grew moist and I thought, like last time, I could hear water running, splashing. I led him down a hallway toward these sounds, toward what I thought was the bath and spring I'd found before. The locked door. But then the sounds diminished. We'd gone too far. We turned back. But this didn't help. The floor we were on was absolutely quiet, cool, dim, abandoned.

Passing a stairwell, Paul thought he heard voices below us. He started down. I followed. I wanted to say something, to hold him back – wanted, now that I think of it, to return upstairs altogether, a sense of panic and disorientation and fear rising in my guts – but I did nothing. I followed the man down.

In short order, we were completely lost. The room we finally stopped in was immense. The ceiling overhead was out of sight, the walls bent around right and left in a long curve, connecting across from us at a distant point, though in the dim light it was impossible to tell. The chamber had, at equidistant intervals in the walls, multiple dark archways, recesses.

It was also difficult to tell what was on the opposite side of the chamber because something in the middle of the room blocked our view. The object was black, conical, with a wide base and narrow top, curved along the edge. It bore a vague similarity to a tee-pee or chapel, only, as I say, for the dimness of the room and for the black surface of the object, it was difficult to say what exactly it was we were looking at.

The room was quiet. Even the distant, ceaseless engine that we'd heard all along seemed to have shut off.

Without a word, Paul Wise walked right in, heading straight for the thing in the middle of the chamber.

The surface of the object looked to be stone. In fact, it appeared to be one entire piece, an enormous formation that the original Drammond House must have been built upon and around.

There was a narrow opening in the rock, a slit rising from the floor to a point high overhead in the darkness. We stopped before going inside. The partition was full of steam or smoke, the vapors shifting, curling slowly in the darkness.

There's something in there.

Very quietly, hardly breathing at all, Paul said: "Have you smelled that before?"

"No. What is it?"

"Ethylene. And hydrogen sulfide," he whispered. "They might have used it to heat and light the house." And then, thinking, trying, it seemed to me, to remember something: "They once thought it had healing properties."

"Does it?"

He looked at me closely in the darkness, our faces nearly touching, as if seeing me for the first time. A stranger. He put his hand on my shoulder. "No. It makes you hallucinate. I think it's time we go."

"Without Lucy?"

He shook his head quickly, nervously, his eyes wide as saucers. "Lucy's not here. She can't be. We must've taken a wrong turn, missed something."

"I tell you, she's here. I know she's here. In there! And *you* wanted to see her, to find her." I raised my voice and everything I said came back to us a moment later, echoing off the walls, the round ceiling high over head, filling the darkness in a terrified hissing whisper. "And I *told* you. I *warned* you."

He pushed past me and started away in the direction we'd come from, but then stopped suddenly, stiffly. We weren't alone.

The women had appeared quietly out of nowhere, following us barefoot, naked and filthy, covered head to toe in what looked like black grease, the whites of their eyes burning in the dimness.

Our way was blocked.

"He sleeps," one of the women said.

"He feeds," said another.

"He sleeps, he feeds, he sleeps. On and on and on."

Their voices surrounded us.

He sleeps, he feeds, he sleeps, he feeds, on and on and on and on –

A woman on my left approached quickly, gently took my arm, and said: "This is a sacred place." She glanced from me to him, her glistening chin swinging back and forth, her teeth and gums flashing: "I'm sorry."

"We were just going," Paul said.

"I'm sorry."

"I didn't mean to – " he said.

"I'm sorry," the woman at my side said, reaching for my cheek. The others closed in.

Paul said: "Who are you?"

"Who are *you*?" the women said in unison.

One of the women sobbed loudly and started whining like a child. She clenched her fists and pounded them in the air. She stomped her bare feet like a child, crying, turning around in circles. A tantrum, her naked feet slapping loudly against the stone floor.

The woman holding my arm began to pull herself closer, her face up to mine. She opened her mouth. Long black teeth in the dim light, the flicker of a thick tongue: "Thank you," she said.

"Thank you!" they intoned.

"But we're – " Paul was stammering, growing frantic, trying to push his way through the crowd. But they had him. They were all around him, pressing against him, pulling at him, at his clothes, at the flab of his cheeks and neck, at his hair. "Ray! Let's go!"

"But you can't," said the woman before me, as she turned her attention to the other man, as she released me and stepped toward him. "This is a sacred place. Because you've come here. You, Paul, make it sacred."

"But, but, but – "

"So you can't leave."

"Raymond!"

I walked away, straight out of the crowd as they concentrated on, swarming like insects around the frantic, porcine lover of my wife. He was fighting with them, swinging, slapping, *hitting* these women, swinging them around by their arms, kicking at them, bones cracking in the air.

"Unhand me!" the man said sharply. "You have no right to... I'm only here for *Lucy*, for Lucy Byrd, *that man's* wife. Show her to me and I'll – "

But if it was any attempt to distract the horde from their attention on him, this curious declaration of purpose, it didn't work.

Or, I should say, I don't think it worked. I can't be certain about what happened next. Because I didn't look back.

And I left the Drammond House, as before, alone.

And though I didn't *see* what finally happened in that room, to Paul Wise, I could hear them. And even after I'd put enough distance between them and me, climbing those stairs as fast as I could, running and climbing, running, running until I thought I couldn't take another step, until I was seeing stars trying to catch my breath – even then, outside, in the silent vastness of the world at night in the mountains, even then I could hear them.

Until I die, I imagine, I will hear the sounds those women made as they took Paul away. I would cut my ears off, snip the part of my brain from my head that lets us hear and remember, if I thought it would help. But nothing will help. It's in my blood now, in my DNA, like a virus, this memory, the sounds they made.

They were singing.

~ 34 ~

Why didn't I call the police after that?
I guess I still thought that either things would realign themselves on their own – that Marianne and Lucy, and maybe even Paul, too, would reappear – or that what I had experienced at the Drammond House was some bizarre trick, hallucination, or dream. Of course, these people were missing, but who knows – I told myself – maybe they were all in on it.

And I hadn't, as far as I could tell, broken the law. Or broken any important laws.

In any case, the weeks following my trip with Paul Wise to the house were increasingly stressful. I was beginning to feel something – psychological strain, let's call it – for the Drammond House. It was finally getting to me, under my skin. The house itself, obviously, but more particularly *not knowing* what had happened to Paul Wise, not knowing what had happened to Lucy or Marianne. The simple fact that these people had *disappeared* inside the Drammond House was beginning to drive me mad.

Nobody from Lucy's office called. Not Betty. Nobody. I caught myself wondering, sleepless in the middle of the night, if the woman – Betty, I mean – had ever existed in the first place.

Then somebody did call.

It was late one night. This would have to be almost April, first week of April. I was watching TV, the volume up loud, all the lights on in the place.

I didn't hear her the first time she spoke. I had to gather my wits, turn off the TV, sober up in a flash.

"Come again?"

She spoke very quietly, with this weepy voice, like a dying mouse. "What did you do to my husband?"

"Who is this?"

"What did you do to Paul?"

"Paul? Who is this – "

"If you've *hurt* him... I swear..."

"I think you have the wrong number."

"He went to talk to you. Raymond... *Byrd*. He said he was – "

I hung up on the woman. I turned the TV back on and when the phone rang again I unplugged it.

But I could still hear it. The phone, that mousy woman. So I went out, for a burger and beer at this place in Silver Lake. To be around people, to busy myself with eating and drinking.

Early the next morning a man came to my door. He was tall and blond, blue eyes, deep tan, a million dollar smile. The Hollywood Joe or Cam or Brad type. *Troy*, it turned out to be. Troy Beckmann, P.I., his card said, his teeth sparkling in the fresh morning light.

Who comes up with these things?

"Help you?"

"Where's Paul Wise, Mr Byrd?"

"With my wife, I assume."

"You know where I might find them?"

"In fact, I do. They're at the Drammond Institute, up in the mountains. Heard of it?"

He was taking notes, biting his tongue, nodding.

"That's *drammen* with a *d*, like *Dramamine*?"

I turned to step inside, half hoping Troy Beckmann, P.I., might follow and we could talk about it over a cup of coffee. I'd have liked the company. "I got a brochure here somewhere. Why don't you – "

"Byrd," he said, snapping closed his little notebook, tucking it away in his jeans, smiling like he meant it, "I think that's good for now. A place to start. Anyways, just wanted to drop by and say *ciao*. Introduce myself. So."

"And might I ask, Mr..."

"Beckmann, Troy Beckmann, but call me Troy." That smile.

He actually seemed like a friendly guy. I felt momentarily guilty for doing what I was doing – letting him go like that, without further explanation.

But it was just for a moment. There's no stopping some guys, once they get a notion. *A place to start.*

"And now, if I have any more questions, I know where to find you," he said.

"Sure you don't want a cup of coffee?"

The man pressed his lips tightly together, a firm straight line. He raised his eyebrows, said, "You know – I don't drink the stuff. It's just too acidic for me. So tea's all I take in the morning, *green* tea with a pinch of sugar. And after noon, nothin' but water."

"Sounds healthy."

He nodded. "You should give it some careful consideration, what exactly you put into your body. You know what coffee can do to a man's stomach?"

"I have no idea. But I heard about his Japanese guy, he drank so much hot tea every morning, he got throat cancer."

"Impossible," Beckmann said, shaking his head. "Tea cannot cause cancer. But coffee?" He raised his eyebrows, gave me this look. "They did this study, with rats – "

"We're not rats."

"Coffee will eat a hole in the lining of your stomach. That's a fact. Scientifically proven."

I was getting tired of Mr Beckmann's confidence. I caught a breath, blinked, thought about the thousands and thousands of cups of coffee I'd consumed in my lifetime, about the lining of my stomach, which, last I checked, was still intact. "So you'll go up there? Find them? Talk to them?"

Now Beckmann looked thrown, out of sorts. We were talking about coffee, stomachs, rats. *Science.* It was only an instant. "I'll see what I can do."

"They're scientists, you know. They work together. That's how they met."

"So I've heard."

"Genetics. DNA. Building blocks of *life.*"

"Right," the man said, nodding, tired of me. "Beyond my ken. I just find'em, know what I mean."

The man laughed, his lower jaw rising and falling piston-like in his face.

"They're sharp," I said, "my wife. Mr Wise. Or so I gather. What little she told me before she left."

"Safe assumption."

"So..."

Beckmann waited for me to finish my sentence, his brilliant blue eyes sparkling. Then he raised his chin and poked his face forward in a way that gave me the impression that he was very slowly coming in for a kiss.

"So don't be discouraged, I wanna say, if you don't find them. At first," I said. "They want to be alone. With their work."

The man closed his eyes, opened them, rebalanced himself, flashed me his prize-winning smile, said: "Of course they do. But I'm good at what I do, Mr Byrd, and I'm sure, asking the right questions to the right people, I'll track him down before long. And we'll find some proper closure to the whole situation. Mrs Wise is terribly distraught." He nodded for a moment, agreeing with himself, and then turned on a heel and started for the street, a white Porsche convertible parked at the curb. He said over his shoulder: "Nice talkin' to you, Byrd. Don't be a stranger. And don't take any sudden trips out of town nei- ther." And then: "I'll be in touch."

~ 35 ~

I called Troy Beckmann, P.I., the next morning. Someone else, a man, answered the phone. I asked for Beckmann and the man said he was out. I asked if he knew if Beckmann had left for the mountains, on the trail of Paul Wise, and the man said he couldn't say. Then he asked me to identify myself, which I did.

"He have your number? When I see him I'll tell him you called," said the man.

Beckmann called back a few hours later. "Something come to mind?"

"No," I said. "But what if I joined you. Up to the Drammond place. I know the way."

"You been there?"

"Once."

"Uh-huh. Okay..." The investigator paused. I pictured him stirring a pinch of sugar into a mug of piping hot green tea. I thought he had more to say. He didn't.

"So I'll join you," I said.

"I'm thinking about it."

"I don't see why it – "

"Why'd you go up there, Byrd?"

"To see her. Talk to my wife."

"Of course. And did you?"

" ... Yes. Briefly."

"Briefly. I see. And did you speak to Mr Wise at that time?"

"No. I didn't see him."

"Okay. So you went up there, made this long trip – how long does it take, did you say?"

"I didn't."

"And only to talk with your wife for a minute. Was she angry with you?"

"Yes."

"I see. Would you say she was surprised to see you?"

"Yes."

"I see. Well," he said, and I heard him doing other things, covering the mouthpiece of the phone, whispering to someone else in the room, *eating* something. Nuts, or ice. And then: "Last thing. When was this – that you went up there, saw her?"

I thought about it for hardly a second and then named a Monday a few weeks earlier, some days after Wise and I had made the trip.

The man on the line continued eating. Chewing, swallowing, he said: "It's not a bad idea. Come by the office. Friday. Noon. Don't be late."

"See you then."

After I hung up I thought about the days, if I'd counted right.

When had the missus called? *He went to see you...*

I didn't give it too much thought. I figured if I were wrong in my arithmetic Troy Beckmann, P.I., would be there to politely correct me.

The investigator's office was on the top floor of a run-down building down in Hawthorne. The street level was taken up by Asian beauty parlors, the windows completely blocked by enormous head shots of these radiantly smiling Chinese women, heads afloat in cherry blossoms and clouds.

At the elevator an old janitor stepped out of a closet and told me it didn't work. "Where'ya goin'?" he said.

"Beckmann's."

The old man nodded. "That's the fifth floor. Doesn't go past the fourth. Take the stairs."

But just then the elevator dinged and this older woman, rounded out in furs and sunglasses, a snarling chihuahua in her hands, stepped out. She directed the glasses at me and then at the janitor, smacked her lips, put her nose in the air and left. I took her place. "I'll take my chances." The doors closed as the janitor barked something else and started laughing.

The old man was right. At the fourth floor the lift came to a sudden, bouncing halt, and the machinery overhead rattled, gears grinding, groaning. After a moment something in the motor sighed miserably, coughed and quit. The box bounced on its line once more and the doors opened. I stepped into a dark hallway, mildew rank in the air. A TV played somewhere. A child wept. I found the staircase at the end of the hall and made my way up. The fifth floor was little different from the fourth. The ceiling was falling in, dusty tiles swinging by threads. On the roof just overhead, the loud coo of pigeons, the shuffle and beating of their wings as they hunkered down in the morning sun.

Beckmann's office was orderly enough. There were two desks, each before two tall windows, the shades lowered to head level. One desk was clean. The other was a disaster, covered corner to corner by teetering piles of paper, manila folders, newspapers, books, wire in and out baskets, various flattened gimcracks and gewgaws, a hat, a cactus, an ashtray. Near the center of the desk was a magnificent electronic typewriter, a small desklamp craned over one shoulder, a rotary phone at the other. A man sat behind the desk, turned to the side, a paper in his hand, up to his nose. Much older than Beckmann, the man had a dark gray mustache, weathered yellowbrown skin. He wore a white shirt, coat and tie. He hardly moved when he spoke: "What is it?"

"Beckmann in?"

"You Byrd?"

It was the man I'd spoke to on the phone.

"That's me. I was meeting Beckmann at noon. Guess I'm early."

I wasn't late, anyway. I knew it was before noon when I found the building. And just then, somewhere in this derelict quarter of the city, a church bell hammered out the hour.

The man lowered the paper he was reading, looked my way, turned in his chair to align his body square with mine. He licked his lower lip. "You missed him."

"Missed him?"

"That's what I said."

"You mean he left?"

"Looks that way."

"He asked me to come along."

"No use crying about it. He's not here. Plans change."

"He told me noon."

"Like I say. Plans change. Anything I can you help with?"

Plans change. Don't be late, he said. And then he goes and...

So there's more to pretty-boy Beckmann than meets the eye.

"No," I said, turning to leave. "Tell him to call me."

I'd hardly stepped out the doorframe into the hall when the man at the desk said: "So you do it, Byrd?"

"Do what?"

"You know. Kill the guy."

I turned back, regarded the man behind the desk, behind his piles of papers and typewriter, wondering if I'd misheard him. I stepped into the office, took hold of the door as if to close it and then realized that we were alone, that Beckmann and his man had the run of the place, the entire rotten floor to themselves.

I took one step toward the man's desk. He had deepset, dark blue eyes. He said very calmly: "Look, fella. You can tell me. What am I gonna do? *Go and tell the police?* They got better things to do than listen to anything I have to say. The story of a story. And the stories I could tell... Just imagine if they took seriously every old man that came in off the street wanting to tell them what they knew, of who did what."

"You were a cop?"

"Imagine that... Nah. Never a cop. I'm not cut out for –"

"Just the guy's secretary."

"I wouldn't call it that. But it's basically what I do, sure. He gets to drive around town asking all the questions. Filling in the details. I – I take numbers, keep the days in order. Invoicing, payroll, taxes. You know."

A siren, spinning distantly, monotonously for a minute, grew suddenly louder and then, as suddenly, stopped just outside the building. The vehicle's radio chirped, the muffled voice of a woman barking orders. A door closed. It was a bright and clear spring day.

"You gonna answer my question?"

"No. I didn't kill anyone."

The man smiled, his mustache opening up like wings. "Then you got nothing to worry about. Right?"

"Mr ..."

"Abergast."

"Mr Abergast. I was supposed to meet Beckmann here at noon."

"Yeah. You said that."

"I didn't... I didn't expect him –"

"To stand you up?"

"– to go up there alone, see."

"But he didn't go alone, Byrd."

I looked at the man, his piles of papers, the gargantuan typewriter set in their midst, and then at the more or less empty desk of his partner.

Abergast went on, chuckling to himself, twisting his chair about ninety degrees, crossing his legs, talking to a corner of the room. "Troy, you might have guessed, likes company. And he has no problem finding company. You see his Porche? I mean – " The man looked at me, his small mouth falling open. "So he has some new doll every week it seems. And this time – get this – she's a journalism student, over at USC, and she wants to do a story – ... I mean, when I heard this ... – on *true crime.*"

"True crime."

"I said to her, because she was right there, where you're standing, I said, 'What's that? True crime.' And she says, all serious, god bless her, 'As it actually happens.'"

Maybe I wasn't listening to the man, thinking suddenly about Beckmann, the move he'd pulled, the girl he'd decided to take up there, but I couldn't make heads or tails of what Abergast was going on about. "True crime," I heard myself repeat.

"That's right," he said quickly, getting worked up. "*As it actually happens.* But what other kind, I said to her, of crime is there? Crime happens. Not in our imagination. Not in a hypothetical *other* world. But here, in this world, I says."

If they'd left at nine, ten, then I was two hours behind. He'd need to stop, ask for directions. She'd want to stop, eat something, drink something. No hurry to get there and come back, right?

Maybe they'd even stay...

"She says, 'TV.'" The man raised his eyebrows and stared at me. "TV, the girl says. Ah. Of course. How it's done in TV. And how it's done in real life. Now I get it, I tell her. And she, standing right there, *where you're standing*, pretty little thing, can't be twenty-five if she's a day, she *beams at me*, like the understanding I've just come to, in her simple explanation, means *everything* to her. Like she's just taught me how to say *thank you* in Ancient Greek. TV," he said, raising his left arm, open palm to the ceiling, "and real life," looking into the open palm of his right hand, "naturally!"

Abergast stopped, dropped his hands, cooling off, watching me, his old self returning.

"And what'd you say?"

The man swallowed and looked down at the paper he'd been working on when I arrived. "I said 'Darling. The real thing is just not that interesting. That's why they don't make TV shows about it.'" He poked at some keys on the typewriter. "Wouldn't you agree?"

I told him I'd think about it. He snorted, cleared his throat, stroked his mustache, nodded several times, took up the page he'd been studying, and said he'd tell Beckmann that I'd come by and that I was nonplussed by his change of plans. Then he resumed reading. I pulled the door closed as I left.

~ 36 ~

Leaving straight from the office, I drove without stopping, pulled up outside Rosalee's at half past three. I hadn't seen Beckmann's Porche on the way up and didn't see it there, outside the diner.

I stepped into the place to see if Jillian, the waitress, was around. She wasn't. The other girl was there, the oval faced Mexican. I asked her if this movie-star type fellow had come into the place – tall, tan, blond, million-dollar smile, maybe a girl under his arm, studious type, tortoiseshell glasses, slacks, turtleneck. The waitress looked at me blankly, not understanding a thing I'd just said.

So he didn't stop and ask for directions. Maybe the girl, the journalist, knew about the place, knew how to get there. Or maybe he did, doing some research, but I doubted that. "He drives around, fills in the details," Abergast had said: "I just take numbers."

Abergast, who didn't act like he knew what the Drammond place was about, who knew little more than the name of the missing person. Which meant Beckmann hadn't said much about our brief exchange.

Filling in the details.

Beckmann, if I had to guess, was the kind of guy who wouldn't get his hands dirty so long as he didn't need to. The kinds of the things he's asked to do: Take some pictures, ask a few questions, sit and connect the dots for the wife over tea. That'll be five hundred dollars, please.

Which meant he met the journalism student before he came to talk to me. And when he mentioned to her, maybe that same day, "Drammond," the girl lit up like Shirley Temple. *She had her story.* "We've gotta go!" And he couldn't say no to that. And he couldn't, obviously, say "*All right* but we're taking along the man I'm investigating, because, I'm guessing, he'd like to show me where the bodies are buried. Or try his hand on me. And you."

He couldn't have said that. Could he?

To this USC journalism student? He just might have. But, then again, the prospect of getting away with her for a night alone in the mountains, letting her take charge and tell him everything she's heard about the place... *The bodies can wait.*

I stopped on my way out of town to get gas. I'd paid at the window. Returning to my car, someone ran up quietly behind me. "Hello, stranger."

I turned. It took me a moment to recognize her without an apron around her waist, without a counter between us.

"Remember me?"

Jillian Veldt, I could hear the housekeeper saying, the time I went up there with Lucy. *We know her.*

~ 37 ~

I asked her if she wanted to go to the diner, get a bite to eat. "You're kidding, right?" she said, sneering. "I get a day off you fuckin' think I wanna go to that place? Come on. I cook you something."

She drove an old Ford F-250 pickup. I followed her to her place, a one-story cabin in the woods on the edge of town. There was a light on inside. Smoke rose from a stovepipe in the roof.

"Who's dat!?" someone said on our entry.

"Nobody, grandma. Just a friend."

Jillian looked at me, gestured at a table in the middle of a small kitchen. She pulled out a chair. "Sit." Then, at the sound of giggling in the other room: "My grandmother," the girl said, rolling her eyes. "She's sick. Can't see very well, so stays in most days. Gimme your coat."

The old blind woman was in a La-Z-Boy recliner in the other room, big feet up in the air, *Jeopardy!* on the tube. She turned her dead eyes my way when I looked in the room, sniffed the air like a dog, said, "Howya doin', fix me a drink," and then turned back to the TV.

In the kitchen Jillian handed me a glass of ice, rum and coke. I brought this to the old woman, who held out a quivering hand expectantly. I took the hand, gently pressed the old fingers to the glass. "Thankee, thankee," said the woman, bringing the glass to her lips, slurping at the drink. And then, bellowing the word: "Hypotenuse!"

"What is the *hypotenuse*?" Alex Trebek calmly asked, to applause.

In no time at all Jillian fixed a couple cheddar cheese omelettes, microwaved a bag of frozen French fries, and chopped up some iceberg lettuce for a salad. "All I got is Coors."

So we drank Coors with our omelettes, fries and salad.

"Tell me about the house," I said.

"What house?"

"You know the one."

She smiled. The girl had a beautiful smile. Narrow face, fair skin, dark red hair. And a smile that could make the sun blush.

But then it faded, her eyes dropping to her plate. Flat, indifferent, "I told you not to go back there."

"I did."

"I know. I see that. You wouldn't be here if you hadn't. You goin' or comin'?"

"Neither. Tell me what you know."

"Neither." She laughed. She attacked what remained of her omelette, slicing it up, thrusting pieces quickly into her mouth, eating like she'd just learned how. She got up from the table still chewing, went to the fridge a pulled out a couple more beers, went to a drawer and took out a pack of Camels. She took a cigarette and tossed the pack on the table.

I opened the beer, said, "People go missing up there."

"That a question? Course people go missing. People go missing everywhere."

"But around that house particularly."

"*Particularly* shit. And you mean *inside* the house. Not around. You've been in there. A number of times now, I take it."

"I have."

"How many people have you brought up there?"

"... Two."

Her head tilted to a shoulder, raising an ear. "I think you're lying to me but it doesn't matter. So. You've looked around. Been in the basement?"

"Parts of it."

She sat down, opened her beer, drank, tipped her chair back and drew on her cigarette. She didn't say anything for a minute, smoking, eyes elsewhere.

She closed her eyes, stroked her eyelids. "Place is big as fuck," she quietly said.

"I know."

"You have no idea."

"No. I think I know."

"No you don't. Listen to me. *Big* doesn't even begin to describe it. It stretches out – like this," she said, opening both of her pale hands, fingers out, over the table, "tendrils and veins going everywhere. All over the mountain."

She drank, tipping her head back, puffing out her cheeks, the muscles in her throat flexing as she swallowed loudly. When she'd finished she slammed the empty can down and wiped her mouth on her wrist. She said:

"This one line, it goes from the house under the lawn in the back, down the hill, down to Sam Gretton's cabin – I'll just tell you this, but nothing more 'bout the inside because, well, honestly, it scares the shit out of me just to bring it up, and anyways this is something you might need to know someday – ... And it comes up there, through this hole in the floor in his cabin. It's covered by a little wooden door, and it's underneath the rug, under the piano. Got that? Don't forget what I just told you. It'll save you."

I smiled. "You're telling me there's a tunnel that goes from the house to that old man's cabin. That beneath the grass, behind the house, there's a hundred meters of tunnel connecting the two buildings."

She stared at me, said nothing.

"... How do you know that?"

"Because I've seen it!"

"What else you seen? Tell me."

There was something silly about her tone and posture, how she'd roll her eyes, how she drank so quickly. But at the same time I never had the impression she was faking it, putting on a show for me. Not even close. Rather,

I think what she wanted to tell me was so complex and frightening that she was overwhelmed with how to proceed, where to begin. She was whistling in the dark.

"You a detective?" she asked.

"No."

"A journalist? She has a thing for journalists."

"*She* being – "

"You know."

"... I'm not a journalist."

We smoked for a spell, listened to Alex Trebek in the other room. I thought the old lady had fallen asleep. But then, roaring to life, cackling like a lunatic, "*Fat Man,* you idiot! *Jeee-sus!*"

~ 38 ~

"**I**s it haunted?"

"Everyone asks that. Even you asked me that, once. The first time. Surprises me that that's what you'd think of, about the house. Having been inside. I don't know. Do *you* think it's haunted?"

She'd opened two more beers. We'd finished those and moved on to a bottle of the grandmother's bourbon, Four Roses. Jillian did the dishes. I stepped into the other room and found the old lady tipped back in her La-Z-Boy fast asleep, her enormous ankles up in the air, her head turned far to the side, like she wanted to look over her shoulder. I turned the TV off but then – Jillian shouting at me from the sink, "Leave it on!" – flipped it back on. Apparently the old woman couldn't sleep without the TV on. Silence bothered her.

I didn't think the place was haunted, but I couldn't say why. It *felt* haunted but that didn't seem like enough to go on. I hadn't actually seen –

You make it sacred.

"It's not haunted," she said. "It's not that, not that at all."

You, Paul, make it sacred.

"Although, that *housekeeper*," she went on, "Corinne Kearn. I take it you've met her. Piece of work, that one. *To keep* the place... As if it needed keeping, or even *could* be kept."

She raised her glass, caught her breath, warming up. Shaking her head, "The things you hear – "

Tell her about what you saw in the basement.

"The old dude, Sam Gretton. He's the groundskeeper. You've met him too, I assume. He never steps foot inside. You know why? Cuz *he* thinks the place is haunted. Full of demons, bad spirits. But he's a little nuts himself, so... And from what I've heard, Kearn never comes out. Into his territory. So it's kind of a ying and yang for the place. Some say the two are related, brother and sister or father daughter, but that's only a story, and from what I can tell there's nothing to it... Except for," she said, raising a finger in the air, "the trick of ancestry, common blood, that sometimes helps us make sense of the insensible. Meaning. If they *were* related, then..." She lowered her chin, raised both hands palms-up in the air. She held the pose for a moment. Then she took her drink, leaned forward, went on: "A lot of it, the Drammond House, boils down to that. Fitting the pieces together. The old man who stays outside, the woman he fears who's always inside. Making sense, making the place and its people *fit* into some logical scheme." Her glass was half-full. She set it down, pushed it gently across the table. "You want this? I've had enough."

She stood, left the room, came back a minute later with a small bag of weed. She sat down, started rolling herself a joint. "Haunted houses," she said, "come with women." She licked the edge of the rolling paper, pressed the joint closed. "Bet you didn't know that." She lit the joint, took a deep crackling drag, said, holding her breath, "You're staying her tonight, no question... I want the company... Talking about that place."

She coughed violently, blood rushing to her face, tears in her eyes. She held the joint out over the table and gasped, "Mendocino!" but I waved it off. I finished my drink, finished hers. Still thirsty, I poured myself another.

After a minute, her voice slower, thicker, she went on. "It's a woman's story, the haunted house story. It's a spirit that won't go outside, into the world. With its dirt, and filth. All this *nature*... The spirit of a woman who wants to *hold on* to the place, to keep the place her own forever and ever. Made in her image."

They swarmed. They surrounded him, stripped him, covered him.

She was staring at me.

"Argue with me," she said.

"Go on. I'm listening."

She blinked, puffed on the joint. "The woman of the house, she *fills* the place, keeping it for so long. It becomes a part of her, her residue all over it. *Its* residue all over her. You can smell her in the woodwork... So you ask. Is it haunted? A better question, Raymond, would be, is *she* haunted? To be so... *obsessed* with her house." She stared at me, her eyes sparkling, reddening. "While *a spirit* might inhabit the house – haunting it, as they say – *that* is just a story, something to frighten children with... What's *not* a story is how a spirit inhabits *a person* – someone like you, or me, or her, or my grandma... So I ask you, Raymond – is *she* haunted?"

"Possessed, you mean."

Jillian took a final drag on the joint, studied it for a minute, twisted it out in the ashtray. She licked her lips, looked across the room at the sink, exhaled and slowly got up. She went to the sink, filled a glass with water, came back and sat down. She drank her glass of water. She said: "It's a good point. There's an important distinction to make here."

I drank my bourbon, watched my philosopher-waitress carefully. I couldn't tell if she'd asked me a question, and was waiting for me to say something, or if she was thinking, about to go on. "Seems to me," I said, "that a haunt –"

"A house," she said, interrupting, "can be haunted." She put her hands on the table, fingers spread, regarded the space between her thumbs. "At least, we tell ourselves this in stories." She leaned over the table on her forearms, looked me in the eye and said with extraordinary clarity:

"In reality, a haunted house doesn't make a whole lot of sense. Because what we mean by this is that the house is *occupied* by something frightening we can't identify.

There's someone or something *in there* that doesn't want to be recognized. It hides, it lurks in the shadows, showing itself only when it needs to frighten off invaders, those who would try to claim for themselves what is already claimed, that is, what is *hers*."

"You've thought about this."

She blinked. Then she held still, frozen, like a person wanting to disappear. "In this sense," she continued, "we're talking about possession, about ownership. Which is more to the point. If *haunting,* Raymond, is a kind of *hunt*, a moment of surprise, terror and pursuit, it will have its resolution. The prey gets away or gets consumed. But what remains in the end, always, is a question of possession. What is mine and what is yours. What is hers, and what we'd like to call ours. And if you think about it, think about it for a moment, you will see that *possession* is much more powerful... much more frightening in its potential... than *haunting.* You can get away from the haunt. But once you're possessed..."

As suddenly as the analysis had crystallized in her mind, it started to dissolve. The thought escaped her. A lose end, at *possessed,* a dead end.

She closed her eyes, sat back in her chair. Drowsy, heavy, stoned eyes. The light in her eyes, blue and electrified as she told her story, flickered and started to fade. Her chin lowered, her lips trembled, a girl on the verge of tears. She said nothing more.

I put some wood in the stove. In the other room I stretched out an old couch. At first the babble of the television kept my attention, leading my thoughts this way and that. *Dead ends.* And then in an instant it was gone, and I was in that great emptiness of a dreamless sleep.

~ 39 ~

I awoke to a presence, a figure directly before me, between me and the grandmother and the TV. Her hair was dripping wet, hanging past her face down her arms, her body wrapped in a black towel.

"I'm not finished with you. Get up," she said. "This way." She left the room, started down a dark hallway. "You'll sleep better here," she said over her shoulder.

I sat up, stretched my legs, followed her.

She was sitting on a bed in the dark, her long white back to me. She was drying her hair.

I lay down and closed my eyes, listened to her rubbing her hair with the towel, to her breathing soberly in the dark. I was nearly asleep when I felt her lay down beside me, turn and face me, felt her watching me in the dark.

"One time," she said, "this guy tried to burn the place down."

I opened my eyes. The darkness in the room was nearly perfect but her face, inches from my mine, was sharp, clear, white, lit up as if by a ray of moonlight. Softly, nearly in a whisper, she said:

"His name was Simon Lawson. He came out here from... Philadelphia or someplace. Said – when they took him away – that he'd *dreamt* of the place, that the place – that house – and this was all in the papers – was *inside* him... *It's in me! I can feel it!...* Fuckin' nuts... He caught the housekeeper. It wasn't Corinne then. 'Twas another woman, I forget her name. Anne... Anne Dashell – Drezzle? I don't know what. It's in the papers. But he took her, beat her up, tied her up. Put'er in the closet. Locked her in. *Nailed the door closed...* She's all screaming, *You can't do this! I'll die! I'll die if I stop! Die if I stop! I'll die! Don't! You can't!...* But he did. And he'd planned it. Going up there with a *truckload* of gasoline. And with the housekeeper locked up, out of the way, he goes down to his truck, starts unloading – twenty, thirty, forty, I don't know how many of these jugs of gas. He carries them, one in each hand, up into the house. All of them. And he goes room to room, everywhere, covering everything in sight, drenching the place in gasoline. Downstairs, upstairs, the hallways, the stairways, the elevator, as many rooms as he could... *Even on the closet door he's nailed shut...* Going *ape shit* with the stuff..."

I'll die, I'll die if I stop! Simon, please! Please! Don't! I'll die if I stop!

"And he lights it up. He's singing to himself, running around the place, lighting and tossing matches everywhere in his path, the house going up in flames around him. And he's down there in the front yard, singing and dancing, his arms up like he's *conducting* the burning of the Drammond House, the burning of *that witch*, Anne Drezzle, the housekeeper..."

Burn! Burn! Burrrn, you bitch!

"The place burns all night. The fire chopping at the sky at dawn. They say they could see it on Mount Palomar. That's like two hundred miles away... And the fire engines coming up at dawn. Slow, heavy, big machines crawling up the mountain. But there's no hurry. It's like – they've done this before. Like – every decade or so some screwball goes up to the Drammond House, hearing voices in his head, and lights the place up... *And it never works.*"

She stopped. Her body was feverish, sweating in the bed. Her lips were chapped. Her teeth clicked, shivering, chattering. I put a hand on her side, to calm her, but she brushed it away.

"The house is too big, Ray. It's too big to burn. The fire burns out on its own, in time. You try to burn it down, and it will burn and burn and burn, and then the fire, it gets tired – and it slows, petering out. And finally it dies. And what's left. *The Drammond House...* There it is," she whispered. "Still there. More of it. On and on and on – Drammond House after Drammond House after Drammond House... They found Lawson sleeping at the bottom of the yard, in the bushes, curled on his side like an animal. When they woke him, and he saw the fire engines, and saw the fire he'd started had gone out, he starts screaming *Don't! Let it burn! Fools! You fools! Let it burn!* ... But they hadn't stopped it. It stopped itself, as it always does...

They took him away. Part of the house burned down that night. Some part of some wing... They found the house-keeper in a broom closet. She didn't burn but the heat and the smoke... They say she lived awhile. I mean when they found her, she was still breathing. They did what they could. But then, of course, she died... They say Lawson was pleased to hear that."

"What happened to him, this man?"

Jillian closed her eyes, opened them. She reached out and touched my forehead with her finger, stroking a line there. She smiled. She was coming back, the Jillian I'd met before – not the strange thing that'd emerged as we started talking about...

"Fuck if I know what they did to him. It's just a story, Ray."

~ 40 ~

I woke a few hours later. I could hear the TV in the other room.

I was alone in the bed. I sat up, looked around. The darkness in the room was heavy and stifling. My head was ringing, the early phase of a mean hangover.

I could hear her in the room but barely make her out, not ten feet away. The faint white line of her naked back, her ass and legs. She faced the opposite wall, her hand up on the wall, fingers moving, waving.

"Jillian?"

She was scratching at the wall.

I went to her side.

She was asleep, but talking quietly. Scratching gently at the wall, her eyes closed, she said: "Michael."

"Jillian, wake up."

"Michael." *Scratch, scratch, scratch.* Stroking the wallpaper, gentle as a cat.

"Jillian."

Slowly she turned, faced me, regarded me with her closed eyes, her shut face. "Michael," she said.

"Jillian. You're dreaming. It's Ray. I'm Ray."

"Only one gets away."

"Come back to bed."

"Only one gets away," she said.

I helped her back into the bed, covered her with the damp sheet. When I lay down beside her, she, on her side, facing me, quietly said: "Only one gets away... So get away from me. *Get away from me! Get away...*"

She was mumbling, dreaming. Her eyes trembled, turning frantically. Then she was suddenly quiet, calm, breathing slowly, deeply, asleep.

~ 41 ~

High up on the wall, dim milkblue light in the window. I could see pine trees, tall and thin, swaying in the wind.

I'll die if I stop.

Jillian was gone.

Her blind grandmother stood in the middle of the kitchen sipping a mug of coffee, a blathering transistor radio tuned to some Christian ministry station. From Exodus, the construction of the tabernacle.

"Where's Jillian?" I asked.

"Work."

"Didn't hear her get up."

"She's quiet like that. Tip toeing around, trying not to wake me. But I hear her. She thinks I don't but I do. I hear just about everything that girl does, everything that goes on round here. Who she brings around."

I took a cup from the wash board, filled it with black coffee.

Still in the middle of the room, addressing an obscure point between the fridge and the entry to the other room, the old woman went on. "Heard you two talkin' last night. 'Bout that house."

"I had some questions."

"So I heard." She took a breath, reached out for the kitchen table. She set her mug down on the edge of the table. She said: "I'd 'preciate you don't bring that up round her, don't come around and talk about that stuff."

"About the Drammond House."

"She gets so worked up."

"Why's that?"

The old woman took a ragged breath, sucking in her teeth. "She's lost so much. Just don't bring it up anymore, will you. It hurts her. Maybe you can't see it but it does."

"What's she lost?"

"Just don't bring it up."

" ... Who's Michael?"

The woman turned her head, her blind eyes searching the room for me. She leaned on the table, sighed, groaned in her small chest.

"Your name's Raymond, is it?" she said.

"Ray."

"Ray, then. You ask me about this Michael. Yes, I've heard about him too. I wish I could tell'ya more but – she's brought so many by."

"Boys, you mean."

"Boys, girls. Men like you."

"By here?"

" ... Let me ask you. She asked you to go with her yet, up there?"

I thought about that. In all the stories she'd told me the night before, going up to the house – a natural proposition, I thought – hadn't actually come up. "No," I said.

"That's good. Don't. Do me a favor. She asks you to go up to the house – don't let her go. And above all, should she fight with you, and insist on going, and get away from you, which she will, wily creature that she is – *don't go with her.*"

"Why's that?"

"She doesn't need to go out there anymore. She's done enough. It's done enough. Anyways... Can't you see? How she is? She doesn't *need* to go there anymore. What it's done to her. And someday..."

"... Someday?"

"True as Christ's my savior, Ray, someday that girl's gonna take someone up there and *she'll be the one who doesn't come back.* And it'll kill me. She's all I got. We're all that's left."

The old woman didn't say any more after that. She sat at the table and swallowed her coffee.

I finished my cup, took my coat, thanked the woman for her hospitality, to which she simply raised her chin, her blind eyes in my direction, and left.

I'd just got into the car when the old woman came to the cabin door and waved at me, swatting the air. I got out, went back to her.

"Get some wood for me, will you," she said. "Jillian must've forgotten this morning. The shed's around back."

I did as she asked, bringing an armload of firewood into the cabin, setting it down by the stove. I opened the stove door, stirred the ashes, put in some wood. The cabin was cold.

I'll die if I stop.

I could feel the old woman behind me, watching me with her dead expression, her withered hands clasped at her navel.

I turned, faced her, said: "One question. One last thing."

She raised her chin.

"Talking with her last night, Jillian, listening to all these stories, she said something I've heard now several times, about the house, these words the woman there is supposed to say. *I'll die if I stop.*"

The old woman slowly drew back, her face tightening up, her jaw swelling.

"What's that mean, you think?" I said.

Slowly the old woman turned, aimed her face at mine, her flesh rippled eyes digging at something inside me. I had to look away.

"Why you ask such a mean question of an old woman?"

"I'm sorry, I didn't – "

"Thought you were smarter than that, Raymond. Struck me almost as a gentleman, you – "

"Listen. Forget it – "

"Nah. You said it. And poor Jillian won't have the answer. So let me try. This old bag of bones."

She went to the open door, stood by it, waiting for me to follow. I did. I stepped onto the porch. A light rain had started blowing in the pines overhead, the sigh and whistle of the wind in the trees calling to mind the ocean, the coast a hundred miles away.

Her chin down, the old woman said: "You ever built something you cared about, something that needed your care, something helpless, wanting your constant attention?"

I thought about it. Nothing came to mind. Not a single thing.

"Sure," I said.

"Well – that's it," she said, her chin tucked down at her chest, blind eyes on my feet. "Answer to your question. Now get outta here." And, as I walked back to my car, as she was closing the cabin door, her voice, more quietly even than before, an afterthought: "Men."

~ 42 ~

I was thinking of getting a ticket for Hawaii, to the island of Hilo. I have an old friend, he's got a place on the mountain there. He was a priest, and then he fell in love with this girl. So he quit the priesthood, married the girl. A few years pass. They're no longer in love. They get a divorce. He didn't know what to do then. So he goes to Hilo, lives by himself up in the clouds, in the rainforest. I get a card from him now and then, pictures of the place.

You can keep your doors and windows open all year round, practically live outside.

But what if Lucy came back?

Three months had passed. In fact I wasn't thinking too much of Marianne or Lucy. They'd stayed. They'd left me, not the other way around.

And so they'd come back. If they wanted to, they'd come back. Right?

It was Paul Wise and, more specifically, Troy Beckmann, P.I., who'd gone up there looking for the man, who were keeping me awake at night. Because there, with him—

You make it sacred.

– there, I felt, was potential. An opening. A partner-ship.

I was expecting him, Beckmann. He'd be at the door, the moment I got up, all vibrant and confident, firing his dopey questions, giving me health tips as he stepped aside to let the cops finish up what he'd started. Filling in the details. Like Columbo, you know. Telling the story at the end – making it all fit. I could picture him seated at my dining table, tipping the chair back, a pen twirling be-tween his fingers, a steaming cup of tea before him. Giv-ing the ABCs to the sergeant, flashing that winning smile of his. His huge white teeth.

Because, from a certain angle, and it's a big angle, what I'd done was plain as day.

Then again, what *exactly* became of Paul Wise, I can't say. I wasn't there. I can *imagine*, as any of us could, what became of the man. But such a description would amount to little more than a frightening story. Something for the kids, as Jillian would say.

Speculation.

I am not guilty for what *may* have happened beneath the Drammond House.

I didn't force him. I didn't threaten him. He followed, willingly.

So where was he, Beckmann? A week passed. And then another week. And another. And I began to wonder: Is that it? Does nobody else want to know where these people are, will nobody else come around asking questions, say to me like that woman who called,

"*What* did you do?"

The missus, Paul's wife. She'd hired Beckmann.

I hadn't heard from her either.

But it wasn't Beckmann who finally caught up with me. It was his partner, the deskman, the phoneman.

I was downtown, down at that gallery I mentioned. The Samaniego Gallery. The day Lucy left I made a trip down there to look at this painting, the one by Heinrich Manning. The one I have on my office wall? I know I mentioned this. We've talked about this.

Well, I went down there again, to see this painting I'd turned down twice before. But not because I was thinking of buying it. Or not that alone.

I guess I was hoping that that woman would be there. The assistant, Graham, Charlotte Graham, remember her? I wanted to talk to her, to learn something about her, about how she found Manning, or how he found her. Even if it was only for a few minutes, to talk with this woman, to look into her eyes and listen to her, and maybe recover something of my previous life, from before I lost Lucy, and Marianne, from before I'd even heard of that place...

She wasn't there. Neither was the painting.

I thought at first that it had sold. But then, looking around, I saw that *all* of Manning's things were gone.

There was a girl at the desk. She was bent over reading a comic book, her nose down at the page.

"Like comics?" I said.

She looked up, squinted at me. She had a silver ring in her bottom lip. "It's a graphic novel!"

"Sorry. Say – they used to have these paintings here by Heinrich Manning. You know..."

The girl shrugged, pouted, shook her head. "Sorry, dude, I just started. Night shift."

With the tip of her tongue she swung the ring in her lip one way and then the other.

"Enjoy your graphic novel."

"I will. It's fuckin' rad. By Alan Moore, man. Fuckin' genius!"

I wandered around the place for a minute. It seemed like a different gallery altogether. Fallen, spiritless. With crap on the walls and *this kid* behind the desk. But it was the same place. I'd stood in this spot, and looked at that painting – those lines drifting off to the left, fading, drawn toward a point off the canvas. I'd stood there, thinking: "You stand back, it's one thing. You come in close, it's something else."

And *he'd* stood there with me, the first time I saw the painting. "It *pulls!*" he'd said in my ear – the old man's hands in the air, demonstrating, tightening a knot in a rope.

Anyway, the woman I was looking for wasn't there. So I left.

Just down the street, I hadn't been in the car a minute, this VW Thing – remember those? Like army jeeps – pulls out behind me, tails me home. Making no effort at all to conceal itself, this guy follows me, right on my bumper, all the way home.

~ 43 ~

"You're telling me you've lost your girlfriend, you've lost your wife, and this fellow, Wise, all in this house – you spend the night with some kid, getting drunk – you even *consider* for a minute *the legality* of the situation you are in – and then – *and then* – you're telling me, you go after this other girl? You go back down to this gallery lookin' for – ... I mean. Help me, Ray. Help me understand this."

The Japanese man, in the corner all morning, not saying a thing, he'd moved suddenly, come over to the detective, touched him on the shoulder, said something to him. They stepped out of the room.

Raymond Byrd sat by himself for almost an hour. He got up, looked out the window. It was about two o'clock, a beautiful September afternoon in LA.

He thought about Charlotte Graham, where she could be.

Mexico City. She got away. She's waiting for you.

Then the detective and the Japanese man returned. Everyone took their places.

"You were saying," said the detective. "Why you went back to the gallery, after this girl."

"I wanted to see her. I wanted to see the painting, and her, too. If she was there."

"Would you say you were a good husband?"

The question surprised him. He'd anticipated some of their questions, but not this one.

"I don't know," Byrd said. "But good or not – how's that relevant?"

"Heh. *How's that relevant.* Maybe it's not. Humor me."

"... I don't know what a good husband is. What makes a good husband? But – yes. I cared for Lucy, if that's what you mean. I never hurt her. I never gave her any reason to... do what she did."

"You a womanizer, Ray?"

"A *womanizer*!? Good husband, *womanizer*!? Where do you come up these things?" He looked at the Japanese man. The man was inscrutable. "I like women. I enjoy their company. I like the way they talk and think. I like how they feel and how they smell. I like having sex with them, if that's what you mean. If that's what being a womanizer means, enjoying sex with women, and going after it – then yes, I'm a womanizer. I womanize. But that's not what you mean, is it?"

~ 44 ~

She wasn't there, as I said. And this guy follows me home in a VW Thing.

Momentarily, I thought it was Manning. Maybe he'd been outside the gallery, seen me walking away, wanted to come after me, talk to me, make me an offer.

But the driver was a smaller man. Square head. In a hat I thought I'd seen somewhere.

At my place, I hadn't even got out of the car when the driver quickly stepped from the VW, came to my passenger side window. I recognized him though it took me a minute to remember his name.

Abergast.

I lowered the window, looked up at the guy.

"It's Max Abergast," the man said louder than he needed to, announcing himself to the entire block, "I'm with Beckmann, remember?"

"I do. Nice car."

The man frowned, drew in his lips, squinted. "It's a classic. It's a very good car. Not everyone appreciates such things anymore."

Going to my door, he followed on my heels like a hungry dog.

"What do you want, Abergast? Seen Beckmann?"

The car comment aside, the man seemed in rather good spirits.

"Sure I seen him."

"You have?"

At my door I turned, looked at the man. He was a different man standing than he was when behind a desk. He was short, for one thing, and broad in the shoulders, with a head narrow at the temples, thick and fleshy in the jaw. He had tired, dark gray eyes. A long sad mustache hanging from his lip. He wore a bucket hat.

"Sure. That surprise you?" he said.

"No. It's only that – I was wondering..."

Abergast smiled kindly. "No need to say any more. I perfectly understand. But tell me, Mr Byrd... I was checking on some things." The man waited, as if for a cue. When I gave him nothing, he said: "Finances."

"What sort of finances?" I said.

"Yours."

"Can you do that?"

"I dunno. I did. Nothing happened. Now my question is, Mr Byrd – you laid off?"

"That's not really your question, is it?"

"Just answer the question. You working now?"

"No. I lost my job."

"And what is it you were doing?"

"... Why do I think you already know the answer to that question?"

"Don't answer my question with questions," he said quickly, coolly. "Answer the question."

"Computers. Development. That's what I *did*. Now I – "

"What's that, *development*? You mean construction? Like nuts and bolts. Chips?"

"I worked for a company that found resources for other, emerging companies. Most of those companies dealt in computers."

The man smiled, his mustache tilting at a sharp angle. "Ah! *Emerging* companies. That's rich. So yer one of *those* guys," he said, shaking his head. Then he was quiet for a moment, watching me, thinking. He said: "Then you lost your job."

I almost turned my back on the man, went inside without another word. "What does this have to do with anything – with Wise or my wife or – ?" I didn't turn on the man. I knew how that would look. And presently – said a voice in a far-off corner in my head – I needed to be polite, and needed to answer this man's questions.

"I'll get to that," Abergast said. "But first – you lost your job?"

"I don't want to sound condescending, but – "

"Try me."

"People in my line of work don't lose jobs. They follow money. Change teams."

"So you quit, that's what you're saying? To move on to something else?"

" ... Sort of."

"What's that mean, sort of?"

Be polite.

"That means I left before I was asked to go."

"I see." Abergast closed his eyes, opened them, scratched at his cheek with his stubby fingers. "Why would they ask you to go?"

"I was in a relationship."

The man stood still as a statue, hardly breathing at all. Then he sighed, a gentle expression coming to his face, his eyes. Like everybody's favorite uncle. *Uncle Max.* As if he'd heard it all before.

I was expecting a follow up question. Regarding this relationship and its connection to my job. Surely something awry and titillating with that. But he backed up. "You were good at whatever it was you did, in ... *development?*"

A better crook, a wiser man than I, would lie. "No," I said. "I was average. A run of the mill techie. But still. When I want to work again, I'll get placed, and work for a bit, and make an unspeakable amount of money, and then I'll quit. Look for something else. Start anew."

"Must be nice."

" ... Has its moments."

Abergast stepped back, took a deep breath, his chest rising, smiled, said, "Well I thank you for your candor,

Byrd. I don't meet many people – like yourself, people in your position – who're so forthright."

"So we're finished? That's it?" I was turning the key in the lock.

"Guess so. Always nice talking to you."

I stepped quickly inside, closed the door. Then I immediately opened the door, looked out into the night, the cement of my front yard. The man hadn't moved. He was looking upward, his fat chin pointed at me. You'd think he was admiring the stars except there are no stars in the city. There's nothing up there.

The chin dropped. "Forget something?" he said.

"You didn't say. When's Beckmann coming back? He coming by? Gonna call?"

The man smiled cheerfully, his mustache swinging up, hanging from his cheek. "You didn't ask, Byrd. ... And I wish I knew. But even if I did... Boy's busy, hard at work."

"And his journalist friend? She write her article?"

The man snorted, chuckled, his whole body heaving. Then he grew quiet, solemn. "Must be a fascinating place up there," he said. I thought he was referring to outer space, to stars we couldn't see. "With how many times he's been back. Back and forth, back and forth."

"You mean to the mountain, to that house. The institute."

"Whatever. I tell you... He's putting that Porche to good use. Among other things."

"You don't say."

"Thinking of going out there myself," he said. He turned, started back to the street. He paused, turned. "I'd have to rent a car, of course. Don't think the VW would cut it. It's at altitude, right?"

I didn't know what to tell him, didn't know what to think – *Beckmann's gone to the house a number of times now?* Almost like nausea, what I felt was curiosity, of course, about what Beckmann was up to, about what he'd discovered at the house, but also, strangely, terribly, *envy.*

"No. Right. I'd rent something," I said.

Abergast nodded, turned, took two steps to his Thing, climbed in, slammed the door and drove away.

~ 45 ~

Curiosity and envy, I soon realized, was getting off light. I'd rather envy the guy than sit around anticipating his return. Let him go.

That's what I did. And I began to think, over the following weeks, that the story of the Drammond House was coming to a close, that I'd never hear from Marianne or Lucy or Troy Beckmann, P.I., ever again. Even the envy I felt for the guy, if we can call it that – that he might actually find the women and come back with an explanation – that too began to subside and diminish, as if I were driving away from the house, across an enormous plain, watching the house in the rearview mirror grow smaller and smaller and smaller. And, as evening turned to night, and darkness came over me, the house would be gone.

What a happy thought. Repeat that to yourself, Raymond. Close your eyes, tell yourself: It's just a dream, a bad dream. When you wake, it'll all be over.

"I'LL DIE IF I STOP!"

I couldn't sleep through the night. When I closed my eyes I felt that my bed was moving, that the walls were moving, coming in, drifting apart. The house was transforming in the dark. I'd get up, go to the bathroom, reach for the light switch and find it wasn't there. It'd be in the other wall, on the right of the door, not the left. Or, where once there was *one* step between the garage and kitchen, there were then, I discovered, almost breaking my neck, two.

How's the song go? "This isn't my house. That's not my wife. Those aren't my kids."

The cats, the old one and young one together, noticed this too. They started sleeping in the bedroom, with me, at the foot of the bed, which they never did before. And I could hear them, as my skin tingled, feeling something in the house in the small hours of the morning, hear them growling at shadows, at things in the dark that only they could see.

A month passed. And nothing. Nobody. Not Beckmann, Marianne, Lucy, the wife – *nobody*. I was going out of my mind. I felt, without them, who would believe me? Without, even, *a body* –

It was like none of it had happened. It was like, very simply, they'd left me. Moved on. Forgotten about me. Like *I* was the only one holding onto the memory, the only one wanting an explanation.

You asked me why I'm here telling you this...

August first. I decided to leave, to get out of LA. I'd sell the house, move to Hawaii, find my friend up on the mountain.

I called a realtor, an acquaintance of Lucy's I met some years ago. She said she'd come by, look at the place.

"How *is* Lucy?" the woman said.

"Can't say. She left me."

"I'm so sorry!"

But the day I expected her, there was that accident on the 605, that spill, and the pileup. She couldn't get around, through it. The city – you remember – it was like we were cut in half for twenty-four hours.

The woman called that evening, said she'd check in with me later in the week.

"And what's your *timeline* like, Ray?"

"My what?"

"When were you thinking of – "

"Immediately."

"Oh-*kaaaaay*. I'm going to recommend we *waaait* – "

"No. I want to sell it now."

"Oh-*kaaaaay*. I'll see what we can do. But, first things first, obviously, I'll need to come by and see – "

"Call me."

"*Will* do."

But she doesn't. Not at the end of the week. Not the next week. I call her, she doesn't answer. I leave a dozen messages.

I could've gone after her. But then what? If the woman didn't want to talk...

Now I've gotta find somebody else. If I'm gonna get away before...

I'm not a criminal. Even if what I've done can be called a crime, I'm not a criminal. But in those days, waiting and waiting and waiting to *hear back* from someone, from anyone, who might help me find *closure* for what had happened – I think I felt what many criminals must feel. This *intense* anxiety for the future and for not just answers but *logic.* To make everything make sense.

But I'd stopped sleeping. Nothing makes sense when you stop sleeping.

The sun sets, I turn on *all* the lights in my place. I sit at the table. I have something to drink. I smoke a cigarette. I pick up the phone, check if it's working. I put on some music and turn it up really loud. I try and eat something. I drink a little more. I turn the music off and check the phone again. Silence in the house starts getting to me, makes my skin crawl. I can hear, with the stereo off, this far-off rumbling. Like thunder, or I got water in my ears. But the sky's clear. I turn on the TV and flip through channels for hours and hours. At some point I go out, driving, looking for people. I come home alone. I can't meet anyone, can't talk to anyone. I couldn't even get a *realtor.*

She sensed it in me. The infection, the...

Then the sky starts to turn. Dawn. I'm weak in the legs with happiness. Because in the sun, nothing happens, nothing moves. Everything is as it should be, in its proper place.

So I climb into bed, close my eyes, try and sleep.

But it's there, still, behind my eyelids. In my head, in my dreams.

This is not my house –

Then, late one night – this is maybe a week ago, around the first – the phone rings. It's been almost a month, I don't know how long since I spoke to the woman, since I spoke to anyone. I pick up.

But no.

I should have forgotten the place, the people there, the women. Everything. After Paul Wise – I shouldn't have thought twice about it. Should've come home, packed my things, gone down to the bank, taken out as much money as I could, gone straight to the airport and gotten on the next plane to Hawaii, gone out to Hilo, climbed that mountain, joined my friend, let my beard grow out, taken up yoga, started writing poetry. Forgotten about the house, my house, *that* house, *Manning's* house, it suddenly occurred to me,

"It's a very *complicated* house," the old man had said –

forgotten them, *all* of the them, everything. Shut the door. Turned. Walked away. A new man. A clean slate.

But nothing could be so easy. Not about what I'd done, or about what Lucy or Jillian or any of them had done. In fact, what I'd done was nothing, of such little consequence in comparison to what I was about to do, in comparison to what was about to happen.

"Who was it? Beckmann? He got a body."

"No."

"The wife, then. Wise's."

"No."

"*Lucy*, then. She wants to come by and get her things."

"You enjoying this? No."

"Marianne."

"No. No, no! They're gone, they're..."

~ 47 ~

It was Charlotte Graham. The painter's assistant, the woman I'd gone out looking for.

Manning was dead. Turned out he left something for me, wanted me to have it.

It's like – with some things – no matter what you do to avoid them – *they find you.* They happen.

A glass is going to break. You bump it with your elbow, but you catch it before it falls. But then, two minutes later, *bing* - something slips, and down goes the glass. *BANG!*

It was going to happen. With some things, there is *nothing* you can do to stop their destiny.

The man put it in his will. My name and *that* painting, partner to the one in my office. There was nothing I could do about it.

I said: "I would've bought it. Paid what he wanted."

"Sure," she said. "But you waited. He was an old man. Now it's yours. Lucky you."

"... So. What now? Where is it? I went by the – "

"You'll need to sign some things. It's not at the gallery any longer. Everything's here, at the house," she said. Then, quietly: "You'll have to come by."

Part of me, I realized, was waiting for such an invitation.

"Maybe," she said, "you'll find something else that interests you. Before it all disappears. And you can..." She paused, sighed. "If you're so inclined, you can give your money to the estate. The Mannings, his son and daughter."

"I didn't know – "

"Why should you? But don't wait too long, Mr Byrd. You miss good opportunities. And then you're left with nothing."

The woman on the line laughed briefly. Her words were slow and thick. She was drinking. She sounded sad and tired.

"When can I expect you?"

Part Two

The House Inside

~ 1 ~

It was a week ago, last Monday, I went out there, to Manning's. She met me on the porch, took me into the kitchen. She'd made coffee.

She pushed papers at me. "Here," she said, pointing at a line at the bottom of the form. "And here." Another page, another after that. "Here. Here."

Charlotte Graham looked haggard, like she hadn't slept. A long face, bags under her eyes. Like she'd been fighting with spirits through the night. Nothing like the woman I'd seen at the gallery months before.

I signed what she wanted me to sign. "Why did he change his will? So recently, I mean – "

"I don't know," she said. She looked into her mug of coffee, at the table between us, these neatly stacked forms. She looked up at the window, what remained of the afternoon quickly diminishing. A line of eucalyptus trees on the hill between us and the ocean stood tall and motionless. "He worked on it frequently," she said. "I would say his relationship with his children had a lot to do with it. He was quite torn about them... about how he'd treated them."

"But giving me a painting that I didn't... That can't help–"

"As I said." She looked at me and shrugged. "His children... distressed him, to say the least. But as to why he decided to give *you* this painting... I didn't understand half the things he did. And I learned to stop asking for explanations."

"You've been with him awhile?"

She stood up, leaned on the table with one hand, rubbed her eyelids with the other. When she looked at me again, despite the dimness of the kitchen, I saw in her face a momentary flash of the beauty I remembered.

Very quietly she said, "Seventeen years." She walked around the table, passed me. "This way. Follow me. I'll take you to it."

We walked across the yard. In addition to my Volvo, there were two other cars parked there. A black, filthy and battered BMW, and a bright red, brand new Lincoln. A rental.

We followed a path down the hill, a steady breeze off the ocean at our backs.

There's a barn down there, in the gully. I don't know if you noticed that.

But it's not a barn, I saw on entering. It's Manning's studio. Inside is a wide clean space. Lamps of various sizes fastened to vertical posts, suspended from the ceiling high overhead, scattered about on the floor. Easels. Platforms. Canvases. A row of sinks. A couch. A large square wooden table.

A dozen or so works were set against one wall. Mine, I noticed immediately, was among them.

Overhead, covering half of the room, was an open loft. A steep stairway clung to one wall. "The archive," she said, going upstairs. I followed.

There was not a lot of space in the loft. Huge paintings, in rows to the left and right, were stacked up against each other like boards, lumber. There was a narrow alley between them, and at the end of this, rising to the ceiling, a tall metal cabinet.

"Forty-five years of work," Charlotte said. I helped her pull some of the paintings out, leaning them, one at a time, against the others.

Barren landscapes, cluttered interiors. Colorful, expressionist. A woman taking a bath. A woman getting dressed. A woman reading a book. A woman standing at an open window – the room is dark, full of shadow, large obscure objects around her, around the window. The only light enters the room from outside, behind her, over her shoulder. She's turning, looking over her shoulder at the observer.

Forty-five years, I thought. I'd never seen so much work – of any kind – done by one person, piled like this in one place. Painting upon painting upon painting. I remembered looking once at the man's hands. Thick, dirty appendages.

What have I done with my life?

In 1999 I made eight point four million dollars sitting at a desk, talking on the phone. If you asked me today what exactly I did to earn that money, as if you, or I, could do the same again, repeat this phenomenon, I couldn't tell you. Not because it's a secret. But because I really don't know. I *made* money but, in Manning's studio, up there in that loft, seeing half a century of work, I tell you – I *made* money but I didn't *make* a damn thing. *Zilch.*

I looked at this painting, the woman by the window, very carefully, at the curve of her neck, her back, her hand on the sill.

"That you?"

Charlotte was smoking at the railing, her eyes elsewhere. Listening, it seemed to me, to something distant.

The realism faded with the decades. Everything of the painter's last years was abstract, minimalist. As simple, in a few cases, as blots of ink scattered on the canvas.

"Why does he have so much?" I said. "Here, I mean."

"Why aren't these paintings in a museum, or a gallery?"

"Right."

She glanced toward the painting of the woman at the window. She smoked. She turned away.

"We took everything from the galleries. As you discovered."

"But – "

I went up to her, stood at her side, looked over the railing into the empty space of the studio. She was hiding something. But it wasn't about the paintings, or not only about the paintings.

I was suddenly, inexplicably nervous, unable to formulate the question I wanted to ask her.

She said: "But why is all *this* still here? Why weren't they sold thirty years ago?"

"Right. Wasn't he – "

She looked at me. She turned, looked behind us at the painting of the woman in the window. "He worked a lot, Raymond. He was always working. He was always painting. Until he stopped, that is. Then..."

"So he *did* sell," I said.

"What are you asking me? What is it you want me to say?" She stepped toward the painting, toward the stairs. She started down. "Of *course* he sold. He..." She paused on the stairs, looked back at me.

It had to be the same woman.

A smile in the corner of her mouth, in her eye. "He couldn't ask what he asked *of you* if he didn't sell."

She was downstairs, crossing the room, approaching the wide open door. Because of the structure's low position behind the hills, the light outside was fading quickly. The sandy yellow of late afternoon had turned in a matter of minutes to the dark blue of evening.

"Why'd he stop?" I asked, raising my voice.

"There was something else he wanted to do."

The roof above me rattled in the breeze.

"And why did he want everything out of the gallery?"

She looked up at me but didn't say anything. I returned downstairs. Approaching her I asked her again, "Why did he – "

"I heard you, Raymond. But what business is it of yours, what Henry..."

"I'd just like to understand why he's *giving* me – "

"He knew it was coming."

"Knew what was coming?"

She closed her eyes, shook her head. "Why," she said, "his..."

Then she was looking at something over my shoulder. Her face adjusted, pulled inward, hardening, a shadow coming over her.

That was the end of our conversation.

I turned.

In the corner of the room, beneath the loft and at the end of a line of large metal sinks, stood a man. He was bald, pale, all in black. He was a tall man with a long, egg-shaped head, broad shoulders, a thick waist. He wore very small, rectangular glasses.

"I'll arrange to have someone bring the painting by," the woman at my shoulder quietly began to say when the man spoke, his voice filling the space:

"I would appreciate it, Char, if you kept the issue of my father's death to yourself. I thought I made that clear. It's hard enough having to explain what he did – over and over again – as an artist to all of these *parasites*... What makes you think explaining his *death* should be any easier?... And *every fucking time* you open your..."

The man stopped, his lipless mouth, it seemed from the distance across the room, flexing creature-like inside his head. He looked down. He looked up, directly at me.

"Who's this?"

Charlotte began to speak. I said: "I'm Raymond Byrd. I've come for a painting."

The man didn't move. His shoulders lifted as he took a deep breath. Softer, calmer, he said: "She told me."

Up in the house, a telephone began to ring. I glanced back, as did Charlotte. She had a dark freckle beneath her pronounced jaw bone, on the right side. A beautiful, strong and long throat.

The man went on. "A surprise to everyone. Seeing as you walked away from it twice before."

"He – "

"I'll take it off your hands."

"Sorry?"

The telephone continued to ring.

"Don't you have something you should be doing, Char," said the man. Then he took a step back, into a recess at his shoulder, and vanished. He said, his voice rising but muted, from a distance, "Name your price, Byrd. You didn't even want it. So let me give you a chance to..."

But I couldn't make out what he said.

Charlotte, nearly my height, suddenly seemed very small beside me. Reduced proportionally to a smaller version of herself.

Neither of us spoke. She seemed to be holding her breath, perfectly still.

I said: "That was his son?"

"Yes. Joseph."

"Kind of..."

"Don't say it."

I approached the corner the man had appeared in. "So there's a downstairs, I take it." Halfway across the room, I stopped, looked back.

The phone up in the house was quiet. Outside the barn the world was winding down, darkening. The hush of the breeze, the far-off cry of a seagull.

Hesitating, she took a step forward. She approached me. Passing me, she said: "Yes. There is." I followed her toward the corner of the room.

She stopped, turned, faced me. "I'll show you what's down there. I have no reason to. And... this will certainly only *provoke* him... Because, what Henry's built, as you'll see..." She looked down. "It's hard to explain. But now," she said, turning on her heel, leading me to a dark recess in the corner of the room, "I *have to* show you. Because you know there's something down there and you'll never," she said, glancing coyly over her shoulder, "ever get to sleep if you can't see it with your own eyes. And maybe, who knows, you can come to some agreement with the son."

~ 2 ~

I followed her toward a long counter, a row of deep metal sinks along the back wall. In the corner, after the last sink, was a narrow doorway. Through this, immediately on the left and deep in shadow, was a huge iron door, open, a large black key hanging limp in its keyhole.

We stood shoulder to shoulder atop a long flight of cement stairs. There was a light on in the room at the bottom.

I went down before her. She followed. I couldn't hear her behind me, and I didn't turn to look or say anything – something curious and uncanny about this long and straight descent suddenly, as in a dream, killed any remaining reason for banter – but I knew she was there, at my back. I could smell her, this mix of tobacco on her breath, and perspiration. It was cold on that stairway, and getting colder as we approached the bottom, but she was sweating. Feverish, frightened.

If I close my eyes, I can hear her breathing, hear her heartbeat. I can see the glowing entrance to the room beneath us getting larger and brighter. I want to turn and touch her, and take her hand – *and go back* – but I can't. It's done. The *present* is an extraordinarily fragile thing. We approach it, we enter it, and we break it. There is no going back, no returning things to the way they were.

There is a room under Heinrich Manning's barn. It is an undivided square space nearly the size of the structure above it. This room is very well lit. It is clean and orderly, with a ceiling at least fifteen feet high. There are no windows. There is a kitchen area with a stove, oven and fridge. Along one wall there is a large couch, a desk, a bed, a bookshelf, a stereo on a shelf over which, built into the wall, are other shelves, mostly empty, though books of many sizes lie stacked here and there. Beneath the stairway, through a crooked door, there's a large bathtub, sink and toilet. Lying in the bath one could study the underside of the cement stairs and think all sorts of strange things.

In the center of this room, and filling most of the space, on a gargantuan square table, countless legs fashioned of two-by-fours and four-by-fours holding it up, and lit beneath a dozen lamps, is the model of a house. You wouldn't recognize it as such on first seeing it, for its extraordinary dimension. It could be a city. And you might take a stroll, walk around the structure for an hour or two, and still not understand what exactly it is you are looking at, what you are seeing.

But I'd seen it before. I knew in an instant what it was. And I knew – although I couldn't say it at the time, and perhaps I couldn't *see* it, precisely – I knew what was going to happen. At the bottom of my soul, I knew it. Because I knew the house, and I knew why a man would build a model of it. And I knew that anything *he* touched, and anything *it* touched, would be infected, and would go to hell.

It's inside of me!

To the right of the entrance to this room, down the length of the wall, seated in a wooden chair next to a small round wooden table, one long leg hooked sharply over the other, was Joseph Manning, Heinrich's son. On the table beside him was an empty bottle of Johnnie Walker scotch, an empty glass, and a large wooden mallet.

The man's eyes, deepset behind narrow, rectangular, sharp black glasses, twitched, vibrated nervously. Hardly moving, he said: "Left alone down here a minute longer, I might've destroyed it. Taken this hammer and *smashed the shit out of it*... Just to see what would happen."

Then the man moved, his long oval head turning. He looked at us, standing in the entrance.

Charlotte came around me, walked quickly along the wall toward the kitchen area, which was opposite us, across the ...

Joseph watched her proceed, his large head turning. He said loudly: "There's nothing for you down here, Char. So – thank you for showing our guest in, but now, why don't you..."

He stared at the woman across the room, his head craned up and out on his thick neck, as if to detach itself from his body and follow his words to the woman. He struck me immediately as the kind of man who was used to being obeyed.

I stayed put, near the door. Clearly I had stepped into something, between these two. And although my sympathies were with Charlotte, I was unsure how, to what extent, I should make this apparent. It seemed – *aggravating* the man might not be in my, or her, best interest.

When Charlotte didn't respond to his taunts, he looked my way, appearing suddenly tired and weak. "Mr Byrd. I guess my father's given you... that *abstract* thing, the one... What's it called, Char?"

From across the room, Charlotte said, "It's untitled, Joseph." She'd found another bottle and poured herself a drink. She stood behind a long yellow formica counter, one hand around a glass, the other pressed flat on the counter's surface.

"It's un-titled," Joseph said. "Right. I'd forgotten."

Charlotte looked at me momentarily, sipped her drink. She said to Joseph, cool and poised, "Care for another, Joseph? There's more. He's got enough here – "

"No," he snapped. He took a deep breath, uncrossed his legs, sat up straight in the little chair. "I can't sleep if I have too much."

"Works the other way with me."

I approached the model, reached out for it, wanting to touch. Pulling back.

The man laughed. "It won't bite! And there's nothing *fragile* about it."

I made my way around the room, following the path Charlotte had taken. Moving in close to the structure, stepping back. I leaned down, hands on my knees, put my eye to a tiny window, looked into a room on the tenth or eleventh floor. There was furniture in the room: a sofa, a table, a chair, a bookshelf. An empty vase. A piano. A music stand. All of this carved and made from wood. All of it small enough to fit in the palm of your hand.

Through this room I looked through an open door, into a hallway. At the end of the hall was a closed door. I kept my eye on the door, waiting, for no sensible reason, for it to open.

"I'll buy it," Joseph said. He'd stood up, come over to me. "What's it worth to you?"

He was a tall man, broad in the shoulders, like his father. Except for the head. He was nearly bald, what little hair he had left shaved down like a Buddhist. He wore a black turtle neck, black slacks.

"Buy it?" I said.

"The painting."

"It's not for sale."

I don't know how much the man had had to drink, but standing beside me he spoke with surprising clarity and strength.

"But if it were," he said.

Charlotte said: "He said it's not for sale, Joseph. It's Mr Byrd's now. And he doesn't want to sell it."

"Everything has a price."

"In fact," I said, "I have something similar, at home. It's partner, your father called it. Something I picked up a few years ago. So now, I'd – "

"It's *his*!" Charlotte said, nearly screaming, something quickly coming over her. "Joseph! Accept it! Your father gave this man a painting because he *wanted him* to have it. Get over it!"

Throwing her head back, she finished her drink. Over the rooftop of the model, on the other horizon, as it were, Charlotte leaned on the counter with both hands. Her eyes lowered, fixed on something on the house.

Joseph crossed his arms over his chest. His head tipped slightly to one shoulder. He glanced at me in the corner of his eye. He said: "It's not a question of *acceptance*, Char – I think you're making a much bigger deal out of this than it actually is. It's just a transaction we're talking about, what I'd like to propose. Isn't it?"

The woman didn't answer. She stood up straight, took a step back, looked away from us. She held an empty glass at her breast, her small hand wrapped around it so tightly her fingers looked like bone.

"What exactly is it that you object to, Char," Joseph said, raising his voice, "in my wanting to talk with this man about something of his that I'd like to buy – what is it?" His thin lips spread into a straight dark line across his face.

Charlotte remained silent. Then she quickly set her glass down and started around the room, heading for the stairs.

Joseph's enormous mouth dropped wide open. "Don't walk away from me! Tell me what – " but she did, she had, going quickly down the opposite side of the model, passed the bathroom, and then down, nearly running, that length of the room, passed the table and chair Joseph had been in, to the exit, the bottom of the stairs. She quickly disappeared around the corner. "Tell me!" Joseph said, smiling at me, "what's wrong with my wanting to *pay* this man – *he* can name the price – for something my father made?"

The man's voice echoed in the room. Echoed, I realized, inside the house, the model.

Charlotte didn't answer.

She couldn't be gone, I thought. Not *that* quickly. It was a long way up those stairs.

Joseph, nostrils flaring, closed his eyes, catching his breath, opened them. He was listening. As loudly as before, he said quickly, "At least tell me what you want to do with *this*, Char."

We waited. I started around the table, to the kitchenette, that open bottle of Johnnie Walker. I took Charlotte's glass, filled it halfway, drank. I didn't set the bottle down. I poured another. I drank. I poured again.

I thought it was over, their spat. But then her voice, quiet, clear, somewhere up the stairs: "The model, you mean."

"It's a monstrosity!" he cried, almost singing.

"It's yours," she said.

Before he said another word, Joseph looked at me, this coolness in his eyes, a sharpness to the corners of his mouth. As if he had a secret to confide. As if I were about to be witness to a magic trick. Cutting the woman in half.

His jaw shifted to one side of his face. Then it swung to the other. Then it centered, locked in place. He said: "It *is* mine. But Charlotte – you were here all along, these past – what's it been? – ten years, did you say? – as it was built. You've been with it all this time, with *him* as he did it... So part of it, I think – let's be fair – belongs to you, Charlotte."

No response.

"Charlotte?"

After a moment, her voice, from up the stairs: "So cut out the part that you think belongs to me."

Joseph took a breath, his jaw dropping, his mouth opening into a huge black hole. "Ha! Cut out the – ... What a *brilliant* idea. My kind of thinking, Char! Sometimes, darling, you do surprise me. I always wondered what he saw in you. But sometimes – yes – *cut it out!* – yes – sometimes you hit it *right on the head.* Cut it out. I should've thought of that before. All this time. Sitting down here thinking *Now how on earth am I gonna get this out of here?* Why – we'll cut it into pieces. Of course! And give Char her fair share."

I was watching the house, considering this solution, her portion. To quantify her role in its invention, and then to settle upon a division, a line, simply *a place to cut.*

Impossible. The inside is –

Joseph had come around to my side. His back to the counter, facing the model, arms folded over his chest, he was coming down, cooling off, that tired look returning to his eyes.

– infinite.

"Fact is, Raymond," he said gently over his shoulder, "I don't give a fuck about it. Whether she wants it or not. Suppose I can't just *give* it to her. She'd have to pay for it. But still... We come back to the question of *removing* it. How he – "

I found another glass under the counter. I started to pour the man a drink. He noticed this, waved his big hand over the counter, like brushing off a fly. "None for me. Can't sleep if I have too much. And I'd like to sleep. But I've probably had too much already. So here we are. Back again."

I looked across the room at the little table he'd been seated at when we came in. The empty bottle, empty glass, that mallet. In my imagination I was lifting it, feeling its heft.

I finished my drink. Still thirsty, I poured another.

The man watched me carefully, attentive to the bottle. A comment on his lips, in the way he smirked.

He took the empty glass and poured himself a drink. "So you knew my father."

"We met a couple times."

"Why'd he give you that piece?"

"I've no idea."

"He tell you he was going to give it to you?"

" ... I was going to buy it. We'd talked about it off and on. Goin' on two or three years now. I was about to call him."

The man, facing the model, his ear to me, lowered his chin to his chest, fat in his neck rolling up. He said: "Your offer?"

I looked into my empty glass. There appeared to be a hole in the bottom of it.

I wanted another drink badly – to keep some distance from Manning's son, to dampen the sound of his voice, to blot out what was directly in front of me.

But I also had to get home.

I realized suddenly, without a doubt, that I didn't want to go home. I wanted Charlotte, to leave with her immediately, to protect her.

Fuck it.

I poured myself another splash. There was only a little left. I said: "I can't recall. But it doesn't matter. I'm bringing it home, Joseph." I then added, thinking his father's line of reasoning, which I'd never understood, might make sense to the son, "I have its partner on my office wall. It'll make a nice union."

We looked at the model in silence, like two strangers in a museum.

I was beginning to appreciate the booze, a warm drowsiness coming up, I could feel it in my cheeks, in my eyes.

When I looked again, he was looking away, at the entrance to the room.

"Charlotte's angry," he said, "because she thinks she deserves more than she's getting."

"What's she getting?"

He turned, leaned a hip against the counter. He pushed his glasses up the bridge of his long nose. "He left her some money."

"How much?"

"Two hundred thousand. Three hundred thousand. Something like that."

I sipped my drink, listening, calculating as best I could. Before I said anything, he said: "Cash."

"Cash?"

"In a bag."

The man turned, faced me, pressed his hands into the counter, leaned toward me. He smiled, started to giggle like a school boy. Lowering his voice, dropping his chin, swaying in like a boxer, he said, "In a *fuckin'* bag. Like carry-on luggage. Cash."

"Three hundred thousand dollars," I said. "What's your father doing with a bag of money like that?"

He pulled back, stood up straight. He looked left and right down the length of the counter. Charlotte must have left her cigarettes down there. In three big steps he was at the end of the counter, took out a cigarette, looked around for a lighter. I tossed him a book of matches. He lit up, slowly came toward me, said: "She told me he stopped using banks, credit. Wanted to extricate himself from the finance institutions. God knows why. But he was like that. Born into a certain world. You might drift out and away. But in the end, you come home." He looked away. Turned, faced the model. He blew long streams of blue smoke over the rooftop. I thought he was finished. He went on. "Cash under the mattress. For a rainy day." He chuckled to himself. "And that's what *she* gets. And she doesn't like it. Not at all."

"She lived with your father for almost twenty years. They could've been married."

"She was his assistant. A manager."

He took a step forward and placed his large hand on part of the model's roof. He leaned in. "Maybe they fucked now and then. Early on in the partnership. Wouldn't surprise me, knowing him. Though I hardly knew him, after all... Doesn't change the fact. She wants more. She feels *entitled* to more." Eyes down on his hand, through his hand, his thoughts somewhere inside the house, he finally said: "Where does that come from, Ray? Americans and their sense of entitlement."

"You're American. You tell me."

He was now pressing down hard on the model, putting some weight into it. Something in the house whined, stretching, strained. He turned his eyes my way, over his shoulder, the corner of his mouth tightening in a grin. "I haven't lived here for years," he said.

"No? Where you from?"

"Berlin."

Of course. I'd heard it, the German, in his voice all along. The glasses, too, gave it away. You can't find glasses like that in America. Germans and their specs. It's like English and their teeth.

"Charlotte's Welsh," I said.

His eyes still on me, red in the face, the tip of his tongue between his lips – *Look what I can do.* – he was practically climbing atop the structure.

Something cracked, near his stomach.

He grinned, winced.

Then he stopped. He stood up, stood back, hands against his hips.

"She's been here forever," he said. "Wherever she came from. It's washed out. She might as well be one of us."

Elaine, the maid, that creature up at the house, suddenly came to mind. She couldn't talk but she had no trouble repeating things she'd heard.

I'll die if I stop –

The man was going on and on.

– DIE IF I STOP!

"I'll talk with my sister. But she won't budge. They *hate* each other. So the best thing *now* would be for Charlotte to gather her things and prepare herself for a new life. That would be best."

He was looking at the house, nodding to himself. When I didn't respond, he looked at me, a childish emptiness in his soft face.

I said: "What did she get, your sister?"

"The house. The property. A self-portrait."

"And you?"

He took a breath, his eyebrows rising and falling quickly. His hairless cheek curled into a smile. "Everything else," he said.

"His paintings."

He looked down in a kind of embarrassment. "If it's not in a museum, Raymond, it's mine. All of it."

I was feeling it then, the scotch. Suddenly, violently heavy on one side of my body, light on the other. This tug-o-war with gravity.

The thought of those stairs made me shiver.

I said: "Except for... "

He looked straight at me. Hard, cold. Big man from Berlin.

"Yes," he said. "Except for one piece. A certain abstract painting that has no title."

~ 3 ~

"You driving home?"

"Why not."

"You could stay here," he said. "There's a bed. I'll bring you more blankets, a space heater from upstairs."

I managed a laugh. "Nice offer, but ... I'm not sleeping down here. In the bunker."

With that!

We made our way up the stairs.

It was dark outside. The sky, edge of night, held on to a hint of blue, remainder of the day.

The air smelled good, refreshing after being in the barn, with the model.

Still, making my way up the hill, I had to slow down and catch my breath. My head was spinning.

Up on the rise, Manning's place was dark. Charlotte was either gone or already asleep.

"You okay?" Joseph was looking down at me, his big hand on my shoulder. I couldn't keep his eyes from sliding in and out, together, apart, together again.

"How'd your father die?"

He pulled back, diminishing. I could have been talking with a man a hundred meters away.

Very quietly, like pebbles being thrown into a deep dark well: "He took his own life. He couldn't face…"

We stood there, on the path between the barn and bungalow atop the hill, for at least a minute. He wasn't going to say any more. Then he turned and went on without me.

In the driveway, I was nearly at the porch when I tripped on something and fell flat on my face, skidding along in the gravel. I heard him rush back, felt him drop his hands on my shoulders, pick me up and drag me the rest of the way up to the porch, inside the house.

We staggered in loudly, breathing hard. He sat me down at the kitchen table.

It was cold in the house. Dark, silent. I vaguely wondered if Charlotte was upstairs.

It was a small place, after all. Comfortable, perhaps, for two people. But no more.

Couldn't imagine living there with Joseph. A man his size. And he was big. In more dimensions than height and mass. A man who took up space. Like his father.

But *not* like his father. Where the old man *made* things – paintings, thousands of them, that model – what did the son do?

Name your price, Byrd –

Talk. Order people about. He was all words.

He was suddenly directly before me, a hulking shadow over me. He thrust a handful of paper towels in my face. "Wipe yourself off."

I'd cut my chin. I pulled the paper away from my face full of blood, surprised but at the same time, removed, indifferent to the event. I felt almost nothing.

He said: "You know where the bathroom is?"

My head was spinning. He brought me a glass of water. "Drink this."

I did. He helped me stand, guided me from the kitchen into a dark, narrow hallway, to a small door. He reached into the room, flipped a switch. A sink, toilet, shower. "See." Then he took me further down the hall, through a larger door into a living room. Through a large window I could make out the sparkling orange and blue lights of the city.

There was a futon open on the floor. A small lamp next to it. He crouched, turned on the lamp. There was a magazine on the floor. An ashtray. "You sleep here," he said. "I'll go back to the barn. Take a heater down there. I'll be fine. I like the quiet."

I didn't know what to say. Part of me, out of some kind of politeness, wanted to insist on going home or sleeping in the car. But I could barely manage a word, barely thank the man for his help.

He put a hand on my shoulder, squeezed, leaned down, in, searching my face. It was unsettling just how big the man was, Joseph Manning. I felt like a child under his gaze. He said something, muttering, I can't recall what. He stood there, holding me up, it seemed, watching me carefully, waiting for something to happen. And then he was gone. I heard the door in the kitchen open and close.

The house was silent. The house was so quiet I felt momentarily out of time, in a place without a beginning or end.

I tried to say Charlotte's name but, as before, I couldn't speak, couldn't move my tongue except to emit a kind of gurgle and growl.

I touched my chin, looked at my fingers. I was still bleeding.

I went to the bathroom and cleaned myself off. I'd cut the palm of my hand and scratched the side of my brow, over my eye, as well, falling on the driveway. I started to laugh at myself in the mirror. But in a second what I'd found amusing turned the other way, and the spinning, bleeding, laughing faces in the mirror were anything but funny.

They were mad.

"I didn't even *want* the painting."

No. You wanted it. You just didn't know *that you wanted it. You wouldn't admit it to yourself.*

"Well, now I got it."

Sure as shit you got it.

"Learned my lesson."

And what lesson would that be?

"To know what I want."

You sure about that?

"Sure I'm sure. Isn't that what we're talking about?"

I don't know. Is it?

"Course it is. I got the painting. And you were right. I wanted it *all* along. And now I got it... for nothing."

Nothing comes from nothing.

The model. The sheer *size* of it. One man, not in a hundred years, could build such a thing. Could know *so much* about the place.

Sure it's nothing he's asking for it?

"He gave it to me. It's mine."

In exchange for...

"He gave it to me!"

... You're going back there.

"I won't."

You're going back.

"I won't! If they want to, let them. But I won't!"

You will. You have. In fact, Raymond –

"Stop it. Shut up."

– Raymond, in fact, who's to say –

"It's impossible. Shut up! Don't – !"

– you aren't already there?

The magazine by the futon was an issue of *Architectural Digest*. It was an issue on castles, these firms in Europe that were refurbishing them. Making homes for the astronomically wealthy.

This one castle, it was situated right in the middle of an Alpine lake. There was a picture, from a bedroom, off a balcony, of this beautiful lake. Crystalline, dark water. Mountains all around, up to the purple evening sky, and down, in reverse, in the water. In the olden days, I remember thinking just before I put out the light, they'd need a boat to get to the mainland, and a boatman whose job it would be to ferry people back and forth across the water.

A brilliant defensive mechanism, a deep lake like that.

Only, if your enemies killed the boatman, then how would you get supplies? They'd starve you out. A *siege,* I think it was called, in the olden days. They had a lot more time back then, I suppose.

I woke to the sound of someone in the kitchen. I could smell coffee, a cigarette. I could hear, very softly, what sounded like one of the Brandenburg concertos.

Charlotte was in the kitchen, at the table, her back to me. A large book was opened before her, under her chin. A steaming mug of coffee. Slowly she raised a piece of toast to her mouth.

"What's that?"

"*JESUS!*" she said, jumping six inches out of her chair. When she landed she caught her breath, put a hand on her chest. She looked up at me. Big unknowing eyes. Then she turned back, eyes to the book. "Can't you wear a bell or something. I live here alone, you know. Except for him."

Joseph, I assumed she meant. Whose bed I'd slept in.

"What happened to your face?"

I'd forgotten. I touched my chin. The skin was rough.

"I fell. Coming up to the house."

"Walking give you trouble?"

"... I tripped. In the dark. Anyways, *you* left me down there alone with him."

"So it's *my* fault you fell on your face?"

She smiled, got up, took a mug from the washboard, poured me a cup.

I sat at the table in the opposite chair, turned the book she was reading around. It was a notebook, page after page of drawings, what looked like blueprints, designs. Handwritten notes in the margins. Numbers, calculations, and lists: the parts of a house, furniture, bathroom items, kitchen things. Now and then, sometimes in the margin, and sometimes within the drawings themselves, framed, as it were, by the lines of a room, names.

George. Lydia. Clarice.

I opened to a random page and found myself looking at a hand-drawn, simple diagram of a room, a hallway, a twisting stairway, another room, a bed, a window –

Elaine's crying upstairs.

"What is this?" I said, closing the book. The leather cover was blank.

"It's a real place, you know." She sat down across from me. She finished her toast. On a plate, with a small knife, she peeled the skin off a green apple. The flesh inside, almost instantly, began to turn brown, oxidizing.

"What's a real place?"

"The house. What he built out there."

"Is *that* what it is? A house?"

Nodding quickly, childishly. "Yea. A house. The Drammond place, they call it."

When she finished skinning the apple, she sliced off a piece, slipped it into her mouth, chewed. She sliced another piece, reached across the table, and set it down before me, tips up. Knife still in hand, she pointed at the book between us. "And that's it. A map of it. Or at least ... what he remembers of it. A catalogue of rooms would be a better description, since ... He told me once. It can't be mapped."

I opened the book again, to the first page. There was no title, no introduction, no contents. Just sketches, notes in the margin. Early on, naturally, was the entrance hall. And the atrium, the glass domed ceiling so high overhead. Those surrounding floors, countless, spiraling staircases going up and up and up...

On another page, under a handwritten heading, *The Breakfast Room,* the very room I'd sat in with Lucy, where she ate a muffin, had a cup of coffee, *that woman* at her shoulder, behind her, watching me.

On another page: *The Library.*

Another: *The Great Staircase.*

And: *The East Stair. The West Stair. The South Stair.*

The Reading Room.

The Elevator.

"That's an interesting one," Charlotte said quietly, pointing at the page with the tip of the knife. Slowly she leaned forward, her big chin coming over the table toward me, her eyes down on the book opened between us. "He showed it to me – "

"You've been there?"

Her eyes, big and dark, gentle, warm, on me. "No," she said. "He showed it to me *down there*. In the model. Watch this, he said, unusually excited..."

~ 4 ~

This was early on in the project. It was much, much smaller then. Years ago, now. Must've been ... one of the last times he let me down there.

Come here, he says. Watch this.

And he shows me. The elevator, it's up here, high up on some floor, the twentieth, thirtieth, I don't know where, nothing's numbered – *high up there* – and, looking across this terrace, through a door, I see the elevator.

Watch, he says.

The elevator doors close.

He'd pressed a button. A lever. This *tiny* device he'd made up, to make the elevator go. He showed it to me. In a little shed, behind a tiny door, up here above a gable, there's a motor. What looks like a motor. And there, in the motor, is a very small *spool of thread*. One end of the thread is fastened to the top of the elevator.

So out plays the thread. And down the elevator goes.

Now, it's dark in the house. There's no light, no electricity in there. The only light is the light in the room, where he works. From the lamps. So *on top*, the house is bright enough. But as you go down, these beams of light filling the place, crossing each other, mix with lines of shadow every which direction – as in, it now occurs to me, *an aquarium*, like a reef diffracting sunlight as it falls to the bottom of the sea.

But the elevator shaft, it falls in a straight line down through the building. So light, from above, has this unobstructed path. Straight down. Over the elevator *car*, that is. Beneath the car, obviously, it's dark. Above, it is light.

You can see this. As the car passes a floor, *behind closed doors*, a paper-thin line of light between the doors extends, falling from the top of the building, down. The elevator car has passed. Down it goes.

And down, down, down. Slowly, steadily, perfectly.

He was a good inventor, Henry was. If it was mechanical, he could solve it. It was good for him, finally ...

"Good for him?"

To stop painting. To begin work on the house. Because *that* was the only way he would ... answer the questions he had ... the questions *he'd been asking* all along.

"What questions?"

... When the elevator reached the ground floor, it stopped. I could see it there, behind its doors. This tiny dark box, about the size of the nail on my pinkie. It had stopped. It was waiting.

Why don't the doors open? I asked him.

He smiled. This flash of light in his eyes that always told me he was up to something, *hiding* something.

"There was someone in the elevator."

No, don't be silly. Nobody *lives* in the model. It's not a *doll* house. Not something to *play* in. No...

It's said that we get a second childhood in our last years. As everything goes. ... Henry didn't. He was far from that. A long way to go...

You listening?

It was this. *Watch,* he says. So, again, I lean down, my eye to this window on the ground floor, and I watch. And the elevator, *which I can see,* between these closed doors, this small black box, which I have seen, following with my eye, descend from someplace way up here, to this level, the very bottom, the ground, down the hall from the entrance to the house.

It's there. It's right there.

And down it goes.

Alright, you're thinking. The house has a lower level. A basement. Okay. Makes sense. But we're talking, here, about the model. That thing he has out in the barn. And the model *does not have a basement.*

Silly me, I bend down lower, *looking under the table.* Of course there's nothing there. Legs. Sticks. Saw-horses. It was all much smaller then.

But no elevator. No tiny box dangling from the end of a string.

I stood up. I checked that motor he'd devised. That spool of thread.

It was turning. The string running down through the house.

Where is it? I finally asked.

He looked at me. Now his eyes were flat, expressionless. He could have been as perplexed as I was.

Henry, I said, *where is it?* Where's it going!?

It had to be a trick. Somehow ... Something ... It was ... Pulling, see, on the string. Drawing it in. Another motor, a device just under the line of sight, beneath those closed elevator doors on the ground floor. Just under the floor. ... A trick.

"And how did it work?"

He never told me. At first I thought he was playing games. Showing off. I'd let him be. He could have his secret for the time being. But then, later, I asked him again. He still wouldn't say. I asked him why it was so important that he *play* this trick on me, that he keep me in the dark.

But he wouldn't say. And the more I pressed him, the more the matter seemed to grow out of hand. Become an argument about other things. And the more – I only suspected it at first, but then, and this was a year or so after, it became clear, very clear – the more *sad* it seemed to make him. It *pained* him, my questioning him. About that *stupid* elevator. About the house. *Pained him.* Because he couldn't explain what he was doing, couldn't explain what he'd done ... What *it* was doing to him.

After awhile, he stopped talking to me. He stopped coming up here. He *lived* down there, in that hole. Working, working, *working.*

He disappeared one time. I hadn't seen him or heard him at night – he would sometimes come in the house after I'd gone to bed. A premonition comes over me. A sense, indeed, that now *I am alone.*

In the morning I went out there. Our car was in the yard.

I went down to the barn, over to the door to the basement. It was locked. I knocked, I pounded on it. *Henry! Henry! Are you alright!?* But nothing. Of course, I then realized, there was no way to get in there, no way to open the door. If something had happened - if he'd fallen, passed out - there was no way I'd be able to help him.

I looked through the keyhole. The stairs were dark. I put my ear to the keyhole. Nothing.

But I wasn't worried, exactly. I wouldn't call it that. He's an independent man, a quondam crazy man. He's gone off without telling me before.

The car was in the yard. And we have only the one car, and I'm the one who drives it, most of the time.

But this *feeling* I had. That something had happened to him. I couldn't shake it.

Days passed. A week. And nothing. I was sure, then, that something *bad* had happened and that I would soon get a call from someone, telling me that they'd *found* him. Dead in the woods. Drowned on the shore.

But that didn't happen.

I tried to open the door, to pick the lock. I hooked a clothes-hanger through, trying to reach around and...

I gave up. If he was dead in the basement there was nothing I could do about it. I'd smell him eventually. Call someone...

Then one evening, as the sun is setting, he comes up the driveway, his hiking rucksack on his shoulder. He looks tired, *bearded,* which he never is, but none the worse for wear.

Where have you been?

Doing research, he says. A trip to the mountains.

To the mountains! Without telling me!

I didn't mean to be gone so long.

In his bag, I find his camera, its equipment, film, his notebooks, pencils, and so on. In the notebook, I see sketches he's made of the mountains, trees, various structures, and then parts of *this house.* This thing he's been obsessed with all his poor life.

So you went up there *again*, I say.

"He went to the house."

Where'd you think I'd gone, he says.

You said you wouldn't –

"He goes up to the house."

Raymond, he's been there I don't know how many times. How do you think he made *that thing*? From scratch? *An idea?*

"He goes inside?"

Of course he goes inside.

"By himself? He stays there?"

How would I know? He's never brought me. He brings other girls, I'm sure of it. But never me. And God knows I've asked.

~ 5 ~

The Pantry. The Dining Hall. The Terrace. The Master Bedroom. The Master Bathroom. The Servants' Quarters. The Wash Room. The Sauna. The Gymnasium. The Ice Room ...

"He's brought other women there," I said.

"I don't know if he has. He's mentioned names. You know, I get a *feeling* about it, about what goes on at this house. And frankly it wouldn't surprise me. His having these other women. It's not like we were married, Raymond. I was his assistant. Nothing more."

"But you asked to go. And he never brought you?"

"No."

"And did he say *why* you couldn't go?"

The Laundry Room. The Linen Room. The Coat Room. The Men's Hall. The Women's Hall. The Salon. The Sun Room. The Billiard Room. The Ball Room. The Recital Hall. The Parlor ...

Charlotte said: "I told him that I wanted to go, to see the place. 'Absolutely not,' he says. 'Take me,' I say, 'Let's go for a weekend, you and me.' 'I won't. And you *won't* go up there on your own. That's it. Listen to me for once.' 'How can you – ' 'There is *nothing* to see, Charlotte. Nothing! It's a ruin. That's it.' 'But *you* went,' I say. 'So what?'

'Why'd you go?' 'To take pictures.' 'Bullshit,' I say, 'There's *a woman*. She meets you there!' 'There isn't.' 'You rent a car and pick her up and take her there! Don't lie to me!' '...'

"We were not married, and when we met, Henry was already an old man. But I loved him. I loved him very, very much. And I wanted to be *his*, his alone. I was, for a time. When we first met. He had other models, of course. But he didn't care about them in the way he cared for me. I know that. I *knew* that then. And so I didn't care about these other women. They were just *models*. Bodies. Granted, that's how I started. But he liked me, he liked listening to me, talking with me. I don't know why. He was a very smart man, and a handsome man, and a *pure* artist in his soul. He could have had a much better woman than I. A more beautiful woman, a smarter woman. Even a more caring woman. But he didn't. He had me. He chose me. And for a time, we were happy together. Absolutely in love with each other. It was around that time, nineteen ninety-two, I think it was, that I stopped being his model and began being his assistant. I sold his paintings... I did a damn good job of it. ..."

So Heinrich Manning had gone to the Drammond House. He'd taken pictures of the place, sketched the place in his notebook. Exploring – on his own? with someone? I don't know – its interior, these *endless* halls, all of these rooms.

I was thinking of the painting he'd given me, of what he'd said about it that time we met: "It *pulls.*" Draws the eye to this –

Nothing comes from nothing.

"And I could be jealous," Charlotte said, "even if we *weren't* married. And even if, in the last years, we hardly saw each other... I still loved him."

Telling her about the house, telling her, I mean, the *whole story* about the house... He could have lied, I suppose... But he loved the woman – and if she knew...

They argued, Charlotte told me, about this matter many times. Her wanting to *see* the place, and his forbidding it.

Maybe he should have just let her go. Prohibition, I mean – isn't it just a sly form of permission? It makes things possible, the *don'ts* we tell ourselves.

Because she went anyway. Charlotte did. Up to the house.

She disappeared for a few days, as Manning had. And, as the old man had before her, one evening, he's in the kitchen frying eggs and sausage – he'd eat breakfast in the evening, before going to work – she comes through the door.

"You went to the house, didn't you?"

"Yes. I did."

"I told you not to."

"I know."

"But you went anyway."

I'm not a child, Henry!

I don't know what she said then, or what he said, or what finally came out of the argument. What's done is done.

It's hard for me to see Heinrich Manning being angry with the woman. He was big, and he had this deep, rumbling, *loud* voice. But I don't think he was the kind of man who would *show* his anger. Never *act* in an angry way.

"What I didn't tell him," Charlotte said, "was that, while I did *go* to the Drammond House, I didn't go inside."

The Valets' Hall. The Maids' Hall. The Servants' Dining Room. The Upper Kitchen. The Lower Kitchen. The Finishing Kitchen. The Garden Kitchen. The Bakery. The Scullery. The Abattoir. ...

"You didn't go inside?"

"No. I made it there, sure enough. I had to ask around, for directions. But I had a general sense of where the place was, from things he'd told me. And in fact, once you get up in the mountains, seems everyone knows something of the place. It's an open secret.

"But no, I didn't go inside. I parked at the end of the driveway, by the gate. Walked up the hill. It was getting dark, then, and I was quite tired, and hoping to find a place to stay the night. No... I remember going up the driveway, feeling excited about the whole thing, coming to this *mysterious* house that I'd heard so much about, checking in for the night. Sitting by a *warm* fire, having a hot toddy. There was something fantastic about the trip, about *finally* getting there, and seeing the place. Not that

I hadn't *believed* Henry. I'd seen the notebooks he'd kept, the pictures he'd taken. And heard the stories.

"When he was a child, he told me – twelve years old – he went to the Drammond House for the first time. There was a girl with him. After lunch, they'd eaten outside with their parents, the housekeeper having prepared something for the visit, the two children went exploring. The woods were dense, thicker, darker then than they are now, he told me. But they were children. Everything is larger and stranger when you're a child.

"In a tree they found a wild animal. A badger, or a raccoon, it leapt out, attacking the girl! And he laughed. And *oh was she sore* about that, angry at him only in the way a twelve year old girl can be angry at a boy. At once *loathing* him and *wanting* him like mad.

"They went inside. At first, he said, it was thrilling. Trespassing in such a beautiful home, in such a *magnificent* structure. Running around like they *owned* the place, a prince with his princess. Not a care in the world.

"The girl, her name was ... Nancy ... I forget the surname ... she got lost. Separated from him. And he couldn't find her. Was she playing? Getting back at him for the trick he'd played *on her* at the tree, with the animal? He called out to her, and she replied, but from deep in the house. And each time he called her name, she would respond, *Henry! Henry! I'm here! Henry!* but her voice was getting softer and softer, farther and farther away in the house.

"He was *petrified*. He could hardly move for fear, for sadness, having lost her in there, for having *trespassed* and then lost his friend in this forbidden place. ... *Petrified*.

"He made his way back outside, to where his parents, and her parents, and the housekeeper, sat at the table, talking under the trees, finishing their dessert.

"Interrupting, he told his father what had happened. ..."

The Workshop. The Garage. The First Arcade and Second Arcade. The Hothouse. The Glass Hall. The Wood Room. The Observatory. The Mill. The Diversion Room. The Nursery. The Map Room. ...

"But they found the girl," I said.

She'd stood up, moved to the sink, to where there was a window looking on the yard. Whiteblue morning light on her face. She lit a cigarette. She raised her chin toward the window. "Here he comes," she said.

A minute later, Joseph Manning stepped through the door. He came forward quickly, stood at the end of the table, took a long deep breath, smiled tightly.

"Feeling better?" he said to me.

"Coffee?" Charlotte asked him.

The man turned, his colossal body pivoting, addressing her. "Thank you but no, Char. My stomach hasn't been right since the funeral. Acid reflux. I'll have some water. Toast."

"How'd you sleep?" I said.

"Like the dead. It's *a tomb,* basically, what he built out there. And I'd still be asleep but for a meeting I have at UCLA in an hour. Char, I'll be back by noon. Then I need the phone. Ingrid wants to talk. There's a man coming Friday to see the house. Before then, you and I will need to arrange a few things. So... This afternoon?" Then, swinging his shoulder around, turning, his gaze fell on the book before me. The man paused, stepped forward. He reached out for the notebook, dragged it to the table's edge. He flipped through the pages quickly. "More of my father's work. More of that *house...* God, it never ends, does it – we'll be finding these things for years." He regarded me over the rim of his glasses, said in a hushed tone, man to man: "I'll let my sister deal with it." Then he stood up straight, spun on his heel, and in two large steps was back at the door. Over his shoulder he said, "Pleasure meeting you, Raymond. I hope the painting meets your standards. And if you change your mind about my offer, do call. Charlotte has the number." He glanced back at the two of us, his long egg shaped head hardening, vessels in his temples flexing. Then he stepped through the door. A moment later the Lincoln in the yard roared to life, backed out, sped away.

Charlotte was still at the sink. She lowered her head, closed her eyes, raised a hand to her brow.

"To answer your question," she said. "Yes. They found the girl."

"And was she okay?"

Charlotte looked at me for a spell before speaking. She seemed drained, half the woman she'd been minutes before, before Joseph's entry.

"She was fine," she said. "Henry told me... She wasn't hurt. But she wasn't the same. Something had happened to her in the house. And when Henry would ask her about it, the girl couldn't say. Wouldn't tell him. They drifted apart after that, as teenage boys and girls do."

I turned a few more pages in the notebook. *The Armory. The Infirmary. The Morgue.*

"What happened between you and Joseph?"

The Gallery. The Family Room. The Banquet Hall. The Smoking Room. The Drawing Room. The Ossuary.

On one page, a simple, rectangular image: *The Back Corridor.* Next to this, in quotation marks, these neatly inscribed words:

"Backbone of the staff's quarters."

And beneath these words, in the lower right corner of the page, in three eloquent lines, a sketch, the profile of a girl.

When Charlotte didn't respond to my question, I pressed on, tried a different course. "So you didn't go inside."

She sighed, leaned down on the back of the chair across from me. "There was nobody there. As he said. Nobody answered the door... And then... It was cold up there, and night came on *very* quickly. So I didn't wait around. I left. I stopped at a Motel 6, out in the desert. So, no. I didn't go inside the house. I've only seen it from the outside. And only seen the entrance, that face of the building."

I was looking at the book, at this sketch of a girl.

"She reminds me of someone," I said, touching the image.

"Drawings tend to do that."

"There are names on some of these pages, in his notes..." I flipped back, searching for an example. I couldn't find any. I assumed she'd seen them. I looked up at her, said: "Did he ever mention someone named Michael?"

Charlotte stood over me, smoking. "No. Why do you ask?"

I was reluctant to say more. I wanted to tell Charlotte about the house, about what I knew of the place. At the same time I wanted, somehow, to take Charlotte away, to somewhere far away, somewhere safe. Because it felt like we were – but *she* was, particularly – on the brink of something disastrous. It felt like, though the Drammond House was at least a hundred miles away, it was there, around us, outside the door. As though the model, *what we all recognized as just a model,* was more than that.

It was an extension.

It's big as fuck! Jillian had said, opening her hands, her fingers spread out like claws.

Creeping, reaching...

~ 6 ~

"I should be going," I said.

"You sure? It's early still. Stay for another cup. Have some toast. You must be starving."

The Drying Room.

A curved line connected two walls. From this hung articles of laundry, what looked like long pajamas, thermal underwear. Byrd eviscerated husks.

I closed the notebook, pushed it away, turned my eyes to my host as she went about brewing another pot of coffee, slicing some bread for toast. The domestic company of a woman was a pleasant change. On the radio Debussy's spring rains, a rising creek, had replaced Bach's charts and graphs.

"Do you know why," I said, "Henry left me that painting?"

"I already told you. I don't. But I'm sure he had his reasons."

"Is it true, what Joseph told me, about the other things? The paintings."

"I don't know what he told you, Raymond."

"That – "

"It's none of your business."

She put butter and jam on the table, toast, coffee, a small carton of cream. We ate in silence.

I said: "What will you do?"

She tilted her head toward a shoulder. She brushed her long bangs aside. "So many questions."

"You invited me to stay. And now I'm... I'm a little – "

Her eyes on me, waiting. Her large jaw held perfectly still.

"A little puzzled, is all," I said.

"Puzzled?"

"About this house, and – and that painting and..."

"And?"

"Why he didn't give *you*..."

"That's none of your business, Raymond. Now – "

"And what about the model?"

"What *about* the model?"

"What will you do with it?"

"Why? Do you want it?"

"No, but – "

"It's for Joseph and Ingrid to sort out. But make him an offer, if you're interested. Offer him the painting, Raymond. He wants it."

"I – "

"If *you* want the model, offer him the painting. They'll take it. He and Ingrid. The model is a throwaway. It's unfinished and, in *his* view, and in hers, I've no doubt, it's the only false note in an otherwise flawless performance.

Heinrich Manning was a painter, in the end. An extraordinary one. He was not a sculptor. In any case, the model can hardly be called *sculpture*. It's ... I don't know what to call it. A study. An exercise in *obsession*. By which I mean that foolish hope of discovering beauty through blindness, deprivation and self-sacrifice."

I ate the toast she'd offered me. "You've thought this through."

"I lived with it for nearly a decade! Most of my adult life, Raymond, I've been listening to him talk about *the house* in one form or another. It was *all* about the house, about this little girl he lost in there, about something *of himself* he lost in there, taken by that woman – *all of it*, Raymond, came down to that. So, yes – I have thought this through."

"You don't like it, do you."

"*Like* it? What the fuck kind of question is that, Raymond? It's not vanilla ice cream or jazz. You don't *like* something like that. You *live* with it, you put up with it, you hope it doesn't burn the house down. Fucking Christ – *like!* I can't believe you say that. The old man *died* building the goddamn thing, but it's not like he suffered alone, in his hole. Not like *madness* doesn't infect those it touches."

Neither of us moved. I stopped eating. She didn't touch her coffee. She wouldn't look at me. Then she rose suddenly, walked into the other room, turned the radio off.

I didn't want to leave her alone. But I knew she was going to ask me to, and I knew that I would.

She went upstairs. I could hear her cross the room, floorboards in the ceiling creaking, stop, cross back. Stop.

I waited. Without the radio, there was something hard and honest about the silence that filled the house.

After a minute I stood, prepared to leave. Maybe I'd call her, take her to dinner, a movie. Before she disappeared, that is.

But then she came back into the kitchen. Her face was pale, her hair damp on her brow, by her ears.

Quietly, she said: "Raymond, I'm sorry. I shouldn't have ..." Her eyes on the floor, she said: "You need to be on your way. I'll phone to arrange for the delivery."

I went to the door and opened it. It was sunny and warm outside. A large white seagull sat on the railing at the end of the porch.

"You could destroy it," I said. "Burn it."

To my back, her voice, gently: "It's crossed my mind."

"If it would help you forget it. What's happened."

Take your money and run. Start a new life.

"I don't care one way or the other about Joseph," she said. "I don't know if I made that clear. But I do care about Henry and about what he did and how he's remembered. As much as I might want to destroy the thing he built, because it hurts me to see it and to think about it and to remember what it did to him, I can't. I would never be able to. It's a part of him." She added: "I'm leaving soon. Joseph wants me out. And I don't want to see Ingrid. Which is fine. Get away, let all of this go. That's the best, I think, that I can do."

She followed me out to my car. A breeze blew her hair across her eyes. She wrapped her arms around her body, cold.

"What will you do?" I asked.

"After this? I'll find something."

"You'll stay in the area?"

She shrugged. "Mexico City," she said. "I know people there. It's a good place to disappear."

I couldn't imagine Charlotte Graham disappearing. I didn't want her to disappear.

"When does Joseph leave?" I said.

"Monday morning."

Then I asked, because I had to ask it: "Why not take him to the house?"

"... To the mountains, you mean? To the Drammond House?"

She said it like it was the last thing she would have considered.

Because she doesn't know.

"Why not? Show him. Tell him, 'See! It's real. The real deal. Your old man wasn't so crazy after all.'"

"Joseph won't care. And he wouldn't go. He can't stand the wild, anything across the city border. So much as a blade of grass outside concrete confines... however the poem goes."

I got in the car, turned around, drove away. Charlotte remained in the yard, watching me off. Before going over the rise, facing the city and the ocean, I raised a hand, waving. But the figure in the rearview mirror didn't move. Hard and small, wrapped around itself. Then I hit a bump, and the world in the mirror bolted violently skyward and the woman, what was left her, vanished.

~ 7 ~

Why didn't I ask to see the photos Manning had taken?

Of course. But what for? I believed the woman, every word she'd told me.

So Manning had piles of pictures of the place. What would looking at these pictures, which were probably taken years ago, years before *I* ever got up there, tell me about the house that I didn't already know or didn't already suspect?

I might've seen what was beneath the place, in that hole.

I might've. I might've not.

I might've discovered *something else* about the house, something I hadn't considered or thought possible.

It grows. It sleeps and feeds.

What would learning more about the house, at this point, mean to us? Will a better understanding of the house – a better understanding of the house's *structure*, I should say, because isn't that what the pictures would offer? – help us... find Lucy, Marianne, Paul Wise? Others?

You assume that there is something familiar, finally, about the Drammond House, assume that it *looks* and *appears* like other houses you've been in. You assume, furthermore, that the things that go on inside the house, its *domestic life*, so to speak, has something in common with the goings on out here, in *this* world. And you assume, finally, that Lucy, Marianne, and Paul haven't reappeared because, simply, they're lost, still inside.

I didn't ask to see these photographs for the same reason I didn't tell Charlotte what I knew about the house. Before going out to see her, I was ready to leave everything behind, to get as far from the house and what had happened there as I possibly could. And talking to Charlotte about the house, *answering* the question Manning and his model seemed to have set up for me... would only further complicate the situation. I would be *adding* to the story, enchanting and confusing Charlotte all the more. Because she would realize, then, that Manning's *gift* of the painting was not as straight forward as it seemed. Because he wanted me to see...

Still, there was Joseph. And the sister, Ingrid. Driving Charlotte off, casting her aside. A bag of money – for what she'd done? The years she'd spent with the man, helping him, caring for him? I'm not saying it's wrong or right. I'm saying...

The solution seemed simple enough. Joseph would have no idea what was coming, what was about to happen.

But this would require *my* persuading the man to come with me to the house. Charlotte was right in this regard – Joseph would question me every step of the way. *He had no reason to go to the house.* He couldn't care less whether the model had its foundations in fact or fiction or something else altogether. And he was smart enough a man to see through any ruse I or Charlotte might come up with.

In any case, he was leaving in a few days. Which meant, for all intents and purposes, the issue would resolve itself. Charlotte would be gone, off to Mexico City, and Joseph Manning, now a millionaire many times over, would return to life in Berlin, where, I later learned, he lived with a woman named Hannah Kode – with a K – a professor of classics at one of their universities, and where he worked in a firm as a civil engineer. Piping was his thing.

That is the conclusion I'd drawn. I would let things follow their natural course.

I waited for Charlotte's call, to arrange the delivery of my painting. And I waited for Monday – today – when Joseph was to return to Germany.

Neither of these things happened.

Saturday night, not having heard from Charlotte, I decided to call. No answer. I tried again early yesterday morning. Joseph picked up.

"Joseph," I said.

"Who is this?"

"It's Raymond. Is Charlotte – "

"Raymond who?"

"Raymond Byrd. Listen, Joseph – "

"*What?*"

The man didn't sound right. Something had happened, something was coming undone.

"I'm calling about the painting. Charlotte was – "

"What painting?"

What painting?

"The one you – we talked about this last week – expressed some interest in."

" ... "

The setup was changing. Charlotte, I suspected, was completely out of the picture. Which meant I'd have to deal with Joseph. Which meant – first – careful words, and second, one last chance. I pressed on:

"You asked me to – "

"I know the painting. Go on."

"I've had a change of heart," I said. "Still interested?"

"I'm listening."

"It's yours... For the model."

The man on the line took a long deep breath. He said: "You want the model. Not the painting. Is that what you said?"

"Yes."

"Why do you want the model?"

"No reason, Joseph. I slept on it. I changed my mind. Let's trade."

"You were so keen on the painting. What happened?"

" ... I wasn't *keen* on anything. Honestly, I just didn't want *you* to have it."

The man on the line snorted, laughed once. "He puts the cards down."

I was in my kitchen. I looked through the sliding doors into the backyard. I'd neglected things for weeks and weeks. The lawn, so high and green in the winter months, was now a dusty yellow, withered. The deck was falling down, pulling away from the house. It occurred to me that repairing the deck, and cleaning up the yard, making plans of any sort for the future, for next summer, were pointless. In short order the place would be empty. I could feel it.

"I'd like to see it," I said. "Make some measurements."

The man snorted again. When he spoke it was almost in a whisper. "You can't."

"Can't what? Make measurements?"

He sighed. He said: "The painting's yours. You'll need to arrange the pickup yourself. Charlotte's gone."

"Gone? When?"

The man was quiet for a moment. There was static in the line, the faintest, distant sound of other people, other languages. He cleared his throat and said: "Saturday morning she destroyed it. The model. Completely destroyed, Raymond. There's nothing left. It's... Then she took her things and... She's gone. She left."

I listened to the man breathing on the line. I didn't know what to say. He started to speak. I interrupted him. "I'm coming out there."

"Don't come. There's nothing – "

"I'm coming out. Now. I want to see this."

"Don't, Raymond. It's – "

In the yard, my old cat crept out from under the bushes. He hobbled forward on his bad legs. Then he spotted something in the grass, something I couldn't see. Slowly he lowered himself, his fat tail rising, serpentine, stirring the air, back and forth.

I said: "I know where she is." To which Joseph had no response.

~ 8 ~

The red Lincoln was in the yard. The BMW was gone.

I didn't bother going up to the house. I wanted to see the model, this complete destruction.

I followed the path down to the barn. The door was wide open. It was dark inside.

I heard Joseph hustling down the path behind me. "Hello!" he said.

In the barn, large wooden crates were lined up and stacked against one wall. All of the paintings, mine included, and everything from the loft, which was empty, were gone, packed away.

Someone's been busy.

I made my way quickly across the open space of the ground floor, toward the corner, the entrance to the stairs.

Joseph was shouting as he came into the barn. "Wait! Please! Raymond!? I thought I told you – "

Without turning, I said: "I'd like to see the model. Or what's left of it. It's hard for me... I just can't see how – "

"There's nothing – "

"I'd like to see for myself."

The basement door was open. The key, I noticed in a glance, was missing.

It was pitch dark at the bottom of the steps.

A moment later, Joseph Manning appeared behind me, a step above me, enormous, his front a slab of tangled shadows. I could hear him breathing horse-like through his nose.

"The lights?" I said.

If the man had reached out, placed a finger against my brow, and pushed, it would have been the end of everything. I would have fallen, head over heels, all the way to the bottom.

He was breathing hard, having ran down the hill after me. In a quiet dry voice, he said: "They're at the bottom. Right of the entrance."

I glanced over my shoulder. It was a long way down. The stairs disintegrated into darkness.

Joseph closed his eyes, sighed. The spirit apparently had passed. Gently: "If you insist. I'll show you." He stepped down, toward me. He wrapped his large hand over my shoulder, brushed me aside.

Down he went. I followed.

Near the bottom of the stairs, the only light cast down from the entrance behind us, he said, "Where is she?"

"This place in the mountains she told me about."

"Where's that? Look, Raymond, I'm – "

"I'll take you, after – "

He turned on the lights in what had been the model's room. At first they buzzed quietly, eight coiled filaments hanging in the air, a soft brown, warming and building, glowing brighter and brighter until they burned a blinding white.

In the center of the room, where the model had been, was now, wall to wall, a pile of splintered wood. A tornado could've passed through, ripping everything to shreds.

"See," he said. He stepped past me, into the room, kicking aside debris.

I saw but I didn't believe.

"Do you see," he said again, the temper rising in his voice once more. He spread out his arms, rage flashing in his eyes.

"Charlotte," I said, almost whispering, my voice cracking, "she did this?"

He looked at me and nodded pathetically. He was blushing. I could see blood under his skin rising up his neck, covering his enormous naked head. "I couldn't stop her," he said.

"*You* couldn't stop her."

"She locked herself in."

The air stank. Was that glue, smoke, piss?

He stared at me, holding his breath, waiting for a reaction, for me to question his lie. Then it seemed he was looking through me, beyond me. I wasn't there. It was something else, something past, that caught his eye.

Then the act broke down, or shifted into a different phase, different character.

He moved, stepped aside, raised a hand, wrapped his fingers over his brow, took a deep shuddering breath, as if on the verge of tears. "Look at what she did! And I couldn't stop her..."

Even the chair and small table that he'd been sitting at when I first met him had been destroyed. "Take this hammer," the man had said, sitting *right there*, "and smash the hell out of it. Just to see what happens."

I made my way around the room, trying to find in the ruin something familiar, something I might grasp to remind myself that what I had seen only a few days before had not actually been a delusion. It seemed incredible even that a structure the size of Manning's model could be destroyed in such short time.

"Where is she?" he said.

I spoke but at as if from outside my body: I was watching myself on a stage, in a performance of the present reality. "Where's my painting?"

"Your *what*?"

"You know what. The painting. It was upstairs. Along with some others. *It* is mine. What's happened here – " I kicked pieces of the model out of my way – rooms, floors, balconies, a staircase, a turret – "is between you and her. Give me the painting."

At first the color drained from the man's face. His lips turned momentarily blue. Then a quick splotchy red filled his cheeks. And he smiled, his enormous mouth opening and spreading, splitting his huge head into two. Eyes closed in glee, he said: "Give me Charlotte. And the painting's yours."

~ 9 ~

"Thing was, trying to give him the benefit of the doubt, I couldn't picture Charlotte destroying the model, causing *that* much destruction. Not a short woman, she was maybe taller than average, but she's thin, small boned... Even if she could have used the hammer... that mallet, or something else... it would've taken her... I don't know – a *day*, a couple days to... Anyways – she'd told me she couldn't do it."

"Who you gonna believe?" said the detective.

"I had no reason to doubt her."

"And him?"

"Who else?"

Byrd looked at the detective across the table from him. He looked at the other man, a younger man, a white man, thin and gaunt, who'd come in a couple hours before, sat down next to the detective, started taking notes.

"Question is," Byrd said, "why? And why blame Charlotte?"

The sun was setting. A lovely orange rectangle of light appeared on the wall beside them. It crept upward, adjusting, elongating as the sun descended.

The man in the corner – Matt Suzuki was his name, he was a sergeant – seemed more interested in the setting sun than in what was happening at the table before him.

"Maybe it was an accident," Byrd said. "One thing led to another, and then... He'd meant to disassemble it. To cut it into parts. He wanted to get it out of there and see it in the light of day... But something went wrong. He broke a piece. He didn't know where to begin, so... But he *had* to start somewhere. And so, rather than tell Charlotte of his plan, ask her advice, or even ask me for help, rather than waste any more precious time racking his mind trying to solve this puzzle, he just started. And he broke a piece... I imagine the man standing there dumbfounded, shocked at what he's done, looking at this splinter of wood like... Like he's found, you know, a severed finger in his garden. Thinking *What now?*... It would take too long to disassemble the house, piece by piece, floor by floor, room by room. And reassemble it upstairs. He'd need a manual, a description of the place, his father's books. But he was leaving in a couple days. And there were *a thousand* other things to settle first... So. Where to start? *Fuck it.* He breaks off a piece. He's thinking, *I don't need this.* Let the sister deal with it. He wants – all he wants – is to get back to Germany. To get away from this place, his dead father's house, the old man's things, out of the country he'd proudly left behind years before. To get back to Hannah Kode, his professor lady-friend. Go back and tell her stories about the place, about his crazy father, about *the thing* he'd spent the final years of his life building in his basement. Would she believe him? Would she care? Would he even be able to describe it, the model, and the room it was in, his sitting there before it trying to *take it all in*... Or would it come out as... something idiosyncratic, extravagant, and finally – imagine his *disgust*, his *embarrassment* at the thought – American? With Disneyland just down the street... She wouldn't care. She'd glance up from her work, over this slip of glass balanced on her nose, nod once, 'Hmm,' stare at the man as if trying to remember his name, and then look away. Back to work... He was embarrassed by it. 'Where does it come from,' he'd said, 'Americans and their entitlement?' No. He'd cut himself off. Wanting to deny his past, put it all way behind him. And coming back for the old man's funeral, except for seeing the coffin into the ground, and sorting out *his* things from his sister's, apart from that – he wanted nothing to do with the place, the people, the memories, the art. *Charlotte.* An embarrassment... And the more he thought about it, then, holding that splinter in his hand, the thing spread out wall-to-wall before him, having broken this piece off the model his father had spent almost ten years building, the more he realized how impossible it would be to get the thing out and, not only that, explain it to others. He was afraid of this, I suspect. Having to answer questions about the thing. To fit it into the man's, what's it called – it's French for the man's work – "

"His oeuvre," said the gaunt fellow.

" – Thank you. Because there was something inexplicable about it, as if it were the hand of someone else, not this painter. Or was it that, as Charlotte said – the model had been there all along. *All* of his work, *all* of the paintings, Joseph is thinking, had been in anticipation of the appearance of this *thing*, what the old man'd envisioned for the last seventy years of his life. Which is to say, the paintings amounted to, not *nothing,* but something subordinate to this structure, this sprawling, inscrutable and terrifying *house.*"

The Japanese man in the corner of the room was looking at Byrd. Byrd couldn't tell if the man was listening but he seemed to have the man's attention.

Byrd lifted a plastic cup from the table, drank what water remained in it, set the cup down. The white man at the table quickly got up, took the cup, crushed it, left the room, came back not a minute later with a new cup and a plastic bottle of water. He set these on the table, returned to his seat. Byrd opened the bottle, filled his cup.

"There was something to it, see," Byrd said. "It was not a work of art. The paintings, sure, were art, nothing else. But the model... Nor was it simply the result, as Charlotte said to me, of a man obsessed. Inside Joseph's thick head, I see him thinking, the model was the result of a man *consumed* by an idea. But the model, incomplete as it was, was only the beginning of the expression of this idea, this larger plan. This is not obsession, which is usually about repetition, or possession, Jillian would say. This is about *execution*. About *doing* something, about building something *for* a future move... I think Charlotte knew this, though she didn't say it. And I think Joseph knew this. And that's what troubled him most, holding that splinter of wood in his hand. That the model could never be finished and put out, like sculpture, for the viewer's pleasure... It was never meant to be like that, like sculpture, like a painting. No... It was more like, I think, a *script*, something for a person to read and perform, something for a person or people *to enter,* so to speak, and *activate.* But activate what? It's just *a model*, nothing more than a giant rat maze. Right? Uncertain about the answer to this question, Joseph was nervous. Something was coming. Because if the model were a sign of something to come, of something that his crazy father had in the works, what *on earth* could this possibly be? And so we ask – "

"Did Joseph," said the detective, "know about the – Drammond...?"

"Good question."

"Charlotte could've told him."

"But he wouldn't have listened to her, wouldn't have cared."

"She told *you*."

"She told me because I showed interest... in the model, and in that notebook. She saw my reaction. She saw her opportunity. She needed to tell someone. Before going. Needed to get it off her chest, the things the man had done and said. She needed to *warn* me – us."

"But Joseph also saw the notebook," said the gaunt fellow. "That morning. You were there." The man referred to his notes, licking a fingertip, flipping a page. "*More of my father's things,* he said, *we'll be finding –* "

"Joseph *saw* it, yes, but didn't realize what it was."

It is right in front of you. And still you do not see.

"Or if he saw it," Byrd went on, "he *chose* not to recognize what it was he was looking at. Because it reminded him of something. Something he didn't want to think about, something he'd rather not remember... He had only a few days to go. And then, the paintings catalogued and sorted out, the house emptied and dusted off and put up for sale, and Charlotte gone, back to Germany he goes, back to Kode and dark, honest Berlin, *millions and millions and millions* of dollars essentially his in the future sales of the collection... The man is counting the minutes before his plane takes off. He doesn't want to – "

"Wait. Wait, wait," said the detective, holding up a hand. "What you're saying is, now, he knew what the book was, what it was about."

"Yes."

"He knew about the house. The Drammond House."

"He'd never been there. He only knew the place through the story his father told him when he and his sister were kids. And whether Manning meant to frighten the kids – what *he meant* by telling them this story doesn't matter. Because he *did* frighten them. He scared the hell out of them with the story of this house and the people and things inside, of the little girl who went off on her own and *got lost* – "

"But you said she got out. They found her."

"Got out. Sure she did. But what came out of the house was not entirely the same girl."

"What're you saying?" said the detective. "She was missing a part? She was hurt?" The white guy snickered.

"No. It's simpler than that. She was just a different person. The house *did* something to her. And the model, I've come to think – and this is *a scenario* that they, Charlotte and Joseph, *must have* considered... was meant to be a kind of map for him, Manning, to help him return to the place in order to recover what he'd lost... But wait, you're thinking –that doesn't make much sense at all. Because *the girl* got out. And because we're not talking about *a girl* any more, we're talking about an old man who's remembering a time some seventy years back. So what we mean here by *saving the girl* is saving something else, something, I think, much closer to him, something – "

"I get it," said the gaunt fellow. He was from the Midwest originally. Minnesota, Wisconsin.

"You do?"

"You mean his innocence. He was – what was it? – twelve."

The black detective nodded his head thoughtfully.

Raymond Byrd looked at the white man. He said: "I think it was actually – its opposite – a question of understanding. Not innocence but – wanting to know what happened to the girl, wanting to know what was inside that house. Because there was – *there is* – something there. Some kind of machine. And it *does things* – it's *doing things* to people. And as an artist, Manning wanted to see it, whatever it is, to see how it worked, to see what it did to the people it touched. The girl – Nancy was her name – was an opening. She'd been worked on, done over by what was in the house. And he wanted to understand this. He wanted to see how it was done... I bet Joseph knew this. I bet Joseph, splinter in hand, knew exactly what the model was, and exactly what needed to be done."

"So you're saying, now," said the detective, " – and I'm sorry to keep interrupting, but I wanna understand this and – you know, it's a tricky story you're telling us here, Ray, so – I just wanna make sure I'm following – so you're saying that he, Joseph Manning, *knew* about the house. The real house, I mean."

"How could he not? If the model was the culmination of a seventy year long nightmare, how could the son or the daughter grow up and *not* know about the place. The old man *must have* told them something, disguised it, perhaps, as a story, but he had to have said something. The house, as Charlotte told me, was a part of him. It was inside of him. It *transformed* him that afternoon in nineteen twenty whenever, when he and that girl took a walk in the woods and decided to play at being adults – *trespassing inside the house of a stranger*... He told Charlotte stories because she asked, she wanted to know what was happening.

He told his children stories because *he had to*, because he had to say something and to tell the truth would have hurt them, *terrified* them... No. Joseph knew. Even if he didn't realize that he knew. In his heart, it all came together... So he locked himself in the room, took that mallet, and he destroyed it... And then, realizing what he'd done, he needed an explanation for his sister, who he'd told about the model. And what's the easiest explanation?"

"Charlotte."

"Charlotte Graham."

~ 10 ~

The men in the room sat in silence for a minute. Mc-Neal, the black man, looked at Raymond Byrd and thought: "He's lying. Lying, lying, lying. He's had too much time. He's talking too much. He's enjoying himself, telling us this story."

Quietly, very clearly, the sergeant, Matt Suzuki, said: "Why would he want Charlotte Graham?"

Byrd looked at the sergeant, surprised by the sound of the man's voice. "Why would Joseph want Charlotte?"

"Why would he want you to take him to her?"

"He wouldn't give me the painting. He was stealing the painting. And he knew I couldn't stop him. So he used Charlotte as leverage."

The sergeant thought it over. He said: "Leverage for what, if he already has what he wants? Mr Byrd, if you couldn't stop him, and if he knew you couldn't stop him, then why didn't he just leave? Why bother with the woman?"

Byrd closed his eyes. When he opened them he noticed, again, that the Japanese man had only one arm. The way the sleeve of the man's jacket was folded concealed this fact. But if you looked closely, you could see it: The man had no left arm. "There was something else he wanted. Something she had."

"Something she took from him?"

"Yes and no. Something she knew, knew about him."

"That he had wrecked the model of the house?"

"Yes, that, but also..."

The sergeant and detectives waited. Occasionally Raymond Byrd had to pause and search for the word.

"It was also," he went on, "his father's affection, his love. Charlotte got it. All of it. The children didn't. They got all the things, yes, the art and the house and the land, but she got, you know, *the man*. A life with him, an understanding. And he, Joseph, couldn't understand that. He couldn't look at this woman and see the connection between her and his father. But he knew there *was* a connection. And this troubled him as much as, maybe more than, the model itself."

"He was jealous," said the gaunt fellow.

Byrd couldn't help it. He smiled. "Sort of."

"Would he hurt the woman?" asked the sergeant.

Byrd blinked. "Yes."

"Would he hurt you?"

"... Sir. In different circumstances, I think Joseph would have killed us both."

The sergeant nodded once. He turned, looked out the window. The skin on his face, in the evening light, was blue and brown.

He took one step forward, toward the table in the middle of the room. He took a deep breath. He said: "Do you know where Charlotte Graham is?"

"No," Byrd said. "I do not."

"Do you know where Joseph Manning is?"

"Yes. Yes I do."

~ 11 ~

He left before me. Slouching, sulking like a child, he passed me in silence and disappeared up the stairs.

The mallet was on the counter. It was wooden, with a large square head, a handle worn smooth with use, about a foot long. The face of its business end is soft, like skin. The tool is heavier than it looks. I imagine it fit perfectly in Joseph Manning's large hand.

I looked at the remains of the model, this pile of wood. I thought about Charlotte, her hands, her arms.

Joseph shouted something from the top of the stairs. He was in a hurry, naturally.

I turned the lights off as I left.

He was in the house, Manning's bungalow. I waited outside. After a few minutes I climbed the porch steps, went inside, into the kitchen. It was as cool and quiet as it had been the last time I was there.

On the table, otherwise empty, was a black backpack.

"This going to take long?" Joseph said, strapping on a wristwatch as he entered the room.

"I don't know. A few hours."

"Because I need to be back for..."

He swung the backpack up on a shoulder. I looked at him. He flashed a quick tight smile.

Like a good boy scout. Always prepared.

What was he expecting? A hike in the woods?

"What's in the backpack?" I said.

"A book. Something to eat."

"You watch your diet."

"Not especially. But American food. It can hardly be called food. The GMOs. And sugars."

"I see. Bring me anything?"

He blinked, tightened his jaw in a way I was beginning to recognize. All business, Herr Joseph Manning, pipe specialist.

For the record – I disliked the man very much. For no good reasons – though I have reasons – I despised him, and I despise his type.

If I could, Charlotte or not – because, in fact, I was only guessing that I'd find her at the house – I would take the man to the Drammond House, lead him into the basement, with its filthy occupants, and abandon him. Not out of any loyalty to Charlotte, or to Kearn, the housekeeper – but just for the hell of it.

Take that hammer, I could still hear him saying, *and smash the hell out of it. Just to see what happens.*

He was frozen. Tightening up. His blue eyes dimming behind his pretty specs.

Going out to the car, I said: "Charlotte take her things?"

"Yes."

"Everything? There was a book, a notebook."

"I'm telling you. There's nothing left. Not a stitch."

He was telling me, sure, but only what he wanted told. I didn't have any choice. Anyways, I was getting what I wanted, if taking him to the Drammond House could be called a plan of any sort, so why push my luck?

"Explain to me," I said, pulling into a line of traffic on the 101, "after she wrecked the model, where were you? At the door, waiting for her?"

" ... I'd gone inside."

"And then what? She just comes in like it's any other day, goes up stairs, takes her things, and leaves? That how it happened?"

Something cracked in the man's throat, on his palate. He was licking his thin lips. He said: "Listen. Just drive. You don't have to make small talk with me. I don't care. I don't know you. I don't want to know you. I prefer the silence to listening to you."

So I drove.

He said a minute later: "I didn't think she could... Would actually... Bring me to her and we'll settle things. You'll get the painting, and I..."

The man took a big book out of his backpack. Then he took out a small leather case. His reading glasses. Carefully he switched glasses. Then he took a long yellow pencil from the backpack. He sat up straight in the passenger seat, opened the book, and read. When he started making a note in the margin, I said:

"The painting is mine, Joseph. Charlotte was to arrange for its delivery. She hasn't. What you've done by – "

He turned a long pale face to me. His bald head nearly touched the ceiling of the car. "I never said the painting *wasn't* – "

"If I *had* the painting, we wouldn't be in this situation. And you'd be – "

"Raymond, please!"

"What do you think she'll do when she sees you? Just what do you expect – "

"Please!" The big man's voice broke. His face was bright red. He was sputtering, gasping, trying to speak but the words wouldn't come. Finally, his eyes closed, mouth wide open, nothing but these great big square teeth, the word came: "Enough!"

I didn't know Heinrich Manning, the father, that well. We met only a couple times, as I've said.

His son, seated next to me, crying like a school boy, *paled* in comparison to the other man. I glanced his way one last time, wondering who his mother could have been, because the father had been so different, so strong and determined and unaffected, it seemed to me, by the presence of others.

But the son, behind the shouting and the posturing presumption that everyone, because they were smaller than him, would get out of his way, had the backbone of a worm.

I didn't say another word. For risk of losing him, frightening him off. Because I needed him to trust me, to come with me just a little farther.

~ 12 ~

In Maiden, I stopped at Rosalee's. Jillian was behind the counter. She poured me a cup of coffee, walked off without glance.

Joseph was in the bathroom.

I'd finished my coffee and was beginning to wonder about the man. It was getting dark.

Then I heard him, by the bathrooms around the corner, where a payphone hung from the wall. German, whispering. Like a pit of snakes.

Some minutes later he came back, stood at my shoulder like an idiot giant, tapping his foot.

"Want anything?"

He shook his head. As I stood, took my coat, paid, he left the diner, walked quickly out to the car, climbed in. He stared at me from behind the windshield.

"Who's he?" Jillian said.

I looked at her, her soft blue eyes, her red hair pulled back in a ponytail.

"Some guy," I said. "Picked him up on the side of the road. Car trouble. Says he was supposed to meet someone at a place called the Drammond House. Heard of it?"

She raised an eyebrow. She wiped the counter clean.

Back in the car, I asked him about the phone call. Quietly he told me about Berlin, this girlfriend of his, Hannah Kode. He sounded sad.

"Everything alright?" I said.

"I told her what happened."

"With the model?"

"With the model, with Charlotte, with ... I told her I might miss my flight."

I'd pulled back onto the road. We were climbing what remained of the mountain before the street narrowed, tapered down to one lane. We rounded a bend. Trees, tall and thin, like ancient ruins, hung tipping over the road.

"Why would you miss your flight?"

The man sighed. He leaned forward, peered out the windshield.

"We're high up now, aren't we?" he said.

"We are."

"I can feel it. The air's different."

He looked at me. I watched the road.

"When's your flight?"

"I need to be at the airport at six thirty tomorrow morning."

There was the gate, the driveway.

"We'll make it," I said, pulling over.

He opened the door, got out quickly, stood in the open door, hands on his lower back.

He was in a hurry to get the house. Before I'd even got out of the car, he'd passed under the brick archway to the left of the gate, started up the hill.

"Wait." I called after him. He didn't reply.

I had to run to catch up.

"Joseph," I said. "There's a house..."

"I know where we are."

He was marching, swinging his arms, eyes dead ahead.

"But it's – "

"I said I *know where we are*."

I stopped. I watched the man continue up the hill. The afternoon had worn thin and the cold of night was coming up fast. There would be no dusk. What little light remained on the driveway, under the trees, would be gone in an instant.

It would be a long night.

"Have you been here before?" I said.

That slowed him down. But he didn't stop. He looked over his shoulder, said: "No. I haven't."

"But you know what's up there."

I had to hurry to keep him within reach. If we were separated before going inside the house, I'd never be able to find him, and I wouldn't know what became of him.

Quietly, chin down, he said, "My father used to tell me stories."

"About the house."

"Yes. And when I saw the model, I realized..." He stopped, turned, looked down at me, catching his breath.

"I realized many things. One. That the place was real. The stories *weren't* stories, or weren't *just* stories. And so..."

Through the trees, far up the hill to our left, in the damp final light of that day, I saw the orchard Lucy had discovered. And once again, the old man, Gretton, the groundskeeper, was there, a dark clipper opening and closing in his hand. But this time he wasn't alone. Seated on a stump directly behind him was a little girl, a child. The man looked down at us, his thin face full of shadow. And the girl, leaning to the side, looked around the man's heavy arm at us, still and distant as a statue.

"And so?" I said.

"And so," he said, taking a deep breath, a white cloud of air covering his face, steam rising from the back of his neck, "so when she destroyed the house, and took the books, I thought she might retreat here. To the actual place. Where I'd never be able to find her."

"But – "

Expressionless, he went on: "I knew you would call, Raymond. Because you were expecting to hear from her. And you knew, or I thought you knew, when I'd be gone. So when you didn't hear from her, you called. I knew why you were calling. And I knew you'd come out. That was the easy part. What I wasn't sure about was whether or not you knew where she went."

"She told me she was going to Mexico."

He smiled, his fleshy eyes pressed shut. "Yes. She told me that too. And maybe that was the plan. But... "

"What makes you think she isn't there?"

He lowered his voice, leaned in. "Because you told me, before I'd even asked, that you knew where she was. What was supposed to be a secret... Right?"

I thought about it. I guess he was onto something. A smart guy, finally, even if he did have the backbone of a worm.

I said: "But how did you know that I knew about this place, and that I'd take you here?"

He blinked. "I didn't. I was guessing. Look. Put yourself in my position, Raymond." He pivoted. Eyes over my shoulder, on the woods. His hands came up, framing, holding two sides of an invisible box. "I had *my* reasons," he said, "for thinking she might come up here. And she has *her* reasons for retreating here. Based on this alone - *if you weren't in the picture* - I might have done it myself. Come up here anyways." He dropped his hands, stood up straight, looked me in the eye. "When you said that you knew where to find her, that settled it. Of course she told you about Mexico. But that was before she wrecked the model. When she did *that*, things changed. Because I could find her in Mexico. But here... She was betting she could disappear. Or at least be protected. Because... Assuming that I wouldn't dare come up. After what my father told me of the place... And maybe I wouldn't have, alone. Maybe it was a good bet. But then you called, and said that you knew where she was."

"And if I'd said Mexico?"

"I'd know you were lying."

"How?"

"Simple. Because she told you about this place. The real thing. I know she did. Filling your ear. I saw you. That morning, with the book – that expression on your face. Should've seen yourself. Unbelievable, Raymond. Truly. Touching."

"But – "

"No *buts,* Raymond. No argument. She's here."

Joseph lowered a shoulder, drew back his arm, swung around his slender backpack. Slowly, with the routine movement of a schoolboy arriving at his desk, taking out his pencils and books, Joseph opened the bag, reached inside, and pulled out a small pistol. He held it momentarily, arm bent, the muzzle pointed down at his feet. He seemed to be weighing it in his hand. Then he looked up, his face stretched out as if in wonder, eyebrows high on his forehead, a long mouth and chin.

The light was low. Beneath the trees it could've been night already, so at first I didn't recognize the gun in his hand as a gun. It was too small to be a gun.

But then he pointed it at me, like this, and I understood what was what.

He said: "You're meeting her here. Aren't you?"

"What're you – "

"*Aren't you!?*"

"Yes," I said.

"I knew it. She gave you directions."

"Yes."

"I knew it. And she forced my father to leave you that painting, didn't she?"

"What?"

"Didn't she!?"

The man was transforming before my eyes. "Yes," I said. "She did. I hadn't thought of that. But... You're absolutely right. It's the only explanation."

"Just as I thought," he said. "Just as she did with the money, which my father *never* would've..." The man's long hairless face contracted into a tight-lipped V, smiling with satisfaction.

The house was up the hill, at his back. He took a step aside, cut the gun horizontally between us. "Go," he said. "Lead the way." I stepped forward, before him. He pressed the muzzle of the gun into the flesh of my side. We stood so close I could smell him. Beads of sweat speckled his upper lip, his pale head.

He said: "You will take me to her. You hesitate, you try anything, and I'll kill you. I'll leave you out here in the woods. They'll never find your body. ... But if you bring me to her, I'll let you go. My business is with her, only her."

I walked up the hill. I paused. He stepped into me. The muzzle of the gun rubbed a bone in my back. "Joseph." I turned to face him, but he snarled, stepped back, raised the gun. Turning back around, I said over my shoulder:

"Joseph. I don't know if she's here. You're right about everything, but... It's too early. We weren't going to meet until – "

He pushed my head forward, my chin down, with the gun.

"If she's not here, then you are out of luck. Now move! I got a plane to catch."

I moved. A minute later I stopped. He stopped.

The yard was cold and silent. The woods had vanished. In their place, the house, instantaneously, like an animal leaping from the dark, surrounded us.

~ 13 ~

There was a light on inside. Someone was playing a piano.

Corinne Kearn, the housekeeper, opened the door. She looked at me quietly, taking a moment, I felt, to remember who I was. Then she looked at the enormous man behind me. Then she looked back at me. Dark gray, questioning eyes.

Behind her, across the entrance hall, and far down a corridor, Martin Sanchez appeared. He came quickly forward, head down.

The music stopped.

In the corner of my eye, Joseph moved. It was the gun, at my ear, pointed at Kearn.

She hardly moved. Her chin fell, eyes lowering. Then she looked at me again.

"We are here," Joseph said, "for Charlotte Graham."

The man gently pushed me across the threshold. The housekeeper, without a sound, took a step back. Her hands, which had been folded one over the other before her hips, came apart, arms straight down, the fingers of her right hand moving, curling, flexing plantlike at her side.

Sanchez, the tap of his shoes on the parquet growing louder and louder, was nearly upon us. If there was any doubt in the housekeeper's mind about what was happening, there was no doubt at all in the houseman's. Then Kearn, backing into the light of the entrance hall, began to address the houseman over her shoulder. But Sanchez started first. He was almost at a run.

"There is no need," the houseman said, coming directly at me, his eyes over my shoulder, raising a hand, "to –"

Joseph pushed me aside an instant before the gun went off.

It was a slapping sound, the sound of something tearing. And somewhere a woman, Elaine, it must've been, sobbed, began to cry.

The houseman fell straight the floor, turning, writhing, moaning.

Joseph was breathing hard, his eyes huge and wet in his long face. He was studying his work.

Sanchez rocked back and forth on the floor, both of his small hands pressed hard against his chest, high up, directly beneath his throat. He was gasping for air. The color was gone from his face. Blood was seeping up between his fingers and spreading out in a dark pool beneath him. He was slowing down.

"Graham," said Joseph softly, the gun snapping up, arm firm, in Kearn's face.

With his free hand he took me by the shoulder of my coat.

Someone was coming up behind us.

"What! What's that!" the old man, Gretton, cried. "Martin!? Martin?"

Joseph whipped around, pointed the gun at the groundsman. The old man ignored him, fell to his knees as he entered the room, clambering like a creature over the floor to where the houseman lay. "Martin! Martin! Please!"

The houseman was breathing his last, coughing, gasping loudly, fear in his eyes, his twisted face.

Kearn said: "This way."

She took one step backwards and turned and walked away from us.

Joseph snorted, shoved me forward, took an exaggerated step around Sanchez's body, the blood gathering on the floor.

We followed the housekeeper into a dark hallway.

"Sara! Sara! SARA!" Gretton said behind us. I glanced back. A little girl stood in the shadow of the foyer. "Go," the old man said, "down the hill. Get help. Go, go, now! As fast as you can!"

I'd looked away. Joseph was practically lifting me single-handedly into the air, rushing to keep up with Kearn.

I heard the pitter-patter of the girl run off, out the door, down the dark driveway.

Sam Gretton was crying, sobbing.

Kearn stopped. We came to a door. Kearn looked at Joseph, reached for the door, opened it, took a step back.

Stairs winding down. Damp, familiar darkness.

She looked at me momentarily, indifferently. I kept my eyes on the stairs.

"She's here?" Joseph said. "Down there?"

Kearn said nothing.

Joseph was growling in his throat, something bubbling, rising.

"*Is she here!?*" the man said to Kearn. He shook me, stabbed me in the side with the gun.

"I told you," I said. "I was to meet her here." I looked at Kearn. For once, she seemed to be listening. "But not for a few more days. I..."

He was breathing quickly through his nose. He pulled at my jacket, pushing me back, away from his body. The gun, such a small device, almost like a toy in his hand, coming up –

Quietly, calmly, absolutely in form, "Mr Manning," Kearn said. "There's no need to hurt anyone else. The woman you are looking for is here, at the house. I will take you to her. Please."

She raised a hand, palm out, for Joseph. Soft smooth skin. The hand of a marble masterpiece.

The man was calming down. He turned his eyes to the stairs, the darkness around the bend. He closed his eyes, opened them. I wondered if he'd been here before, seen this hallway, this door, these stairs. He'd never been in the house, I was sure, but still – in the stories his father had told. Could he recognize the place?

He pointed the gun at Kearn, gestured. "You first."

The woman nodded once, glanced at me, and took the first step. Down we went.

~ 14 ~

It sounds like someone sleeping. A man, breathing easily in his sleep. It's almost a sigh. The rhythm is steady, not too fast. It's not very loud. Far off, always distant.

But it could be a machine. Some kind of respirator, like in a hospital.

It's hard to tell. You don't hear it at first, going beneath the house. But then you do. It starts rather suddenly. Silence. And then this sound, this machine or man asleep, all around, its source impossible to determine.

After awhile – there's nothing else down there, no other people, I mean – you get used to it, the sound, and it disappears. It's *there,* but, like white noise, gone, not there.

It's very quiet.

The temperature was going up. We were in one of the halls I'd visited before, at some numberless level beneath the house. The light, through small apertures near the floor, was dim, yellow and orange, warm.

Kearn was far ahead of us. At the end of the hall she stopped, turned, looked back. Gestured, beckoning. "This way," she said, her gentle voice immediately with us, between us.

Sounds – it seems to me now – had this strange, flat quality. Dim, close, clear, present. The woman could be fifty feet away but her voice was here, at your shoulder, in your ear.

"You've been here before?" Joseph said. He was just behind me.

We continued forward, Kearn waiting up ahead.

"I've been to the house," I said.

After a moment, Joseph: "But here, I mean. Down here. With her."

She was watching us. Calm, poised.

"No," I said. "Never."

We passed a room, its door open. There seemed to be a window on the far wall. Light flickering, as through trees, outside. But that would be impossible. Something else, then. Reflecting or emitting this milky light. Across the room – we saw only in glance – in a long dipping horizontal arc, wet clothing hung from a rope. Dark, dripping coats and pants and shirts. I'd seen something like this before, I recalled, in a picture, in one of Manning's drawings.

The Drying Room.

Joseph said, swallowing, whispering: "Laundry. It's just laundry."

But it wasn't laundry hanging in that room.

We'd almost caught up with Kearn.

Joseph, hardly breathing, said: "Are you scared, Ray?"

I wanted to stop. I wanted to take the man by his shoulders, and tell him, eye to eye, that *he'd* asked for this, that it was *his idea* to do this, to pull a gun, to *force* his way into the house like this. To hurt them. To threaten them.

Kearn smiled as we came up to her. A beautiful woman, despite everything. She could charm the most savage thing with that look, those eyes, those lips.

"There's nothing to be scared of," I said, turning, looking up at him.

"Ready?" she said.

~ 15 ~

In the center of the chamber, still some distance off, was an enormous rock, a black boulder several stories tall, hewn into the shape of a pointed dome.

We approached it, the sounds of our steps echoing off the stone walls. The floor was hard and clean, a dark blue-black stone or cement.

There was an opening in the object. A long, black split, a narrow crack down the front. But this, like the object itself, grew in dimension as we approached. In fact, when we finally stopped, the opening into the rock was wide enough to let ten men stand shoulder to shoulder across it.

The air was hot, moist, smelling of the earth, thermal vapors. Paul Wise knew the technical term.

"Omphalos," Joseph suddenly said, his voice rising into the dark of the room, echoing ghostly around us.

That got a reaction out of Kearn, who raised an ear, smiled.

"It's an omphalos," the man said again.

"Very good," Kearn said. "A learned man. Like his father."

"And what's that?" I asked. "The *om* - "

"They were girls, often, just children," Joseph said. His eyes never left the opening in the rock. "This was a *long time* ago. Ancient days. Hannah told me..." Kearn, a pinprick of light flashing in her eye, watched Joseph carefully.

"Imagine," Joseph said. "Precocious, strange kids. Nobody knew what to do with them. They didn't *act* like kids, not in the ways kids should. They were different. And in those days they didn't waste any time. Life was too short... So they killed them. Had to start over." He looked at me, his eyes swinging back and forth, thinking, remembering. "Ever see *Oedipus Rex*?"

"I've heard of it."

"So imagine. Your kid misbehaves. Says things she shouldn't say. Everybody knows. So one day the police come. They'll take her. They say to you –

> It's the knife
> or the hole.

"And you, her father, you love your daughter, you don't want her taken away, killed. You say – if there's *any chance* that it will save her – you say,

> The hole.

"Off she goes. Virgin priestess. She lives in the wild, up in the mountains. With the gods. *Pythia*, they were called."

"What were?"

"The girls. Prophets. *Seers...*"

Joseph took a step forward.

Inside of the rock, like a well, only much, much larger, was a hole. Stairs, clinging narrowly to the inner wall, spiraled downward.

It seemed that time had stopped. We stood there under the rock, staring into the hole, at the stairs descending, disappearing into the earth. When I sensed that Joseph was about to speak again, I almost turned, seized him, to stop him – *to throw him,* if I could, over the edge.

Not another word!

The man looked aside. At me, then at Kearn. To the woman, he said: "She's in there?"

Kearn lowered her chin, nodded. She was no longer smiling. Sweat beaded on her brow, at the base of her throat. A strand of her black hair clung, curling, to her cheek.

Joseph turned on his heel, raised the gun, thrust it in my face. "You first," he said.

The light was so faint inside of the rock – I could barely make out the stairs. And one false step –

Kearn, quietly: "Mr Manning. I'll take you. But Mr Byrd needs to stay behind."

He looked at her, something shifting his face, in his lips. Baring his teeth. He said: "I *want* him to come with us. He *needs* to be there!"

My eye fell on the hole, those gleaming stairs wrapping around, serpentine, downward into the earth. It seemed – somewhere in my mind – it was speaking to me, the hole was, a voice from below hissing in my ear:

Do it! Now! Take him!

Kearn looked at me sharply, her composure for an instant failing.

"Joseph," she said, stepping toward the man, coming close to him, looking up into his eyes. "He can't. Men..." She closed her eyes, took a breath, opened her eyes, whispered: "Men are not allowed. I've already – "

She'd positioned herself between us. I took a step backwards, moving out of the entrance to the rock, away from them. Joseph noticed but he seemed, suddenly, helpless, his face softening, relaxing.

She reached for him. With one hand she caressed his cheek. With the other, she gently took his wrist, pushed the hand with the gun down to his side.

"It's a sacred place," she said, "here. Down there. I can show you. But *only* you."

His eyes were on the opening, the stairs. He looked like a child: desperately curious, but terrified.

"What's in there? What is it?"

Even his voice was changing. Soft, relaxed, pure. Without the contempt, the mean certainty that inflected everything he'd said before.

Almost –

"My master," Kearn said as she took the gun from his hand.

"And she'll be down there? With him?"

hypnotized.

"Yes, Joseph. Charlotte's there. She's waiting for you. Now come. Take my hand."

They stood together, chest to chest, close as a bride and groom. Without taking her eyes from his, she extended her arm around his side, held the gun out for me.

I was reluctant to touch it. But I did. I took it. I couldn't stop myself.

And a moment later, the woman stepping before him, her right hand in his left, step by step, they started the descent.

Joseph was still talking, quietly asking her questions, which she calmly and simply answered.

I went to the edge, looked down.

They moved very slowly, the steps being damp and steep and narrow. But in no time at all they were nearly out of sight. Then they stopped. Joseph had said something. He looked up, directly at me. He raised his free hand, as if to wave.

"Ray?"

At Kearn's word, they continued.

The darkness came over them.

~ 16 ~

I left the house through a salon, a theater. There was a stage, curtains. The vast room was empty.

The house was dark and quiet. Night had fallen.

When I made my way around to the driveway, I saw that the front door remained open. I could hear Gretton inside. Talking to himself, crying. I guess he was alone.

I still had Joseph's gun. It occurred to me that if Gretton saw me with it, he'd attack me. And one of us would end up dead.

I set the gun down on the porch steps.

Very quickly I left, running in the dark down the driveway to my car.

I didn't expect Rosalee's to be open still but there was a light on inside. The little girl was there, Gretton's girl, slumped over the counter, and Jillian too, beside the girl, her hand on the girl's back, and the cook, Nico, still in his apron, hunchbacked behind the counter, a phone to his ear. In the corner of my eye I saw Jillian turn, look out onto the dark street, watch the passing car.

I went home. I showered. Tried to fix something to eat. I wasn't hungry. I had a couple beers. Turned on the TV.

Nothing doing. Unemployment is on the rise, the president doesn't know what to do, a Chilean man, down in Miami, accuses a Santiago professor of having tortured him one night in 1973.

The cats came around. I fed them. The old one looked at me in total disgust, eating slowly but with murder in his eyes.

"She's not coming back."

I went to bed. I lay awake listening to the cats creep around the house.

I called Manning's number, on the chance that Charlotte might be out there – having come out of hiding, seeing me take Joseph away.

But no.

Joseph's flight was in the morning, in a few hours. In two days someone would start asking questions, making calls. If I was going to find Charlotte it would have to be in that time, in the next forty-eight hours.

She's never coming back.

I fell asleep watching *Murder, She Wrote*, Jessica Fletcher explaining to the police how the poison had been applied to the glue on the envelope. "And he knew," she said, "that she would write back *the moment* she received the letter and learned that he was free."

~ 17 ~

There's a closet in our bedroom. It's Lucy's. She never closes the closet door, not all the way. She also tends to leave dirty things on the floor, in the entrance of the closet.

I got up early this morning, wanting immediately to return to Manning's.

Dressing, I noticed that the closet was closed.

I would have noticed this before. I know it's been months since it happened, but I would have noticed it.

I must have closed it.

Cleaning up after her, I would sometimes do that, close the closet all the way. I've done it many times

I opened the closet. There was some clothing on the floor. Pants, socks, black nylons. It had been pushed inside when the door was closed.

Now *that* is something I never do – close the closet door without first picking up her things.

I looked at her shirts, sweaters, pants. In some ways, I recognized nothing. They could've been the shirts and pants of any woman. Still, I had the feeling that something was missing, that someone had come by and taken something of hers from the closet.

There was too much space.

Then, driving out to Manning's, it occurred to me that Lucy could have come home when I was out. She could have come in and taken some of her things, her favorite shirt or blouse or jacket, some underwear, so little but maybe just enough to hold onto a part of herself from before, from her life with me.

Where was she? Was she with anybody? Was she alone, a prisoner? Was she waiting for me? Was she dead?

I was beginning to think returning to Manning's was the wrong thing to do. I should have stayed home, gone over the place more carefully. Maybe she'd left me a clue. Maybe she'd been taken against her will, and left a hidden message for me.

Don't be silly, Ray. She's gone and she's never coming back.

In any case, that's where you found me. And so I'll probably never know if what I saw in the closet this morning was real or – or a figment of my imagination.

Part Three

The Body Temple

~ 1 ~

"**W**ould you like something to eat?"

It was night already. Was it possible that he'd been talking all day? The sun was setting last he noticed. Now the window was dark.

"Sure."

They brought him a hamburger, fries, a coke.

The sergeant, Suzuki, stood by the door. Byrd thought the man was leaving but then he'd stopped, turned and looked at him. "I want you to stay here tonight."

"You mean in jail?"

"You'll have your own room. There's a bed. A toilet."

Raymond Byrd ate the hamburger quickly. He shoved fries into his mouth. "You think," he said, chewing loudly, "I'm going to... go somewhere? Try and escape?"

The Japanese man didn't say anything. He blinked three or four times. He raised his right arm, the sleeve of his black coat sliding down his wrist, exposing a watch. He glanced at this. He looked at Byrd. He reached into his coat pocket, took out a pack of Marlboros, shook it, bounced it in his hand, finally extracting a cigarette with his lips. He replaced the pack in his pocket. He reached under his coat, in the pocket of his slacks. But the detective, McNeal was his name, came at him first, a lighter illuminated in his hand. The sergeant leaned forward, lit up, inhaled deeply. He said: "Mr Byrd. It's not that. It's in the morning, there are a few more things we need to do. I want to make sure I understand everything you've told us today."

Byrd finished the burger and fries. He drank his coke. He was still hungry. His fingers were wet and greasy. "But I'm not under arrest," he said.

"Technically, no. Technically, I can keep you here for twenty-four hours."

"Then I'm free to go. Now, I mean."

Suzuki was tired. There was a heaviness to his face, to how he moved and held his body. He hadn't slept well the night before, a short night. Nor had he slept well the night before that. Fact was he couldn't sleep much more than four or five hours before waking up, unable to go back to sleep. Sometimes, on Sundays, when he stayed home, he'd take a nap in the afternoon.

"You're free to go," he said. "We'll come for you in the morning, if that's what you decide. Early."

"I'll stay."

"Very good."

After a moment the sergeant turned, faced the door, opened it. "If you need anything, you ask for Officer Pearl." The sergeant looked at the detective, the black man. The detective nodded. Suzuki went on: "William

Pearl, we call him Billy, you'll see why, has the night shift. You need anything, you ask for him. Only him. Don't talk to anyone else. That clear?"

Detective McNeal remained in the room with him. The detective sat motionless across the table, his eyes down on an open notebook. The pages were dark with notes. The detective's eyes, Byrd noticed, were moving rapidly back and forth. The man was reading or thinking. If he'd been asleep, Byrd would guess he was dreaming. Then the detective, a tall man, suddenly stood up, reached out and swung his hands together over the surface of the table, crushing the burger wrapper and fries container and empty coke cup swiftly into a compact ball. He left the room with Byrd's trash. He came back with a cup of water.

McNeal sat down at the table and flipped through the notebook, handwritten notes. They were either his or Suzuki's or the other guy's. Byrd didn't know, couldn't tell. It seemed all of them, at different times – even that woman who'd come in for only a few minutes – had been taking notes.

McNeal said quietly, eyes on the notebook, "So. Joseph Manning. And before him, Troy Beckmann. Paul Wise. Lucy Byrd, your wife. Marianne Heaney. Am I forgetting anyone?"

Byrd drank some water. He looked into the plastic cup and wondered if he'd have to do it all again, all through the night. He remembered from movies that they sometimes would do that, ask a fellow to tell his story twice, three times, to different people, to catch him in a slip. "It's McNeal, right?"

The man across from him nodded.

"No. That's it. As far as I know."

"And this – *Michael*, was it?"

"You'd have to ask Jillian Veldt, up in Maiden."

The black man nodded, eyes on the notebook.

"Are they dead, Ray?"

Byrd kept his eyes on the detective. The man hardly moved, eyes down on the notes. He was a big man, tall and fit. He spoke in a curious way, gently, patiently, rather clearly, unlike any other black man Byrd had ever met. Still, he thought he'd misheard the man. He thought: "Why would he ask me *that*, are they dead?"

"You asking me," he said, "if I, if I killed anyone? No. I did not kill anybody. Joseph did. He shot Martin Sanchez. I should say, I saw him shoot Martin. Whether he lived or not..."

"Did he look like he was going to die?"

Byrd nodded.

McNeal waited. He had large lazy brown eyes, flared nostrils. He said: "And the others? Joseph? Paul Wise?"

Byrd noticed how greasy his hands and fingers were. He wiped them on his pants but they still gleamed, stank of salt and oil. Holding up his greasy fingers: "You think I could wash my hands?"

"Later. Tell me about Paul Wise."

Raymond Byrd sat back, sighed, dropped his head. He was exhausted. He actually looked forward to seeing this room the sergeant had made available for him. "Since I'm not under arrest, you'll understand... my reluctance to speculate. I don't want to confuse things, about what might have happened. Are they dead, you ask. What I saw was, last night, Joseph Manning shoot Martin Sanchez. I saw the man fall to the floor. He was holding his chest, here, like this..."

McNeal watched Byrd's demonstration.

"What happened then," said Byrd, "I can't say. What happened to Paul Wise – I can't say."

"They're dead, aren't they?"

Byrd coughed, put his hands down, gripped the edge of the table. He looked at the table, at crumbs, at the mess he'd made. He wondered how many men had sat in this chair, answered similar questions to those put forward by Detective McNeal, eaten a dinner similar to the one he'd just had, making this kind of mess. Lucy once told him that in the future they'd grow hamburger in vats. Protein coils that looked like burger and tasted like burger but didn't come from a cow and didn't require all the resources a cow requires to make meat. They'd grow it, like a mushroom.

"Paul Wise," he said, his eyes still on the table, "isn't coming back. You can tell his wife that. I think it's safe to say."

"Isn't coming back because he's left town or because he's dead?"

Raymond Byrd continued, his eyes still on the table between them. "I didn't *see* what they did to him... But I heard, I could hear what... So. To answer your question, detective... I have not seen the body, alive or dead, of Paul Wise since that time, since I saw him in the basement of the Drammond House. But if what I *heard* was an indication of what happened to Wise... then I'd say the man is not coming back *not* because he's skipped town." He looked the black man in the eye.

"Can you take us to where this happened?"

"I can."

"Would you be willing to do that?"

"Are you giving me a choice?"

The black man took a deep breath, sat back in his chair, slouched. He too looked worn out. Quietly he said, "Why not make it easy on yourself, Ray?"

"Easier for you, you mean."

That elicited a smile in the black man. His superior, Sergeant Suzuki, came off as no-nonsense. The man never smiled. But this one, you could see it, liked to argue. He'd been quiet most of the day. He'd interrupted Byrd a few times, wanting some explanation. But that was logical and tactical. The impression he otherwise gave was of a man who knew how to listen carefully and to wait his turn. And now, for a minute, he was getting his chance.

It seemed so casual. It wasn't, and Byrd knew that. It would go on and on and on until they got him to say what they wanted him to say, exactly as they wanted it said.

"You think this is easy, Ray?" said McNeal. "You think there's an easy way and a hard way to do this?"

Raymond Byrd said nothing.

"Let me tell you something," said McNeal, leaning back, his eyes rising up to the ceiling, a corner of the room. "Now that you've said your bit, my turn. Listen," he said. "Think of it like this. For you nothing is going to be easy. It's hard or it's harder. For us, it's all the same. What we do is try and find missing people. That's in theory. In practice, as I'm sure you can imagine, it's something else. Some we find, many we don't. But before that, you know, in order to get to that point where we can say he's here or there, or she's not coming back... before that, you know, it's basically a lotta shit to go through. The problems people have – their lies, their anger, and then more lies, and more anger. It never ends. All the shit, toxic waste of life. Day in, day out. You wouldn't believe it. You'd think someday, cleaning up after all these people, you'd find a gem. Something to go on. Something to *help you* understand what makes people click... No way. There's no explaining it. No bottom to it. It just goes on and on... Now is that to say things are easy or hard for us? I don't think so. You get used to it. It's like purgatory, Ray. All this wickedness. And still," he said, clasping his hands together under his chin, "nothing extraordinary. Normal people – you, me,

Suzuki – they do stupid things. You put them in a situation, light the fuse, see what happens." The black man shook his head. "But there is one important difference between you and me – if you're thinking the monotony of what I have to go through is anything like the so-called choice you're being asked to make. And that is this. I get to go home at the end of the day. I get to sit on my deck and look at the Pacific and not think about anything, for a minute, too heavy. I can just sit there and watch the waves come in and go out and," he said, touching his temples, "let everything out. Put all of this behind me for an hour or two. Drink a beer. Invite a girl over if I want company. – But *you*... Let's talk about the future, Ray. Let's talk about this loneliness you've described. I would say – and I think you'll agree with me on this – I would say that in the coming years you won't be thinking much about loneliness anymore. Because you'll have lots of company. You'll have company all the time. Men like us, these fellas you've seen here today – police, investigators... not to mention *the shrinks*, the doctors... And when they're gone there'll be others to take their place. A whole line of them, *crowds* of them. So many men like us you'll think back on these days, this place, fondly. When you could wake up, make yourself a cup of coffee, sit and talk to your cats and think about all the women you'd like to lay and not be disturbed by... I... I get sidetracked so easily... And the things I've heard... Listen, Ray. For the remainder of your life, the way this is going, you'll always have company. Good company.

If that's what you want. Always have *at least* one other fella around. In a cell in Pelican Bay, smaller than this room, some angry dumbfuck gangbanger sleeping right there in your face. For the rest of your life... And you talk about being alone? Man." The detective shook his head. The corner of his mouth rose, his cheek dimpling in a hesitant smile. "And the *women*," he said. "Needless to say, none of those where you're going. And what *will* you do then?"

WRONG! Raymond Byrd was thinking, looking into Mc-Neal's pleasant carefree face. It wasn't between hard and harder he was being asked to choose from. It was between one impossibility or another.

Those women, those men, everyone who went into the Drammond House and didn't come out – *they're not coming back!* And no amount of detective work, no amount of questioning and clever argumentation was going to change that fact.

Bring them up there, *take them to the place beneath the house* where you last saw Paul Wise –

It would mean the end of everything, all of them.

He wanted to say: "Sitting on that deck, watching the Pacific, the waves come in, night falling, stars in the sky. You remember that. Hold onto that, McNeal. Because if we go there, to the house..."

He closed his eyes. Joseph Manning's face was there, small and distant, at the bottom of a pit.

He said: "I'll take you. I'll show you."

"Excellent," said McNeal, clapping his hands once, smiling brightly as he rose to his feet.

~ 2 ~

His room was a cell. Like many rooms, it had four walls and a door, but it was a cell all the same. A short narrow bed took up most of the space. There was a toilet and a sink. A small, slightly used bar of soap. A roll of toilet paper balanced on the edge of the sink. The door had a small square window in it.

Not long after they showed him to the cell, and he'd closed the door, the fluorescent overhead light went out.

The door remained unlocked. He opened it once to look into the hall, where lights remained on. The hall was empty, quiet. There were other cells in the hall. He wasn't sure if they were occupied.

He slept surprisingly well. The temperature in the room was comfortable. And the place, until early the next morning, was without a sound.

He woke up suddenly from a deep sleep. There was a commotion down the hall, in the station. Men shouting. Then it was quiet, as if everyone had gone outside, left the place.

The light in his room flickered and went on. A minute later he heard someone in the hallway, walking toward his cell. Then Sergeant Suzuki said through door, "Mr Byrd? Are you awake?"

"I'm here."

Byrd opened the door. Suzuki and McNeal, side by side, stood waiting in the hall. McNeal's eyes were terribly bloodshot. Suzuki, who looked exactly as he had the day before, said: "Come with us."

They went back to the interrogation room. Suzuki took a seat at the table and lit a cigarette. Byrd sat down across from him. McNeal came in the room with two small cups of coffee. He set one before Byrd. The other he drank loudly.

Suzuki smoked and stared at Byrd. Then the sergeant sat up straight, leaned forward over the table, and said, "You haven't heard but this morning, two hours ago, there was a terrorist attack in New York." The man watched Byrd, waiting for a reaction. "They hijacked airplanes and flew them into the Twin Towers. Nothing is confirmed. But they're saying thousands of people are probably dead."

Byrd sipped his coffee, thought about what the man was saying. He didn't understand. It sounded like a movie he'd heard of. But Suzuki, if he'd heard him right, wouldn't make something like that up, and would have no reason for saying such a thing. "Who was it?"

"I'm telling you this," said the sergeant, "because you'll hear it from the others. They're going to be excited. It doesn't matter. I need you to do some things for me. And then, for the time being, you'll be free to go. If you know people in New York, you can call them then."

The sergeant and his assistant watched Byrd drink his coffee. When he was finished, McNeal brought him his jacket, and guided him down a hallway. The sergeant followed behind. The three of them passed through a door at the end of the hall and stepped outside into a parking lot. It was early morning, the sun still low in the east.

Suzuki's Mercedes was directly in front of them. McNeal opened the back door of the car and the sergeant climbed in.

McNeal said to Byrd: "Sit in front." Byrd did as he was told.

But McNeal didn't get in the car right away. He went back into the station.

The sergeant, seated directly behind Byrd, lit a cigarette. He tapped Byrd on the shoulder with a pack of Marlboros. Byrd took the pack, took a cigarette, handed the pack back over his shoulder. The sergeant handed him his lighter.

The two men smoked in the cool silence of the Mercedes. Byrd looked at the golden blue sky over LA. It was empty, clean, infinite.

McNeal appeared a minute later. He quickly got in the Mercedes, started it, and pulled away. They were on I-5 in no time. There was no traffic. LA was behind them in twenty minutes.

At one point on their way up to the Drammond House, McNeal turned on the radio, spun across the dial. He stopped on the news. The reporter sounded out of breath, frightened. Apparently it was true, what Suzuki had said. The Twin Towers, in Lower Manhattan, had collapsed. The place was on fire, in total chaos. Body parts everywhere, it could be inferred from what the reporter said.

"Turn that off," the sergeant said.

McNeal turned the dial and the radio, with a click, went dead. The hard steady purr of the car's engine filled the cab. They were doing ninety, easily. There was hardly another car on the road.

The village of Mojave, where he'd stopped with Marianne so many months ago, came and went. Only approaching Maiden did McNeal slow down. Then, following the narrow, winding road up into the mountain, Rosalee's Diner came into view. The sergeant said, "Pull over. I'm hungry."

McNeal parked the car outside the diner. There was only one other car, a Ford F-250, in the small lot.

The sergeant said: "I'd prefer going in alone."

McNeal nodded, his eyes on the man in the rearview mirror.

The sergeant got out of the car and made his way to the diner's entrance. He pushed open the door and went inside. From the Mercedes, McNeal and Byrd watched the sergeant take a seat at the counter, and saw the redhead waitress, the one Byrd had described, Jillian was her name, come down the counter and talk with the Japanese man in the black jacket.

There didn't appear to be any other customers in the diner. The waitress and the sergeant talked for a long time, for much longer than one would expect, given the situation. The man wasn't ordering coffee. At one point the waitress opened her mouth in surprise or shock, covered her mouth with both hands, shaking her head, closing her eyes. The man made a gesture in the air over the counter. Then both appeared to be quiet, their eyes down. Then the man said something and the waitress smiled suddenly, and then she laughed, once again covering her mouth with her hands.

The sergeant's shoulders shook, as if with laughter, but the two men in the car couldn't tell what exactly he was doing. His back was to them.

McNeal turned the radio on. The reception was terrible. He spun the dial. He stopped on what might have been a news station. There was static. Through this a woman was crying, talking incoherently.

They listened for a minute, trying to understand what the woman was saying, what the story was about, waiting for details about New York. Then McNeal turned the radio off. He took a deep breath.

"He's taken a particular interest in this case," he said. The leather of his seat crackled as he shifted his weight. "In this house that eats people up."

Byrd wanted to correct the man but didn't say anything. He tapped his pockets. They were empty. He looked at McNeal. "Got a cigarette?"

McNeal was staring at him. "I don't smoke."

Byrd looked at the detective in the corner of his eye. They watched the sergeant and waitress talk inside the diner.

"He had a kid," McNeal said. "A little girl. Yoshiko. She disappeared in nineteen eighty-five, when she was six. Someone took her. They were at the supermarket. He took his eye off her for a moment. And next thing he knows, she's gone. He was already with the force then, a patrolman. The police did everything they could. To help him – as a father, but also as one of their own. That didn't change anything. The kid was gone. Without a trace... I guess we almost lost him. He really... It's only what I've heard, understand. But can you imagine? *Your child.* You raise this little girl. She's a baby, then she's a person. A little girl, you know. Seeing her grow, dreaming of her future. Then it's taken away from you – *just like that*... A month goes by, nothing. Six months. Nothing. Statistically speaking, at that point she's never coming back. Very seldom does it happen. Doesn't mean the girl's *dead.* Just that probably, very probably, we'll never see her again."

Raymond Byrd closed his eyes.

"But is that any different," McNeal said, "to the father, the mother? Dead or never seeing her again... They're very different, if you think about it. If she were dead, and they knew this was the case, because they had a body, then – well – maybe they could look ahead. Bury her. Try and forget it. But not knowing if she is or not... Think about it."

Raymond Byrd glanced at the man next to him. McNeal was watching the diner, his eyes on the sergeant inside. Byrd thought: "I'll get out of the car, get some air, get a cigarette from the sergeant. I don't need to hear this."

"The man didn't sleep *for years*," McNeal said.

"Why are you telling me this?"

"For *years*," McNeal went on, "he searched for his daughter. He'd work, sure, come to work like a zombie. Do what was asked of him. But then he'd go back, back to his own mission, this search. Didn't sleep. Years and years he's looking for her. But then, you know, he had to stop. His wife left him, went back to Japan. He was all alone, killing himself with this obsession. So he accepted the situation for what it was. Accepted the fact that his little girl was gone and never coming back, accepted the fact that he would never, ever find out who it was who took her, who did that to her, did that to them, to *him*... Then one time he thought he saw her. You believe it? And of course it would happen like that. He's accepted the fact that she's gone. He's moving on. When one afternoon, in the parking lot outside the supermarket, the *same* market where she disappeared five years before, he thinks he sees her. This girl getting into a car. He goes after her, wanting to see her face, wanting to be sure. He's like a mad man. Scares the hell out of the girl's mother, who's also in the car... It's not her. Figment of his imagination. You think about it long enough, hard enough, you begin to see what you want to see... Ghosts."

The sergeant came out of the diner. The waitress looked after him from behind the counter. Her eyes passed over the Mercedes but it didn't seem to Byrd that she saw him. Had the sergeant said anything about him?

Once the sergeant was back inside the car, McNeal started the engine and said, "We going the right way?"

The sergeant said nothing. Byrd turned, looked at McNeal, listened carefully for the man seated behind him. Then the sergeant said: "Yes. We are."

"What'd she say?" asked McNeal.

"To what?"

"To what you asked her."

"I asked her for directions," said the sergeant. "She gave me directions." McNeal pulled the car onto the two-lane road, pointed it up the mountain. "Sweet kid."

~ 3 ~

At the end of the driveway Byrd was surprised to see two LAPD cars, a cruiser and a truck, a K9 unit. Three uniformed officers stood by the cars. One of them, a stout Mexican man, had a German shepherd on a leash. The dog lay calmly at the officer's feet.

McNeal brought the Mercedes to a stop behind the police cruiser. The three men got out. Suzuki introduced the officers to Raymond Byrd. There was William Pearl, a thin young man with fine, whiteblond hair. He looked friendly but tired, the flesh beneath his eyes shaded and swollen. He'd done the night shift at the station. Byrd could only guess as to why he'd been asked to come along. Then there was Officer Tom Dobson, a middle-aged man with a round pock-marked face, a crewcut. He was expressionless behind sunglasses, black lenses. The Mexican officer was Jaime Ortiz. He smiled and said cheerfully, "And this is Tony," at which the dog raised its head and looked Byrd in the eye. It was a rather ambiguous move by the dog. Byrd was glad to see it on a leash. He'd never liked dogs, especially German shepherds.

Suzuki did all the talking. The officers, except for Ortiz, regarded Byrd in silence. They seemed tense, expecting the man to do something. Then they turned and faced the hillside, the woods, the ancient gate closed over the driveway. Officer Pearl went around to the other side of the cruiser and opened the rear door. A woman got out of the car. Long straight brown hair covered part of her face. She turned and looked at Byrd over the top of the police cruiser. Her right eye was black and blue, swollen closed. Her cheek was bruised, stone blue. A thick line of dried blood crossed the bridge of her nose.

Byrd blinked. He watched the woman come around the car, led by the police officer. He closed his eyes, uncertain. He opened them.

Charlotte Graham.

McNeal said to Pearl, "No need for those." The woman was in handcuffs. The men watched as Pearl removed the cuffs from the woman's wrists. She rubbed her wrists, touched her face. She looked at the ground.

"Charlotte," Ray said.

She glanced up at him but that was all.

Quietly Ray said, partly in wonder, partly as a question: "What'd they do – "

"Pure coincidence, Mr Byrd," said the sergeant, "that we should find this woman only a couple days before meeting you. An interesting story, hers, and one that, as I am sure you know, has a lot in common with what you've told us. I think that's a good thing."

Ray took a step toward Charlotte. McNeal dropped on a hand on his shoulder.

Reaching for the woman, Byrd said, "Who – "

Almost in a whisper, her eyes still down, she said: "It was Joseph."

"Joseph did this to you?"

The woman said nothing. She began to look up at Pearl but then hesitated, dropped her chin. Nobody spoke. It was cold in the mountains. Clouds high up in the atmosphere were beginning to cover the sky, the golden blue of the coast becoming a wet cement gray.

The woman said: "Can we get on with it? Let's get this over with, please."

The six men, dog, and woman went up the driveway in silence.

When it came into view, the Drammond House looked old and abandoned. Much of the front of the building, the porch, the steps, the long dark windows, was covered in dust, a thick layer of pollen and dirt and ash. Huge brown leaves rolled about the yard, collected in corners of the steps and to one side of the porch. Sam Gretton, the groundskeeper, had been neglecting his duties. Maybe he was away.

"This the place?" said Ortiz, looking the house up and down. The others looked at him in a mixture of despair and disgust. Even Tony, the German shepherd, seemed uneasy, pulling in different directions at the end of his leash, whining nervously.

Ortiz pulled sharply on the leash. "Cállate."

Suzuki and McNeal climbed the steps, approached the front door. McNeal raised the iron knocker in the mouth of the satyr and let it fall.

They waited. McNeal pounded his fist on the enormous front door. It made hardly a sound.

When the detective tried the door, it swung open in silence. There was the foyer, the entrance hall cast in shadow. Byrd could see the place where Martin Sanchez had been shot, where he'd fallen. The floor was clean.

They looked inside, through the open door.

Across the entrance hall, at the end of a long narrow passage, Raymond Byrd saw something flutter in the dim light, a shadow shift as if someone stood just around the corner, waiting, coming up to the edge to listen and then retreating a step.

Byrd came up to McNeal quickly. Suzuki, who stood in the entrance, turned, looked at the two men.

Byrd said to McNeal quietly: "Don't go in."

"We have to. We have no choice, Ray."

McNeal was a tall and handsome black man. He seemed, as best as Raymond Byrd could tell, like a thoughtful and level-headed man. In fact he'd never met a black man as patient and articulate as McNeal before. Was it Suzuki's doing? Or was it a result of the man's own efforts, his own self-discipline? *Sui generis.*

"Listen to me," said Byrd. He was now speaking between McNeal and Suzuki. "Please. Don't do this, don't go in there. Wait... At least get some back up."

Suzuki smiled, laughed deep in his chest. "Back up!" he said, giggling. "Listen to him," he said to McNeal. "Too many movies, you," he said, looking at Byrd.

"Why would we need back up, Ray?" asked McNeal.

Byrd held McNeal's gaze. "Haven't you heard anything I've said? Do you think I *made it all up* – what goes on in this place?"

The German shepherd was growling behind them, whining, pulling viciously at its collar, the leash. Ortiz, Byrd saw in a glance, had something in his hands, a small shirt that looked remarkably similar to something he'd seen Lucy in some time ago. A lavender blouse.

Byrd said to McNeal: "They won't come out. *You* won't come out. She only lets..."

Suzuki stepped into the house. The other men were coming up quickly, following. The sergeant said over his shoulder: "Bring him. We've wasted enough time. Move." Then he raised his voice, saying, "Officer Pearl! Bring Miss Graham up here. If Mr Byrd can't show us the way, maybe she can."

Byrd said, "But she's never been here before. She doesn't know!"

Officer Pearl and Charlotte entered the building. As she passed Raymond Byrd, Charlotte looked at him and hissed, "Why are you now so goddamn *reluctant* to go inside? Can't you see what they're doing? *They're giving it to you.*"

"Stay with me," Byrd said.

But she was already moving ahead, directly behind Officer Pearl, who seemed eager to keep up with the sergeant. She said, a quick glance back: "I'll take my chances."

"Charlotte!"

Byrd reached out for her. McNeal turned, wide-eyed, about to intervene.

The woman hissed, pulling back, sidestepping the man, her good eye flashing darkly: "Get away from me."

Raymond Byrd stopped, stood dead still. He'd seen his wife in the gesture. Heard her. It was happening again.

You'll lose her.

"Ray," said McNeal, who was waiting for him in the entrance hall. "We need you. I'm sorry, but... Now you have to show us where it happened. Where you last saw Joseph Manning, Wise, the others. We can't do this without you."

So they went into the Drammond House, the six men, the dog, the woman. It was a quarter to twelve, the morning of eleven September, two thousand and one.

Around three that afternoon, they emerged from the house, returning to where they started. Sergeant Suzuki moved stiffly, limping slightly, showing his age. He stood in the yard, lit a cigarette, looked up at the Drammond House. The sky was gray, heavy with cloud.

They found nothing inside. Not a soul.

They had entered what looked like a basement, a long series of windowless rooms beneath the house, but found nothing like the rock Raymond Byrd had described, nothing like the bath-house, the hot spring, nothing like the hole descending further into the earth.

The air outside had a cool scintillating quality. It was transforming, breaking from day, taking on night. The transition, Byrd knew, would be a quick one.

Tony, the German shepherd, lay on the ground behind Ortiz, putting the man between itself and the house. The dog didn't make a sound. Its black eyes flitted quickly one way, the other, noticing things only a dog could discern.

McNeal said: "Where's Pearl?"

They looked around in the halflight of the late afternoon.

William Pearl was not with them.

Charlotte Graham seemed particularly animated. She looked around frantically, going so far, before Dobson caught up with her, as stepping into the woods at the edge of the yard. "Billy!" they heard her cry. "Billy! Billy!"

Dobson brought her back. She was crying, pale. Dobson pushed her forward, to the sergeant. Suzuki, hardly moving, said to the woman, "He was with you."

"I know he was!"

"Where did he go?"

Charlotte faced the man, her grotesque black and blue eye turned up for all to see. Her shoulders rose and fell.

The sergeant was breathing hard. "When did you last see him!?" he snapped.

Meek, she said: "I don't know."

The sergeant looked at his men. "Who saw him last?"

The men looked at each other, at Raymond Byrd, at the ground, at the house. Nobody could say when William Pearl was last seen.

Suzuki was changing color, his cheeks flushed. He reached up, hooked a finger in his collar and pulled. McNeal placed a hand on the man's shoulder. The sergeant regarded his colleague, and then turned his gaze to the others, the men, one at a time, contemplating.

Something stirred inside the house. The people gathered in the yard, at the foot of the porch steps, caught their breath in unison, looked up. Was it wood, glass, something breaking far off in the house, something dropped? But then the house was silent. Suzuki turned quickly, facing Byrd, raising his hand for the man, about to say something, when Dobson said sharply: "There." The man pointed upward. Every head turned to see.

High up on the building, rising upward from a small window, was a thread of black smoke. Then the window, with a gentle, distant crash, broke, the pane shattering outward, shards of glass falling lazily through the cold air, landing on a terrace still many floors above them. Then a figure filled the window frame. It was a man. He was waving at them, calling to them. But he was so high up...

"Who is that?"

"Pearl?"

"That's not him. It's not him."

The man above them turned quickly, looking over his shoulder, into the building. And momentarily he returned inside, climbing back through the broken window.

"You know that man?" McNeal asked.

Byrd thought he did. The name wasn't immediately on his tongue. It seemed so long ago, as if from a different world, the experience of a different man.

But then the name was there, and he was about to say something when a flash of light up on the building blinded him, blinded everyone – their turning away, wincing and covering their faces in unison as a sheet of fire filled the sky above them.

The room the man had disappeared into exploded. The flames seemed frozen in the air; shards of glass and rubble from the house fell, slowing, holding photographically in the instant of recognition. Even the man, falling, his arms and hair ablaze, seemed to pause in flight, some odd contorted form in juxtaposition to the massive squareness of the building, before finally returning to life and finding its purpose, as it were, in falling.

Then, the moment before the figure fell out of view overhead into an unseen part of the house, Byrd recognized the man. That toothy, movie-star grin, the practiced, chiseled cheeks: Troy Beckmann, P.I.

The sergeant took out his pack of Marlboros. He was having trouble whipping a cigarette from the pack to his lip. McNeal reached out and helped the man. The sergeant smoked for fifteen seconds. Warm cinders, bits and pieces of the house drifted in the air around them. The sergeant said: "Dobson. Take Ortiz and the dog and go up. Find the man. Bring back what's left of him." The sergeant raised his arm in the air, the sleeve of his jacket sliding down his wrist. He looked at his watch. He said: "I give you forty five minutes."

The sergeant's men said not a word. With the dog they went into the house.

Suzuki, McNeal, Charlotte Graham and Raymond Byrd followed. In the entrance hall they saw Dobson and Ortiz ascend the main staircase to the second floor. Part of the floor wrapped around the entrance hall. The men followed this passage, moving quickly and silently. Tony, the dog, was out of sight. Then the men turned sharply and ascended another staircase. They disappeared momentarily. They reappeared behind a railing on the third floor. They were moving quickly, almost at a run. But they seemed smaller, and the light was dim. One had the impression that an optical illusion was at work: the faster the police officers ascended, the smaller they became.

On the fourth floor Dobson appeared to pause, looking at something on his left. The man stepped out of view.

Distantly they could hear Tony barking.

Suzuki led McNeal and the two suspects to the door he'd previously used in accessing the basement. At least it appeared to be the same door. It was quite easy to get lost inside the Drammond House. In fact it was a very, very large house. The sergeant hadn't understood this about Byrd's story. He'd thought the man had been exaggerating, at best, and more likely lying.

Before descending, Suzuki turned to the others. "Officer Pearl was with us when we were in the basement. I know he was because I saw him. He was with you. You and he were talking," he said to Charlotte. "What we need to do is to go back to the place where we last saw him. You will remember, Miss Graham, where this was. When we come to it again, you tell me." The sergeant blinked quickly. Then he was looking at none of them, but remembering, grasping in his thoughts. Quietly he added: "Help me, Miss Graham. We must find him. I can't do this on my own. We aren't leaving here without him."

With that, they took the stairs down.

~ 4 ~

They sense his strength, Raymond Byrd thought as he watched the things beneath the Drammond House quickly circle and dispatch McNeal.

Suzuki was gone. The Japanese man had been there one moment, at his shoulder, but was gone when next he looked. Vaguely Byrd recalled hearing the man say something, slowing down, falling back a step. Hardly a second passed. But it was all it took. The man was gone.

He and Charlotte, before they realized what was happening, found themselves separated by the horde. McNeal was yelling, walking backwards quickly, his eyes shining, wide with terror. He raised a gun, pointed it one way, the other, shouted warnings. Then he started shooting.

Charlotte was screaming, calling to Raymond from across the room. "Run!" he said. "To the stairs! Don't stop! Don't look back!"

Of course, *the stairs* could be anywhere. They hadn't dropped crumbs along their way. Nor unwound thread, as Ariadne had done to save the hero Theseus. (Or was it the other way around?)

They had been in the basement for a long time already.

Then again, as Byrd reflected on the matter – retreating at a run down a straight and narrow hallway, a dangerously smooth floor beneath his feet, the air growing cooler as he descended by the slightest degree further into the mountain – he'd never had a particularly hard time of it, finding ways out of the basement. There were certainly *many* ways out, and being alone, he thought to himself, running as hard as he could, as fast as he could move his soft feeble legs, was probably an advantage.

One had to act quickly, decisively, without deliberation. *That* was how to get out of the Drammond House. Company, the presence of others and their obligations, worked like a law of nature against this principle.

Hadn't Jillian said something about an exit via the old man's cabin? A tunnel connecting the house to the cabin?

It stretches out, everywhere, like this...

A vision of the waitress's hands opening before him. Such small, lovely, white, caring hands.

They were getting closer. He could hear them, the click of their nails on the floor, the wheezing laugh – *hey-hey-hey, hey-hey-hey* – they emitted in unison once excited, following him so closely the creatures could be just over his shoulder. And he could smell them, all of that filthy, grisly flesh, a dark mass of it, as if they slept as one, labored as one, ate as one, defecated as a single entity, its countless appendages reaching out with the indifference and ineluctability of roots over everything.

Still, the man was calm. The running helped. The straightness of the hallway, antidote to the chaos of the house, helped. So though his heart raced, his mind was level, empty.

The passageway came to an abrupt end. He nearly ran headlong into a cinder block wall. A finger of light overhead had given it away, caught his attention at the last second.

Through a hole in the ceiling of the chamber, just above his head, a medal ladder descended. He reached up, took hold, lifted himself, climbing.

They're getting closer –

The space was tight. He pressed his body up against the ladder, bowing his legs out like Charlie Chaplin for the proximity of the earth at his back.

The light he'd seen, an angled ray of it as he came closer, came through what looked like a small, square wooden door above him, through a hole in its edge where the wood had dried and warped with age.

"Sam!"

He struck the closed door with the side of his fist.

"Gretton! It's me! Open the door! *Open the door!*"

Then the creatures were below him, gathering quickly in the room. The air around him was filling with their heat, their stink, their clicking and clucking.

"Sam, please!"

It was just beneath him, the first of them – *Hehehehehe-hehehehe* – its claw scratching at his ankle, pulling at the fabric of his sock, the hem of his pants –

"SAM

The door above his head opened without a sound. The old man was there, his face an inch from Raymond's. Without a word the groundsman reached down, grabbed Byrd beneath the arm, and lifted, pulling, extracting the man from the hole and dropping him on the floor. As both men fell, Gretton kicked the trapdoor closed.

There was a key in the large brass lock of the door. The old man stood up quickly, took a deep breath, bent down, a hand on his knee as he drew the key from the lock. Then he stood over Raymond Byrd.

"Find what yer lookin' for?" he said.

"What?"

"Those women."

"Sam..."

Byrd was having a hard time catching his breath.

"What were their names again?"

The old man shuffled away, into the other room. Through the open door of the cabin Byrd could see the Drammond House, like a golden crown, up on the rise, atop the slope of the lawn. It was on fire, bright red and orange and black, blowing, blazing, reaching up into the night with its furious and mysterious energy. Dark figures, thin humanoid shadows, cut frantically in silence one way and then the other around the base of the house.

Marianne. What have I done?

When Gretton returned to the room he had a double barrel shotgun in his hands. He dropped in two cartridges, closed the breech with a loud snap. "It's Raymond Byrd," he said, "isn't it."

"It's me."

Byrd started to get to his feet.

Gretton said, swinging the gun his way, "Stay put."

The old man smacked his lips. He scratched his bristling chin.

Beneath the door in the floor, inches from where Byrd lay, a tapping, clicking sound.

"I remember a Mary," said the old man. "Was that it? The first?"

"Marianne was her name. Marianne Heaney. It was her idea – "

"Marianne. Right. You think I give a rat's ass whose idea it was?"

"But she wanted to – "

The old man stuck the muzzle of the gun in Byrd's face, and the man on the floor closed his eyes, became very quiet.

The thing behind the door in the floor knocked quietly at the wood, scratched at the metal lock.

Raymond Byrd was short of breath.

"You asked me once if I'd seen'er," the old man said.

"I did."

"You did, right out there. Remember that day? There was a leak. When was that, again?"

"It was February."

"That long ago?" The old man's eyes narrowed down the barrel of the gun. He was thinking, incredulous. "And I told you then that I'd seen her, that she'd come down and spoke to me."

"You did."

The old man's upper lip folded inward. "I lied to you Mister Byrd. I'm sorry to say. But I didn't see her that day. After you left. I just wanted you to get away, is all. To go back."

"You didn't..."

"I didn't see the woman. Haven't seen her since then, since you left. You shouldn't have been here in the first place! Yer friend running off like that."

Byrd didn't say a thing. He looked at the gun, at the old man's steady hands, his dark beady eyes.

"And then there was – the second one was – "

"Lucy was my wife."

"Your wife! Of course she was. The missus was fond of her, I must say."

"So you've seen her?"

Gretton blinked. Someone, a man, was shouting outside, up at the house.

"I haven't," said the old man. He added, "But I don't go into the house. Not unless I have to."

The thing behind the door in the floor struck the door sharply. It cackled, murmured to itself in its own language.

Byrd moved back, slid himself toward a wall of the cabin, his back up to a large low-slung leather chair. A book was open, face down, on it.

Gretton took a step toward him, the gun pointed at a relaxed angle between them. He said: "And then there was– "

"Sam, that's it. I didn't – "

"The young one. The redhead. Miss *Veldt*," said the old man with a yellow, toothy grin. "A favorite here."

"I never... I never."

The smile on the old man's face held for a moment and then withered. "Sure you did."

"I know the girl," said Byrd, "but I never came here with her."

The old man looked sincerely puzzled. "I could swear..." He scratched his freckled scalp.

Thump!

They could feel it in the floor, the creature striking hard at the wooden door.

Thump!

Byrd was sweating. His hands slipped over the floor as he pushed himself backwards, crablike. "Sam!" he said, "I don't think..." But he couldn't catch his breath, couldn't get the words out.

Gretton had an eye on the floor. He didn't seem too concerned.

Get away. Run. Don't look back!

Then the old man regarded the man on the floor, semblance of pity in the weary expression.

Bam! Bam!

The creature wanted out.

The old man said, raising his voice: "Why you think I let you outta there, Mr Byrd?"

"What?"

"You think I let you outta there for the kindness of my heart, Mr Byrd?"

"Sam?"

Bambambam!

The old man closed his eyes, opened them. He softly said: "Martin died."

"It wasn't me."

"*It wasn't you! It wasn't YOU! It wasn't YOUR idea - it was hers!*" the old man screamed, turning bright red. "Of course it wasn't your idea! Of course it wasn't you! Poor you, Raymond Byrd, *poor you*. All these women, making life so hard - "

"But you saw what happened. It was Joseph Manning. You saw it!"

"You brought him here."

"He... he..."

"You brought them all here."

Byrd could see the light of the fire outside flicker in the old man's dark eyes.

"I cared for Martin," said the old man. "I gave him..."

Gretton drifted off in thought, memories.

Take the gun. Now!

Byrd straightened himself, pressed his palms into the floor, drew his feet in, tightening, gathering strength. He'd have only one chance.

A woman's voice interrupted them. It said his name – "Raymond." – but so soft and sudden this utterance, he thought he'd imagined it, thought he was beginning to lose his mind.

But it spoke again, beneath the door in the floor: "Raymond."

Glancing up at Gretton, he saw the old man, his eyes wide with fear, watching him, his face transformed. "It's not her," he whispered.

"Raymond, let me out."

Charlotte!

"Raymond," she said quietly, her lips to the other side of the lock, "*please. Open the door.*"

"It's Charlotte," Byrd said, twisting, crawling on all fours to the door. "She made it," he said. "Give me the key. Open it. It's her!"

"It's not her."

Gretton had taken a few steps back. Byrd was almost on top of the door. He reached out, excited: "Sam, give me the key. I *know* it's her. We have to – "

"I tell you," said the old man, his hands beginning to shake, "that's not Charlotte." And then, hardly speaking at all, breathing the words: "It's *her.*"

"Raymond, please!" said the woman. "They're coming for me. *I can hear them. They're coming!*"

Byrd stood up, took a step toward Gretton. Up went the shotgun, the long black barrel stopping Byrd in his tracks.

"Give me the key, Sam! It's Charlotte! It can only be – "

The old man was shaking his head.

"Raymond! *RAYMOND!* Hurry!"

"Damn it, Sam! The key!"

The old man, keeping the gun upright between them, shuffled to the right, moving toward the entrance to the other room.

"*RAAAAY!*"

Byrd moved, cutting a hand through the air, striking the shotgun with the side of his hand, the barrel whipping to the side, as it fired.

Chips of molten cinders burned Byrd's arm, but the shot sprayed everything else behind him, breaking glass, incinerating the leather chair at his back.

His head was ringing painfully. He could see the old man's lips moving but he couldn't hear a thing.

Let me out!

The voice was in his head. He could feel it, her screaming, in the soles of his feet.

RAYMOND! OPEN THE DOOR!

He grabbed the shotgun with two hands and shoved the stock beneath the old man's arm into his side, wrenching the gun from his grip.

The old man threw up his hands, lowered his head. He was babbling.

Byrd turned the gun around, pointed it at Gretton's chest. "Give me the key," he said calmly, clearly.

"No."

"Sam! Give it to me!"

Byrd pressed the muzzle of the shotgun into the old man's chest. He realized that if he pulled the trigger he'd vaporize the man, he'd be digging through guts to find what he wanted.

Gretton kept his eyes on the floor. He shook his head. "No. No. No, no, no, no," he said. He looked Byrd in the eye. "It's not her. It's not who you think it is. You don't realize what – "

Byrd stepped in, raising the gun up, struck the old man in the side of the head with the stock.

Gretton cried out, clutching his head as he fell to the floor. Bright red blood ran over his fingers, pooling on the floor where he lay moaning.

Byrd knelt, set the shotgun down out of reach, stuck a finger into the old man's pocket. He took the key, spun about, pushed it into the lock.

Click.

"I told you," Gretton said. "I told you. I told him – ma'am, I told him!"

The old man lay prostrate on the floor, the side of his face covered in blood, his hands wet and dark with blood.

What rose from the hole in the floor was not Charlotte.

"I'm sorry, I'm sorry, I'm sorry," the old man was saying, his face against the floor. "Ma'am. Forgive me. Forgive me. I am your servant and I have failed you. Forgive me. Please..."

She turned to address Raymond Byrd but the little man was quick on his feet, and had fled into the night.

This was of no concern. Because he'd be back. And she'd deal with him then.

The man had exhausted his resources and was now, as usually happened, only a disruption.

The fire would burn out soon enough. Then they'd need to see about cleaning up and restoring what was destroyed. It would be significant, the damage.

Equipment, materials, and help, the housekeeper thought to herself, watching the Drammond House burn from Gretton's spartan living room.

Two, maybe three more girls. Temporarily. To Christmas. And another man, for inside.

"I'm sorry," said the old man.

He reached out, wanting to touch her foot.

She took a step back.

He, too, finally, it was sad to say, had exhausted his resources.

They had been together a long time.

The shotgun was much heavier than it looked. A terribly strange instrument, up close. All the hinges, levers and locks, hidden buttons. So much steel. The neck was warm, which made her think all sorts of things. She pressed it to her cheek. She had never, in all her years, held a shotgun before.

A man's tool, after all.

"There is one last thing you can do for me, Sam."

~ 5 ~

He ran down the hill through the woods. Branches cut at his face, his body. Roots tripped him up. When he fell, he scrambled to his feet without a word and continued desperately on, furious to get away from the place, the woman.

Somewhere in the darkness a gun discharged.

It didn't slow him. Nor did the impression in his peripheral vision of something running hard beside him in the trees slow him down. Some low four-legged creature leapt through the underbrush. Sprinting, gasping for air, as desperate as the man to escape.

The dog. Tony –

A moment later the trees fell back behind him and he found himself tumbling head over heels down an embankment. His arms out, he caught himself, skidding to a stop, cutting open the palms of his hands, on a broken paved road. He'd split his lip, his mouth full of blood and dirt and gravel.

He was on his feet in an instant, running.

I'll die –

The words crept up in his consciousness, breaking the surface like toxic fumes, spirits released.

- if I stop, die if I -

He took a deep breath, quietly focused his attention on a point in the road ten feet ahead, concentrated on the rhythm and exertion in his legs, the fire in his muscles, his back, his feet.

Don't stop, don't stop, don't stop -

Around a bend, the cars appeared in the darkness, at the edge of the road, the police cruiser, the truck, the Mercedes parked in a line. Cold pine-dusted metal.

The doors were locked. Even had it been otherwise, the men took the keys.

He was about to continue down the road. He'd run all the way to Maiden, find a place to hole up for the night.

Tony, Ortiz's dog, sat waiting on the other side of the truck. It whined, raised a paw, scratched at the door.

"I don't have the keys."

The dog barked gently, seemed to smile at the man.

"I can't open it without the keys."

The dog barked more violently then, loudly, repeatedly. Again it scratched at the truck's passenger side door, digging its nails shrilly into the metal.

Byrd took a step back, down the hill. The dog wouldn't attack him, he thought. Still, he wasn't sure what to do.

If I run?

He walked backwards away from the dog, away from the cars, down the hill.

But Tony wasn't going anywhere. He'd stay at the truck. He barked at Byrd, as the man moved away, but, unable to speak, did nothing else.

When Byrd turned and started to run, he left the dog barking in the night, wanting its master, wanting company, attention, but incapable of finding these. It would wait at the truck until morning. Then it would either go back to the Drammond House and find its way inside and search for Ortiz, who would never turn up, or it would wander down to Maiden and befriend some of the humans there into feeding it and caring for it. It wouldn't be the first time a lost and hungry dog wandered into town.

There was a light on in the diner. Jillian Veldt sat at the counter, in the same place Suzuki had sat hours before. She was drinking a beer, reading a book. Her back was to the door. The door was locked.

He rapped on the window. The waitress jumped in her seat, spun around.

She set the book down on the counter, came to the door, slid the bolt, opened the door.

"That was fast."

He was breathless. His mind went blank. He stared at the girl uncertain about what was happening, what she had said.

He staggered into the diner. When he reached for her his hand was shaking. His legs were unsteady. She took his hand, helped him toward the counter.

According to the clock over the door, it was a few minutes past ten.

She went around the counter, opened a small fridge. She set two Coors on the counter, opened them. She drank from one, leaned back, considered the man seated at the counter. He looked awful. Scratched and bloody, exhausted, frightened.

Byrd lifted the beer but didn't drink. He felt like a man in a foreign country, seeing things for the first time in his life.

The paperback on the counter was titled *Do Androids Dream of Electric Sheep?*

The words came suddenly, logically. "The hell kind of title is that?" he said, pulling the book over, flipping through its yellowed pages.

The girl shrugged, smiled.

He took a long drink from the beer. "What's it about?"

"Robots that look like humans."

"They dangerous?"

"Some are. Others," she said, leaning over the counter, flashing cleavage, smiling, laying it on thick, "just want some loving kindness."

He didn't follow. He drank, closed his eyes. He saw in his head Gretton lying on the floor, his head covered in blood, a shadow coming over them.

I told you.

He said: "What'd you mean – when I came in you said, 'That was fast.' What was fast?"

She stood up straight, said flatly: "The detective asked me about you."

"Suzuki."

"The Chinese guy."

"Japanese."

"Whatever. He asked me about you. Asked if you had stopped by here. You know."

"And you said?"

"... I said I knew who you were. That we'd met a couple times."

"And?"

Jillian raised a shoulder.

They drank their beers in silence.

Then Byrd said: "You didn't answer my question. You said, 'That was fast.'"

The girl closed her eyes, opened them. Her face lowered, suddenly tired, old. "I saw the cars go by. Earlier. The police. And then – you can smell it – the fire. So you ..."

"Guy named Troy Beckmann started it. He was trapped inside."

"Oh. Him."

"What's that supposed to mean?"

"Piece of work, that one."

"You knew him?"

"He stopped by." She drank, finished her beer. "Ray," she said, leaning into the counter, "they all stop by."

The waitress reached down, took out two more beers, opened them one after the other. She took a long drink.

Byrd was thinking, trying to put the pieces together. It was something the old man had said, something about Jillian, about his connection to her.

He thought you went up there with her, brought her there.

"Someone was coming down tonight," she said. "With all that action. No question. Someone'd be coming down."

"So you were waiting?"

Again, she shrugged. Apart from the blind old woman she had to feed at home, the girl had nothing else to do after dark.

So she comes back to the diner to sit alone and read. Wait for some passerby to see the light on, come and knock. And then what?

"I'm glad it was you," she said. "But I knew it would be."

"How's that?"

She drank. She went to the end of the counter, took a hoodie off the coatrack there. Keys jingled. She flipped a switch and the lights went out.

"Come on," she said, going to the door. "I'll give you a lift."

He followed. He said: "But how did you know it would be me? What if ..."

Would she be having this conversation with McNeal? Dobson? Was she like some kind of gate keeper for the house, some – *what's his name?* – carrier of souls from one world to the next?

They went through the door. She turned and locked it. They walked through the dark under the trees to her Ford.

There was smoke in the air. In his imagination – because the mountain was dark, the night sky impenetrable – he saw trees exploding into fiery pillars, saw level upon level of the house blazing black and red and orange, folding, tearing, crying, crumbling inward upon itself.

She turned the ignition, gave the cold motor gas and then let it idle.

"You're good to her," she said.

"To Kearn?"

"And she likes you."

"Not any more. Or not for much longer."

Jillian turned in the dark of the cab, looked at the man. She'd heard similar things many times before.

He said, feeling her scrutiny, unsaid questions, "You weren't there, Jill. You didn't see what happened."

Jillian waited. Would the man go on, explain, tell his story? No. He lowered his head, closed his eyes.

Quietly, she said: "She wouldn't have let you go, Raymond, if she didn't know you'd be back."

"I won't go back."

"Yes you will."

"I won't!"

Jillian wasn't going to argue with him. There was no point. Words didn't matter where destiny was concerned. And he wasn't going to listen, anyways. Come to grips with what had happened, what was going to happen.

Men, she found, had a harder time of it.

She drove him down to Mojave. He said he'd take a cab. But the village was empty, completely abandoned. No cabbie from the city would come out at this hour.

Without a word she drove on. An hour later, in San Fernando, she pulled off, stopped in a bright and empty Walmart parking lot. It was 1:30. Across the street a bar, The Green Door, was still open.

They sat in silence for a minute. Huge halogen street lamps buzzed overhead.

"I'll call a cab there... Thanks for the ride."

He started to get out.

"Buy you a drink, at least," he said. He didn't look at her as he spoke. Eyes down, some strange embarrassment coming over him. "After everything you've done."

She snorted. "Sure. Why not."

She had a cocktail, a tiny red umbrella balanced at its rim. He had a beer and whisky. They looked the place over – it was warm and sparkling and colorful, all plastic and kitchy – but didn't say a word. She used the toilet. He called a cab.

He walked her back to the truck. She said: "So where you off to, where's home? You never told me. I don't even have your number."

He liked the girl. She was subtle, operating on many levels. But sensitive, too. Right where you wanted her. When everything else in the world was breaking down, there she was, open hands.

"Maybe it's best we keep it that way," he said.

She was swinging her keys around and around on her index finger.

He went on. "*Aurevoir*, angel," he said, hearing himself, wondering for an instant who it was saying these words. She'd done something to him. "I don't think we'll ever see each other again. And if anyone asks, I'll say we never met. And you say the same. Ray *who*? You never knew me. But nobody'll ask. There's nobody left."

She snorted, gave him a crooked smile, said, "I wouldn't be so sure." She climbed into the Ford, rolled the window down. She lit a cigarette, leaned her elbow on the sill. "What about the detective? The Japanese guy."

"He's not coming back."

"Then the others. That woman."

"What woman?"

"What's her name – the one with the painter fellow. The tall one."

Byrd felt his heart slow, skip a beat.

Subtle.

"Charlotte?"

"That's the one."

"You saw her?"

The girl drew on her cigarette, said exhaling, her voice grinding: "No. It was something the detective said. Mentioned her."

"What about her?"

"I dunno."

"No, what'd he say?"

"All I'm saying is... Sometimes they get out. The women."

She turned the ignition. Finished her cigarette, twisted it out in the ashtray in the dash. She faced Byrd one last time, held him in her gaze, those cool blue eyes.

The man wanted to disappear. She could hear that in him, sense that. Rightfully so. He thinks he's lost everything, given up everything. Thinks he needs to change his name, move to another country. They all do, at some point.

You only think you have nothing left to give.

But Raymond Byrd, like all men, had resources, energy, a depth of spirit he was not even aware of.

"Don't be a stranger," she said and pulled away.

Something had come over her in those last moments. She seemed sad, far away, much older than her years.

He wondered momentarily if he'd ever see her again. He thought it was unlikely.

When he got in the cab he realized he wouldn't have enough for the fare. He asked to stop at an ATM. The cabbie cut across the street, pulled quickly into the parking lot Byrd had just left. There was an ATM outside the Walmart.

At a couple minutes to three the cab pulled up in front of his place. He paid the man, got out, went inside.

And stepping through the door, closing it, he knew immediately that something wasn't right, that what Jillian had said had been on the mark.

It spreads out. Like this!

The girl's lovely, open hands. Those strong fingers.

The Drammond House wasn't done with him. Not yet. Not by far.

~ 6 ~

There was a man sitting in the dark at his kitchen table. But it wasn't the black heaviness of this figure that first caught his attention. It was the grinding sound of his old cat. It was purring. It never purred.

He touched a switch in the wall. A shaded bulb over the table flickered on.

Max Abergast, the P.I.'s assistant, sat there, a bottle of Macallan whisky opened on the table, a half full glass at hand, and the old cat, sleeping ecstatically, in his lap.

"You've good taste," said the man.

Byrd didn't know what to say. He was very tired, too tired to be angry or surprised by the man's presence. Deep in his soul he felt disgust for the man, how he'd gone into his liquor cabinet, pushed everything aside, looking in the back for this one unopened bottle. Who does something like that? "I was saving that for my anniversary," he said. "Ten years!"

"Hmm."

Abergast finished his drink, set the glass down. He poured himself another. He gently stroked the cat's back. "What's a ten-year anniversary called?" he said. "Feel like

I should know that one." The man thought for a moment, raising his glass. Then he looked at Byrd and said: "But since that's off the docket, what's the point? Wisdom," the P.I.'s assistant started up, "is the capacity to distinguish what's fundamental from what's not. And to then let everything, all of it, the fundamental and the extraneous, go." He sipped his drink, licked his lips, sat back, went on: "To realign objectives according to changing circumstances." The man nodded his head approvingly.

Byrd didn't move. He stood there stooped, dumbfounded, as animated as a saguaro cactus.

"Drink?" Abergast finally said.

"That'd be nice."

Byrd dropped into the chair across the table from the man.

Abergast came up with a second glass. He took his time pouring it half full. With his fingertips he pushed the glass across the table.

"Terrible, what happened," he said.

Byrd drank his anniversary whisky. If you didn't know him, you might assume the man was thinking of his wife or ex, remembering the good times, the bad. All those years. But Byrd's mind in that moment went blank. The whisky, like a candle in a cave, warmed his heart, offered a point of feeling. Otherwise he felt dead inside, a mummy buried thousands of feet down.

He opened his eyes, looked at the man across from him.

"In New York," Abergast said.

"I'd almost forgot."

The P.I.'s assistant nodded, his upper body rocking back and forth. The old cat in his lap groaned, raised its fat head to the edge of the table, eyes pressed tightly closed. The man said: "Probably better if you had. S'not something to dwell on. All those dead. You haven't seen the pictures, I take it."

Byrd sipped his drink. He was hardly listening to the man. New York? Was it *thousands*, they'd said? It seemed like a different time, different era, what was now yesterday, only a few hours ago. His sitting in the car with Mc-Neal outside Rosalee's.

"The president is coming out blaming Saddam Hussein," Abergast said. He studied Byrd, the man's posture, expression, his hands.

Byrd finished his drink. He looked down into his lap, at his dirty pants. He scratched at a spot of blood on his jeans. His stomach was a cauldron, hot embers burning bright inside.

He's come for you. This is it. He's not going to let you go.

"Whatta you want, Abergast?"

"So you go to this house."

"What house is that?"

"This place in the mountains. *Drammond*, they call it. Funny name."

"I've heard of it."

"But you've been there. Several times."

"So?"

"That's where you take them."

"... So?"

Abergast spoke slowly, whisky dulling the edge: "But they don't come out."

Byrd shut his eyes. He was hearing things.

Abergast leaned back, casually twisted the end of his mustache with his free hand. Then he lifted his drink, tossed it back, set his empty glass down. "You take me for a fool, Byrd?"

Byrd reached out, turned the bottle around, poured himself a healthy drink. "I don't take you for much," he said. "But whatever I came up with, no, I wouldn't say you were a fool."

"I *know* these things," the man said, his face flattening out, spreading out, darkening as it lowered out of the light, "and soon – "

"You know these things. Whatta you know, tell me – "

"Know that you took – " It surprised Byrd, the gesture the man then enacted, his ten-year anniversary whisky beside him like a silly prop, a bottle of colored water: the man raised his right hand, a fist over the table and started, with each finger, enumerating his points. "You took, one, a woman named Marianne Heaney up there." He shot a look across the table: "She didn't come back." Then: "Two. You brought *your wife* up there." Another eye-thrust. "She didn't come back." The man didn't blink. "Three. Paul Wise. The lover. ... *He* didn't come back."

Abergast lowered his eyes to the table. He slipped down an inch in his chair, his shoulder slumped. His three points made, he looked suddenly, strangely, defeated.

The old cat tumbled loudly from the man's lap. It landed on its feet, shook its head to clear the stars, and lumbered off sulking.

Byrd thought it over. There wasn't anything there that Beckmann himself didn't know. And the P.I.'d told him. Simple.

So why's he here?

Abergast filled his glass, held it up, stared at it as if it might whisper secrets, lift the fog from all the great mysteries of the universe.

"Your point being," said Byrd.

The man raised his eyebrows, glanced upward. He took a deep breath and said:

"You killed your wife, Mr Byrd. You thought about doing it. And then, Paul Wise comes along, you had your motive. So you killed her and you left her at this place in the mountains. Or maybe you just buried her in the woods out there. Doesn't matter. In the parlor or the garden, dead's dead, the poor thing's gone, not coming back. But the lover does. Stops by one day. As you probably expected him to. Solution's simple. Get him up there, deal him the same. So you do. Then Troy Beckmann comes knocking. Since the wife, Wise's, doesn't believe her fella would just pick up and leave like that. She thinks, justifiably, that you've done something. And Lucy, we find out about that time, also happens to be missing. Doesn't take a rocket scientist, Byrd, to see what's what."

Byrd heard what the man was saying. It made sense, however wrong it was. He wanted to argue but lacked the will. At the same time, the accusation – that he'd killed Lucy – hurt in a profound way. He said: "Marianne. You think I killed her too?"

One of Abergast's rubbery cheeks bent upward in a halfsmile. "No," he said. "You didn't do that, because..." He ran the tip of his index finger around the rim of his glass. "It's an interesting case, to say the least."

"You think she's in on it."

"Troy told me about this woman."

Byrd's heart stopped momentarily. He felt all the blood drain from his face, his brain. A sudden emptiness inside his stomach, beneath him, like the floor had vanished and he was falling –

"It's not Marianne," he said quietly.

"At the house, the woman who runs the place – "

"*That's not Marianne!*"

Abergast paused, drew back an inch. "Whoever she is," he said, "seems to me she's the one we oughta talk to. Don't you think?"

The P.I.'s assistant waited. He didn't move a muscle. When Byrd didn't respond, he said again: "Don't you think we should have a little chat with this housekeeper lady?"

"I'm not going up there."

"Yes you are. Tonight. You're taking me. We'll be there for sunrise."

"I'm not going up there. I'm not taking you, not anyone. Take yourself." Byrd thought for a moment. He added: "Let Troy show you the way."

Abergast's lip twitched. "Troy's gone."

Troy's dead, burned alive! He fell a thousand stories!

"Wha'do you mean he's gone?"

Abergast emptied his glass, gritted his teeth, squeezed the glass and then set it down without a sound. He said: "In August I saw him. Was a few days after my birthday, I remember. Because my boy had come over. My son, he's grown now, younger than you, but he's got all these problems. I think he's a drug addict. He tries, he's trying. Anyways, I never see him, and he comes around, which was actually nice. That he'd remember his old pop. We went to see the Dodger's." Abergast smiled, dropped his chin, eyes on the table. "Anyways, the phone rings late one night, wakes me up. It was, well, about this time. Three. Halfpast three. I was thinking, you know, it's him, Carl, he's in jail or the hospital or worse. Just *a feeling* I had, you know. So I pick up. And it's Troy... Says he has to see me. *Now?* I'm sleeping, right. I mean, if it was Carl... It's this case, this *house,* he says. He's losing it, you know, coming undone, practically *crying* in the phone. So he comes over. He looks different. Frightened. I mean... It's like..." The man raised his hands, touched the sides of his face, the corners of his gray eyes. "I'd seen him just a couple days before, I don't know – a week before – and he seemed fine, his normal self. He told me the... But now... He's all *hollowed* out, traumatized, you know. And Troy, I've known him a long time, since he was a kid really... He's scared of nothin'. He's a tough kid. You wouldn't know it, lookin' at him, I know. But he is. Thick skin on him. But now he's different, all shaken up. I ask him to tell me what's going on, what he found... But all he could say was... This... There's this woman."

Abergast clenched a fist, stared at it. He was shifting, losing the advantage.

Troy's your ticket.

The man laughed once, sadly. He cleared his throat. He went on. "And then he left. The next day. He went back up there. He said he'd... he'd met this gal. Some kid. She'd shown him around. Taken him to the house. Only... only... When he left, she... He said he couldn't find her. Said he was going back to get her, to find her and get her outta there..."

Byrd listened to the man with one ear. In another part of his brain he was building something, setting things up. "The journalist, you mean," he said.

"Not her," Abergast said, shaking his head. "She was... He..."

It was Jillian.

"You mean to tell me," Byrd said, reaching for the Macallan, filling his glass, "that your man went up there with a girl and came back alone. *Twice!* Lost two girls up there."

Abergast shook his head. If it was a denial, it was hardly convincing. "That's not what happened, not what I'm talkin' about."

"Seems to be spreading. Whatever it is. Listen – "

"It's not like that at all," Abergast said, getting riled up, shaking his head quickly, closing his eyes: "Missus Wise, Byrd. Lydia Wise!... Journalists! Fuck the journalist, Byrd, he had them lined up out the door. Yes, sure, her too, but fuck it. *Missus Wise.*"

The P.I.'s assistant leaned back in his chair, his head in shadow, took a deep breath, directed his gaze at the man in the dimness across from him.

Byrd started to speak. Abergast cut him off. "Yes, *that woman.* And he went back for her. And now he's gone. I think he was in, I don't know, two Saturdays ago. The window was open. But I didn't see him. And I haven't heard from him since."

Every one of these people brings me back to the house. They keep me from leaving. If I'm to get away, I'll need to –

Abergast said: "You're taking me to that house."

"I won't. But – "

"I'm not asking, Byrd."

Abergast adjusted his weight. He lowered a hand, lifted a pistol out from under his coat, set this on the table before him.

Byrd stared at the gun, confused. It was the second gun he'd seen that night, the second gun he'd had pointed his way. Far back in his head, in a corner of his consciousness, he thought about odds. *Keep this up and yer gonna get shot before the sun's up.*

"What's that for?" he said.

"We're going to that house and finding Troy," the man said. He picked up the gun, leaned forward over the table, pointed the gun in Raymond Byrd's face.

Byrd lowered his eyes, looked into his lap. He scratched at the spot of blood on his thigh.

"I don't see what there's to think about," the man across from him said. "We go up there, find the man, come back. You're free. Never hear from me again. Or – "

"You expect me to believe that?"

Abergast winced. Lowering an ear, he said, "You don't think I'm an honorable man? I'm giving you the benefit of the doubt, son. What I *should* do is take you down to the precinct. Sit you down with them. You tell them your version of the story, I tell them mine. Who you think they're gonna believe?"

Byrd snorted. "They know everything already. They picked me up for questioning. Two days ago. This come as surprise to you? Guy named Tom Suzuki, a sergeant. We went up there today. Where you think I've been all day? If you're so smart, Abergast. Up there, at the house, with the police. They asked their questions. I answered them. And the people there, they explained everything... It's all copacetic. So listen, if it's not all wrapped up, it's not quite the mystery it was this morning. Furthermore, they let me go."

"Copacetic," the man said, looking aside, lowering the gun, sitting back, "where *the fuck*..." He looked Byrd in the eye. He grit his teeth, his mustache rising in a mean grin. "Meaning," he said, "they won't go looking for you. If you're so innocent. Let's go."

Take him! He wants to go!

The old cat growled somewhere in the darkness of the house.

"Okay," Byrd said. "But first I need to show you something. It'll help us find Troy."

"At the house?"

"It's a different place. The name Manning mean anything to you?"

Abergast rose to his feet quickly. He leaned into the table. He had the pistol in his right hand, at his hip. He stared at the seated man.

Byrd was suddenly sweating, nervous under Abergast's scrutiny. "Look, you got me," he said, putting his hands up, palms out, over the table. "I'll take you to the house. But first let me... I'll show you. There's a map. But we gotta go to this other place. Up the coast. It's not far."

After a moment Abergast said: "Okay. You drive."

Byrd stood up. He screwed the cork back into his anniversary whisky. The bottle was about a third full.

He shook his head, burning resentment coming up. "I can't believe you drank my anniversary whisky," he said.

"Get over it! What're you saving it for anyway!?"

Byrd opened the sliding glass door to the backyard. Cool night air washed over him. He wanted the cats to have a way out. He didn't think he'd be back any time soon.

~ 7 ~

Manning's place was dark and small on the hilltop. A Volvo and what looked like a brand new Lincoln Continental were parked in the yard.

Byrd carefully guided Max Abergast's VW Thing past the parked cars. He followed the trail straight down to the barn. The shocks on the VW were worthless. Decent enough for the well-tended streets of LA they were useless in moving over sandy and uneven ground. The two men bounced around like dolls inside the cab.

Byrd stopped the car outside of the barn and turned it off. He and Abergast sat in the car in silence.

Leaving the keys in the ignition, Byrd got out. "This way."

Inside the car, Abergast looked around patiently. It was a dark moonless night. The barn was situated near the bottom of a gully. Atop a hill to their left, south, was a stand of tall dreary eucalyptus. Atop the hill directly behind them was a small flat house. Beyond the barn, the land rose quickly into a sharp angled canyon.

Abergast got out. Byrd stood before the barn looking his way. Then the man turned, pushed aside the large door of the barn and stepped into the dark structure.

"Wait."

Abergast rushed forward. He didn't want to underestimate Raymond Byrd, but the man didn't strike him as a killer. Smart enough, maybe a little clever, the man was, finally, rather simple and straight forward. And Abergast believed him when he said there was something he needed to show him, before they went looking for Troy.

It was a very, very strange case, and he suspected that Byrd was if not innocent, not entirely guilty either. He was just a man who got caught up in whatever drama it was playing out at this Drammond House, with this woman. There was, in fact, no evidence at all of violence of any kind. Only these missing people.

Still, Abergast reminded himself, approaching the wide dark entrance to the barn, Troy had seen something at the house, and it had terrified him. And now he was gone, like the others.

Under his left arm, Abergast carried a Walther PPK .38 in a holster. He reached under his coat, stroked the gun with a fingertip, checked if the safety was off.

He stood in the entrance to the barn. It was impossible to see anything inside. An instant later, following the loud sharp click of a switch, large lamps turned on overhead. The light was warm and golden, and slowly growing brighter, like the sun at dawn.

It was a large space, nearly empty. Against one wall was a stack of large wooden crates.

Byrd stood near the back of the barn, near what looked like a deep metal sink.

"What is this place?" Abergast said.

"It's Heinrich Manning's studio."

Abergast stepped into the barn. He approached Byrd, his shoes clicking on the hard wooden floor. It didn't look so big from the outside, this barn. It looked like just an ordinary, two story barn. Livestock down here, hay up there.

"He was a painter," Byrd said, raising his voice. "In those crates are his paintings, what remain of them. His son put them there. To do what, I don't know." He added: "One of them is mine."

"This guy's dead, I take it?"

Byrd waited until Abergast was close. Then he said: "Heinrich? Yes. He died. He was old." He looked at the floor, at Abergast's feet. He caught his breath, turned quickly, walked toward the corner. Abergast followed.

Through a recess in the corner they came upon a huge iron door. It was part-ways open. Byrd placed a hand on the door and pushed and it swung inward, exposing a long flight of descending cement stairs.

Abergast swallowed. His mouth was suddenly dry. He thought, reasonably, that he'd gone far enough, that without light, without *a lot of light* he was not going down those stairs. "What's down there?"

"He was building something. A model. It's of the house. Where we're going. Remember I told you there was a map? It's what I have to show you."

Byrd proceeded quickly down the steps, into the dark.

"Byrd, wait up!"

"There's a light at the bottom. I'll turn it on. Makes it easier. Take your time. It's a long way down. You slip and fall, it's gonna hurt."

Max Abergast had a grown daughter, half-sister to his delinquent son Carl. One time she'd given him a keyring light, this little plastic job: you squeeze it, this whiteblue LED light flips on for thirty seconds. Helps you find your way, find the keyhole when you get in late and all the lights are off. But it was a piece of crap, as those things usually are. He kept it on his keyring for a time, but then it stopped working, so he took it off. Threw it in a drawer.

Why hold on to something like that? Why's it so hard to throw away some things?

In any case, Abergast thought, taking another step – the steps were deeper than usual, and there was no hand railing; his knees were beginning to ache – in any case, his keys were in the car.

"Byrd!"

A light turned on at the bottom of the stairs. He was right. It *was* a long way down. It took almost a minute to come to the bottom.

Inside of the room – it was hard to take in at once – was an enormous, tangled pile of wood. Splinters, tiny, tiny pieces, millions of them stacked up about three feet high. There was a little space along the walls of the room, but otherwise it was just this fantastic mess.

"I thought you said he made a model."

"He did," said Byrd from the opposite wall, his feet hidden by the rubble. "This was the house my friend Manning built. His son, Joseph, for reasons we'll never fully comprehend, destroyed it."

"And you're saying this was... It was a replica of the..."

What was it called again?

"That's right. And it was about here," Byrd said, kneeling down, lifting a piece of the wrecked structure, "that Troy died."

Had he heard him right?

"What did you say?"

Abergast made his way around the room.

"Watch your step," said Byrd, "there aren't any nails but some of the splinters are sharp."

"What did you say? You said Troy – "

Byrd was on one knee. He balanced a thin piece of the model upright. Very slowly the man began to rise.

"Look," said Byrd.

Abergast, tripping once, stopping, quickly catching his balance, made his way around the room to Byrd. The man seemed different. He was quiet, distant, sad, speaking in a tone you might hear in church or in a hospital, in the presence of forces far greater than man's understanding or reach.

He was looking at what he'd set up, this piece of the house. And it *was*, evidently, part of the model, the house. There was no mistaking that.

The thing had to have been enormous.

Abergast's brain started racing.

Troy had said something about that, the size of the place.

"You get inside," he'd said, "and... it just goes. On and on and on. It's not really a house," Troy said, "it's... like *another world*. A world outside of..."

"He jumped," Byrd said. "Look." Byrd pointed at something in the house, in the piece he'd arranged. There was a window.

"What're you talking about?"

"I'm talking about Troy. Beckmann. The man you're looking for!"

"What do you mean he jumped?"

"He jumped from this window. Look."

Abergast was having a difficult time. It was too much to process at once. *Troy – dead? He jumped?* And Byrd was beginning to look and sound just a little bit crazy.

"He must have fallen – I don't know – *will you look at the building, damnit!*"

Abergast was staring at Byrd as if this were a different man, not the man he'd been drinking with an hour before, not the man who had promised to take him up to the Drammond House, to help him find Troy.

Something's happened to him.

When Abergast turned to look at the piece Byrd had stood upright, at this small window the man was pointing at and seemed convinced was the very window Troy had apparently jumped from, and through this window onto more and more and more of the same, other windows, walls, floors, doors, rooftops, *tiny* pieces of wooden furniture, a pile of rubble, the model of a house this man, the artist, must have spent years constructing, completely ruined, Byrd moved quickly, spinning.

He had a large wooden hammer in his hand. He swung this around with incredible speed, striking Abergast square in the forehead, cracking the man's skull. The P.I.'s assistant gasped, staggered backwards into the cement wall and fell straight to the floor, arms out.

Byrd bent down, reached under the man's jacket, took the gun from its holster.

Abergast's mouth was open, his fat tongue hanging limp on his lower lip. His eyelids fluttered. He was having trouble breathing.

Turning the gun over in his hand, back and forth, appreciating something, he couldn't say what, of its antique beauty, Byrd said to the man on the floor: "I did not kill my wife. I did not kill Paul Wise. I did not kill Marianne Heaney, Joseph Manning, Charlotte, any of them. The house did. It would have killed Troy, too, but he managed to escape. Only... he had to jump. That was the only way out. Sometimes you have to jump."

Byrd couldn't tell if Abergast was listening. He didn't think he was dead. The man didn't appear to be unconscious. He wanted to apologize to the man for what he'd done, and began to, but the words failed to appear.

Then he shot the man through the heart.

~ 8 ~

It would be improper to leave the body in the room. The wreckage of Manning's model was something in its own right. The corpse added nothing and was only intrusive, insulting.

The blood, on the other hand – Byrd reflected, heaving the corpse on his shoulders up the stairs – was as abstract as the splintered wreckage of the house. Wreckage it was, too, but of a different order.

When he reached the top of the stairs he had to stop, set the corpse down, sit and catch his breath. He was so tired he could have fallen asleep then and there, finished the job in the morning.

"I didn't want to do it," he said to himself, his voice filling the emptiness of the barn. "I could have let you go. We might have settled things." He thought about how they might have done that, but came up blank.

Abergast wouldn't have listened. He was that kind of man. Persistant, headstrong. There was no way out of going back to the house. No way out apart from killing the man, this connection.

Byrd did what anyone in his position would have done.

437

It took him awhile to find one, but then, outside, behind the barn, in a lean-to, he found a spade. There was also a wheel barrow. He put the spade in the wheel barrow, took these around to the front of the barn. He loaded up the corpse. He followed a path along the side of the barn, up into the canyon.

He buried Abergast in the canyon. He worked in the dark frantically, exhausted, sick to his stomach. Finally he stopped, dropped the spade, grabbed his knees and vomited.

He examined the hole he'd dug. Sand kept falling back in. It was not very deep. But he wasn't going to do any more, not at that hour, not in his condition. He dumped the corpse into the hole and covered it with sandy earth. It left quite a mound. He slapped at this with the back of the spade, trying unsuccessfully to crush it flat. A sickening sound emerged: liquid sloshing about in the dead man's stomach.

He returned to the barn, leaving the wheel barrow and spade inside. He returned downstairs and retrieved the gun. He turned the light out.

He pulled the VW into the barn. He wiped the gun off with his shirt, as he'd seen done in movies. He left the gun in the glovebox of the car and walked up to the house. Before going into the house he drove his Volvo down to the barn and parked it inside, next to the VW. He closed the barn door.

Outside, the air was cool and refreshing. The sky was just beginning to change. He took a deep breath. End of another day. A job well done.

In the house he took a long shower, went upstairs, collapsed in the bed. It had been Heinrich Manning's bed for many years. Charlotte had slept there with him. Then she'd slept there by herself.

He pressed his face into the pillow, smelling the woman. He imagined Charlotte lying beside him. But this came to nothing. Following the shocking realization that he was absolutely alone, he dropped into a deep, dreamless sleep.

He woke a few hours later to the sound of a ringing telephone. He was too tired to get out of bed to answer it. He vaguely thought he shouldn't answer it because he wasn't supposed to be there, in the house, in Manning's bed. But then it stopped and he fell asleep.

Later, the phone rang again.

It was late in the afternoon when he got out of bed. He took another shower, soaping his entire body, scrubbing hard, rinsing, soaping himself again, scrubbing, rinsing. He trimmed his finger nails and toe nails. He shaved, combed his hair. In the medicine cabinet he found a bottle of aspirin. He swallowed four tablets. There was also a small bottle of Drakkar Noir cologne. He splashed some of this on his neck.

In the living room he went through Joseph's things. The man's clothing was too big for him. He liked black, apparently. And turtlenecks. There was also his passport, his itinerary. He should have returned – what day was that? – the tenth. Two days ago. Someone will be calling.

Someone is *calling.*

There was also cash in the luggage. Two manila envelopes full of bound hundreds and fifties. The man had probably taken the money from Charlotte before she realized what he was doing, what he had planned.

Why hadn't he taken more? Why hadn't he killed her?

They were questions he'd never be able to answer. But that didn't matter because, regardless of whatever you came up with, the money, for all intents and purposes, was now his, as was everything else in the luggage and in the house. Only, he couldn't stay. He had to take what he could fit into a bag, and go.

I'll die if I stop.

He took Joseph's red Lincoln Continental.

LAX was more of a circus than usual. It was like a war zone. Military Humvees were parked at the curb. Soldiers in Oakleys embracing sub-machine guns stood at the entrance to the international terminal.

Byrd didn't think twice about it. He saw the soldiers, the Humvees with their turret machine guns – weapons powerful enough to cut a car like his in half in a matter of seconds – and he kept going. He pulled right through, nice and easy. He took I-5 to the border.

In San Ysidro, with only a few miles to go, an enormous helicopter, one with two blades spinning overhead,

caught his eye. It was out over the Pacific, low enough disturb the otherwise calm waters. What could they be looking for?

It occurred to him suddenly that they wouldn't let him
through. Not only was the status of his car a potential
problem – the car was overdo, and rented in Joseph's
name – but it was very likely that *his* name would be in
their computer.

*Do they check every ID? What reason do they have to suspect
me? I'm just a man taking a holiday in beautiful Mexico.*

The investigation into the whereabouts of Paul Wise,
Lucy Byrd, and Marianne Heaney, not to mention Troy
Beckmann and that journalism student he brought up
there and – *don't forget* – poor Missus Wise, and all those
cops, Suzuki and McNeal and what's-his-name and
what's-his-name and that dog – *am I missing anyone?* –
and Charlotte Graham... though temporarily delayed, had
been, and certainly still was, underway. No. His name was
out there, no question.

So use Joseph's. It's his car, after all. You have his passport.

"I don't look anything like him."

Doesn't matter. They hardly look at those things anyways.

"But it's German. They'll look. What's a German man
doing driving to Mexico?"

Taking a trip. Germans love *taking trips.*

"Wasn't one of those hijackers from Germany?"

Traffic was gathering, everything slowing down. In the
rearview mirror he saw red and blue lights. A moment

later, engine roaring, a highway patrol cruiser sped past on the shoulder of the road. Then a second car, a black sedan, doing at least seventy, two of its wheels off the road, whipped by, red lights blinking on and off in its rear window.

Something was happening up ahead.

His stomach suddenly clenched up painfully. He hadn't eaten anything, he realized, in days. The burger and fries in the precinct was his last meal.

And when was that?

A sign on the edge of the road read "Last Exit Before Mexico." He took the off-ramp slowly and, after a hundred meters, pulled into a Chevron station. He parked outside a dusty market they had there, at the corner of the building, where the asphalt met the desert. The ocean wasn't far off.

He walked as casually as he could into the market, gritting his teeth for the pain in his stomach.

In the bathroom he stood over the toilet bowl, hands on his thighs, waiting. Nothing came. He undid his pants, stood back to pee, and waited some more. He closed his eyes, emptied his mind of all thoughts, and took a deep breath. When the urine came it came in a dark fragrant torrent, pouring out of him. He urinated for well over a minute. Then he zipped up, went to the sink, washed his hands. He let the cool water run.

"Go back." There was a small square mirror over the sink. It was tilted downward, meant for a man much shorter than he was, because all he could make of himself in the reflection was his chin, an ugly brown scab. The chin moved, speaking. "Go back. Turn around. Return to Manning's. Wait. Like the man said. When circumstances change, reassess. Tomorrow you try again. What's a day or two?"

He turned off the faucet. The air dryer was broken. A filthy towel hung from a nail in the wall. He reached for it and then hesitated. He wiped his hands on his pants. He glanced once more at the mirror, crouching and peering into his bloodshot eyes, took a breath, grabbed the wet doorknob and prepared to face the world. He paused. On the back of the bathroom door was all sorts of material: graffiti, names and numbers, penned and knife-scored tits and genitals. There were also stickers advertising various things. One, it had been torn, partially stripped from the door, read "Alien Catho" in neon green block letters. Beneath the words, a cartoonish buxom blond was bent over, looking over her shoulder and covering her mouth in surprise or fear, since something like E.T. (the creature'd been effaced) had its claw hooked in her white panties. At the bottom:

For an out of this world experience!

Area 51 – Armagosa NV

"Nevada," he said. It sounded good, saying it. "Nevada." It sounded natural and honest and practical. "They'd never think you'd go there. Because what's there? No. You're in a hurry. You're going for the border. Or an airport. A train station. Not Nevada. There's nothing in Nevada. Desert. Salt flats. Casinos. Would you go to a casino? Why on earth would you go to a casino – too closed, too many people. No. You'd never go to a casino. It's space that you want. Being outside, in the desert, where you can – "

In the market an old Mexican woman was selling homemade tamales. He asked for two: one with beef, one with green peppers. He ate them furiously, standing before the woman. The old woman sat in a plastic chair unmoved, her wrinkled eyes closed. He complimented her on her cooking and asked for two more. He ate those just as quickly as the others, blowing on the tamales, licking his fingers.

"Mmm!"

When he tried to pay the woman, however, he realized that he had nothing smaller than a fifty dollar bill in his pockets. He had a thick roll of them.

He held the money in his hand embarrassed, nervous. He owed the woman six dollars. He peeled a fifty from the roll and held it out to the old woman. She looked at the money and shrugged. Then her head began to shake, twitching quickly.

Now he was attracting attention. People in the market, there weren't many, were looking his way.

He took the fifty dollar bill to the cashier, a fat Mexican girl. Her t-shirt was too small for her and rode up her sides. Brown waves of fat hung over the waist of her tight jeans.

"Can you break this? I need change for the tamales."

The girl looked offended. She pulled her chin in, doubling up rolls of fat in her neck. "Buy gas, man! Jeez!"

Ray whipped up the fifty, put it in his pocket, turned on his heel, stepped outside.

He could hear that military helicopter in the distance, down near the border. There was now a traffic jam on the highway, a colorful string of motionless cars.

Around the corner of the market the Pacific, warm and calm and clear, greeted him. The sun was blinding, reflecting off the water. Far out at sea a long dark vessel broke the horizon, a cargo or oil ship up from Panama. He held a hand to his brow, squinting. They were birds, not a ship, a flock of pelicans flying just over the surface, on the horizon.

The space he'd used to park Joseph's Lincoln Continental was empty. He couldn't believe his eyes.

He looked at the ocean once more, wondering if maybe it was a mirage, the empty parking space, a trick of light, or maybe he'd parked at the other end of the market. He looked again. Nope. The car was gone.

Raymond Byrd listened to the military helicopter hovering in the air down the way.

Inside he told the cashier: "My car's stolen."

"No way!"

"Way."

He turned, pointed out the murky window. "It was there, right over there. Now it's gone."

"But how!?" said the cashier.

He looked at her.

She said: "You leave the keys in it?"

Byrd realized that he probably had. He'd come in wanting to vomit.

"I might've."

"Well, hey man – " The girl threw up her hands like Jesus at the last supper. "Kinda stupid, mister, leaving your keys in the car. You know Mexico's right over there, right? You know how many cars are stolen in Mexico *every day*?"

The girl blinked her dark little eyes.

"It was a rental," he said. "Just call me a cab."

The girl nodded. She took the receiver, punched some buttons in the phone. She spoke quickly into the phone, identified the station, hung up. "Be here in twenty minutes."

"Thanks."

"Now what about the tamales?"

He looked at the girl. He looked at the old woman, who appeared to be asleep behind her table. He went over to her, asked her how many tamales she had in the box. Eyes closed, the old woman leaned forward in her chair, reached into the box, muttered to herself. She looked up and very quietly said: "Catorce."

"What'd she say?"

"Fourteen," the cashier said.

"I'll take them."

The old woman lifted them out one by one, set them on the table. They looked like pipe bombs lined up, ready to go.

The cashier came over, looked at the old woman's tamales. She said: "Mister, you taking all those?"

Ray said: "I can eat two more. That leaves twelve for you. And the others. You got brothers, sisters?"

"I gotta a kid!"

Ray looked at the cashier. She couldn't be more than eighteen.

"So take'em for the kid. Your friends," he said. The girl nodded, pouted. He said: "I'll wait outside for the cab."

"You owe her thirty dollars," said the girl matter-of-factly.

Ray blinked. There's no argument. He took his two tamales, one with beef and one with peppers, set the fifty dollar bill on the table, and walked out of the market.

~ 9 ~

It was nine when he got back to Manning's. The cab cost him three hundred and twenty dollars.

At the kitchen table he took all the money from his pockets and wallet. He counted it, what he'd taken from Joseph's stash minus what had been stolen with the car.

About three thousand dollars. How far can you go on three grand?

Go home. Turn up what you can there –

"They'll be watching the place."

Then here. Turn it upside down. Manning had other hiding places –

"Joseph took care of that."

Then wait for Charlotte to come home.

"She ..."

He found pork chops and tomatoes in the fridge. In a pantry he found an onion and some wrinkled, soft potatoes. There was also an unopened bottle of red wine from Paso Robles. He put on some music, Miles Davis' *Sketches of Spain,* perfect cooking music, and fried the pork chops and onion and potatoes. He sliced the tomatoes, salted these and drenched them in olive oil.

He ate quickly, desperately. He drank three-quarters of the bottle of wine. Then he went outside to smoke.

It was a lovely late summer night. Quiet and cool.

He walked up to the top of the bluff, looked down onto the Pacific, along the coast to greater LA.

"In a million other scenarios, I could do this and still be a free man," he thought. "Only in *this* scenario am I who I am."

If you'd just bought the painting the first time!

He was rewriting his past when, distantly, the telephone in the house began to ring. He tried to ignore it but it was impossible to ignore. Then it stopped.

He walked down to the barn. As he came to its entrance he heard something behind the structure, in the canyon. Scratching, hissing, a soft cry.

He followed the path up into the canyon. He suspected what had happened before he saw it. But sure enough. A dog was digging up Abergast's corpse. He could only make out its back, its shoulders.

He picked up a rock and threw it, missing wide. The creature looked up from its work. Glowing green eyes, its snout black and glistening.

The man shuddered, closed his eyes.

He bent down, picked up another stone. This time he hit his mark, catching the dog in the throat.

The animal cried out shrilly and ran off.

It had only dug up the top half of the corpse. It'd eaten the face off, picking Abergast's cheeks and forehead smooth. Byrd didn't look too closely.

He walked back to the barn, retrieved the spade, returned to the grave. He reburied the body. Then he rolled down some large boulders and set these atop the grave.

In the back of his mind he didn't think the rocks would do much. If the creature was hungry enough it would simply dig around them, under them.

Walking back to the barn, the spade aloft over his shoulder, he remembered seeing, when he was kid, how pensioners in the neighborhood would put white bleach bottles at the corners of the lawn to keep dogs away. Whether the bottles had bleach in them or not he was never sure. He seemed to remember them being empty. The smell alone must've been strong enough to keep the dogs away.

He looked around the barn.

The loft was completely empty except for a tall metal locker. Inside of the locker he found, in addition to paint, half-a-dozen cans of turpentine. There was also an old toolbox.

At the grave he splashed turpentine on the mound, over the sandy earth. He contemplated lighting it on fire but thought he'd wait and see what the dog did. Fire was always an option, the next line of attack.

That night he dreamt of the house. At least he thought it was the house. He couldn't get out. When he came to a closed door, sure that it opened onto the outside, Jillian – he couldn't see her, but it was her voice – told him not to open it.

"She's coming," the girl said. She didn't sound frightened. She sounded excited. "She's coming!"

He turned to look for her, Jillian, but he was alone. When he turned back to open the door he woke up.

Fog had come in. The window onto the yard was blank, dappled with moisture.

He went downstairs and wandered about in the dark. The fog moved outside the windows in curious ways: collecting, dispersing, spinning, stratifying.

He was returning upstairs when the phone began to ring. He stared at it, willing it to stop. It didn't. He wondered if it might be Charlotte trying to reach him. He was going to answer and not say anything, and wait for her to speak, when it stopped. He went back to bed.

In the morning – he'd made coffee and toast – the phone rang again. Without thinking about it, he answered. "Hello?"

"Joseph?" It was a woman. He didn't recognize the voice. "Joseph!"

Could it be Hannah? She didn't sound German.

"Joseph? Joseph!? Are you there! Can you hear me! *God damn it! What is –*"

Without a sound he hung up.

The fog had lifted but the sky remained covered in cloud. The morning was flat and cool, everything perfectly still.

A small white car drove up, some insignia on its door. Two people, a white man and a large black woman, both in uniforms, got out. They looked around the yard, up at the bungalow, down at the barn. They walked side by side up to the porch and up the steps to the front door. The woman knocked powerfully.

They did not look like police officers.

"Good morning."

"Mr Manning?" the woman said.

Byrd had a mug of coffee in hand.

He smiled at the visitors and said, "No, I'm sorry. He's not here. But please come in, out of the cold." He stepped back.

The woman returned his smile. "Thank you."

The man seemed reluctant to come inside, but then he followed his partner.

"Coffee? It's fresh."

The man, a towering figure, quietly accepted the offer. The woman declined.

The visitors stood by the large wooden kitchen table. Byrd leaned against the sink. The man sipped loudly at the coffee, raised his eyebrows, raised the mug in the air level with the tip of his nose as if to toast the host.

NPR was on the radio in the other room. A man named Scott Simon, in a mournful register, was reading the news of the day. None of it was good.

"We're looking for..." The woman opened a notebook, consulted a form. She had on dark red lipstick. "Joseph Manning," she said. She looked at Byrd.

"Joe's in Mexico," he said. "He and his girlfriend went down a few days ago. Puerto Vajerta, Cancun, all that. Told me – "

"Is that right?" said the woman loudly. She was huffing and puffing, like an old smoker. She didn't look like a smoker. She was big, ovaline, with narrow shoulders, little feet, magnificent breasts.

"Yep," said Byrd. "He told me that since he didn't get out here much – it's his father's place – the old man died some weeks ago, you probably heard – ... Heinrich Manning, the painter? – ... No? Well. Joe's here from Europe and while he was so close he thought he'd get away for a bit. So you missed him."

"And you are?" said the woman.

Byrd sipped his coffee. "Raymond Byrd," he said. "I'm a friend of the family."

"You're watching the place while he's away."

"That's right."

"And do you know when he's returning?"

Byrd frowned. "I'm sorry but... What does this – "

The woman giggled. Her entire bulbous body quivered and shook. Her partner took one step forward and rather shyly held out a white card to Raymond. His name was Robert Delaney. They were US customs agents.

"Oh it's nothing that serious," the woman said, smiling widely. She had blue gums. The tops of her teeth were stained red with lipstick. "It's just that, well, Mr Manning seems to have missed his flight."

Nobody spoke for a moment. The woman was no longer smiling.

"Olivia," said Robert Delaney.

Someone on the radio was weeping violently.

Delaney finished his coffee and set the empty mug down on the table. "We just had some questions for Mr Manning regarding his stay here. But if you say he's in Mexico... I guess we'll have to wait until he comes back. So _ "

"I could," said Raymond, looking once again at the card the man had given him, "give you the number he gave me, where he's staying."

"That won't be necessary, Mr Byrd. No need to bother him if he's enjoying himself, taking a little R and R. Before he goes back to *Berlin,* of all places." Delaney grinned. He was from the south. Texas maybe. "Nah," he said. "Let's let him be. And when he comes back... We'll talk to him then."

The woman consulted her notebook again, turning a page, reading quickly. Then she snapped it closed, looked at Byrd, smiled beautifully. "Thank you for your time."

The customs agents left.

They'll be back. It's just a matter of time now.

There was no thinking about it. He'd take the VW Thing to Nevada. He could pack up, stop by Abergast's place – *he lived alone, nobody would've reported him missing, not yet* – take what he could, and get out of town.

At the barn, directly outside the door, a mauled human ear lay in the dust.

"God damn that dog!"

Byrd picked up the ear and ran into the canyon, up to the grave. The dog, a thin mangy mutt, calmly sat further up the path. It had disinterred the entire body, torn it to pieces.

"I'm going to kill you!"

The dog was unimpressed.

He'd use Abergast's gun. He'd lure the dog up close and then shoot it through the head.

He ran back to the barn. He'd have to burn Abergast's remains. It was the only way.

From the glovebox of the VW he took the Walther .38. He jammed this into his pocket. Then he took the can of turpentine he'd used the night before in one hand and the spade in the other.

"A lighter. Matches."

The lighter was in the house.

"Something for the dog, too."

Slow down. One thing at a time, kiddo.

Byrd stopped, considered himself. For all he knew the gun in his pocket could discharge at any moment, blow a hole right through his leg.

And then what?

The dog would come for him. It would wait until he was on edge of consciousness and then saunter on in.

Raymond Byrd closed his eyes and took a deep breath.

"Nevada," he said to himself. "That is your mantra. *Nevada.*"

He replaced the gun inside the VW. He stepped out of the barn with the can of turpentine and the spade. He set these down at the corner of the barn and started up the path to the house.

There was a car in the yard. Small, silver, clean.

Someone was in the living room. He heard her before he saw her. His heart raced, his body warming with a sense of vindication, of closure. Everything was working out as planned!

Her back was to him. Head down, straight brown hair covering a cheek, the woman regarded the mess on the floor, Joseph's gutted luggage, the unmade futon, the ash-tray, an empty glass tipped on its side.

Charlotte!

When she turned, looked at the man, it wasn't surprise in her eyes. It was a patient expression full of contempt, disgust, a kind of ownership, as if Joseph's things were *her* things, Heinrich Manning's house *her* house. As if Raymond Byrd, interim keeper of the house, had been negligent in his duties, and had let things fall to such a state of disarray that order, any time soon, would be very difficult to restore.

~ 10 ~

The woman was tall and pale. Her face was long, lined with fatigue. There were large dark divots, like muddy thumbprints, pressed beneath her eyes. Her straight brown hair fell around her face like a hood.

"Where's Joseph?" said the woman.

Byrd wiped his hands, one over the other. He wiped them on his pants.

It was the woman who had called.

"You must be Hannah," he said, approaching her, extending his hand.

"No!" she said breathlessly, her eyes flashing, taking a step back. She paused, this vicious curl in her lip. Then she opened up, like a wasp nest falling to the ground and exploding, she started: "Hannah? I'm *Ingrid*. Joseph's *sister*. I've been traveling for THREE FUCKING DAYS to get out here. I slept in the fucking Chicago airport for two goddamn fucking nights, every fucking flight cancelled! You can't fucking imagine what fucking goddamn airport fucking hell I've had to go through to get here! They flew me to fucking Miami! And then Seattle! I mean – FUCKING CHRIST! I've been calling and calling and calling and nobody fucking answers the goddamn telephone! And now where's my brother? He's not supposed to be here but I see that he is. For God's sake. So where is he? So I can *see* him and get this over with and go home and be with my family. Ugh!" she said, taking a breath. "I mean – who the fuck are you, by the way!? Where's Joseph?"

"I see," said Byrd. "Of course. I was... It's been so crazy here this last week." He sighed, smiled.

The woman stared at him, her cheeks puffing up, mouth agape like she were watching a talking chimpanzee. "What?"

"So I was, you know, after Charlotte left – "

"*Who are you?*"

"Oh. Sorry. I'm Ray, Ray Byrd. A friend. I knew your father." He smiled as best he could. Psychologically he had no problem burning the body of the man he'd shot, and then luring a hungry dog up close before killing it, but this Ingrid Manning was something else. Rather surprising. After losing his car, and finding the ear, and the customs agents, he was getting tired of surprises.

He looked into the dark hole of the woman's mouth, held out his hand.

Ingrid Manning's eyes dropped a notch, considering the hand. "So Charlotte's gone?"

"Yes. She left. I was just... helping a little, doing what I could." Byrd left the room, started for the door. "Joseph's down here."

The woman followed. "He missed his flight."

The man and woman started down the path to the barn.

"Well," said Byrd, "with all the work that still needed being done here, you see, he decided..."

The woman slowed down, followed the man a few steps behind. She had on expensive black leather shoes. Over his shoulder, Byrd said, "Did he tell you about the model they found? What your father was building?"

"He told me."

"It's really something. Anyway, I'm sorry to..."

He'd left the barn door open. He could see the two cars, his Volvo and Abergast's VW Thing, parked there, side by side.

Where's the gun?

"Sorry?" the woman said.

He stopped, looked at the ground, cupped his hands, one in the other. He looked at Ingrid. "There was an accident. Some kind of... disagreement, I guess, between your brother and, um, Charlotte."

"Yes, I know. That's why I'm here."

Byrd looked into the woman's eyes. They were brown, like Charlotte's. She had a small sharp chin, small thin lips. She'd had lipstick on at some point but had since wiped it off. Now her lips were chapped, flaking, pink.

"So he told you what happened?"

The woman puckered her lips, breathed through her nose. She tapped a foot in the dust. "Yes. I spoke to him. I guess Charlotte..." Her cheeks had flushed momentarily.

Then they drained of color. She snorted, said: "Why am I talking to you? Where's Joseph?"

"She destroyed it. Charlotte destroyed it."

Ingrid was having trouble keeping her eyes steady. She was looking over the man's shoulder, into the barn, and then back up the hill, at the house.

"Destroyed what?" she said.

She's nervous.

Something awful then occurred to Raymond Byrd. Nobody knew that Ingrid Manning was there with him, talking with him. Except for the customs agents – and their understanding of the situation was superficial at best – nobody knew that he was there, at that moment, at Manning's place, talking with Manning's daughter.

In his imagination the woman before him began to disappear, to disintegrate and go up like smoke.

"The model," he said. "It's gone. She wrecked it. Every last bit of it." He turned, continued on his way into the barn. "Come," he said, "I'll show you. Anyways, Joseph's down here. Trying to fit the pieces together."

~ 11 ~

It was not dark in the barn. Milky sunlight came in through windows high overhead. But it would be dark downstairs. He'd turned the light off after taking care of Abergast.

The woman followed closely. She glanced at the crates stacked against the wall. She looked carefully at the two cars parked side by side.

"Whose are these?"

"That's mine," Byrd said, pointing at the Volvo, "and the other belongs to Max, a dealer Joseph called out. He's around here somewhere."

Byrd began down the stairs to the basement without stopping. Ingrid paused at the top.

Then Byrd stopped, turned, looked up. "You've been here before, haven't you? You've seen his..."

"In fact I've only heard of it. No. I haven't seen it yet. The last time I was here..."

Byrd waited for the woman to finish. Apparently she was finished.

Ingrid stood at the top of the staircase, framed by the large rectangular entry, her face in shadow.

461

Byrd continued down. He said: "There's a light. But he must've closed the door or something. Let me check."

After a moment the woman followed the man down the stairs. She moved slowly, cautiously.

In the basement, Byrd turned on the lights. The woman on the stairs was saying something.

There was blood on the floor.

Nothing you can do about that now.

"Is that blood?" the woman said, still descending.

Byrd took a deep breath. "Yes, it is. It's Charlotte's."

"But what happened?"

She sounded genuinely concerned.

"Joseph, he..."

"Are you sure?"

"Of course I'm sure!" Byrd said, turning to face the woman as she came into the room, eyes wide, mouth agape, in absolute wonder and confusion at the sight. The ruined model, blood all over the floor. "I saw her. I saw what happened."

"But – how?"

Ingrid stood in the entrance to the room, her hands out. She looked like she didn't want to get her feet wet.

"She came to me," Byrd said. "Called me."

"But, I thought – "

"I knew her. From before. Anyways. Long story. But, yes. Your brother. I guess he kind of lost control for a moment. He hit her."

"*Hit* her?"

Tight lipped, Byrd nodded.

"But *why*?" she said.

"Well." Byrd made a sweeping gesture, arm out.

"She..."

Byrd nodded. After moment, looking about the room, he said, "It's going to take some serious time, tremendous commitment."

"You mean. To – "

He faced her suddenly. "Of course."

I'll die if I stop!

"To restore it," he said. "Ingrid – *I saw it*. The original thing. It was *magnificent. Un-believable!* You have no idea... Of course I mean to build it again. From his notebooks. Your father's."

The woman's eyebrows bent inward, the skin in the center of her pale brow folding. "Where's Joseph?"

Byrd considered the woman. She had no connection to the Drammond House, as far as he was concerned, so he had no reason to kill her. Still, he couldn't just let her go. And surely she did *know* about the house, from stories she'd heard as a child.

He feigned mild surprise. "He *was* here a moment ago. He must have gone upstairs, to the loft. Or to the beach. He *did* say... I'm sorry, Ingrid." Byrd smiled, showing teeth. "I was... I was busy with something else. I bet he's down at the beach."

Raymond Byrd started up the stairs.

Ingrid remained in the basement. She'd never seen such a mess, such a violent pile of wood. And with the blood on the floor, on some of the wreckage. There was even blood, over there, a streak of it low on the wall.

The woman shuddered. She wasn't frightened, exactly – there was something consistent about the mess, and the blood, and the possibility of Joseph's hitting Charlotte – he'd *never* liked the woman – with everything she knew of her father and brother. But she was exhausted. And after what she'd gone through in the past forty-eight hours, to have to deal with something like this –

She started up the stairs. She was about to say something apologetic to Raymond Byrd when she saw the door at the top of the stairs quietly, with a click, close.

She stopped in place. Words always came easy to her. But in that moment she couldn't figure out what to say.

"It's simple," she thought. "A breeze must have shut it."

Then she heard the metal bolt in the door loudly turn over and drop into place. And she heard the key, on the other side, slide with a jingle from its hole. Then everything was very quiet.

~ 12 ~

"Nevada, Nevada, Nevada, Nevada, Nevada..."

The sun had come out. It was turning into a beautiful day.

He had to get a second can of turpentine to burn the body. He also gathered up some sticks and brush for kindling to start the blaze. But once it was going, it was quite a blaze. Hot, splattering with grease. He was drenched in sweat by the end of it. He'd need to change his clothes, take a shower before going.

He watched the corpse burn down to white ash and bones. With the spade he chopped through the spine, lifted the skull out, set it aside to cool. He buried the rest of the skeleton.

The dog was a no-show.

Wrapping the skull in his shirt, he brought it back to the barn and dropped it on the passenger seat of the VW.

"FUCK YOU ASSHOLE! LET ME OUT!"

He backed the VW out of the barn, turned it around, pointed it up the hill, got out, went back to the barn. From the Volvo he took the registration and license plates. Any investigator could still identify it as his car but this would buy him a little time.

"YOU KNOW WHO I AM!? YOU FUCKING CUNT! FUCK-ING CUNT! YOU'RE A COWARD! A COWARD! LET ME OUT! LET ME *OUT!* LET ME OUT OF HERE!"

Boom! She struck the iron door. *Boom! Boom! Boom!*

He left the barn and pulled the door closed.

"Help! Help me! Help!"

Joseph's sister had a surprisingly powerful set of lungs. Even with the barn door closed one could still hear her.

He looked up at the line of eucalyptus trees on the crest of the hill, shimmering in the breeze, half expecting to see a man with a rucksack over his shoulder come sauntering down toward him.

"Hello, friend!"

There was a state park nearby. It was only a question of when the good samaritan would make his appearance.

He needed fifteen minutes. Twenty, if he wanted a light lunch.

"Help me! Let me out of here! HELP!"

He drove the VW up the path to the house and parked it beside a silver Hyundai. He opened its door, looked inside. No: She'd taken the keys.

That's what you do when you leave your car. You take the keys.

Byrd chuckled to himself, thinking about Joseph's red Lincoln, the lucky bastard who got away with it. If he'd gone to Mexico, they probably got him at the border.

Which would mean they had Joseph's papers. Which would mean –

The man who'd stolen his car didn't take it to Mexico. He took it to a place where it could be stripped down and rebuilt with switched-out parts and shipped across the country. He probably got ten grand for it, a nice day's work.

He went inside the house. He took a shower. Under the water it occurred to him that if he destroyed the remaining records of the house, he could retreat there, and take Gretton's place, work outside. She'd have him. She'd need him.

It was an option worth considering.

He dressed in some of Joseph's clothes, pulling on the only button down shirt the man had in his luggage. It was black, long and loose around his body.

He made himself a sandwich. He finished the Paso Robles wine he'd opened the night before. He had a cigarette. He closed his eyes calculating, visualizing the steps he needed to take.

Outside, even atop the hill, he could still hear the woman going on. Her cries were small and distant, but audible, unmistakable.

"Help me!"

Boom!

"I'm in here! Help! Let me out!"

Boom, boom, boom!

For reasons we'll never know, Raymond Byrd then, all set for his trip to Nevada, went back down to the barn. He opened the door and went inside.

"I'm here! Please! Over here!"

He glanced once at the crates full of paintings stacked against the wall. One of those was his, he reminded himself. Maybe someday it would come back to him, find him. If it was meant to be.

He sighed.

Let it go.

It's what Abergast would've done. At least in theory.

He stood in the recess in the corner, faced the tall iron door. He heard nothing. He listened carefully. He thought about opening the door but then realized that he didn't have the key. He didn't know where it was, in fact, now that he thought of it. Maybe it was in the house.

He touched the door, the long lever over the wide keyhole.

She spoke. "Please," she said. "Please let me out. I'm sorry. I didn't mean what I said. Mister – " She was directly on the other side of the door. He thought if he stuck his finger in the keyhole he might be able to feel her. "What's your name again?"

"Ray."

"Ray. I'm sorry, Ray, about what I said. I didn't mean to be rude with you. It's just been..." The woman sobbed. She cried quietly. She was sitting right there, at the top of the steps. "It's been *so* hard. I can't..."

He took a step back, bent down so that he could look through the keyhole. It was dark on the other side of the door. He adjusted his position. Nothing.

Had she turned the light out? Blocked the keyhole with something?

"Please," she said.

"I can't."

"I have a family."

He thought he could make out her lips through the keyhole. He leaned closer, up to the door. A cold wind, a stream of air the width of a pencil blew out the keyhole. His eye began to water. He blinked.

"Please," she said, "I'll die... I'll die if I stop."

His body reacted before he even realized what had happened. He'd seen it coming, and yet, hadn't understood what it was.

The woman had found a thin piece of wood in the wreckage of the model, and peeled off what was essentially a very long sliver, rapier-like, and had sat waiting for him on the other side of the door to do exactly what he did. Then she rammed the piece of wood through the keyhole, wanting not only to blind the man but to lobotomize him.

His body, however, quick to react, pulled back, twisting and collapsing in a kind of seizure, but not before the point of the sliver had pierced his eye.

It blinded him. Even turning away, Raymond Byrd wasn't fast enough to avoid the needle-sharp end of the piece of wood as it tore open the cornea and ciliary body of his eye, at which point the vitreous humor spilled out onto his cheek and the eye, like a popped balloon, collapsed. It hurt terribly. Crumbled, curled on the floor holding his head, he could see bright flashes of red light, yellow stars exploding in his head. He could feel the gelatinous contents of his eye covering his cheek.

"I'll die if I stop, die if I stop, *DIE IF I STOP!*"

The woman on the other side of the door was laughing at him.

"Why did you do that?" he said, gasping in pain, crying, "I might have..."

"LET ME OUT!"

It was not Ingrid's voice. It was not Ingrid on the other side.

"LET ME OUT! *RAYMOND!* OPEN THE DOOR! OPEN THE DOOR! *OPEN THE DOOR!*"

He staggered to his feet, backed up. His body was suddenly cold, shivering, tightening, clenching. He had to get away, but his legs locked up, his knees shaking violently beneath him.

Move it! Go! Nevada Nevada Nevada Nevada...

"You can't get away from me, Raymond. I *have* you, Raymond. *I HAVE YOU!*"

It seemed to take forever, getting out of the barn. And then he wasn't sure if he was inside or out, for how dark it was. Like night, as if he'd been in the barn all day.

Then he realized that he'd closed his eyes so tightly that the muscles in his face were numb, locked up. Slowly he tried to open them but the pain was overwhelming. He pressed the palm of his hand hard against his cut eye, and tried to open the other. He could see but still, even in the good eye, through the flow of tears, there were flashes of bright light, red and yellow starbursts.

"You can't get away from me."

She could have been directly behind him, beside him, inside him. She was whispering in his ear.

"You can't get away. *I won't let you.*"

"I can," he said, turning, facing the barn, knowing instantly what needed to be done.

It took him two slow trips up into the loft but then he had the remaining cans of turpentine lined up outside. Four cans, plus some that he didn't use burning Abergast's body.

He circled the barn, carefully splashing the solvent against its wooden surface. He was so sparing in the first round that he started with the same can going around a second time. That brought him a quarter of the way around. Then he opened a second can and continued on his way, around and around.

The fumes were heady and colorful. He reminded himself to slow down, turn away from the barn and catch his breath. The last thing he needed to do was pass out in the sun, in a pool of turpentine, that woman going on and on in the basement. He was beginning to think she'd never stop, go on screeching until the very end, till the fire totally consumed her.

With two cans left he went into the barn. He tried to push one of the wooden crates down, to slide it over against another wall, position it beneath the loft, for instance, but it was too much. His vision remained dangerously unsteady, and waves of dizziness were increasingly forcing him to stop, kneel, pause and count to ten.

"Raymond?"

She was whispering. She wanted him to come closer.

"Raymond, it's me."

Charlotte?

"Please," the woman said. "They're coming. They don't know I'm here, but... They'll find me. Please. You've got to open the door. Hurry."

"But, but, but Charlotte, I..."

"Raymond. Get the key. *Help me.* Open the door. Once I'm free, it will all be over. We'll stop them together – "

"Charlotte. But I thought you... I thought I left you – "

He stood at the iron door, a can of turpentine in hand.

"Love," the woman said, "you didn't. You didn't leave me. You did what you had to do... to escape. But I got away! You told me how to get away, and I did! And I came back. Maybe you didn't see me – "

"I didn't. I was looking. I was waiting for you. I must've..."

"Please, Raymond. You *must* open the door. I'll die, Raymond, I'll die if..."

His teeth were chattering. The can of turpentine in his hand was suddenly so heavy it started to slip from his grip, its metal handle cutting into the fatty skin of his hand, his fingers. Sweat, he noticed, was dripping, pouring from his face, from the ends of his hands, pooling on the floor at his feet.

Calmly, as logically as he could manage, he tried to explain to Charlotte what had happened, how he'd been forced to kill Max Abergast, the P.I.'s assistant, because of what the man was going to make him do, because of what he knew, and then how he'd tried to escape, but then his car was stolen at the border, and then this dog kept digging up Abergast's remains, so he'd finally had to burn them, but then this woman, Joseph's sister, had popped up, come out of nowhere, just when he thought everything was settled.

"I was going to Nevada," he said. He'd sat down with his back to the door. In a far off corner of his mind he pictured Charlotte doing the same but on the other side, like two prisoners talking through the night, or lovers separated by an unsurpassable wall. "I think I could've gotten away, in Nevada. It seems so open, the place. You can live outside, see things coming from miles away."

"I'll go with you," said the woman. "But first, love, you need to get the key that's in the house. The big key, the one made especially for this door."

With his back to the door, the man's right eye, the dead one, was closer to the barn's entrance than his left. It was also the closest to the door's keyhole, which was just overhead and to the right. Although he sensed, as a man with a phantom limb senses a tickling sensation in the arm he doesn't have, movement close to his face, he saw nothing. It was as if, with the woman's words came a gesture, a finger with which she was directing him, pointing.

She touched him. Very gently she stroked the man's brow, ran the tip of her finger down the side of his face. A mother's touch.

But it wasn't a finger that had crept out, extending from the keyhole, reaching down for him. It couldn't be, he thought, a chill running down his neck as he slowly turned and reached up, wanting to feel it, to see it, this warm and damp and bristling –

It whipped back like an amphibious tongue in the blink of an eye. And the thing behind the door started gurgling, furiously giggling, breathless and insectoid,

Heeheeheeheeheeheeheeheeheeheehee

Byrd threw himself over, tipping the can of turpentine, spilling it all over the floor, onto himself, his pants, his hands suddenly tingling in cold liquid. Gasping, crying, babbling curses to himself and to the demon trying to escape, he jumped to his feet, kicked the can aside, ran for the entrance.

"*LET ME OUT!* YOU CAN'T DO THIS! YOU CAN'T! YOU CAN'T!"

Burn it. Burn it. Now Raymond, douse the paintings and burn them, burn everything!

"*CUNT! YOU CUNT!* YOU CAN'T STOP ME! YOU CAN'T STOP ME!"

Very methodically, Raymond Byrd stepped outside, lifted the last can of turpentine, brought it into the barn, opened it, and poured it liberally over the wooden crates Joseph Manning had lined up.

"I'll die if I stop, Raymond. I *can't* stop, can't stop. I'll die! I'LL DIE! I'LL DIE IF I STOP! OPEN THIS FUCKING DOOR!"

The lighter slipped in his hand, the skin of his thumb slipping across the surface of its metal wheel. He couldn't get a grip! He dropped it, fumbled for it –

"LET ME OUT!"

– he could barely see it then, for the sweat in his eye, for the turpentine fumes surrounding and suffocating him. Then he took the lighter in two hands, concentrated, forced his hands and arms steady, and pressed down hard, and it caught, the lovely white flame jumping up attentive, ready for work.

The crates went up first. Then the floor caught. And as he noticed his pants igniting, and blue fire mysteriously wrapping snake-like about his hands and arms, a stream of fire zigzagged across the room to the corner, where, before the loud basement door, it exploded without a sound into a healthy blue and orange blaze.

He rushed outside, the fire following obediently along.

Rolling about in the dirt, digging his blistering hands into the earth and kicking off his pants, he watched amused as the barn burst into flame. It did so so quietly that he wondered if he'd lost his hearing, wondered if the demon had done something to his ears, touching him in the way it did.

"RAAAAAAYMOND!"

Nope. It's just the fire. The nature of fire. Quiet business.

"RAAAAAAYMOND!"

Without a word of complaint, without comment, without flourish. It does what it knows how to do and nothing more, nothing less.

In less than a minute, the entire structure was ablaze. The air around him heated up, pulled over him suddenly, drawn to the inferno. He backed up, climbed the hill toward the house, turned, sat and admired, in a way, what he'd done.

His Volvo exploded. The force blew out part of a wall. When he flinched, covering his face, he noticed that the skin on his hands was burned black, peeling off. The tissue underneath was white, wet and smooth as glass and very sensitive.

The roof of the barn began to sag, fall inward.

A thick plume of black smoke filled the sky.

Raymond Byrd would have stayed and watched the destruction to the end but he had to be going. It would take him at least three hours to get to the Nevada border, and with only one eye he didn't want to try driving in the dark. Even dusk would be a challenge.

But first he needed some pants.

Inside he ran cold water over his burned hands. He soaked a towel in water and pressed this against his eye.

He took some of Joseph's trousers. They were too big for him. He rolled up the cuffs, cinched the waist tightly with a black leather belt. He also put on one of Joseph's turtlenecks. It was also too large for him.

When he left Manning's house that afternoon he looked from a distance like a boy dressed up in his father's clothing. Like a tramp.

"It's not a beauty contest," he said to himself as he got into Abergast's VW Thing. He looked down in the passenger seat at the round heap he'd left there. His shirt, the man's skull. A corner of Abergast's empty eye-socket peeked out at him. Byrd uncovered the ghastly thing and examined it and wondered what he was turning into. He touched the crown of the skull. It was warm. There was a dark crack, like a lightning bolt, in the forehead, above and between the eyes. He'd struck a dead-on blow, swinging hard, as hard as he'd ever swung anything. Pure luck, catching Abergast right there. "It's not a beauty contest," he said again.

His vision was improving. Normalizing, at any rate, his brain adjusting to the loss of his right eye. He was no longer seeing stars or flashes of white light.

What he saw, then, suddenly, pulling from the yard, was a large red fire engine. It was blocking his path. He pulled the VW out of the way, onto the sandy shoulder of Manning's driveway. The truck passed him quickly, with tremendous noise. A second truck passed in the dusty wake of the first. A third was rapidly approaching, its horns screaming like it was Judgment Day.

Byrd tried to get the VW back on the driveway, to more quickly and properly get out of the truck's path. But the VW's right rear wheel was caught in the soft shoulder and spinning, and the car began to rotate leftward ninety degrees such that before he realized what was happening his vehicle was perpendicular to the road and nearly beneath the oncoming fire engine. His dazzled one-eyed reflection looked back at him from the truck's bright chrome bumper.

He looked one last time at Abergast's skull, as if the bone might explain things. He looked at the glove compartment, where he'd put the .38.

A fireman stood outside the car, at his window, the young man's face bright red. "What *the fuck* is wrong with you!?" he was saying. "Get *the fuck* outta there!"

The fireman opened the VW, grabbed its driver by the shoulders, lifted him out, tossed him aside. A team of other firemen quickly set upon the VW, tipping it over and rolling it out of the way. Then fire engine after fire engine, a whole fleet of machines, came blazing down the driveway, raising clouds of dust and smoke so thick you couldn't tell up from down, day from night.

~ 14 ~

"What happened to your face?"

The sheriff's name was Veen. Gentle fellow, soft spoken. He came in with a cowboy hat on. He took it off when he sat down, set it on the table.

"Oh. That," Byrd said, reaching for his eye, not touching it. His hand was shaking. "An accident. I was... trying to... and..."

"What happened to your hands?"

"I burned them."

"When you lit the barn on fire."

"Yes."

They were talking in the kitchen, across from each other at the wooden table there. A deputy stood behind Raymond Byrd.

The sheriff tipped his chair back, folded his hands on his large stomach, crossed his legs. He was in no hurry to ask the man questions. They had all day, all of tomorrow. The guy wasn't going anywhere anytime soon.

"What're you doing out here, Mr Byrd?"

"I work for Henry Manning."

"Heinrich?"

"Yessir."

"He died, didn't he?"

"Yes he did."

"And so?"

Nevada suddenly seemed a long ways away. If he left by nightfall – *but, still, you won't be able to see anything! driving at night...* So tomorrow morning, then. Get an early start. You could be across the state by evening. Utah. Zion.

"I was tying up loose ends," he said.

"That include burning his barn down?"

"Yes. Yes it does."

"Heinrich Manning asked you to burn his barn down?"

"Well, not exactly, no. But it's what he wanted. You'll see," Byrd said, hooking a finger into the neck of Joseph's turtle neck, pulling, suffocating. "It's in the basement. His last project. But his son destroyed it. It wasn't finished, see, and we agreed that unfinished it shouldn't be shown. So – "

"Manning asked you to burn his barn down?"

"Well, no, but I'm explaining – "

"Don't sit there and fuckin' lie to me, young man."

The sheriff's face hardened, grew very still. It was a heavy face, porous, thick tan skin.

"I'm... I'm not lying."

The sheriff blinked, took a breath through his nose. He opened his mouth and stuck a finger inside, picked at something in the back. Quietly, he said: "The barn has a basement?"

"Yessir."

"What was in it? That his son – where *is* his son, by the way?"

A man in a uniform came into the kitchen, walked quickly past the table where the sheriff and Byrd sat talking, approached the deputy. They conferred. Then the man left as quickly as he'd come. You could smell the fire on the man.

Byrd waited, watched the man behind him in the corner of his eye. He started to say, "Joseph went to Mexico," but then the deputy spoke, saying:

"There was someone in the barn, sheriff."

Veen took a long deep breath, his chest expanding, his shoulders rising. Then he relaxed. He seemed drowsy, like it was time for his afternoon nap.

"*Someone*," he said, "meaning they found a body in the ashes?"

The deputy didn't answer. Byrd didn't know who the question was directed at.

The deputy moved toward the door. The sheriff, his eyes shifting, noticed his deputy's departure. Then he faced Byrd. Very slowly the sheriff's eyes opened wide, the entire top half of the man's sunburned face stretching out, opening up. There was some kind of light inside the sheriff's head, the whites of the man's eyes beginning to glow. Then he relaxed again, settled back into place.

"You can stay here or you can come out with me. If, perhaps, you think it might be a bit – what's the word?

– overwhelming for you to be out there and look at this thing they've taken from the barn..." Now the sheriff waited. Let the man speak, set things straight. He didn't seem like the criminal type. He seemed, actually, kind of crazy – gone too far. The sheriff continued. "Then I suggest you stay here. Count slowly to one hundred. Then come out and let's talk."

You can't go to Nevada, Ray, you don't have a car! You blew up the Volvo.

"I'll stay here."

What you're going to do –

"Very well."

– is get back to Maiden, back to the house. She needs you, she needs a groundskeeper, a man outside, and you're just the man for the job. And they'll never, never think of looking for you there.

~ 15 ~

If there is a kind of relationship we have with our homes, with the places we inhabit, if, after many years, it can be said that a house comes to know its inhabitants, and vice versa, such that I might walk through my home in the dark of night, knowing, without seeing where I put my feet, where and how to move my body through the doorways and hallways and rooms – if we can make such conjectures about what it means *to live in a place* and agree that such claims are not utter nonsense, then I do not think we could say the same of *that* place. It is different. It is not a house in the way we think of houses. It is something altogether different.

The longer we live in a place, I've heard, the more the place becomes a part of us, an extension of us. The house becomes a part of the family. It has a smell and a feel, an attitude, it makes sounds of approval and disapproval, it expresses joy and sadness. The house, over time, takes on a life of its own.

That's *our* place.

It's the place we come back to in the evening, after work, the place we come back to gratefully after a long time away.

We take care of these houses, homes, these structures we entrust our families to. We look at them fondly, up close and from afar. We talk to them when we're alone.

You wake up in the middle of the night and pass in the dark from the bedroom to the hall and to the bathroom. You know the steps, you could do this in your sleep.

You trust the house. And it rewards your trust with its integrity. It doesn't run off when you turn away, doesn't betray you in the night.

In this way, the house becomes a part of you. It functions in your thoughts, in your imagination, in your subconscious. This is why you can walk through it in the night, in the dark, hardly awake. Because you can see all of it in your head.

There is the physical structure of the house. And there is this mental image of the place inside your head. The first is no more important than the second. They operate together, the physical confirming the mental, and the mental, let's imagine, breathing life into the physical.

This is the house inside. It is the house that holds your body, the house that makes of your body the person you think you are, that makes of your body something structured, something secure and balanced and supportive. The house lets you have such things as laws and ideals, such things as a bedroom, a study, a basement and attic, such things as a family.

Animals don't have houses. Of course, we give the dog a house. *The doghouse.* But this too only aims at bringing this animal, already quite a domestic thing, further into the fold, to make of him something like us.

Dogs also live, remember, without houses. We say of such animals: "He stays outside." "He's an outside dog." "It's wild."

And we find it amusing, the challenge for the poor creature between being sometimes outside and sometimes, on the coldest nights, inside. Amusing, because we see in this challenge its struggle between being something wild and being something domestic, of the family, like one of us.

Raymond Byrd had been confused since coming back from the Drammond House, confused about where exactly he was. Like a dog, he was nervous about being indoors, nervous about the rules he thought he must obey. Outside such rules did not apply. Thus the appeal of a place like Nevada.

"Where am I? What have I done?"

It did that to him, the Drammond House. It took the house he had inside his mind, the place where he lived, and covered it, replaced it.

"It's Manning's place. You're in his kitchen. Sheriff Veen is waiting for you outside."

But it didn't feel right. He suspected that if he got up and went to the door and opened it and stepped outside on the porch, he would not find the porch there, not see the yard out there, with the fire trucks and ambulances and police and sheriff cars.

He'd see the Drammond House. He'd find himself in a room in the Drammond House. Manning's place was no more. The little two-story, hilltop bungalow was gone.

Afraid to see if this was actually the case, Raymond Byrd sat very, very still.

~ 16 ~

He started counting. He stopped around fifteen, sixteen. Silly exercise. A hundred or not he'd have to go outside, face them. Look at what he'd done.

He stood at the door, looked outside. There was a man on the porch, his back to the window. There were a dozen cars in the yard. The fire marshal. An ambulance. A couple police cars too.

You'll have to steal one of them. It's the only way.

Byrd stepped out the door, came up quietly beside the deputy standing there. He was a tall, heavy Mexican. The deputy hardly moved, his thumbs hooked through belt loops on his pants. The radio on his shoulder chirped, a distant voice, static, commenting on the situation.

The barn was no longer burning. There wasn't much left to burn. The remains smoldered, pushed into a black wet pile. There was the smoking frame of his car, something he'd had for almost twenty years. He couldn't think of anything else he'd held onto for so long. And though he'd never tell himself he cared much for the car, seeing it burned down to nothing, he realized that he had. He'd spent a lot of time and money on that car, that simple, ugly machine.

There was also, curled and collapsed together like enormous decks of cards, the burned remains of Manning's work.

The notebook. Did Charlotte take it? Is it in Joseph's things?

A group of men stood in a huddle in the barnyard, the sheriff among them. There was a gurney and on this a figure covered in a white sheet. They'd strapped a transparent mask to her face, giving her oxygen, he guessed, which meant she was still alive.

The sheriff started up the hill. He hadn't come very far when a man appeared beyond the smoking ruin of the barn, coming down the path out of the canyon. He called to the sheriff and the sheriff stopped, turned, looked at the man. He started that way. Several others started that way.

They went up into the canyon. A few minutes later they returned. Bouncing ahead of them, its tongue flopping from its mouth in sheer glee, was a dog, the creature Byrd had meant to kill.

Up until this moment Raymond Byrd hadn't felt, if that's the word, very much. He was a man going through the motions, waiting for his next opportunity. But with the sight of the dog, his jaw clenched, a sourness came up his throat, acid filling his mouth. A cold black shadow came over his line of sight.

"You crazy sick motherfucker," said the big Mexican next to him. "What'd they find up there? All the bodies?"

Byrd had to look up at the Mexican, his round fat face. The Mexican didn't even turn when he spoke, his eyes on the commotion down the hill, on the men coming up the hill on the sheriff's heels.

"You didn't think you'd get away with it," said the Mexican, the pitch of his voice rising. He laughed once, quietly. He had a boy's face, the body of an ox. "Did you? Man... Listen, I don't know you. But if you aren't crazy, just plain *wacko*... Then you gotta be one of the stupidest... You burned the barn down! Man – this is *California!* Not – fuckin' – Mississippi. Where it rains in the summer."

The man started to turn, to face Byrd, but then stopped.

The sheriff was giving orders. His men nodding obediently.

"I had to," Byrd said. "I couldn't let it out."

"Let *what* out?"

"This thing..." His voice almost broke. He couldn't name it, couldn't say her name because –

She's alive. Right there. They're bringing her –

– it didn't seem right, blaming her for what had happened. Because it wasn't her fault. It was –

"Inside the Drammond House," Byrd started to say.

At that the Mexican looked down at the suspect in the corner of his eye and took a step aside, down off the porch.

"The Drammond House," Byrd said after him. "In the basement. There's – "

But nobody was listening.

The men were arguing in the middle of the yard. The sheriff looked his way, called his name.

Raymond Byrd slowly stepped off the porch, approached the men. He liked Heinrich Manning's house, the bungalow. Walking away from it, sadness came over him. He'd never be back, never see the place again.

They'd brought the body up the hill. She was right there, on the gurney, covered in a white sheet. Her skin was black. Her hair looked different, wet and greasy.

One of the deputies grabbed Byrd firmly, turned him around, cuffed him. He and another man led Byrd toward a car.

"Wait. Can I..."

Byrd took a step toward the gurney. A medic in a bright orange jacket stood in his way. Very gently Byrd came up to this man, stood at his arm. The man let him in.

The sheriff, his voice different now, said at Byrd's shoulder, "I don't have to tell you what they just found up in the canyon."

Her eyes were closed.

"Byrd," said the sheriff. "Tying up loose ends? You gonna explain to me how that man they found up in the canyon got himself decapitated and burned and buried? Byrd? *Byrd!?*"

Then she was looking at him. Calmly, as if waking from a soothing dream. Instant recognition in her brown eyes. He'd been there, in the dream, about to say something, about to reach out and –

None of the men there, and a few of them had been doing emergency for twenty years, had ever seen anything like what then happened. This woman: she'd been unconscious when they found her down in the basement, in a bathroom under the stairs, in the bathtub. She'd wrapped herself in wet towels. She would have suffocated, and then boiled as the pipes exploded around her, and then, eventually, gone up in smoke with everything else. But by some twist of fate she didn't. They got to her soon enough.

That happened, sometimes.

But what never happened was that a woman in her condition wake up and move with the kind of speed and energy that she then did. Took everyone by surprise.

She was screaming, her arms out, the IV torn from her arm as she grabbed Raymond Byrd by the hair, pulled herself into his face, closed her mouth over his, *biting* at his lips. She got a mouthful, spitting blood, screaming.

When she threw him down, leaping on him, her hands around his throat, they heard not only the crack of bone as something snapped in the man's arms but the woman's strange words, a kind of gurgling and hissing, a different language altogether.

She was working on his ear.

I'll die if I stop, die if I stop, die if I stop!

"Thought you could stop us, Raymond? Stop us, burn us, get away? Stop us, burn us, get away!? That what you thought?"

Byrd was speechless, helpless as Ingrid Manning devoured him.

The woman managed to gouge out Byrd's other eye with her thumb before they could pull her off him and strap her down.

"What'd she say?"

"Nonsense, man. Fuckin' babble. She's – "

"No, she said – "

"Dude, she's gone. Totally – "

"It was – "

"Will someone *please* clean him up. Get him out of those cuffs. Get the doctor over here. That eye?"

The medic held Byrd's head firmly between his hands. He seemed to be massaging Byrd's face. A moment later they were helping him stand.

But the second Raymond Byrd got to his feet, he turned, broke away, and ran. He couldn't see where he was going, but he knew he had to get away –

She needs you. She needs a groundskeeper. Now that Gretton–

– and he knew exactly where to go.

With the wind in his face, he felt, despite the exquisite pain in his shoulder and ear, momentarily free, saved. He could smell the ocean. It wasn't far off.

"I know the way!" he cried out. "I know the way!"

"Where's he going?"

Joseph's pants, which he'd rolled up for their length, came undone. He tripped in the excess material, fell flat on his face, splitting his lip, chipping a tooth. The earth was hot and salty. He could hear something underground, deep down, turning, making its way up.

⌂

Note to the reader:

I first self-published *The Body Temple* in 2018 as Max Ruen. It was available on Amazon on and off for a couple years. What you have just finished reading, except for a handful of minor edits, is the 2018 novel.

Glenn   and   Natalie   -->   **Thank You**